CONTENTS

ALLAN BOROUGHS

Illustrated by Fred van Deelen

MACMILLAN CHILDREN'S BOOKS

First published 2015 by Macmillan Children's Books
an imprint of Pan Macmillan
a division of Macmillan Publishers Limited
20 New Wharf Road, London N1 9RR
Associated companies throughout the world
www.panmacmillan.com

ISBN 978-1-4472-3600-9

1 3 5 7 9 8 6 4 2

A CIP catalogue record for this book is available from the British Library.

Printed and bound by CPI Group (UK) Ltd, Croydon CR0 4YY

For Miss Howe, my Year 6 English teacher,
who started a fire that refuses to go out

1 THE TECH-MINE

India Bentley tapped the delicate meter and frowned as the hair-thin needle flickered gently. In any other location such a tiny reading would not have been a cause for alarm. But this, she reminded herself, was no ordinary place.

She straightened and peered uneasily through the gloom of the deserted factory. The light outside barely penetrated the high windows, illuminating broken machinery and rusted chains hanging in long swags from the roof like jungle vines.

Once, a factory like this would have been alive with the mechanical heartbeat of well-oiled machines. But that was before the Great Rains had drowned the world. Now, it was just a corpse of a place, rotten and decayed with rafters like broken ribs poking against the sky.

India snapped out of her daydream and turned her attention to the sounds of grunting and boot-scrambling coming from a hole in the floor. She took up the slack on the climbing rope and wiped the sweat from her forehead, wishing, not for the first time, for the deep cold of a Siberian winter.

The noises grew louder until a slim brown hand emerged from the hole and heaved a small wooden box out on to the concrete. Next came a pair of elbows, and then the grinning face of Verity Brown, her long hair in disarray and rivulets of sweat carving channels through the grime on her face.

'Hot damn!' she said, hauling herself out. 'I was right. Plasma chargers! These were the state-of-the-art in power generation before the Great Rains. Just one of these babies has enough juice to power a small town for a year and there must be two dozen of them down there. They'll fetch over five thousand apiece in Sing City.'

India peered into the hole. 'So it's a tech-mine?' she said. 'For real this time?'

'Damn right,' said Verity triumphantly. 'There's a small fortune down there.'

India grinned as she helped Verity to brush the worst of the dust from her clothes. It had been over a year since they had discovered the lost fortress of Ironheart in Siberia and Verity had taken on India as her assistant. In that time India had got used to a life of searching drowned cities for working examples of old technology. But it was tough work and they had not had a decent find for several weeks.

India fixed her eyes eagerly on the box as Verity prised off the lid with her knife. 'So how come no one ever found this stuff before?' she asked.

Verity shrugged. 'Just lucky I guess. This factory is in an active earthquake region which probably kept most of the tech bandits away.'

She pushed aside the packing material and let out a low whistle. Nestling in a bed of straw were two sleek metal tubes the length of India's forearm. Each had a black handle and an oval glass window set into the side. Behind the glass, thick blue liquid swirled and glowed with its own light.

Verity crouched down to inspect them. 'They're intact. Let's hope the others are all in the same condition.' She moved back to the edge of the hole. 'I'm going back down. We need to salvage as many of these puppies as possible before we attract any unwanted attention. There are still cannibal tribes in this region and those guys have no idea how to treat a lady.' She picked up the rope and swung her legs over the side.

'Well, if it's so dangerous,' said India, biting her lip, 'then maybe I could get myself some protection when we get to Sing City?'

Verity sighed wearily. 'Nice try, India, but we've been over this a hundred times. There's no way I'm letting you have a gun.'

'But why not?'

'Because I promised your father, for one thing, and it's way too dangerous for someone of your age.'

India kicked a stray piece of metal across the concrete. 'Well, Sid had his own gun and he was only two years older than me.'

Sid the Kid was the young outlaw they had met in Siberia. He had a deadly reputation and most people had breathed a sigh of relief when he'd been lost in the explosion that had also killed his father, the ruthless and brutal Lucifer Stone.

'You're using Sid as a character reference?' spluttered Verity. 'That boy was a psychopath.'

India's brow furrowed. 'He wasn't so bad,' she muttered, kicking at a loose stone. 'It was just that his dad was so awful to him.' She shivered as she remembered how Stone would beat his son mercilessly.

'Sid's the perfect example of why you *shouldn't* have a gun,' said Verity, swinging herself out over the hole. 'Forget it, India. You've got your shock stick and you've got a good head. That should be more than enough to keep you out of trouble.'

'Great!' said India sarcastically, peering after Verity. 'So if the cannibals turn up while you're down there I'll just hold them at bay with some witty conversation, shall I?'

Verity laughed. 'I feel sorry for any cannibals that try to digest you, India. Concentrate on keeping an eye on those seismographs; I don't want to get caught down there if the building starts shaking. And put those plasma chargers somewhere safe; if one of them gets dropped it'll make a crater a hundred yards wide. And relax, you're perfectly safe!'

India snorted. She thought of asking Verity why it was OK to leave her holding an explosive device in a cannibal-infested earthquake zone but too dangerous to let her have a gun, but she thought better of it.

Instead she pulled out her shock stick and turned it over in her hand, taking some comfort from the thought that it could deliver a stunning electric jolt to anyone who upset her enough to get jabbed with it. As she did so, a flash of light on her arm caught her eye and she pulled back her sleeve.

Curled around India's right wrist was a smooth metal bracelet, a gift from her friend Calculus, who had been Verity's android bodyguard. When Calculus was alive the bracelet had allowed him to communicate with India. But when he had been destroyed by the ancient machine they had found beneath Ironheart, it had stopped working altogether. Yet now it was pulsing with a blue light like the heartbeat of some tiny creature.

A light fall of dust from the roof made her look up. Remembering what she was supposed to be doing, she glanced at the seismograph. To her dismay, the needles were flickering wildly.

'Verity,' she said in a small voice. 'I think you'd better get back up here.'

There was muffled cursing from deep within the hole. 'Damn it, India, I told you I'm not discussing it any more. Now just let me concentrate on . . . What was that?'

A rolling shiver ran through the factory building and a shower of rust flakes fell from the roof. Verity scrambled quickly back out of the hole. As she reached the top the building began to shake violently, shattering panes of glass and sending a steel girder crashing down from the roof. A wide crack opened up in the concrete.

'Holy cow, the floor's going to cave in!' shouted Verity over the din. 'Get moving. Leave the equipment and go!'

India did not need telling twice. She sprinted across the factory floor with Verity behind, clutching the plasma chargers as pieces of the roof showered the floor around them.

'Move it, India,' yelled Verity. 'If that floor collapses on top of the other plasma chargers – this whole place will be vaporized.'

India wriggled through the narrow doorway, emerging into a brilliant wash of mountain sunshine. The factory was in a bad way. Its corrugated roof had begun to buckle and the walls were being pounded by huge rocks that were bouncing freely down the mountainside.

'Get to the jeep,' shouted Verity as she squeezed out after India. 'We need to put some distance between us and this factory, pronto.'

They ran down a slope of loose rock towards a battered, dust-covered jeep, an old-world relic that had cost them most of the money they had saved up for the expedition. India vaulted the driver's door, turned the ignition and rammed the gear stick forward. The car made a grinding noise and jumped like a startled kangaroo, causing Verity to lose her footing as she clambered into the back and drop one of the plasma chargers.

'What the hell are you doing, India?' she yelled, as she

tried to grab the charger rolling around the floor. 'You're not old enough to drive this thing!'

'I don't think anyone's going to be asking for my licence,' India called back.

'Well at least put it into second gear,' barked Verity. She succeeded in grabbing the loose charger and clutched it to her chest like a small child. India yanked back the gear stick and the car lurched forward again, slithering and sliding over the rough ground as it picked up speed. At the bottom of the slope, the track crossed an old iron bridge over a deep chasm.

'Straight across,' called Verity. 'I think we've made it—'

The factory exploded in a ball of heat and light, lifting the car into the air and hurling it into the side of the bridge. There was a screeching of metal and India's head smacked against the steering wheel, making lights explode behind her eyes.

She lay still, feeling the pink warmth of the sun against her closed eyelids. The explosion had subsided and the ground had stopped shaking; somewhere she could hear a bird singing.

'India.' Verity's voice sounded soft and close by. 'Whatever you do . . . don't make *any* sudden movements.'

India opened her eyes a fraction and a spear of pain lanced her skull. Her face was pressed against the dashboard, her lip felt fat and something salty dribbled from the corner of her mouth. She raised a hand to her chin and the world lurched.

'I said don't do anything sudden,' said Verity. The urgency in her voice brought India fully awake. She raised her head and looked out of the windscreen. At first it looked as though they were flying high over a dry river valley. Then she gasped as she registered what she was seeing. The car had burst through the railings and was hanging over the edge of the bridge, see-sawing playfully in the breeze. India lurched back in her seat and the car swayed sickeningly.

'Very slowly,' said Verity's voice, 'climb into the back seat with me.'

India's breath came in short gasps as she imagined the horror of falling from the bridge with the certain knowledge that you would be smashed to a pulp on the rocks below. Fighting down panic, she edged her body backwards over the seat, never taking her eyes from the deadly drop; then slid carefully on to the tailgate beside Verity. 'That's good,' said Verity, 'Now, both together, jump!'

They leaped from the back of the car with Verity still cradling her deadly cargo. For a split second, the jeep teetered on the edge, then, with a tortured groan it pitched forward into the gorge, tumbling in a slow ballet until it hit the rocks below with a distant crash. 'Well,' said Verity, breaking the silence, 'I'm sorry to say, Miss Bentley, you have failed your driving test.'

India swallowed hard and blew out a long breath. She looked down at her trembling hands and, as she did so, noticed that her bracelet had stopped flashing.

The Beach View Bar had no beach and no view to speak of either. At one time, the bar had been at the top of a great glass tower, high above Sing City, and beautiful people had come there to watch the sunset as waiters in crisp white jackets glided between tables with trays of jewel-coloured cocktails.

But then the Great Rains had come, torrential and relentless. They swelled the dirty brown waters and drowned the cities until all but the very tallest buildings were lost in their depths and the waves lapped hungrily at the steps of the Beach View Bar.

India and Verity sat in the front of a small boat puttering through a floating market towards the shady haven of the bar. India shielded her eyes against the midday sun and tried to ignore the putrid market smells.

'I'm just saying,' she said, 'it's not the first time.'

Verity wiped her forehead and sighed. 'You're reading too much into it, India. It's a long time since Calculus gave you that bracelet. It's probably just got a short circuit somewhere.'

'But it's happened before,' insisted India. 'Two months ago, when we got caught in that flash flood in Mongolia.'

'I remember,' said Verity ruefully. 'We had to live on roots for a week.'

'Right. Well, just before it happened my bracelet started flashing. I would have told you at the time but I forgot with everything else that was going on. But that's twice it's happened now.'

'Well there you are then, it's just a fault. Give it to me and I'll fix it for you.'

'But both times we were in danger. It was like a warning or something.'

Verity frowned. 'What are you saying, India?'

'Nothing. I mean, I'm just saying that maybe . . .' She struggled for the right words. 'Calculus—'

'Is dead, India,' said Verity firmly. 'No one comes back from the dead, no matter how much you want them to. It's just a loose wire. Give it to me later and I'll fix it so it doesn't happen again.'

She placed a tentative hand on India's. 'I know how you feel,' she said. 'I miss him too. Some days I'd give anything to have him back with us, but sometimes . . . you just need to let go.'

India pulled her hand away and stared sullenly over the side of the boat. What Verity said was true. Calculus had been destroyed as he tried to help the ancient machine-mind that they had found beneath Ironheart. So why was it that lately she could not shake the feeling that he was still out there somewhere?

She looked down at the bracelet again. '*Let go*.' It was what people used to say to her about her father when he went missing in Siberia and everyone thought he was dead. But against all the odds she had found him alive, so why shouldn't the same be true about Calculus?

'If you really love someone,' she said, glaring out over the water, 'you never give up. You never "just let go".' Verity stiffened and India immediately regretted her words. She knew Verity had loved Calculus as much as she did. 'I'm parched,' she said, hastily changing the subject. 'Does this bar sell cold lemonade?'

Verity wiped her eyes and pushed a hand through her long dark hair. 'I seriously doubt it,' she said. 'It only sells two things. The first is whisky that tastes like petrol.'

The boat pulled up beside the bar and Verity handed some coins to the driver. A sign above the entrance read: 'Welcome to the Beach View Bar – the friendliest place in Sing City'. There was an unconscious man lying beneath it.

'What's the second thing?' asked India, stepping over the comatose body.

'Old-tech,' said Verity. 'Sing City is the tech-hunting capital of the world and the Beach View Bar is where all the best hunters come to trade. It's run by a dealer called Two-Buck Tim, he's the best in the business.' She patted her satchel delicately. 'I'm hoping he's going to be interested in what we have here.'

Inside, the bar was crowded with customers clamouring for drinks at the long counter and playing sweaty games of mah-jong that involved a lot of shouting. A group of musicians in shabby dinner jackets were struggling to be heard over the din as India and Verity took a seat at the bar.

In the shady booths around the edge of the room India noticed several sinister figures sporting a grim collection of scar tissue and tombstone teeth. Despite the heat, they wore wide hats and long dark coats that bulged with hidden hardware.

'Freelance tech-hunters,' said Verity in response to India's unasked question. 'They're here to do business, same as us.'

'So is this Two-Buck Tim a friend of yours?' said India.

'Two-Buck?' Verity laughed. 'The man's a dirty little rodent. I wouldn't trust him any further than I could spit.'

They were interrupted by a surly-looking Chinese man who slammed a bottle of brown liquid on to the counter, making them jump. He wore a dirty apron over a ruin of a vest. On his forehead he sported an eyeglass on an elastic strap.

'Hi, Two-Buck!' said Verity cheerfully. 'We were just talking about you. Business looks good at the moment.'

Two-Buck Tim, owner of the friendliest bar in Sing City, made a hawking noise and spat on the floor.

'Damned religious freaks,' he grumbled, nodding towards a quiet-looking group in the corner, dressed in old rags.

'Been arriving in Sing City for weeks now for some dumb fool festival. None of them wants to drink whisky. Bad for business.' He pulled out a cracked and dirty glass and wiped it with a grubby handkerchief before pouring Verity a healthy measure of the brown spirit. It smelled like fuel oil.

'You want a drink?' he said, waving the noxious bottle in India's direction.

She frowned. 'Just some water please.'

Two-Buck shrugged. 'OK, your funeral. Trust me, the whisky is safer.' He reached for a jug and poured her a glass of brown water. India sipped it tentatively, it tasted brackish and gritty.

'I've got a great opportunity for you, Two-Buck,' said Verity, sipping her whisky and wincing. 'Some really high-grade old-tech, fresh out of an undiscovered mine in the mountains.' She reached into her bag and pulled out a random assortment of circuit boards and electronic devices they had unearthed in the course of the previous two months.

Two-Buck poked at the items suspiciously with a dirty finger. He picked up a broken phone and prised the back off expertly. Then he pulled the eyeglass down over his left eye and examined the inside.

'Full of seawater,' he muttered. 'Mos'ly dead circuits. I give you five bucks for the phones,' he said flatly. 'Everything else, just junk.'

'Five dollars!' spluttered India. 'It cost us ten times that to find it.'

'Best I can do,' said Two-Buck. He poked a finger in his ear and examined the residue left on his grubby fingernail. Then he wiped it on his vest, leaving a visible yellow stain. 'You want something to eat?' he said brightly. 'I got sandwiches, made fresh last Thursday.' He rummaged under the counter and came up holding two grey slabs which he squashed on to a greasy plate and pushed to their side of the counter. The bread was curled at the edges and contained something that looked suspiciously like raw liver. Two-Buck's brown fingerprints were clearly visible on the top.

'Er, thanks but we're not hungry,' said Verity, to Two-Buck's obvious disappointment. 'Well if none of that other stuff interests you, what would you say to these babies?' She opened her satchel again, just wide enough to let Two-Buck see the two plasma chargers nestling inside, glowing softly with a faint blue light.

Two-Buck's eyes grew round. He looked right and left and then quickly closed the flap on Verity's bag to hide them from view. 'Where you get those?' he hissed. 'Chargers like that, very rare!'

'That's our business, Two-Buck,' said Verity. 'The point is, can you sell them for us?'

He took another peek inside the bag. 'I need to test properly,' he said. 'Come with me.' He raised a portion of the counter and parted a bead curtain at the back of the bar that led to a small workshop. It smelled unpleasantly of oil and Two-Buck in equal measure.

He squeezed his soft stomach behind a rickety bench,

crowded with tools and metal shavings, and pulled the dust covers from a gleaming machine covered in tiny lights. He took the chargers from Verity and placed them into a steel tray, then peered at them through an eyepiece.

'Electron microscope,' he said proudly, squinting into the lens. 'Got it last year. Means I can spot junk a mile off.' Verity shifted nervously from foot to foot.

'So what do you think, Two-Buck?' she said after a few moments. 'Are they any good?'

Two-Buck flipped a switch to turn off the microscope. 'Top-quality merchandise,' he said looking impressed.

'Great, so how much?'

'Oh, I can't buy them,' he said. 'This is military-grade hardware. Black-tech.'

'So what?' said Verity. 'You always used to deal in this stuff.'

'Not any more.' His face fell and he began to pick his nose absent-mindedly. 'When Lady Fang come to Sing City she tell everyone to stop selling weapons or she would take care of them for good.' He pushed the chargers back across the bench with a sigh. 'Everyone have to do what she say now.'

'It's your bar, isn't it?' said India. 'You can do what you want, can't you?'

Two-Buck gave a rueful 'Ha!' and wiped his finger on his vest again, leaving a fresh green stain next to the yellow one. 'Not any more,' he said glumly. 'When Lady Fang move in, she take over my bar; I work for her now.' He sagged in his chair and stared glumly into space.

'Lady Fang?' said Verity. 'Not the same Lady Fang who used to operate out of Jiangsu province?'

'Who is she?' said India. 'She sounds like somebody's auntie.'

'Only if your auntie is a complete psychopath,' said Verity. 'She was the most ruthless gangster in Shanghai, specializing in selling weapons. They say she collects the eyes of anyone who displeases her and keeps them in a jar. I had no idea she was in Sing City, she must be pretty old by now.'

'Best not let *her* hear you say that,' said Two-Buck nervously. 'Lady Fang is very sensitive about her age.' He dropped his voice to a whisper. 'You could end up face down in the sewers for saying things like that.'

'So, why are we wasting our time talking to you?' said India with a snort. 'Sounds like we should be talking to Lady Fang.'

Two-Buck looked hurt. 'Lady Fang not so easy to see,' he said, examining the black grease beneath his fingernails. 'Very busy lady. But I might be able to get you in to see her, for a small consideration.' He rubbed his thumb and fingers together and grinned a mouthful of slimy, yellow teeth.

Two-Buck Tim led them from the back door of the bar and along a rat-infested walkway between two decaying tower blocks. The passage opened into a wide, watery square, enclosed on all sides by high buildings. It had the sunless chill of a place inhabited by damp things with nasty temperaments.

Moored in the square was a squat-looking junk with blood-red sails. The boat was made of blackened, waterlogged wood with rotten rigging that hung from the masts like cobwebs. At the bottom of the gangplank a man in black clothes nodded briefly at Two-Buck and scrutinized India and Verity before letting them pass. Up on the boat, at least a dozen more men stared down at them and several made a show of reaching inside their jackets as they walked up the gangplank. Two figures, perched in the rigging, trained long rifles on the newcomers.

'Lady Fang sure keeps a lot of security on hand,' said Verity in a low voice. 'Keep your wits about you, India. We might need to make a hasty exit.'

As they stepped on to the deck their path was blocked by a cadaverous-looking man with arms crowded with tattoos. He looked India and Verity up and down and paced slowly around them without saying a word. Despite his skeletal thinness he looked sinewy and strong, every fibre of his muscles visible beneath his skin like taut wires. India noticed several dark shapes swinging from his belt and realized, with a shudder, that they were dead rats.

'Who's this, Two-Buck?' he growled, making the tendons stand out on his neck. His voice was harsh and nasal. 'You were told not to bring strangers here.'

'A thousand pardons, Mr Skullet, sir,' stammered Two-Buck, 'but they have merchandise to sell. Just what Her Ladyship has been looking for, I think?' He looked meaningfully at the thin man and an unspoken communication seemed to pass between them.

The man noticed India staring at the rats on his belt and his face split into a carnivorous grin showing two rows of long teeth, filed to perfect points. 'Do excuse my manners,' he said to India with mock politeness. He swiftly unhooked one of the rats from his belt and offered it to India. 'How about some refreshment?'

She blinked at the matted corpse and stepped backwards with a shudder.

Skullet adopted an offended look. 'No? Very well then. Shame to let a good rat go to waste.' In a swift move he bit off the creature's head with a gristly snap. India and Verity watched in stunned horror as he spat the head over the side of the boat and leaned back to drain the rat's blood into his open mouth, squeezing the body to extract the last drops. When he had finished he let out a satisfied sigh and wiped a trickle of black blood from his chin.

'All right,' he snapped. 'You can come in, but watch yourselves. Skullet's my name and you'd do well to remember that. I'm wanted in five different countries, you know.'

'And unwanted in a whole lot more, I'll bet,' muttered Verity.

Skullet glared at her with murderous eyes. 'Oh, we're just sharp enough to cut ourselves, aren't we?' he growled. He held Verity's gaze for a moment and then flung away the drained rat corpse. 'Follow me,' he snarled. 'Not you, Two-Buck. Get back to the bar and take care of business.'

A look of relief passed across Two-Buck's face and he bowed to each of them briefly before scuttling down the gangplank as fast as he could manage.

Skullet rapped on a cabin door and it was opened promptly by a young girl with a scared face, wearing an ugly black patch over one eye. When they were inside, she bowed deeply and disappeared back into the shadows.

Skullet led them down a flight of steps into the bowels of the black ship. They paused at the bottom to let their eyes adjust to the dim light and India's first impression was that they had walked into a badly lit junk shop. The shelves were crammed with a chaotic assortment of wooden boxes and greasy engine parts. Unidentifiable pieces of machinery lurked under tarpaulins and the air was heavy with the smell of engine oil and rotten wood. India's eye was immediately drawn to a glass cabinet filled with gleaming, steel-blue pistols, slick with a fine layer of machine oil.

At the far end of the room an area had been separated from the chaos by delicate wood and paper screens. A hanging oil lamp cast a pool of yellow light over richly patterned rugs and a silver censer shaped like a dragon's head was giving off musky smoke.

Lady Fang was sitting behind a mahogany desk, smoking a cigarette in a long holder and tapping numbers into a large mechanical calculator with two-inch crimson nails. She wore a red silk dress that contrasted with her jet-black hair and powdered, china-white face.

Skullet led them to a spot in front of the desk, then

stepped back to a respectful distance. She did not look up from the calculator but continued to tap in numbers as though she had not noticed them. A full minute passed before Verity cleared her throat.

'Lady Fang,' said Verity. 'It's a great pleasure to meet you. We are—'

'I know who you are.'

Lady Fang raised her head to look at them for the first time. Her mouth was painted blood red and her eyes were like two black coals set in a white mask. She made a small sweeping motion with her hand. 'You are Verity Brown, notorious tech-hunter and troublemaker.' Her voice was as clear as a glass edge.

She stood abruptly and put out her cigarette, then walked slowly around the desk with the graceful elegance of a cat. 'And you are India Bentley, protégée of Mrs Brown and finder of the lost treasure of Ironheart.'

India blinked in surprise. She had no idea how Lady Fang might know about Ironheart but somehow she didn't think it would be wise to ask. Now that she was close to her, India could see the lines around Lady Fang's eyes, expertly covered with white powder, and the sagging skin of her throat, concealed by her high neckline.

'You are younger than I expected,' said Lady Fang. 'And pretty too.' She extended a single crimson claw until it almost touched India's cheek. 'Lovely eyes,' she said with no warmth in her voice. India shivered.

Verity turned on her most charming smile. 'I'm flattered

that you've heard of us, Lady Fang.'

'I make it my business to know who is in my town, Mrs Brown. The question is, what do you want of me?'

'Two-Buck brought them,' Skullet butted in. 'He said they had merchandise. It could be just what you've been looking for—'

There was a sudden flash of red silk and Skullet's words were cut short as a streak of steel hissed across the room and thunked into the timber post beside his head. India gasped. A small five-pointed star had embedded itself deeply in the wood, barely an inch from Skullet's ear.

'Next time you interrupt me, Skullet,' hissed Lady Fang, 'I will take out your eye and add it to my collection.'

She pointed to a large jar made of fine white porcelain and painted with delicate blue flowers. India shuddered as she remembered the story about Lady Fang's collecting habits.

Lady Fang took a deep breath and folded her hands into her crimson sleeves. She turned back to India and Verity. 'I have a soft spot for the traditional weapons of the East,' she purred with a dangerous smile. 'The *shuriken* is so much more elegant than the gun, don't you think?' She returned to the other side of the desk as Skullet stepped away from the throwing star. He looked shaken, a shadow of the swaggering bully they had encountered earlier.

'So,' said Fang, sitting down and lighting another cigarette. 'Show me what you have.'

Verity carefully took the chargers from her bag and

placed them on the desk. 'These are the best plasma chargers you'll find anywhere, Lady Fang,' said Verity smoothly. 'Top-quality merchandise.'

Lady Fang blew out a plume of smoke and leaned forward to inspect the slender metal tubes. 'Chargers like this are not so much in demand,' she purred. 'But I might be prepared to take them off your hands for, say . . .' She paused to tap some numbers into the mechanical calculator. 'One thousand a piece.'

'Come now, Lady Fang,' said Verity with a fixed smile. 'They'll fetch six thousand each on the open market in Shanghai.'

'But we are not in Shanghai, Mrs Brown,' snapped Lady Fang. Her crimson nails tapped out more numbers. 'Fifteen hundred. No more!'

The bargaining passed back and forth until they settled on a figure that India knew was a lot less than Verity had been hoping for. Skullet hurried away with the chargers and returned with a small roll of thin paper notes, which Lady Fang proceeded to count into a pile in front of Verity.

'So, Mrs Brown,' Lady Fang said when she had finished. 'What are your plans now?'

'Oh, you know, we might look for work, or maybe even do a bit of sightseeing,' Verity replied, rolling up the notes and stuffing them into her satchel. 'We hear there's a religious festival in town.'

Lady Fang's expression darkened. 'I strongly suggest you stay away from those dangerous fanatics. But, if you are looking for gainful employment I might have an opening for two enterprising tech-hunters with a reputation such as yours. What do you say?'

India was mortified at the thought of working for Lady Fang and suddenly fearful that Verity might seriously consider the offer. 'We can't,' she blurted. 'We're busy.'

Verity threw her a sharp look and then turned on her most charming smile. 'A most generous offer, Lady Fang,' she said. 'We'll get back to you on that.'

A cloud of displeasure crossed Lady Fang's face. 'See that you do,' came the icy reply. 'Being turned down always makes me . . . *displeased*.'

India shivered and her eye was drawn again to the jar on the shelf.

'In that case,' said Lady Fang, 'our business is concluded. Go now.'

She clapped her hands and went back to tapping on her calculator as Skullet ushered them from the room. Their audience was clearly over.

As they walked back through the cluttered room, something caught India's eye and she gave a cry of surprise. In the darkest corner of the room stood a slim and smooth figure, wrapped in a flexible metal skin, its face hidden behind a long helmet. But it was not a man: it was something else altogether.

India walked slowly towards the giant android and stared at it disbelievingly.

'Calculus?' she said in a small voice. 'Calc, is that you?'

'Holy mother of all riggers,' murmured Verity. 'It can't be true. I thought Calculus was the last of his kind.'

Now that they looked closer, however, the android was clearly not Calculus. It was pristine with an unmarked visor and flawless matt-black paintwork. The creature stood lifelessly in the corner, like the dark shell of someone they had both once known. Verity reached out to touch the smooth metal skin.

Lady Fang was on her feet instantly. 'Stop!' she barked.

Skullet pushed Verity rudely out of the way and began to haul a tarpaulin over the lifeless android.

'Er, perhaps I might have a quick look?' said Verity. 'I have some expertise with androids, if I could just—'

'I said NO!' Lady Fang's eyes flashed like hot coals. 'That machine is not your concern, Mrs Brown,' she snapped. 'And people who pry into my affairs seldom get a second warning.' She straightened, and folded her arms into the sleeves of her robe. India thought of the sharp fighting star Fang had hurled at Skullet and wondered how many more she might have concealed about her person. She tugged at Verity's sleeve.

'Perhaps we ought to leave now,' she whispered.

Verity blinked and nodded as Skullet began to push them more forcefully from the room. India glanced over her shoulder and caught a last glimpse of the black android, and Lady Fang, glaring after them.

At the top of the stairs, Skullet shoved them out of the door and drew his mouth into a snarl, exposing his carnivorous teeth. 'Get walking down that gangplank,' he hissed. 'Come here again and I'll cut out your livers.' He whipped out a slim-bladed knife and brandished it in the air for effect.

Verity raised an eyebrow. 'Be careful who you point that at, Skullet,' she said with a smirk. 'You might end up losing an eye.' Skillet's grin vanished instantly and he glanced anxiously over his shoulder. With a last snarl at India and Verity he slammed shut the door, leaving them on the deck.

'Come on,' said Verity, 'we've definitely outstayed our welcome. Let's get back to something approximating civilization.'

As they walked away from the boat India stopped and turned to take one last look at the decaying black hulk. 'That android . . .' she said. 'He was just like, you know . . .'

'Yeah, I know,' said Verity. 'He was just like Calculus. I had no idea there were any others. I'd love to see him working.'

'It wouldn't be the same though,' said India hurriedly. 'I mean, another android wouldn't be the same as Calculus, would it?'

Verity gave her a sad smile. 'No, kid, it wouldn't be the same at all.'

'Even so,' said India. 'I'd like to meet him properly.'

They returned to the market, the afternoon sun dispelling some of the chill that had followed them from the alleyways. 'At least now we've got some cash,' said Verity. 'I suggest we get out of Sing City as soon as possible before Lady Fang decides to repeat her job offer.' She glanced at India but the girl still seemed distracted and absent. 'I'm going to pick up a few supplies,' she continued. 'Why don't you head back to the guest house? You could spend some time looking at those circuit diagrams I gave you.'

India snapped out of her daze. 'Circuit diagrams? Thanks, but I'd rather eat one of Two-Buck's sandwiches.'

'If you're going to be a tech-hunter you need to know how stuff works,' said Verity, checking her bag and making a note of the things they needed. 'I'll see you at the guest house in two hours. Now go!'

India watched Verity disappear through the late afternoon crowds, then took a deep breath. Her encounter with the android had left her shaken and in no mood to concentrate on circuit diagrams. Perhaps a walk around Sing City would dispel the awful gloom that had followed her from Lady Fang's boat. If she was quick, she could spend some time in the market and still get back to the guest house before Verity. Feeling cheered by her decision, she shouldered her bag and started out through the crowds.

She was so absorbed by her surroundings that she failed to notice the stern-looking man at a nearby food stall, taking in her every movement. Nor did she see him get up and follow her with the practised ease of someone used to going unobserved.

The market was filled with people taking advantage of the cooler part of the day. India still found it hard to get used to the crowds in this part of the world. At home in London, the population lived in tiny hamlets, dotted around the shores of the drowned city. But here in Sing City, a million people lived in close sweaty proximity on the putrid waters. Even the towers looked different here, overgrown with muscular creepers and linked by spidery networks of rope bridges. Cooking fires burned in the shattered windows, smearing lines of blue smoke across the sky.

She followed the crowds towards a floating market where the air was thick with the shouts of stall holders selling squawking chickens, fly-covered meats and mutated sea creatures with too many eyes. Hawkers waved bags of fried locusts and fat grubs that wriggled at the end of wooden sticks. After some deliberation, she bought a fried scorpion and nibbled at it cautiously.

On the far side of the market the air smelled of oil and scorched metal and a mountainous man in a blacksmith's shop breathed life into a furnace with leather bellows. As India lingered in front of a stall selling rusted guns, she noticed a distinguished-looking man on the far side of the square. He had a deeply lined face and wore a close-trimmed beard with swept-back hair, greying at the temples. When he saw India watching him, he suddenly became interested in one of the fish stalls. Seized with a sudden impulse to leave, India followed the crowds away from the market, glancing back to be sure the man was not following. Many of the crowd had incorporated pieces of junk and old-tech into their clothing. One woman wore headphones adorned with peacock feathers, and a man dressed in a breastplate of circuit boards stalked above the crowd on six-foot stilts. Several people were clothed, not entirely successfully, in nothing but plastic bags.

Music was being played on home-made instruments fashioned from pipes, steel sheets and tins filled with rusty nails, which collectively sounded like a large amount of scrap metal falling down a moving staircase. There was excitement and expectation in the air and India found herself carried along on the human tide, increasingly curious to know where they were going.

The crowd arrived at a wide waterway crammed on both sides with people wearing a riot of reclaimed rubbish. Flags bearing painted pictures of a hand clutching a lighted torch fluttered in the breeze, and a suicidally large number of people clung to the overhead rope bridges. By contrast, the waterway itself was empty as though something important was expected at any moment. India glanced around anxiously to check she was not still being followed.

'Hi there, mind your shoving. There's wee ones down here getting squashed.'

A tall man in a wide-brimmed hat and a leather jacket, like her own, was lifting a wailing, snotty child on to his shoulders. The child understood none of what he was saying but seemed to take some comfort from the sound of his soft voice.

'Excuse me,' called out India, waving to attract his attention. 'Excuse me, can you tell me what's going on here?'

He turned to her as she pushed her way through the crowd and his face lit up with a brilliant grin. He had dark hair and eyes the colour of emeralds in rich soil.

'Well now, it's always good to hear a friendly voice in a strange land,' he said as he handed the child back to its mother. 'And who might you be?'

'India Bentley,' she said, sticking out her hand over the heads of several small children. 'I'm here with a friend of mine.'

'Cael O'Hanlon,' he said, shaking her hand firmly. 'Traveller, adventurer and entrepreneur.'

'Entre-what?'

'Entrepreneur. It means I take my opportunities where I find 'em.' He smiled a row of perfect teeth and the flecks in his eyes caught the sun.

'I was hoping you could tell me what was going on?' said India. 'Who are these people? They seem very excited.'

'Aye,' he said. 'They're trash ferrets. Today's a big day for them.'

'They're what?' India was not sure she had heard him correctly.

Cael handed the small child back to his mother and found a space at the front of the crowd for both of them. 'Trash ferrets. It's what people around here call them. Officially they're the "Divine Brotherhood of Recycling", or something like that. That's their mark.' He pointed to one of the flags with the hand and the torch. 'They're dedicated to recycling old rubbish.'

'Well that's the strangest religion I've ever heard of,' said India. 'What do they recycle exactly?'

'Everything,' said Cael. 'Paper, glass, metal, food scraps, you name it. If no one wants it they regard it as a religious duty to turn it into something useful. They think the same is true of people. They believe when they die they get reborn into a new body.' He grinned again. 'It sounds crazy but it's the ultimate form of recycling, I suppose.'

'It doesn't sound *that* crazy,' said India. 'I once had a friend who could do that.' She recalled how Calculus had once told her that if an android became damaged, its mind could be downloaded into a new body. She noticed Cael giving her a strange look and quickly changed the subject. 'So what happens at one of these festivals then?'

'Oh, the usual stuff,' said Cael. 'First the people "donate" their old rubbish and then the monks hand out whatever they've been making this month. Then the High Priest of

Reclamation makes a speech about everyone's sacred duty to recycle and everyone goes home happy.'

'The High Priest of Reclamation?' said India, laughing. 'Is that for real?'

'Sure,' said Cael. 'He's the big cheese around here. The trash ferrets have over a million followers in this part of the world, and even Lady Fang doesn't dare to bother them.' At the sound of Lady Fang's name, India cast another anxious look over her shoulder.

'Are you OK?' said Cael. 'You seem a bit nervous.'

'Yes, fine,' said India, turning on a smile. 'It's just I thought there was someone following me earlier.'

Cael nodded thoughtfully. 'Well, you're right to be careful. There are people here who'll steal the fillings from your teeth. Believe me, I owe money to most of them.' The crowd surged forward with a roar and India had to brace herself to avoid being pushed into the water. 'You should stick around to watch,' said Cael over the noise. 'It's a grand procession, even if you're not a believer.' He tipped his hat. 'It was nice meeting you, India.'

'You're not going to stay?' she said, failing to disguise the disappointment in her voice.

''Fraid not.' He winked. 'When you've seen one High Priest of Reclamation, you've seen them all. And besides, there's a card game starting with my name on it. Good day now!' He adjusted his hat and India sighed as she watched him saunter away.

While she loved her life as Verity's assistant, it was

hard making new friends. It seemed that you had barely met someone before you were saying goodbye again. She thought of her little sister Bella and her father, back home in Hampstead, and briefly longed for the predictability of her old life.

The cheering grew louder, drawing her out of her daydream. Two long boats were cruising along the canal towards the spot where she was standing. The first boat seemed to have been assembled from an infinite variety of mismatched wood like a floating jigsaw of a million pieces. The bows were decorated with thousands of plastic disks that split the sunlight into rainbow colours, the rigging was a riot of tightly knotted plastic bags, and the sails a patchwork of old rags. Shaven-headed monks in scarlet robes stood along each side, holding empty crates and sacks towards the crowd.

India became suddenly aware that the air was thick with flying garbage, sailing through towards the outstretched boxes. Rotten vegetables, scraps of metal, plastic bottles, tin cans, an old pram wheel and fish heads that smelt like they had been kept in the hot sun for a month – all were deftly caught by the monks. At the back of the boat, more monks were passing out new cooking pots, shoes fashioned from old tyres, and rough blankets to eager hands in the crowd.

'Turning rubbish into useful things,' said India to herself.

But it was the second boat that attracted the most attention. Its bows were covered in burnished gold leaf that blazed like fire in the afternoon. In the centre of the boat the High Priest of Reclamation rested serenely on a throne fashioned from plastic crates in front of an elaborate tapestry, bearing the sign of the hand and the torch.

The High Priest was an elderly man with jowls that moved independently of the rest of his face. He wore a tall scarlet hat and robes woven with threads of copper wire and he peered at the crowd with watery eyes that looked like three-day-old oysters. When India looked closely at the shimmering chain-mail cape that flowed down his back she saw it was made from thousands of tiny ring pulls taken from old drinks cans.

Behind the High Priest stood a young boy who India guessed to be about ten years old. He wore owlish, black glasses and a threadbare robe and he held a velvet cushion on which sat a small, dark stone. He blinked nervously at the crowds around him.

'The poor thing looks terrified,' thought India with a half-smile.

The sight of the procession was so bizarre that she had taken little notice of the faces in the crowd. But, while she was removing some poorly aimed potato peelings from her hair, she spotted a familiar cadaverous face, glistening with oily sweat. Skullet!

Her heart thumped vigorously in her chest. Had Lady Fang sent him here to track her down? But Skullet was not looking in her direction; he was staring at the High Priest with the eyes of a hyena watching a sick antelope. He pulled something from his sleeve that blinked once in the sunlight: the same cruel blade he had brandished earlier.

In a rush of realization, India saw what was about to unfold. Skullet was planning to kill the High Priest, probably on the orders of Lady Fang. She looked around wildly but no one else had seen the danger.

'He's got a knife!' she cried. Her shout was lost on a tide of cheering, but one person had heard her. Skullet wheeled around and his eyes narrowed as he focused on her. To India's horror, he began to push towards her, hiding his knife in the folds of his long coat.

India tried to move away but the crowds were pressing forward to see the boats and she found herself pushed towards the water's edge. Skullet lunged at her and grabbed her arm in an iron grip. 'Got you, you little witch! I'll teach you to keep your mouth shut.'

India struggled to pull away but in her panic her foot slipped from the edge of the walkway. Before she could regain her balance she had tumbled on to the deck of the passing boat, pulling Skullet after her.

They fell heavily on to the wooden deck. The impact knocked the wind from India's lungs but Skullet jumped up like a spring trap. A nearby monk ran towards them, but Skullet whipped his body around and a high kick caught the hapless monk across the jaw, sending him crashing over the side and into the water.

The High Priest began shrieking in a very un-priestly fashion as Skullet clambered towards him. In his panic, the priest became hopelessly entangled in the tapestry behind his throne and collapsed to the floor, trying to fight his way out of the heavy material.

But it seemed Skullet was not interested in the High Priest. Holding the knife in his hand, he advanced towards the boy with the velvet cushion.

India jumped to her feet; however afraid she was of Skullet, she could not stand by and watch him attack a helpless child. As Skullet snatched up the black stone from the cushion, India's full weight crashed into him. The stone fell to the floor and rolled under the throne and Skullet's knife clattered across the deck to plop harmlessly into the water.

Skullet turned on India, a snarling vision of muscle and sharpened teeth, but by now several bulky monks were running along the deck towards them and Skullet had run out of time. He gave India a last, toxic glare and then took off across the deck. He leaped from the boat with an animal howl that parted the terrified crowd and began to climb one of the strong creepers that twisted up the side of a nearby tower.

India climbed shakily to her feet. The High Priest was making faint whimpering noises as he struggled with the heavy drapes, and the young boy was sitting on the deck, his glasses askew, still clutching his empty cushion.

'It's OK,' said India to the boy, as soothingly as she could. 'I'm not going to hurt you. My name is India Bentley. I'm a tech-hunter.' The boy stared at her blankly and she wondered if he spoke any English.

Something caught her eye beneath the High Priest's throne: it was the stone. It was shaped like a segment of a circle and polished to a high sheen. 'Look,' she said. 'This belongs to you.' She bent down to pick it up but as she straightened a sharp pain spiked through her left eye making her clasp her hand to her face.

'Seize her!' screeched a voice.

India looked up and blinked. Several monks surrounded her; one of them pinned her arms to her sides while a second snatched the stone and began to search her pockets.

'It's not me you want,' she cried. 'I didn't attack anyone. It was that man up there.' She looked up at the tower but Skullet had long since disappeared through one of the many broken windows and was nowhere to be seen.

'Assassin!' The High Priest had succeeded in disentangling himself from the drapery and was now pointing a shaking finger at her. His tall hat was pushed to one side, his jowls quivered with rage, and his face had turned as scarlet as his robes. 'Assassin!' he hissed again. 'Heretic! Blasphemer! Unbeliever!' His hat fell off completely and flecks of spittle sprayed the monks nearest to him.

'Perhaps I might be of some assistance, Holiness,' interrupted a smooth voice. The speaker was a dark-skinned monk in black robes who came striding up the deck. India noticed the other monks stiffen and stand to attention as he arrived.

'Brother Amun,' spluttered the High Priest. 'Thank

goodness you're here. This, this *girl* is in league with the assassin who tried to take my life.'

'We found these on her, Brother Amun.' One of the monks handed him the black stone and India's shock stick, which they had removed from her pocket. 'We believe the girl and her accomplice were intent on stealing the sacred stone.'

Brother Amun turned the items over in his hand, a deep frown furrowing his brow. 'Excuse me, Brother Amun,' said a small voice. 'And begging the pardon of Your Holiness, but that's not what happened.' All eyes turned to look at the young boy who now looked even more terrified then he had been when facing Skullet.

'You have something to say, Brother Tito?' said Amun. His voice was cool and measured.

The boy swallowed and bowed deeply. 'Yes indeed, Brother. I saw what happened. I believe this lady was trying to save us. It was she who drove off the assassin and retrieved the stone.'

'Preposterous!' spluttered the High Priest, glaring at the terrified boy. 'She and her accomplice tried to murder me and it was only my cat-like reflexes that prevented it.'

India thought she saw the faintest hint of a smile at the corner of Brother Amun's mouth but he said nothing. He looked again at the items in his hand and seemed to be particularly interested in India's shock stick. He squinted along its length and weighed it carefully in his hand before sparking it alight, much to the consternation of the other monks who recoiled from the crackling blue sparks that sprang from its tip.

Amun snapped off the shock stick and turned his attention to India for the first time. His dark brown eyes drilled into her as though searching for something deep within her soul. 'Where did you get this?' he said, holding up the shock stick.

'It's mine!' she said, a little louder than she had intended. 'My dad made it for me, all right?'

Amun nodded thoughtfully and then snapped his fingers. 'Brother Scrofulous, if you please!' A fat monk shambled to the front of the group, breathing heavily through his mouth. He had a large red-and-yellow boil on the end of his nose and his skin was mottled with scaly red patches that he scratched constantly. 'Place the girl under arrest and take her to the cells,' said Amun quickly. 'I shall question her myself after I have made some enquiries of my own.' He handed the stone and the shock stick to Brother Scrofulous. 'Keep these safe until I arrive.'

The High Priest began to splutter again. 'I must protest, Brother Amun,' he began. 'That stone is a sacred relic and should be returned to the temple as soon as possible.'

Amun gave an effortless smile that failed to reach his eyes. 'As it will be, Holiness. Just as soon as I have finished my interrogation of the girl.'

'But she is an assassin and must be sentenced immediately.'

'I beg your indulgence, Holiness. But my investigations

take priority and the stone is an important piece of evidence. Take her below.'

Before the High Priest could protest further, the monk behind India tightened his grip. She was propelled towards a set of steps at the back of the boat, flanked by stern-looking monks and led by the unwholesome Brother Scrofulous.

India was seized by the terrible thought that Verity had no idea where she was and would have no way of knowing what had happened to her. With panic rising in her chest she turned to plead with Brother Amun. But only the young boy, Tito, remained, staring after her with sad eyes as the monks led her away.

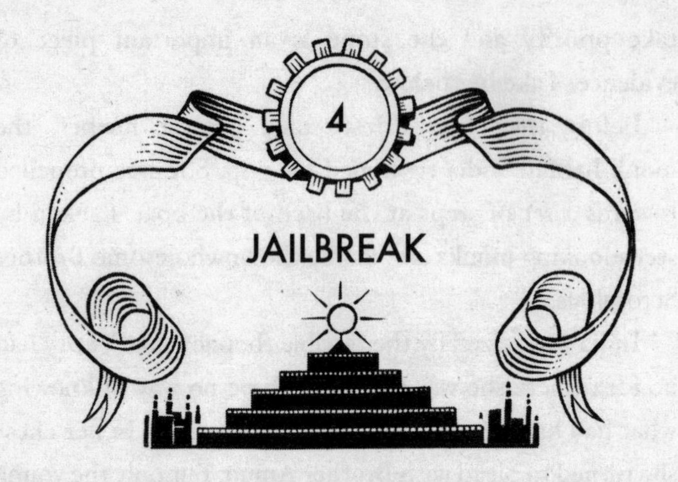

The snow lay like a ghost on the land and she walked with no sense of how she had got there or what had come before.

A lone wolf was waiting for her, snow settling in its fur. It was a wise and ageless creature and even before she looked, she knew it would have mismatched eyes, one the colour of earth, the other of sky.

'Where is this place?' she asked.

'You have been here before,' said the wolf. 'It is the edge of reason, the place where all things meet and where time itself has died.'

'Which way should I go?' she asked, knowing the answer.

'You must go forward,' said the wolf. 'There is no back.'

'Will you come with me?' she said, knowing again what the answer would be.

'I cannot,' said the wolf. 'The last part of the journey is yours alone to make.'

India looked anxiously into the white swirl ahead of them and then back to the wolf's mismatched eyes. She hoped it would change its mind but she knew it would not.

'My friend,' India said slowly. 'The one who died. Will I find him there?'

'You will find what you seek,' said the wolf. 'But at a price you may not wish to pay.'

'What price?' she asked.

The wolf did not answer. For the first time it looked away from her.

'What price?' she repeated.

The wolf scanned the horizon as though anxious to be gone, then turned to look at her with sadness in its eyes.

'You must look death in the face,' it said.

India woke with a start, her half-remembered dreams of death making her heart pound like a drum. She lay in the darkness trying to recall what was giving her such an awful sick feeling. Then she remembered where she was and the fear came rushing back like a cold tide.

She sat up on the crude wooden bed and looked around the dank stone cell. It was swimming with water and cold, despite the heat of the night. She didn't need to panic, she told herself. It was a mistake, that was all. Sooner or later they would come to let her out, she was sure of it.

But still no one had come.

A sliver of moon showed through the high, barred window. How long had she been here? Hours? A whole night? The journey to the jail had been chaotic and disorientating. The monks had kept her in the hold of the boat until they had reached a mouldering, vine-wrapped temple at the edge of the city.

The building was in an advanced state of collapse. Sinuous roots split the foundation stones, roofs sagged and broken archways lay where they had fallen. Sleek brown rats basked on slopes of rubbish heaped against the outer walls and the air was filled with the heavy sweetness of rot and burning rubber.

Inside the temple, the monks had marched India down a flight of steps into a vaulted chamber. Heavy doors were set into the slimy walls and a torch burned in a bracket, casting a guttering light over a small desk. While two of the monks restrained India, Scrofulous carefully locked the black stone in the desk drawer and then examined India's shock stick. India noticed how all the monks seemed fascinated and made appreciative noises when Scrofulous pressed the button to make crackling blue sparks shoot from its tip.

Then they'd pushed her into an empty cell and slammed the door shut with a crash. 'Don't leave me!' she had cried to the retreating monks. 'I haven't done anything. Tell Verity Brown that I'm here, *please*.'

But the monks had disappeared without speaking, leaving Brother Scrofulous still playing with the shock stick and deaf to her cries. Eventually, she had given up and huddled on the hard bunk, wondering what terrible punishments might be in store for someone accused of trying to assassinate the High Priest.

She dozed off briefly, but it was an anxious sleep, disturbed by frightening dreams. Now, several hours later, she was desperate to talk to *anyone* just so long as they would listen to her story and agree it had all been a mistake.

The noise of footsteps made her look hopefully towards the cell door. It sounded like the monks were returning . . . and dragging someone who was singing a loud and tuneless song with them. The door swung open and India started forward. 'Please—' she began.

Before she could get any further, a man was shoved into the cell; he stumbled a few paces and then fell face first into a pool of water. The door slammed shut again.

The man moaned and blew muddy bubbles. India prodded him, half afraid that he might drown and that she would get the blame for that too.

'Are you OK?'

He groaned and rolled over, blinking up at the ceiling. His eyes were red-rimmed and unfocused, his hair was matted and there was a cut over his right eye, but India recognized him right away.

'Cael? Is that you?'

The Irishman sat up slowly. His eyes roamed the room vaguely before settling on India. Then the slow dawn of recognition broke dimly across his face.

'Hey, India,' he declared loudly, breathing whisky fumes over her. 'How's my favourite Londoner?' He looked around the cell. 'The atmosphere in this bar is terrible,' he said. 'What do you say we go somewhere else for a drink?'

'We're in jail, Cael,' said India, trying to avoid his breath. 'I don't think they'll let us out for a drink.'

'In jail?' he repeated, puzzled. 'What did I do? No, don't tell me, let me guess.' He screwed his face up in deep thought.

'I don't know what you did, Cael,' said India irritably. 'You only just got here.'

'Oh yeah, I remember!' he said, brightening. 'A slight misunderstanding over a game of cards. I told them it was traditional in Ireland to carry a spare set of aces in our sleeves. I think that was when they started to chase me with the meat cleavers.'

'The monks chased you with meat cleavers?'

'Of course not! Have you been drinking? It was Lady Fang's men who chased me, I just took a short cut through the monastery. Then I had the call of nature and took a pee in some pond. How was I to know it's where the High Priest keeps his ornamental fish?'

The Irishman pushed himself off the soaking floor and collapsed heavily on to the bunk. 'More to the point,' he said, 'what are *you* doing here? You don't strike me as the sort of girl who would end up in a place like this.'

'It's a long story,' said India. 'Listen, Cael, I need your help. I was supposed to meet my friend hours ago – I *have* to get a message to her.'

Cael did not seem to be listening; he was retrieving his hat from the water. 'Damn it! These monks have no respect for other people's property.' He pulled the damp felt on to his head. 'Sorry, what were you saying?'

India let out an exasperated sigh.

'Oh yes,' he said quickly. 'You were talking about your friend. Hey, that reminds me. You'll never guess what happened after I left you. Someone tried to kill the High Priest. Can you believe that? I wouldn't want to be in that guy's shoes when that story gets out.'

'Cael—'

'The followers of the Divine Brotherhood are a touchy lot. If they get hold of the person who attacked their High Priest, there's no telling what they'll do.'

'Cael! Shut up! It was me. That's what I'm trying to tell you.'

Cael's mouth dropped open. 'You tried to kill the High Priest of Reclamation? In heaven's name *why*, India?'

'It wasn't *actually* me!' cried India. 'It was someone else, an assassin called Skullet. I tried to stop him but then the High Priest thought it was me and then they threw me in here and . . . Oh, Cael, what am I going to do?'

Now that she had begun to talk, the anxiety and fear of the last few hours boiled over and she buried her head in her hands and sobbed. Cael stared at her like a man who had just been sobered up with a bucket of cold water. He placed a tentative arm around India's heaving shoulders.

'Hey, hey, come on now,' he said gently. 'It's not as bad as all that. Look on the bright side.'

'The bright side!' she snapped. 'What's the bright side

of being locked in here exactly? A cell with a view? Three bowls of slop a day?'

Cael looked thoughtful. 'Well,' he said eventually. 'You've got an Irishman for company so you won't be short of conversation.'

India smiled weakly through the tears. 'You're not really helping, Cael,' she said.

She wiped her eyes as Cael settled back on the bunk and tipped his hat over his eyes, then set about inspecting the cell, testing the steel bars on the door but they were solid and immovable.

'Don't waste your energy, India,' muttered Cael, half in a doze. 'They built these places to last you know.' India ignored him and went back to the small window. But when she got there she gave a start. The window was set high up in the wall but it looked out at ground level on the outside. Directly in front of the bars was a pair of heavy black boots and she could hear loud whispering and shushings, as though two people were having a violent disagreement and trying to keep quiet at the same time. A large figure bent down to look through the window.

'Miss Bentley? Are you there? Please make yourself known.' She moved closer to the bars and gasped as she recognized the stern face staring back at her.

'You're the man who followed me in the market!'

'Don't be alarmed, Miss Bentley,' he said earnestly. 'I am a friend. We're here to rescue you.'

India cast an anxious glance towards the cell door

where Scrofulous could be heard snoring outside. 'Don't be alarmed?' she hissed back. 'You frightened the life out of me. Why should I trust you?'

'Because I'm here too.' A second figure bent down to peer in the window.

'Verity!' cried India, a little too loudly. 'Thank goodness! What are you doing here?'

'All in good time,' hissed Verity. 'Now pipe down or you'll bring every monk in the place running.'

'Right then,' said the grizzled man in a business-like fashion. 'Mrs Brown, please be good enough to keep a look-out. Miss Bentley, I strongly advise you to take some cover.'

He placed a small, tightly wrapped tube between the bars that fizzed and crackled at one end, and then ducked out of sight. India stared at it for a full three seconds before she realized what she was seeing.

'Jumping rig pirates!' she yelled. 'Cael, take cover, it's dynamite!'

Cael was lying comatose on the bunk. Unable to rouse him, India hooked her hands under the iron bunk and heaved upward with all her strength. The bunk tipped up, pitching the startled Cael on to the floor as India leaped over the top, hauling the straw mattress over both of them.

The blast slammed them against the wall, knocking the wind from India's lungs and showering them with rubble and grit. She shook her head and spat the dust from her mouth; it felt as though someone had clapped their hands over both her ears.

As the noise subsided, she pushed away the wrecked bunk and blinked through a fine cloud of white dust. Where once there had been a barred window there was now a large and irregular hole. Cael sat up and spat out a piece of rubble. 'Hell, I just had the strangest dream,' he muttered, before slumping back against the wall.

With a clattering of iron keys, the cell door swung open and Brother Scrofulous stood in the doorway, gawping at the wreckage of the cell.

'Stand aside, Miss Bentley,' came a voice from behind India. 'I'll deal with this.'

The grizzled man jumped through the hole in the wall and pulled out a pistol the size of a small cannon which he pointed at the quivering monk. He crossed the cell in two strides, grasped Scrofulous by the collar and marched him to the cell next door where he proceeded to lock the fat monk up using his own keys.

'Now then,' said the stranger when Scrofulous was secured, 'we must move quickly. That explosion will rouse every monk in the temple. Did you see where they put the sacred stone?'

India was taken aback by his request but she showed him the drawer where Scrofulous had locked the stone. As he fumbled with the keys India snatched up her shock stick from the desk. The man opened the drawer and pulled out the stone, holding it up to gaze at it in the flickering torchlight.

The sound of a door opening made him snap out of his

reverie. 'We are discovered, Miss Bentley,' he said, slipping the stone into his pocket. 'Come along now.' He ushered India back into the cell and locked the door behind them just as several monks rushed down the stairs and began to pound on it. Ignoring the dazed figure of Cael, he pushed India out of the hole in the wall.

Immediately someone flew at her from the darkness and two arms wrapped tightly around her. 'India, thank goodness you're safe,' cried Verity. 'When they told me what had happened I was out of my mind with worry.'

'Who told you what had happened?' said India pulling away. 'Who is this?'

'You deserve some explanations,' said the man as he climbed out after her, 'and I will provide them. But first we must get away from here.'

'Well, hello there.'

They turned to see Cael peering from the hole in the cell wall and swaying slightly. He was covered in rubble and dust. 'Nice hole you have here,' he said cheerily. 'Tell me, if you've finished using it would it be available for use by other members of the public?' He flashed a grin full of white teeth. The grizzled man stared blankly at Cael but it was Verity who reacted first.

'You!' she spluttered. 'What the hell are you doing here?' Cael gave her an unfocused look.

'Verity?' He said slowly. 'Is that you?' He scrambled quickly from the hole and peered closely at Verity as though she might be some trick of the light. 'Well I'll be damned, it *is* you!' he declared. 'This is fantastic! We should go and celebrate old times. Why don't we—'

He was cut short as a right hook caught him across the jaw. A brief look of surprise crossed his face before his eyes rolled up into his head and he keeled over backwards. Verity rubbed her knuckles and looked down at him with a scowl.

'Verity!' cried India in alarm. 'What have you done?'

The grizzled man frowned. 'Mrs Brown,' he said sternly. 'I said I would help rescue your colleague. I did not say I would help you to pursue a personal vendetta. What is the meaning of this?'

'He's just someone I used to know,' growled Verity. 'I always swore I'd kill him if I saw him again. I must be getting soft in my old age. Come on, just leave him and go.'

The older man's thick brows knitted together. 'I am not prepared to leave an innocent man to be blamed for our indiscretions, Mrs Brown,' he said. 'We'll take him with us and sort this out later.'

With surprising agility he hoisted Cael on to his shoulders and led them away from the temple at a brisk pace. A bell was clanging insistently from somewhere within the walls and India could hear shouting and running footsteps in the darkness behind them.

'What's going on, Verity?' she hissed as they ran. 'Who is this guy? And why did you punch Cael like that?'

'I'll tell you everything later,' hissed Verity. 'But I warn you now, don't start making friends with Cael O'Hanlon.'

They crossed a stinking stream that formed a boundary to the grounds of the temple and hurried through a warren of foul-smelling lanes until they emerged on to a dilapidated waterfront. At first sight, the little harbour appeared unremarkable; the water slapped thickly against the sides of a few broken-down fishing vessels and the ground was strewn with nets laid out to dry. But when India looked up, she stopped dead in her tracks.

Tied to the end of the wooden jetty was a small airship, straining at its tether. The grey, silken envelope was long and slim with an elegant gondola slung underneath, fashioned in rosewood and brass.

'This is my personal craft,' said the man. 'I find it a more convenient and flexible form of transport when I am in the city. Come along please, those monks are right on our tail.'

Thinking the evening could not get any stranger, India followed him along the jetty and watched as he untied the airship's mooring rope. A hatch swung open in the belly of the gondola and India caught a glimpse of a stern-faced sailor before a rope ladder clattered to the ground.

'After you, dear lady,' said the grizzled man to Verity. She seized the ladder and climbed quickly and gracefully up to the trapdoor. Before India could follow, the sailor leaned out and gave a warning whistle.

A broad skim boat was skipping across the waves towards them at high speed. There was a skeletal figure that could only be Skullet standing in the front and pointing to the airship. The grey-haired man gave a short laugh. 'It seems my airship has also attracted some unwanted attention from Lady Fang's men,' he said. 'Get up the ladder quickly and I'll deal with these miscreants.'

The propeller on the back of the gondola coughed to life and India scrambled up the ladder in an untidy fashion, with the grey-haired man close behind, still carrying Cael over his shoulder. Verity pulled India through the hatchway and they both reached out to haul in Cael's unconscious body.

The man brandished his hand-cannon at the approaching boats. A single blast from the gun rent the night air, sending a jet of orange flame and sparks from the muzzle. The front of Skullet's boat erupted in a shower of splintery wood and it immediately slowed and began to ship water. As the crew jabbered and screeched, the boat sank slowly beneath the waves and India had a last glimpse of Skullet, up to his waist in water, shaking a wiry fist at them.

The grey-haired man hauled himself into the gondola; his face was red with exertion and he was roaring with laughter. 'Lady Fang's men will not be back to bother us in a hurry,' he boomed. 'Please make yourselves comfortable and welcome to my little home from home. My name is Professor Evelyn Augustus Moon; scientist, archaeologist and adventurer.'

The inside of Professor Moon's airship was unlike anything India had ever seen. At one end of the gondola were the airship's controls, where the sailor was adjusting their course by means of a large ship's wheel.

The remainder of the space was a cross between a gentleman's drawing room and an old school laboratory. There were thick rugs and comfortable armchairs upholstered in blood-red velvet and oil lamps that cast pools of yellow light over dark wood panelling. A wooden bench was crammed with gleaming apparatus, and ranks of stoppered, brown bottles stood in glass cabinets. A steel and glass device stood on the bench, partially hidden beneath a dust sheet.

India watched as Professor Moon lay Cael's unconscious body on a small sofa. She thought his neatly kept beard and swept-back hair gave him the air of a sea captain.

'Welcome to my laboratory,' he said, removing his long

coat with a swirl and casting it on to a chair. 'Allow me to get you some refreshments.' He ushered them to a sofa and busied himself at a drinks cabinet.

India gave Verity a quizzical look while the professor's back was turned. 'I don't know much more about this than you do,' whispered Verity. 'One of his crew came to find me with a message to say you'd been arrested and that the professor had a plan to get you out. I had no choice but to go along with it.'

'I must apologize if I scared you in the market earlier, Miss Bentley,' said the professor, uncorking a bottle of wine. 'But I had to be certain of who you were before I tried to make contact.'

'So you *were* following me,' said India, 'I knew I wasn't imagining it. Did you have anything to do with the attack on the High Priest?'

The professor shook his head. 'Certainly not, Miss Bentley. That was the work of Lady Fang's gangsters. You are to be congratulated for your prompt action, by the way, even if the High Priest didn't appreciate it.'

He placed three goblets of ruby red wine on the low table before them and settled into a comfortable leather armchair. India had never tried wine before. She expected it to taste sweet, like blackcurrant jam, but shuddered when she gulped her first mouthful. It tasted of vinegar and cold tea.

'We owe you our thanks for breaking India out of jail, Professor,' said Verity. 'But—'

'But you were wondering why I would rescue a complete stranger?' he said. He took a long draught of his wine and set down his glass. 'I confess I have been trying to find you for some time, Miss Bentley,' he said, looking over at India. 'But before I explain, allow me to show you something.'

He reached into his pocket and pulled out the sacred stone he had retrieved from the jail. He placed it carefully on the table so that India could see it properly for the first time. It had a polished surface of the darkest green speckled with blood-red flecks. It looked like it had been broken from a large disc; the outer edge was smooth and curved but the other sides were rough and jagged and there were tiny hieroglyphs scratched into its surface.

The professor let out a deep sigh. 'The sacred stone,' he murmured to himself. 'I never expected to find this in my lifetime.'

Verity frowned. 'What sort of stone is that, Professor?'

'It is a rare form of green jasper, Mrs Brown,' he said. 'Alchemists believed it drew its power from the sun and the pagans worshipped it as a source of energy.'

'Well, what's so special about it?' said India.

The professor opened his jacket and reached into a small leather pouch on his belt. 'Because, Miss Bentley, it belongs with this one.' He pulled a second piece of red-speckled stone from the pouch and lay it beside the first. It was the same shape and colour, only the faint pattern of hieroglyphs on the surface was different. It was clear that the jagged edges fitted together to make two-thirds of a complete disc.

'This piece,' he said, settling back into his chair, 'was the property of my late grandfather, Sir Vivian Moon. He found it in a burial chamber in the ancient city of Tiwanaku in Bolivia.'

'That's very interesting, Professor,' said Verity, 'but we're tech-hunters, not archaeologists.'

'Perhaps I should start from the beginning,' said the professor, taking up his wine again. 'Have you ever heard of the Cintamani stone?'

Verity frowned. 'I read something about it once. Wasn't it a gift from the gods or something?'

'Very good, Mrs Brown,' said the professor. 'Sumerian legend said it was an ancient artefact and that it was cursed. They said it could not be held by anyone unworthy of its power. So many were killed in disputes over its ownership that it became known by a different name: *the Bloodstone*.'

Verity nodded. 'Well, if it was so ancient, where did it come from originally?'

'From the dawn of human history,' said the professor. 'A time when many cultures told legends of earthquakes and floods that came close to wiping out the human race.'

'You mean like Noah in the Bible?' said India, taking another experimental sniff of her wine and deciding it wasn't worth the effort.

'Precisely so,' said the professor. 'But did you know that there are over five hundred legends from around the world that talk of a great flood? It seems highly likely they all refer to real events in history.' He paused to take a sip of his wine. 'It was during that time of great chaos that a mysterious figure appeared in the ancient writings. He was known by many different names, but he is often just referred to as the Great Teacher. It was said that when he arrived, the earthquakes stopped, the flood waters receded and peace returned to the Earth. He united the warring tribes and taught them farming, mathematics, astronomy and science. His teachings formed the foundation of our modern civilizations and yet no one knows where he came from.'

'So what does this have to do with the Bloodstone?' said Verity.

'I was coming to that,' said the professor with a frown. 'The legends say that after a hundred years of peace and prosperity, the Great Teacher lay dying. He gathered the kings of the three most powerful tribes and presented them with the gift of a sacred stone. He said it was the key to the knowledge of the gods and that whoever owned it would have the sun bow down to him like a lowly servant.'

'That sounds pretty handy,' said India. 'So what happened to it?'

The professor shook his head. 'Jealousy took hold of the three kings,' he said. 'Unable to agree who should hold the stone, they broke it apart and took a piece each. After that all trace of it was lost in the tides of time. Until now, that is.'

India looked at the stones on the table. 'So you really think these are two pieces of the Bloodstone?' she said.

'My grandfather thought so,' he replied. 'The legend became his life's work. After he found the first piece he became obsessed with finding the others. Sadly, he disappeared without trace while on another expedition to find them.' He sighed. 'I have tried my best to follow in his footsteps but after many years of searching I had begun to despair. But then I stumbled upon a clue that led me here to Sing City and a group of monks said to own a sacred stone that fitted the description. When I came to investigate, I found I was not the only one with an interest in it. I witnessed Lady Fang's men trying to steal it and I saw you being arrested.'

'So that's why you broke into the jail,' said India. 'You weren't trying to help me at all, you were just after the stone.'

The professor said nothing.

'So why is this stone so important that you're prepared to risk your life for it?' said Verity.

The professor weighed his words carefully. 'Because this is no ordinary piece of rock, Mrs Brown,' he said. 'It dates from a time when men still lived in caves and mud huts, and yet when I examined it in the laboratory I discovered something that chilled my blood.' He took another sip of wine. 'Embedded deep within the stone I found circuits.'

Verity raised an eyebrow. 'Circuits?'

'Electrical components whose purpose I can only guess

at, hidden where they were never meant to be found. I rechecked my findings, but there is no doubt, the Bloodstone is a twelve-thousand-year-old piece of technology.'

India caught a warning look in Verity's eye. The previous year they had found an ancient machine buried under a mountain in Siberia that had been there for over twelve thousand years. Clearly, Verity wasn't ready to share this knowledge just yet.

Verity gave a casual laugh. 'Really, Professor. Ancient machines? That's all a bit far-fetched isn't it?'

The professor narrowed his eyes. 'Don't take me for a fool, Mrs Brown. I know all about the ancient machine you found at Ironheart.' He leaned forward. 'And I know that Miss Bentley was able to communicate with the machine.'

India gulped. There were only a handful of people that knew about the machine at Ironheart and even fewer who knew that India had spoken to it and persuaded it to stop an asteroid from destroying the Earth.

'W-what do you mean, Professor?' stammered India.

'I'm talking about your ability as a Soul Voyager, Miss Bentley,' said the professor. 'Don't look so surprised. I travel extensively and I always pay well for information. Something as big as Ironheart could not have stayed a secret for long.'

India fell silent; it had been whole a year since she met the shaman, Nentu, in the forests of Siberia, who had told her she had the gift of a Soul Voyager. Who could have told Professor Moon her secret?

'We don't like people knowing our business, Professor,' said Verity coolly. 'So tell me why you're so interested in Ironheart. And what do you want from India?' India noticed Verity's hand move imperceptibly towards her pistol.

The professor glanced at Verity's gun and then smiled. 'Of course, of course, dear lady, I didn't mean to alarm you. But you discovered evidence of an ancient race of beings who lived over twelve thousand years ago. What if the Great Teacher was a survivor from that Elder Race and he came to share his wisdom with us before it was lost forever? The Great Teacher said that the Bloodstone held the knowledge of the gods. I believe it is the key to the secrets of the Elder Race.'

The professor's purpose began to dawn on India. 'You think I can help you because I'm a Soul Voyager, don't you?' she said.

The professor nodded. 'Yes, Miss Bentley, I do. You have a connection with the machines that we don't fully understand. Throughout the ages there have been shamans and holy men who heard the voices of spirits. What if what they were really hearing were the voices of the ancient machines?'

'I'm sorry, Professor,' said Verity, 'I'm not buying any of this. The machine at Ironheart was a mystery but there's nothing to suggest that there are any more of them. And if the Elder Race were *so* important, then why is there no record of them?'

'But there is, Mrs Brown,' said the professor. 'Plato

himself wrote about just such a civilization. He described a mighty seafaring nation descended from the gods themselves. The name he gave to that empire was *Atlantis*.'

India spluttered into her wine. 'Atlantis! I remember that story. The empire was supposed to have lasted for thousands of years but it was lost under the waves in a single night. But it's not really true, it's just a myth.'

Professor Moon's eyebrows knitted together into a thick bush. 'And what is a myth but a truth retold many times over, Miss Bentley?' he said. 'You saw the ancient machine at Ironheart with your own eyes. Atlantis is real, Miss Bentley, and these stones are the key to its secrets.'

India examined the stones. Although she didn't fully trust the professor, she was intrigued by his story. 'Well, what "secrets" does it unlock?' she asked.

The professor was becoming excited now. He jumped up and selected a thick leather-bound volume from the book case. 'I have a theory,' he said, flicking through the pages. 'The Great Teacher said the Bloodstone unlocked a power that would make the sun bow down. I believe he was giving us a clue about one of their most important technological achievements.'

'Which was what?' said India.

'The ability to generate unlimited energy, Miss Bentley. Without a supply of energy no civilization can flourish. Aha! Here we are.' He placed the book in front of them. 'What do you think of that?'

Among the dense text was a fine ink drawing of an

ancient pyramid standing in the middle of a city. A shaft of energy blazed from the top, suffusing the building with a brilliant glow and scattering beams of light across the city.

India frowned. 'What is that?'

'The legend of the Sun Machine, Miss Bentley,' said the professor triumphantly. 'It was said the Atlanteans had a machine that could generate all the energy they needed to power their civilization. At its heart was a unique crystal of unknown origin, called the Heliotrope. It could absorb the rays of the sun and multiply their energy ten thousand times.'

'It sounds like a dangerous thing to have around,' said Verity, raising an eyebrow.

'On the contrary, Mrs Brown. The Heliotrope was the source of great wellbeing to the Atlanteans. Not only did it generate energy, it kept them in good health and ensured they lived long and happy lives.'

India frowned. 'And so the Bloodstone . . .'

'. . . is the key to the machine that harnesses the power of the Heliotrope. Just imagine! If we could harness that sort of energy today we would have no more reliance on oil barons and pirates. We could rebuild our factories, light our cities and grow more food. It would transform our world.' He sat back with a satisfied smile.

Verity blew out her cheeks. 'Well that's quite a story, Professor,' she said. 'Which perhaps explains why Lady Fang is so interested in the Bloodstone too?'

Professor Moon waved a dismissive hand. 'Lady Fang is

no more than an ageing gangster. She has no doubt heard of the Bloodstone and wishes to see if she can make a quick profit.'

India frowned; the professor's words had the feel of a lie about them.

'And where *exactly* do you expect to find Atlantis, Professor?' asked Verity. 'People have searched for it for years.'

'Then quite clearly, Mrs Brown,' he said, 'it must be somewhere that no one has looked before.' He picked up one of the pieces and ran his fingers over it. 'The hieroglyphs on here are written in an ancient language known only to a few scholars. My grandfather translated a portion of the message and believed it pointed to an area known today as the Quartermain Mountains.'

'I've never heard of the Quartermain Mountains,' said India.

'That's because they lie in one of the last great wildernesses on Earth, Miss Bentley, deep in Antarctica, where few people have ever been. It is my hope that the Bloodstone will provide me with the clues I need to find Atlantis.'

'Well, good luck with that,' said Verity. 'But by my reckoning you're still missing a piece and, from what you've said it could take a lifetime to find it.'

'That's where you are wrong, Mrs Brown,' said the professor. He got up and began to pull the dust-covers away from the bench. The equipment underneath was a tangle of wires and tubes. A thick metal column rose from the centre of the bench with a large steel ball at the top. A heavy leather belt on pulleys ran up the column, and the whole device was connected to a small rosewood box by means of red and black cables.

'This is a Van de Graaff generator of my own design,' said the professor, tapping lightly on a flickering dial. 'Some time ago, I happened to pass a small electrical current through my grandfather's piece of the stone. I was surprised to find that it began to give off a signal.'

'What sort of signal?' said Verity.

'A regular pattern of decremental integers with a fixed time period,' he said, prodding the wooden box with a screwdriver.

Verity frowned. 'Er, did you just say it was counting down?'

'Precisely so, Mrs Brown.' He said. 'As far as I can tell, the pieces of the Bloodstone have been counting down steadily for the last twelve thousand years. By my estimates, the sequence will reach zero in approximately three weeks' time.'

'What?' Verity looked incredulous. 'A twelve-thousand-year-old machine is counting down to a date three weeks from now?'

The professor popped his head up from behind the machine and frowned at Verity. 'I believe that's what I just said, Mrs Brown. Really this is going to take a long time if you just keep repeating everything I say.'

'But what is it counting down *to*?' asked India, wishing the professor would hurry up and get to the point.

'Ah, now there's a question,' he said, standing up. 'The end of the countdown coincides with a number of different events. However, the one I believe to be most significant is the occurrence of a total solar eclipse, which will be visible over a large part of the Antarctic.'

'An eclipse in the Antarctic?' said India.

'Now you're doing it too, Miss Bentley. Yes, the eclipse is due to start at the precise second that the countdown ends. Bit of a coincidence, wouldn't you say? However, the countdown is not the most important thing.'

'It's not?' said Verity and India in unison.

'No. I also discovered that the stone was receiving an incoming signal.'

'From where?' said Verity.

'From the second piece of the stone here in Sing City,' he said. 'That was how I learned that the monks had it. I believe that each piece of the stone has the ability to locate the others. It's almost as if they want to be brought back together again.'

The professor made some small adjustments to the cables. 'Now I intend to repeat the experiment to see if I can locate the third piece. This equipment will send a current through the stones and any incoming signals will be recorded on this ticker-tape.' He pointed to a clockwork mechanism standing under a glass dome that spooled paper tape on to the floor. 'I'm hoping the presence of a Soul

Voyager will enhance the signal and improve our chances of success. There.' He stood back to admire his handiwork. 'I think we're about ready to start.'

'Wait a minute,' said Verity. 'The last time we tinkered with a piece of ancient technology, India was nearly killed.'

'There's no reason to suspect the stones are dangerous,' said the professor. 'I've run these experiments a dozen times. We are all quite safe.'

India bit her lip. She had started out feeling sceptical about the professor's story, but the more he talked about lost civilizations and ancient machines the more excited she had become. She looked at the two stones lying side by side on the table. Could these really be connected in some way to the machine they had found at Ironheart? And, if they were, might they provide some clues as to what had become of Calculus?

She gave Verity a pleading look. 'Please let him try,' she said. 'After all, if Professor Moon hadn't helped us, I'd still be in that jail. And besides,' she added, 'it does sound pretty cool.'

Verity sighed and then gave a resigned nod. 'OK then. But at the first sign of trouble I want that thing shut off.'

'Excellent!' barked the professor. 'Let's get started.'

He placed the stones in a steel dish and attached a pair of cables to it. Then he took a deep breath and threw a switch on the front of the box. The leather belt began to move, slowly at first and then progressively faster. A small lamp on top of the box glowed dimly and the room filled with an electrical hum. A blue-white spark snapped suddenly from the steel ball and the air smelled charged and burned.

As the power built up, a high-pitched noise began to vibrate in India's teeth, hovering on the edge of being painful. Without warning, the two halves of the stone snapped together like a child's magnet and the sound increased tenfold, making India gasp and hold her head in her hands.

'Are you OK, India?' said Verity.

She opened her mouth to speak, but nothing came. A brilliant blue flash exploded behind her eyes and with a noise like the sky being torn in two, everything went black.

She walked through the blizzard, feeling more alone with every step, until a shape emerged ahead of her. It was taller than any man, black-robed and dark-hooded. A spectre with no face.

'Which way should I go from here?' she asked.

The spectre watched the pale yellow disc of the sun as a dark bite of shadow appeared in its side. Then it turned to look at her.

'Do you still seek your friend?' said the spectre.

'Yes. Where can I find him?'

With a sweep of its hand, it showed her a lake of ice beneath her feet.

Frozen in the clear blue tomb, she could see a shape, vast and elegant, like a beautiful seashell, shimmering with a thousand colours. And standing beside it she saw her friend, the android, looking up at her. He beckoned her slowly towards him, like a drowning man who knows he is too far from shore.

'I can see him,' she cried. 'I have to go and help him.'

The spectre did not speak. The bite from the sun grew bigger and the light grew dimmer.

'Are you afraid of the darkness?' said the spectre eventually.

'I'm not afraid,' she replied.

The black disc finally slid over the surface of the sun and the shadow of the moon raced across the ground, dropping darkness over them like a veil.

'You should be,' said the spectre. 'Everyone would be afraid of the dark if they knew what lived there.'

The ice beneath her feet gave way, dropping her into the icy blue tomb, a thousand miles below. And she screamed . . .

And she screamed.

'India, wake up!' Someone was shaking her shoulders and cold water splashed on to her face. She coughed and her eyes opened wide; she was breathing heavily.

'India, can you hear me?' Verity knelt beside her, concern etched on her face. 'What did you do to her, Professor? You said this experiment would be safe.'

Professor Moon looked pale. 'It *is* safe,' he stammered. 'I-I mean, this was totally unexpected.'

'I'm all right,' said India struggling to sit up. She forced a smile. 'Really, Verity, I'm fine. I just fainted, that's all.'

The professor picked up the dish which had held the stones and inspected it closely. 'Astonishing,' he said. 'The process seems to have fused the two pieces together. It's as though they were determined to be rejoined.'

The ticker-tape machine burst into life and began chuntering out paper. The professor scanned it eagerly while Verity helped India to a chair. 'You were out cold for about five minutes,' she said.

'I saw Calculus!' said India, remembering. 'He was sort of frozen in the ice but he wasn't dead, he wanted me to come to him. Then the ice opened up and I fell and—'

'Take it easy,' said Verity. 'It was just a dream.'

'No it wasn't,' said India insistently. 'It wasn't a normal dream at all. It felt like someone, or *something*, was trying to give me a message.'

'It's working,' cried the professor. He held up the thin paper ribbon and began scribbling numbers on a notepad. He turned to the globe and jabbed a finger on a remote spot near the bottom of the great blue ball. 'The signal is coming from somewhere around here.'

'That's deep in the Southern Ocean,' said Verity, peering at the globe. 'No one in their right mind has ventured that far south since the Great Rains.'

The professor stroked his chin thoughtfully. 'Nevertheless, it's where I intend to go,' he said.

'Well if it's the Southern Ocean you're going to, then I'm your man,' came a voice from the corner. They turned to see Cael sitting up on the sofa and massaging his jaw. India had quite forgotten he was there and had no idea how long he had been awake.

Cael jumped from the sofa and crossed the room, extending his hand to the professor. Verity scowled deeply.

'I spent a year on a whaling vessel before I came to Sing City,' he said. 'I know everything there is to know about that part of the world. The name's Cael O'Hanlon: freelance expedition adviser, at your service.' He grinned broadly and the light in his eyes twinkled. 'The Southern Ocean is a dangerous place, Professor. If you're going there, you'll need a good guide.'

The professor eyed him carefully. 'And I expect you're about to tell me you're just the man for the job?' he said.

Verity snorted. 'You can't be serious, Professor. This man is completely untrustworthy. He's a liar and a cheat and . . .'

Cael's grin had been growing ever wider as Verity spoke. 'Don't you pay her any attention, sir, she's just feeling a bit of "emotional strain". Believe me, I know everyone worth knowing in the Southern Ocean.' He looked around the laboratory. 'Plus, I'm pretty handy with machinery. I reckon I could be quite useful to you, Professor.'

The professor looked at him thoughtfully. 'Very well,' he said. 'Come and see me on board my ship when we land and we'll talk further.' Cael bowed and then winked at Verity who looked ready to punch him again.

'As for you, Miss Bentley,' said the professor, 'I would dearly like to have the skills of a Soul Voyager on the team. I want you and Mrs Brown to consider joining my expedition to find Atlantis. We leave for the Southern Ocean on the high tide and I'll pay you both well for your services.'

'Thank you for the offer, Professor,' said Verity quickly.

'But we were planning to take a break from work for a while.' She gave Cael a poisonous glance. 'I'd hate to suffer from any more "emotional strain".'

The crewman at the helm cleared his throat. 'We'll be arriving at the harbour in about ten minutes, Professor,' he announced.

The professor checked his pocket watch. 'Well, it's your choice, of course, Mrs Brown. But before you make a decision there's something else I'd like to show you.' He went to the bookshelves and selected a scruffy-looking journal.

'This notebook came from the library of my grandfather.' He thumbed through the pages. 'Look at this.' He pointed to a grainy black-and-white photograph of a stone carving. It showed a circle with rays extending out in all directions and, beneath it, a triangular shape like a pyramid.

'This hieroglyph was found inside a Mayan temple in southern Mexico,' he said. He flicked through more pages. 'Exactly the same hieroglyph was found in the temple of Gobekli Tepe, the Ziggurats of Sumer and the Great Pyramid of Khufu in Egypt. All of them refer to a device that could magnify the power of the sun a thousandfold. I ask you, Mrs Brown, does that not sound like a description of the Sun Machine?'

'Not really, Professor,' said Verity with a shrug. 'It could be anything.'

'In which case,' said the professor with a smile, 'you may be more interested in this.' He flipped over the page. 'This photograph shows a depiction of the demon, said to stand guard over the Sun Machine.'

Verity took the book from him with a sigh and looked at the page. Her eyes grew rounder. 'I don't believe it,' she said in a small voice. India took the book and frowned at the picture. It showed a group of tiny figures, gathered around an altar. But what drew her attention was the figure at the centre. It was a full head taller than the others and its face was masked by a long helmet. The body was slim and, even in such a crude stone carving, it looked powerful and strong.

India blinked at the image. Although the photograph was of poor quality, there could be no doubt that what she was looking was an ancient hieroglyph depicting an android.

6 THE BROTHERHOOD

The first rays of sun broke over the Temple of Reclamation, warming the piles of rubbish heaped against the outer walls and making them steam gently. In the tallest tower of the monastery, the High Priest leaned from his chamber windows to breathe the sweet scent of rottenness and take in the scene below.

In one corner of the temple courtyard, two young monks stood in a vat of glutinous grey sludge, placidly trampling pulp paper, with their robes hitched around their thighs. A dozen yards away a shaggy monk-mountain pulled white hot metal from a brazier and hammered it energetically on an anvil as the sparks nestled in his beard. Others crushed broken glass with pounding poles, sorted ferrous metals with giant magnets or stirred bathtub-sized vats of boiling offal. It was, he reflected, a glorious vision.

He sighed and closed the window. His time as a young monk had been the happiest days of his life. Back then the worst he had needed to worry about were a few rat bites or the prospect of stepping in something radioactive. He sat down and caressed the small golden statue of a garbage god on his desk which was said to impart a sense of deep calm to all those who touched it.

'So,' he said in a tight voice. 'Tell me again, Brother Scrofulous, how you managed to let the girl escape?'

Scrofulous sat across the desk, scratching the scabrous patches on his skin and wearing an expression that made him look like he would have difficulty picking his nose without written instructions. He adopted what he considered to be his best expression of abject sorrow as he rummaged in his ear with an index finger.

'I am most abjectly sorry, Holiness,' he began, 'but it wasn't my fault. The girl had help, she—'

'IDIOT!' Scrofulous dived for cover as the garbage god sailed across the room like a golden missile and cratered the wall behind him. 'Scrofulous, you are without doubt the most pitiful and wretched excuse for a monk I have ever laid eyes on.'

'Yes, Holiness.'

'I have seen more intelligent creatures floating on their backs in the sewers of Sing City.'

'Yes, Holiness.'

'And now you are responsible for the loss of the sacred Bloodstone, stolen, for the second time in the space of a day, BY THE SAME PERSON!'

'Yes, Holiness.'

'Scrofulous, are you trying to send me to an early grave?'

'May your parts be fully recycled and may you always return as something eternally useful,' mumbled Brother Scrofulous, providing the standard response.

Once again, Brother Scrofulous cursed his decision to enter the priesthood, which he blamed entirely on his mother. 'Three square meals a day, Scrofulous,' she had said, 'is not to be sniffed at. And a bath every six months whether you need one or not!' Scrofulous wondered idly if he might be able to earn a better living as a beggar by displaying some of his nastier skin sores in the market. He realized with a start that the High Priest had been talking.

'. . . and I don't need to tell you the consequences if that happens, do I?'

'Er, yes, Holiness. I mean, no, Holiness.'

'You make me sick, Scrofulous. Get back to your post and know that I hold you personally responsible for anything that happens to me.'

'May your parts be fully recycled and may—'

'GET OUT!'

Scrofulous needed no second telling. He hoisted his robes around his fat, scaly thighs and fled the cloister before the High Priest could reach for another sacred relic.

When he had gone, the High Priest closed his eyes and breathed in the soothing vapours from the rotting rubbish outside.

'Are you quite all right, Holiness?' The High Priest opened his eyes and looked wearily at the dark-skinned monk who was watching him calmly from a corner of the room.

'No, I am not all right, Amun!' he snapped. 'Thanks to that septic bag of lard, we have lost a sacred relic that has been in our order for over six hundred generations. How did Scrofulous allow himself to be outwitted by a little girl?' His brow furrowed and he rubbed his flaccid chin. 'Unless of course *he's* in league with the assassin? He's devious, that one; perhaps I should have him flogged to make sure?'

Brother Amun laughed lightly and with the just the right amount of respect. 'Devious? Scrofulous? You overestimate him, Holiness. That fat fool would have trouble outwitting the average chicken.'

The High Priest got up and began to pace, shaking his head, which had the unfortunate effect of making his face wobble like a poorly balanced jelly. 'And what about the girl? Quite aside from having stolen the Bloodstone, how do I know she won't come back and try to finish me off?' He looked at Amun with watery eyes.

Brother Amun smiled reassuringly. 'Have no fear, Holiness, I have information that the girl was seen escaping in the company of one Professor Evelyn Moon, a notorious scientist and archaeologist with a dubious reputation and an interest in the Bloodstone. I believe he is the one behind the theft.'

The High Priest stopped pacing and blinked stupidly. 'A scientist? With an interest in the Bloodstone? You don't think he might be trying to—'

'Yes, I do, Holiness,' said Amun. 'It is rumoured that Moon already owns a piece of the Bloodstone inherited from his grandfather. I believe he might be trying to reassemble the device.'

'Reassemble it?' said the older monk weakly. He groped for the edge of his desk and sat heavily in his chair. 'And he already has a piece?'

'Two pieces if you include ours,' said Amun. 'I don't need to tell you what this means.'

The High Priest's sagging face had turned to the colour of milk. 'This is serious, Amun,' he said in a panicked voice. He jumped from his seat and clutched the front of Amun's robes, shaking them urgently. 'This could mean the end of everything. What are we going to do?'

Amun gently disengaged the High Priest's grip and smoothed down the front of his robe before continuing. 'I have discovered that a vessel registered to Professor Moon is at anchor in Sing City harbour. With your permission, Holiness, I should like to take a small group of our best men to investigate.'

The High Priest nodded and bit his lip. 'Yes, yes, of course . . . that would be the best thing.'

'I will also question the boy,' said Amun. 'The girl spoke to him, briefly, on the boat.'

'The boy? You think he knows something?'

'Trust me, Holiness, the boy may be more important than any of us suspect. If Moon and the girl are collecting pieces of the Bloodstone, then I will stop at nothing to protect our interests.' Amun regarded the High Priest with unwavering brown eyes that chilled the older man's marrow. There was so much fervour in those eyes, so much righteousness, that the High Priest did not doubt for one moment that Brother Amun would do what he said. He felt almost sorry for the girl.

'Very well, Amun,' he said, wearily. 'I'll send for the boy immediately.'

'I have already taken the liberty of sending for him, Holiness,' said Amun. 'Scrofulous will bring him along momentarily.'

'I hope you know what you're doing,' said the High Priest. 'If the other pieces of the stone . . .' He trailed off and cocked his head to one side. 'Can you hear the temple bells ringing?'

They listened to the incessant tolling and a moment later came the sound of footsteps running down the hall towards the office. The door was flung open and a red-faced Scrofulous burst in, panting.

'Your Holiness,' he gasped. 'The boy . . . he's, he's . . . gone.'

'Gone? Do you mean he's hiding in the temple somewhere?'

'No, Holiness. He packed a suitcase before he left. I think he's run away, sir.'

7 THE DOGS OF WAR

'So, tell me again how you managed to let the girl escape?'

Skullet sat before Lady Fang's desk, clenching and unclenching his fists so that the tattoos on his biceps flexed and rippled. Skullet was the sort of man that other men were afraid of. He was quick to anger and slow to back down, and he had the sort of mad-dog look in his eye that said whatever you did to Skullet, Skullet was going to do right back to you, preferably slowly and with the aid of something sharp. That was a reputation to be proud of, he told himself.

So it made no sense to Skullet that his mouth became dry and his hands shook when he was alone in front of Lady Fang. After all, she was just a thin, middle-aged woman who wore too much make-up and smoked like a tyre burner. But, he reflected, it never felt quite that way when he sat here.

'It weren't my fault,' he said haltingly. 'Moon got to her first. Once she got on board his airship we didn't stand a—'

'I don't have time for excuses, Skullet,' snapped Fang. Her voice was calm, measured. It made Skullet even more nervous. 'Your job was simple enough, just get the stone. But you were outwitted by a little girl and that clown, *Evelyn Moon*.'

Fang crossed the room and placed the sharp point of a crimson nail against the corner of Skullet's eye. 'Maybe I should teach you a lesson? Pluck out one of these and add it to my collection perhaps?'

Skullet said nothing but he burned inside. If Fang had been a man he would have killed her where she stood.

Fang began to pace the room thoughtfully. 'My spies tell me the airship is heading for the harbour,' she said, 'and he's taking the girl with him. Once they are on board his ship we will not be able to risk another attack.'

'I could do it,' blurted Skullet. 'Just give me a chance. I'll get on board then I'll find that little witch and I'll—'

Fang bared her long teeth. 'Interrupt me while I'm talking again, Skullet, and I'll have your tongue nailed to your forehead.' Skullet lapsed back into an angry silence. 'Maybe this can work to our advantage,' she continued. 'Moon must be hoping the girl will lead him to the third stone. All we need to do is follow them at a discreet distance. Then we will simply take *everything* we want.'

Skullet scowled and tested the sharpness of his teeth with a finger. 'How are you gonna do that? Once they're at sea there's no way to track their course.'

Fang smiled. 'Maybe not for you, Skullet. But perhaps it's time I put someone else in charge. Someone who knows how to get the job done properly.'

Skullet pulled a face and showed off his shark's teeth. 'What d'you mean, someone else? I'm meaner than anyone else in this town. Tell me who it is and I'll prove it to you, I'll push out his eyes with my thumbs, I'll tear out his liver and eat it in front of him, I'll—'

Skullet's rant was interrupted by a timid knock. The door opened a few inches and Two-Buck Tim peered in.

'Er, is this a bad time?' he said with a wavering smile. 'I can easily come back later? Tomorrow? Day after that, even?'

'Get in here, Two-Buck,' snapped Fang. 'Have you brought it with you?'

Two-Buck took a small object wrapped in paper from his pocket and placed it carefully on the desk. Skullet glared at him poisonously.

'Excellent,' said Fang. 'Are you sure this is the one?'

'Oh, yes,' said Two-Buck, 'this is definitely the one. But I think we should—'

'I don't pay you to think, Two-Buck,' she snapped. 'Go and fetch the chargers.'

Fang went to the far end of the room and pulled away a tarpaulin to reveal the black android, silent and still. Skullet had seen the dead android many times before but it was just worthless old-tech, as far as he was concerned. Why anyone would want to spend a fortune on a mechanical man when the real ones were cheap and plentiful enough made no sense to him.

Two-Buck returned with the plasma chargers laid side by side in a plastic tray. Lady Fang ran her slim fingers across the android's chest and slid back a small panel to reveal a deep, round hole. Skullet frowned; this was new.

Two-Buck slid the first plasma charger into the hole with a soft whisper of expelled air. He turned the handle and it locked into place with a well-machined click. They both stood back.

For a moment nothing happened. Then came the faint clattering of tiny relays and a whispering of pneumatics from deep inside the android's body. The creature shivered, as though an electric current had run down its spine. It held up its hands and clenched and unclenched its fingers so that the sinews stood out on its forearms. Then with a faint whine of servo motors it stepped from its low pedestal and stood poised and ready before Lady Fang. A faint hissing issued from beneath its visor like the opening and closing of a gas valve.

Lady Fang gazed at the android with the expression of a parent watching her child take its first steps, while Two-Buck peeped at it from behind her shoulder. Skullet stared in disbelief at the sight of the creature. It looked graceful, brutal and cold; human in appearance, but completely lacking in humanity. When it looked in his direction, Skullet felt his legs go weak.

'This is Maximus,' said Lady Fang proudly. 'He is a

Matsushito 6000 droid, built for covert operations. I have had him specially adapted to run on plasma technology.'

'If you want a job doing properly you gotta send a real man,' said Skullet, sounding tougher than he felt. 'That ain't nothing but box of gears.'

'This box of gears is your new boss, Skullet,' said Lady Fang. 'So I would be more polite to him, if I were you.' Two-Buck smirked and Skullet made a mental note to remove the top of Two-Buck's skull the first opportunity he got.

'It still don't help you to find the girl,' said Skullet with a note of triumph in his voice. 'How's a robot going to track a boat over open water?'

'I'm glad you asked,' said Lady Fang with a smile. 'Maximus?' The android straightened and at the sound of his name. 'Why don't you show Skullet your little pet?'

With a whispering of hydraulics the android pulled away a second tarpaulin. Skullet craned to get a better look at what was underneath but it was low to the floor and Fang and Two-Buck had immediately crowded around it. They slipped the second charger into place with a mechanical click.

There was a dry scraping of reptilian scales, followed by a ghastly hiss that chilled Skullet's blood. When Fang and Two-Buck stepped back he caught a glimpse of a sinuous body coiled on the floor, so dark it seemed to suck at the light around it. When Skullet leaned closer for a better look, a pair of bile-yellow eyes with slits for pupils snapped open and immediately settled on him.

There was a sudden whirl of movement and Skullet had a brief impression of short muscular limbs, and claws like curved blades, as the powerful coils unspooled with blinding rapidity and vanished from sight.

From behind the crates and boxes came a hideous slithering and scraping that made Skullet's insides turn to water. He tracked the noise around the room, watching the crates move as something scuttled behind them.

'W-w-what is it?' he croaked, trying to follow the sound of the creature. Fang watched Skullet with a curious half-smile, as though observing an experiment. Two-Buck had pressed himself back against the wall, anxious to stay out of the way.

The scraping stopped and the room fell silent; Skullet could hear the sound of his own breathing. He positioned himself as close as possible to the centre of the room and reached instinctively for his knife. The noise began again, behind him this time. He whipped around but it had moved to the shelves high up on his right. A tin crashed to the floor, scattering screws, and Skullet let out an involuntary shriek.

'What *is* that thing?' His voice was high and cracked, on the edge of panic.

'That,' said Fang with fondness in her voice, 'is a Hellhound. The pinnacle of cybernetic weaponry. It is a hunter-killer, telepathically linked with Maximus. It has all of his strength but with advanced tracking and stealth capabilities. Once it has the scent of your flesh, Skullet, it will never stop hunting you. It can track a man for ten thousand miles, staying in the shadows, keeping to the dark places. You will never see it but you will always know it is there. There is nowhere to hide from it, nowhere to run. It is a creature from your darkest nightmares.'

The room had fallen silent again. Skullet cast around wildly, searching for a hint of where the creature might be hiding. A small tic began to pulse in the corner of one eye. 'You can't frighten me,' he gasped.

'Oh, but I can, Skullet,' purred Fang. 'The hound generates infrasonic waves that trigger fear impulses in the brains of its victims. That terror you are experiencing now is the hound *inside* your head.'

'Call it off!' he choked. 'Please, just tell me what you want.'

'Oh, nothing much.' Fang reached into a fold of her robe and pulled out a small, pointed blade on a silver cap that she slid neatly over the end of her forefinger like a talon. 'I just need to be sure I have your complete loyalty, Skullet. You see, I had Two-Buck programme the Hellhound with a sample of your DNA earlier today. If anything should happen to me, if there are any unfortunate accidents or betrayals, then the creature will immediately start to seek you out.'

She fitted more blades over each finger, so that she appeared to possess the claws of some terrible animal. 'You will find, Skullet, that the creature is not nearly as merciful as I am.'

The hideous rattling-and-sliding noise began again, and something unhinged in Skullet's brain. 'Let me go! Let me out of here!' He dropped his knife and fled for the exit. At the same moment, something exploded from the shelves behind him and slammed into his back, pinning him to the floor with its full weight.

'Call it off, Maximus,' purred Fang. Maximus inclined his head a fraction and the weight was gone. Skullet rolled over, panting, and stared wildly around the room, but the Hellhound had vanished once more into the shadows.

An instant later, Fang's arm slipped around Skullet's neck in a choking hold and the tiny-bladed fingers glittered in front of his face. 'You will learn, Skullet,' she said, 'that I do not forgive failure.' Her movement was lightning-quick and Skullet's scream was sudden and shrill. He continued to howl as Fang wiped the finger blades and returned them to the folds of her robe before opening the porcelain jar and dropping something in with a sickening plop.

She sat down at her desk and took a deep breath. The Hellhound had retired to the shadows, Two-Buck stood in the corner, pale and trembling, and Skullet was moaning and clutching at his face.

'Maximus?' she said calmly. The android hissed softly in response. 'Tomorrow you will take charge of my security operation. Use the Hellhound to track the girl, but keep her alive until she has found the stones. After that your little pet can tear her to pieces.' She turned to the shaking Two-Buck. 'All right then, show me what you have.'

Two-Buck picked up the parcel from the desk and unwrapped it with trembling hands, being careful not to touch the contents. Inside was a dirty drinking glass.

'You're sure this is the one she used?' queried Fang. Two-Buck swallowed and nodded.

'Yes, my lady, this is the one she drank from.'

'Good, then it should still have enough of her DNA to take a reading. Give it to the Hellhound then.'

Two-Buck's eyes widened and he licked his lips. He scanned the shadows until he spotted two acid-yellow eyes gleaming from a dark corner. He bent down and gingerly held out the glass with a shaking hand.

The yellow eyes swivelled in his direction and a thin, snake-like tongue flicked out of the darkness and wrapped itself around his hand. For a moment, Two-Buck thought he might faint.

The tongue was rubbery and glistened with something sticky. It explored the glass, leaving a trail of slime behind it, before carefully extracting it from Two-Buck's hand and pulling it into the darkness. Two-Buck gulped as he listened to the creature grind up the glass in its steel teeth. Then it went quiet and only the faintest hiss emerged from the shadows.

'Excellent,' said Fang, smiling benevolently towards the gleaming yellow eyes. 'Now then, go and find me that girl.'

By the time the sun was fully up, the airship was descending steadily towards a bustling sea port. Fresh sunlight filled the gondola and reminded India just what a long night it had been. From her high vantage point she could see a cluster of sun-ravaged warehouses around a stone quayside, and rows of iron merchant vessels moored against concrete jetties.

As they cleared the early-morning cloud they could see the quay was already seething with human activity like a freshly disturbed anthill. The crewman guided the airship gracefully towards a clear patch of ground while Professor Moon cast mooring lines down to the forest of eager hands that gathered beneath them to help.

When the airship was firmly tethered, Professor Moon executed a graceful slide down the rope ladder, followed by Verity and then India. Cael came last, looking like a man with a worsening headache. They were met by a pack of chattering boys thrusting crude trinkets at them fashioned from scrap metal.

'Your guest house was being watched by Fang's men,' shouted Moon over the heads of the crowd. 'So I took the liberty of having your baggage brought here. You can either take it with you or you can decide to join our quest.' He turned the Bloodstone over in his hand before sliding it into the leather pouch at his belt.

'That second piece of the stone isn't yours,' said India. 'It belongs to the monks.'

Moon gave a dry laugh. 'Your sense of right and wrong does you credit, Miss Bentley. However, the two parts are now inseparable and I cannot readily return it to them. Besides, after yesterday I suspect the monks will not be in a very forgiving mood so I will keep both pieces of the stone. Consider it my fee for springing you from jail.'

India thought about arguing, but what he said was true. She doubted the monks would be very pleased to see her, even if she did try to return the stone, and Moon didn't look ready to give it up without a fight.

'Please consider my offer,' he said. 'The *Ahaziah* leaves from Pier Nine in one hour and we wait for no man. Come along, Mr O'Hanlon,' he barked to Cael. 'And tell me why you think I should hire you.' He marched away with Cael in tow, surrounded by a flock of small boys.

Cael looked back and waved to India, though Verity was busy rummaging in her satchel and didn't seem to notice. But when he turned away India noticed Verity follow him through the crowd with her eyes.

They walked in the other direction, mainly to avoid unwanted attention from the beggars who were now competing to show off their skin sores. They bought tea from a man with milky eyes who ran a stall on the waterfront and found a table in the shade.

'I think the first priority is to get ourselves a ride out of here,' said Verity, consulting a map she had pulled from her satchel. 'I thought we could find a merchantman heading north and then try our luck in the tech-mines of Shanghai?'

India looked up. 'I want to go on Professor Moon's expedition,' she said.

Verity sighed. 'Moon's a crackpot, India. All that stuff about legends and stones and Atlantis . . . he's a card-carrying lunatic! Not to mention the fact that he's clearly got some sort of a fight going on with Lady Fang. Believe me, we're in enough trouble with her already.'

'But you saw that photo he had. It was a picture of an android, on the wall of an ancient tomb, and it looked just like Calc.'

'It doesn't *prove* anything, India. Professor Moon could have easily faked those pictures.'

'Well, what about the dream I had? I *saw* Calculus, he was buried in the ice but he was still alive.'

'It was just that, India – a dream.'

'It wasn't. It was a message!' India banged her palm on the table. 'I am a *Soul Voyager*, Verity. The old shaman, Nentu, told me I could talk to the ancient machines. At first I didn't want it to be true but it *is*. What if the machines were trying to give me a message about Calculus? What if he needs our help?'

Verity looked at the intensity in the girl's eyes and felt suddenly less sure. 'It still doesn't prove anything,' she said in a faltering voice. 'Calculus couldn't be . . .' She looked away and swallowed, surprised to find her throat sore and her eyes stinging. 'We both saw the explosion that killed him, India. No one could have survived that. Not even Calc.'

India wiped her eyes angrily. 'But if there's even the slightest chance he's alive, shouldn't we take it? You should never give up on someone you love – never!'

Verity sighed and looked out to sea for a long time. India could be maddeningly stubborn when she chose to be. Ever since she had taken the girl on as her assistant their arguments had been loud and frequent. But like summer storms, they were usually quick to pass. Perhaps, she told herself, this journey made some sort of sense. Perhaps if they followed Professor Moon on his lunatic expedition, India might finally accept that Calculus was gone.

'All right,' Verity said eventually. 'I hope I don't live to regret this. We'll go with Professor Moon. We need to get out of Sing City anyway. But when we get to the Southern Ocean I'll decide whether it's safe to continue, OK?'

'OK,' said India, wiping her eyes and managing a smile. 'So, tell me . . . what's the deal with you and Cael O'Hanlon?'

Verity's face darkened. 'Him? He's just someone I met a long time ago in South America,' she said, becoming suddenly interested in her satchel again.

‘Really? How did you meet him?’

‘Well . . .’ Verity frowned.

‘Tell me.’

‘If you must know . . . I shot him.’

‘You did what?’ cried India.

‘Well, only a little bit,’ said Verity. ‘Besides, he deserved it. I caught him trying to steal from me.’

‘Well, what happened after that?’

Verity looked down and gave a silent laugh, remembering. ‘Well, we sort of travelled around together for a while . . .’ She caught India’s look. ‘All right,’ she said in an exasperated tone. ‘I had a crush on him, OK? I was only twenty and I thought he was the most glamorous man I had ever met. Every time I got mad at him he’d flash that stupid, perfect smile of his and I’d forgive him anything.’

India wore a look of pure delight. ‘Well, how come you two aren’t still together?’

Verity’s smile disappeared abruptly. ‘He dumped me in the middle of nowhere,’ she said. ‘I woke up one morning to find he’d gone. He’d taken all of our money without even leaving me a note.’ She picked up her bag with a scowl. ‘I won’t make the mistake of trusting him again in a hurry. Come on, let’s go and find Pier Nine.’

They fought their way along the quayside, where porters balanced unfeasibly large bundles on their heads and cargo nets swung overhead loaded with barrels of sweet rum and planks of raw teak. There were more than a dozen ships in the harbour. Most were small coastal trawlers but at the far end of Pier Nine they found the ship they were looking for. The *Ahaziah* was a steam cruiser that looked like something from the imagination of a twisted engineer. The hull was constructed of black iron plate, held together with rivets the size of India's fist. Two thick funnels towered over the deck and a heavy gun emplacement stood in the bows.

A team of thickly muscled sailors were ferrying packing crates and fuel drums from the quayside and lashing them down tightly under oiled sheets on the foredeck. At the stern, a dozen men were hauling on ropes to manoeuvre the airship down on to the deck as it strained at the tethers like a fat grub. Professor Moon stood on the quay, barking instructions.

'Excellent news!' he boomed when Verity told him of their decision. He pumped Verity's hand and slapped India on the back, making her stagger.

'Of course, this is subject to agreeing our fee, Professor,' said Verity shrewdly. 'The Southern Ocean is a dangerous place and we expect to be well paid.'

Verity accepted Moon's invitation to discuss their fees on board while India was left with instructions to make sure their bags were safely stowed. She identified their luggage to two barrel-chested sailors who griped at the weight of India's trunk. 'Blimey, lady. What you got in 'ere, a dead body?'

Once she had seen their bags safely carried up the gangplank, she amused herself by inspecting the small mountain of supplies and equipment still waiting to be loaded. She felt her spirits lift as she inspected crates of fresh fruit and vegetables, whole cured hams, and, to her delight, a large box of chocolate slabs.

As well as the food there was all manner of equipment that spelled adventure: coils of rope, heavy boots, ice axes, crampons and several wooden boxes marked 'Explosives'. She wondered what Professor Moon expected to encounter in his search for Atlantis. She peered into every box until the crew lost patience and chased her away with angry words she'd never heard before.

At the top of the gangplank she found a balding, bristly man, wearing a dirty apron, ticking off items on a clipboard.

'Good morning,' said India, cheerfully.

'What's so bleedin' good about it?' he snapped. 'Eighty-four passengers and crew to feed and not one chip pan on the 'ole bleedin' ship. 'Ow am I meant to keep a 'appy crew if I can't make chips? There'll be a mutiny, you mark my words.'

India grinned. 'So are you the chef then?'

'Chef!' he spluttered. 'What d'you think this is, a French restaurant? You bring a chef on board and we'll be drinking a-pair-o-teefs before dinner and eatin' frog's legs before you know it. No, I ain't no chef, I'm a *cook*. Grunion's the name. I can boil things, fry things and on a good day I can make soup out of things but if you want anythin' else then find yerself one o' them fancy *crooze*liners.' He stalked off, muttering to himself as India tried her hardest not to laugh.

When the loading was finally completed, she stood at

the rail and waited impatiently for the ship to cast off, her gloom now completely dispelled by the fresh breeze. As she waited, she noticed a stall at the end of the jetty selling small orange fruits. She recognized them as the ones that she had gorged herself on in the underground gardens at Ironheart and immediately began to crave their sticky sweetness.

'Sorry, miss, no one's allowed ashore,' said the sailor at the head of the gangplank. 'Professor's orders. We cast off in fifteen minutes.'

'But I only want to go over there!'

Her pleading to make the short dash to the fruit stall fell on deaf ears and she slunk away to sulk on the forward deck. But luck was on her side. Moments later a cargo net broke and a falling barrel of treacle burst open on the rear deck. As the sailor on watch went to help his colleagues, India seized her opportunity and slipped down the gangplank.

The strange fruits had attracted a lot of attention. She fought her way to the front of the queue and bartered all of her remaining money for four of the precious globes. While she was stowing them carefully in her bag, the *Ahaziah* gave a loud blast on her horn, scattering seabirds into the air.

'Hell,' she muttered. Glancing at the ship, she saw the gangplank was still in place and breathed a sigh of relief. She hoisted her bag and then froze. A fat man was staring at her from the other side of the fruit stall. He had scaly red skin and wore monks' robes.

Brother Scrofulous stopped cramming fruit into his mouth and gawped at India. 'Ipf her!' he spluttered, spraying several bystanders. 'Thatf her – ftop her – ftop her!'

Without pausing to think, India took off at a sprint towards the ship, barging heavily laden porters out of the way. But after only ten yards she skidded to a halt. More monks were running towards her, cutting her off from the *Ahaziah*. They looked leaner and fitter than Scrofulous and their serious faces were focused on her.

In desperation she sprinted down an alley between two warehouses. A second blast sounded from the *Ahaziah* as India zig-zagged through the narrow lanes until she found an empty crate and clambered in. The horror of being left behind was growing larger by the moment, but she waited for her pursuers' footsteps to recede before climbing out of the crate and doubling back.

As she turned into the last alleyway she came to an abrupt halt. Scrofulous stood at the end of the passage, taking up the whole width of the narrow street. They stared at each other until another blast of the ship's horn jolted India into action. Reaching into her bag, she pulled out one of the oranges. Scrofulous's eyes widened as the girl ran straight at him. When she was less than ten feet away, India screamed at the top of her lungs and hurled the orange with all her strength.

The large fruit struck Scrofulous in the middle of his face and he fell backwards, giving India a most unattractive view right up his robes. She ran straight over the top of the fallen monk, planting a foot in his stomach as she leaped for the end of the alleyway.

Her worst fears were immediately confirmed. The *Ahaziah* was slipping from its berth towards the open sea. But the ship was only ten feet from the pier and moving parallel to it: she could still make it. Gritting her teeth, she sprinted to catch up. A blur to her right made her glance over her shoulder. The dark-robed monk, Amun, was now pounding along the quayside towards her. He was gaining fast and India was running out of jetty.

As the *Ahaziah* pulled away from the pier, Cael appeared at the back of the ship. He took in the scene in a moment and vaulted the rail, leaning out over the water and stretching his free arm towards India. The monk was right on her tail; she could feel his hard breath behind her.

'Jump, India!' cried Cael across the widening gap. 'You can do it!'

Without slowing, India planted a foot on a mooring bollard and launched herself off the pier. Her arms and legs pedalled the air desperately until Cael's outstretched hand closed around her wrist. For a moment she dangled above the dangerously churning waters, before Cael hauled her over the rail to safety and they both collapsed on the deck. The dark monk glared at them briefly from the receding dock – then turned and walked away without looking back.

'You know,' gasped Cael, 'most people find the gangplank a whole lot more convenient.'

'Thanks,' she gasped. 'I really owe you one.'

Cael nodded. 'Well,' he said, climbing to his feet. 'I got the job as the professor's guide in the Southern Ocean. So if you could persuade your boss not to punch me out again for the rest of the voyage that would be just *great*.'

They were interrupted by Verity, running up the deck towards them. 'India! Are you all right?' She seized India by the shoulders and anxiously inspected her. 'You had no business going ashore, you could have been killed!' Verity's concern was quickly giving way to anger and India pulled away from her grip.

'It wasn't my fault,' she pleaded. 'The monks chased me and they would have caught me too if it hadn't been for Cael.'

Verity looked at Cael suspiciously, then gave him a curt nod. 'Thanks.'

'Think nothing of it,' responded Cael with a grin. 'How about buying me a drink to say thanks?'

Verity's eyebrow shot up. 'Buy you a what? Don't push your luck, buster. I—'

'India Bentley!' They turned to see Professor Moon bearing down on them with a face was like thunder.

'Uh-oh,' murmured India. 'This doesn't look good.'

'You have been aboard my ship for less than one hour,' he bellowed, 'and already you have put my expedition in jeopardy.'

'W-w-what?' she stammered. 'I didn't mean to. It's just that I wanted to buy some fruit and then I saw this monk—'

'Silence!' roared Moon. 'Didn't the officer on watch tell you not to go ashore?'

'Well, yes, but—'

'But you went anyway. And, now you have attracted the

attention of the monks who know you are aboard my ship.'

'But I couldn't help—'

'And then one of *my* team had to risk his life to rescue you.'

'I'm sorry,' said India, looking down. 'I didn't mean anyone to get—'

'Quiet!' snapped Moon. His thick brows had knitted together like a bramble hedge. 'You may be important to my mission, India Bentley,' he said. 'But, when you are on my ship and in my employment, you will obey my orders and those given to you by my crew.'

'But, I—'

'First thing in the morning you will report to the galley for a punishment detail with the ship's cook. Perhaps a spell of hard work will knock some discipline into you.' He turned and strode away in the direction of his laboratory.

'Damn it, India,' said Verity as they watched him go. 'I was about to finalize our fee and now he's in a foul mood. You don't make it easy for me sometimes.'

'Well I'm sorry my attempted kidnap interrupted your business meeting,' snapped India. 'Maybe if they'd caught me you'd have had time to negotiate for more money.'

'India!' cried Verity, but her assistant had fled.

Cael leaned nonchalantly against the ship's rail. 'Kids, eh?' He said with a wry smile. 'Do you remember when we used to be like that, V?'

Verity gave him a glare. 'India is tough and brave and *loyal*, Cael,' she said. 'You were never any of those things.'

Cael shrugged. 'People change, V,' he said. 'Now, how about we get that drink and talk about old times?'

But Verity was already walking away. 'I'd rather stick needles in my eyes,' she called over her shoulder.

Cael grinned. 'I'll take that as a "maybe" then, shall I?'

Meanwhile, India had gone looking for her luggage. A deck hand showed her to a tiny cabin near the engine room where she found her luggage already stowed. She tested the bunk for comfort and tried out the taps before deciding to unpack. But when she raised the lid of her trunk, a movement from within made her shriek and jump back in alarm. There was someone inside!

She retreated to the bunk in shock as a small figure unfolded itself stiffly. It was a young boy aged about ten, with a shaved head and round, owlish glasses. He wore a rumpled black suit and tie and held a black felt hat which he kneaded, anxiously, in his hands.

'Who the hell are you!' she spluttered. He jumped visibly at the sound of her voice.

'Please, Miss Bentley,' he said, blinking nervously through his glasses. 'It is I, Tito!'

She squinted at him closely. 'You're the boy from the High Priest's boat.'

He seemed pleased to be recognized. 'Yes, Miss Bentley. Most people do not recognize me in my civilian clothes but you clearly have the well-trained eye of a tech-hunter.'

India looked around wildly as though expecting more

monks to emerge from under the bed, but the boy was alone.

'Do not fear, Miss Bentley,' said Tito, stepping out of the trunk. 'I will not harm you.'

At this, India had to suppress a laugh. The boy was as thin as a rope and looked as though he would be hard pressed to wrestle a spider. 'How did you get in my luggage?' she demanded. 'And what are you doing here?'

The boy looked bashful and wrung his hat some more. 'I climbed into your luggage while it was on the dockside,' he said. 'Please forgive me for intruding upon you like this, Miss Bentley, but I could think of no other place to come. You see, I am no longer fit to be a monk of the divine brotherhood.'

'*What?*' said India. 'Why not?'

'Because I was the stone bearer,' he said earnestly. 'It was my job to protect the sacred Bloodstone. But now it has been stolen and it is partly my fault.'

'Oh,' said India, feeling a sudden stab of guilt. 'Well, I'm sorry about that.'

Tito shrugged. 'It is no matter, Miss Bentley,' he said. 'Since our meeting yesterday, I have realized that I am not cut out to be a monk. I have run away to pursue a new career.'

'A new career?' said India, bemused.

'Yes, Miss Bentley,' he said, proudly. 'I have decided I am going to become a tech-hunter, like you.'

9 THE *AHAZIAH*

The *Ahaziah* sailed south from Sing City, passing through narrow straits where the land on either side was caped in glossy green jungle. A rich mouldering smell filled the air, a welcome relief from the stench of Sing City, and everyone seemed buoyed up by the freshness of the salt breeze.

For India, the excitement of setting out for the Southern Ocean was tempered by the inconvenience of having a stowaway in her cabin. She had to admit, the boy seemed harmless enough and it was clearly too late to get him off the ship. Besides, she did not relish the thought of telling Professor Moon, following his last outburst.

There was also the question of whether or not she should tell Verity. If India was discovered to have a runaway monk hiding in her cabin, Verity might well decide to call off their adventure altogether. On balance, India decided to wait until they were further out to sea and the prospect of turning back had diminished.

'You'll have to stay hidden until we get to a port,' she said to Tito after she had considered the options. 'Then we can try and get you a passage home from there.'

'That will be fine, Miss Bentley,' he said, looking pleased. 'There is plenty of room in here to swing a gnat.'

She looked at him blankly for a few moments. 'It's "cat", Tito,' she said eventually. 'Enough room to swing a *cat*.'

Tito looked around the room and gave her a puzzled look. 'Miss Bentley,' he said seriously, 'for that I think you would need a much bigger cabin.'

India was less than pleased to discover that, to make space in her trunk, Tito had left most of her belongings on the quayside in Sing City.

'You got rid of my toothbrush!' she fumed at him on their first night. 'What am I supposed to do now?'

'In the brotherhood we use a sharpened stick,' said Tito brightly. 'I could lend you one if you like?'

She looked at him dubiously. 'Has it been used before?'

'Only by me, Brother Scrofulous, Brother Chua, Brother Lei, Brother—'

India clapped a hand over her eyes and decided it was best to change the subject before Tito volunteered to share any more of his belongings. 'Tell me about the monk in the black robes,' she asked.

'That is Brother Amun,' said Tito seriously as he unpacked his own suitcase. 'He is responsible for security of the holy relics. He is a good man, very devout, but also very tough. I think he has been sent to hunt for the missing

Bloodstone.' He hung his head. 'My own part in its loss is a matter of great shame to me.'

India bit her lip. Tito clearly had not realized that she and the professor were the ones who had taken the stone from the jail. She considered telling him but decided it was safer to skirt around the truth.

'You shouldn't blame yourself, Tito,' she said. 'Anyway, it's just an old stone.'

'It is not just an *old stone*, Miss Bentley,' he cried. 'The Bloodstone is a precious artefact. It is only taken out during our most important festivals.'

'What about the legend of the three kings who broke up the stone?' said India. 'Wouldn't you like to find the missing pieces and bring them together again?'

Tito's eyes opened wide and he looked aghast.

'Bring them together, Miss Bentley?' he said, horrified. 'That must never be allowed to happen.'

'Why ever not?' said India. 'I thought the stone was supposed to unlock an unlimited source of energy?'

Tito looked horrified. 'No, Miss Bentley, it will not,' he said. 'The kings did not break up the stone, the Great Teacher broke it up himself. He said men were not ready for its secrets and if the pieces were brought together too soon they would bring about the end of the world. He gave a piece to each of the three kings and told them that they must be kept apart at all costs.'

'And you believe that?'

'Of course,' said Tito. 'The Great Teacher was a very

wise man. I have committed all of his teachings to memory and he was never wrong.'

The next morning, India left Tito in the cabin and dutifully sought out the galley. Her punishment consisted of having to peel a very large sack of potatoes while Grunion crashed around the steam-filled kitchen, cursing and dropping cigarette ash in the soup.

Much to her delight, she found that Cael had also been assigned to kitchen duties. He stopped rummaging through a crate of cabbages and winked at her. 'Don't you ever cook fresh vegetables, Grunion?' he said. 'Don't you know about scurvy?'

'Fresh vegetables is all very well,' grumbled Grunion, 'but they don't keep a crew warm the way chips does. And believe me, we'll need chips when we get to the Southern Ocean.' He lifted the lid of a large saucepan to investigate a stew that looked like a pot full of volcanic mud.

'Why is everyone so afraid of the Southern Ocean?' asked India, as she gouged potato eyes. 'What's supposed to be there?'

'Dark things,' said Grunion without looking up. 'Things that spawn in the deepest, darkest parts of the ocean. Leviathans, they call 'em.' He shot India a narrow look. 'I've heard stories they'll drag a ship to the seabed and drown every last soul on board.'

'Really?' said Cael with a grin. 'So who tells the stories then?'

Grunion looked confused. 'What? Well, er . . .' He scratched his head, sending dandruff spiralling into the stew. 'Get on with your work and stop interrupting me.'

India tried not to laugh as she was forced to sit out the rest of her punishment in silence while Grunion added handfuls of salt to everything and Cael made faces behind his back. After three hours of peeling and scrubbing she was finally free to leave and investigate the rest of the ship.

Everything about the vessel was solid and workmanlike. She examined the thick mooring ropes, coiled like pythons in the bows, and tugged at the tarpaulins covering mysterious pieces of equipment on the upper decks. She leaned over the rails and breathed in the fresh air, already several degrees cooler than the sweltering heat of Sing City.

At the back of the ship she found the gondola housing the professor's laboratory had been bolted firmly to the deck and the balloon stowed away. She peered through the darkened windows of the laboratory, but of the man himself there was no sign.

When she returned to her cabin she surprised Tito, who had removed his shirt and was washing at the sink. He gave a cry of alarm and clutched a towel to himself.

'There's no need to be so bashful, Tito,' she said. 'All the boys in our village go skinny-dipping in the summer. And anyway,' she said frowning, 'that's my towel.'

She snatched the towel away, revealing his scrawny chest, and her mouth dropped open. 'Tito, you have a tattoo.'

In the centre of Tito's chest she could plainly see a

design in blue ink. It was a simple orb, like the sun, with a triangle beneath it. The boy hurriedly pulled his shirt back over his head.

'You should not see this, Miss Bentley,' he said. 'It is a secret mark worn only by the monks of my order. The Great Teacher himself had one and it is forbidden for outsiders to look upon it.

'But I've seen it before,' said India.

'That is not possible,' said Tito, buttoning his shirt.

'But I have,' insisted India. 'It was on a photograph the professor showed us. He said it was the mark of the Sun Machine.

Tito stared at her. 'You must be mistaken, Miss Bentley,' he said in a tight voice. He buttoned his shirt up to the neck and would say no more on the subject of tattoos or anything else for several hours. India thought it best to leave him alone and turned her attention to her shock stick.

She hefted the slim metal stick in her hand, feeling its familiar weight. But when she turned it over she was affronted to discover that the fat monk had tried to scratch his own initials into the soft metal while she'd been in jail. She took a small metal file from her bag and spent an hour carefully filing them off and replacing them with her own.

'There!' she said, blowing away the metal filings and holding it up to show Tito. The boy did not answer. He sat cross-legged on the floor with his eyes closed, breathing deeply. There was a small piece of cloth on the floor before him, adorned with the picture of the hand holding a burning torch.

'What are you doing?' she asked.

'Meditating,' he said without opening his eyes. 'The Great Teacher said we should meditate on the meaning of life every day.'

'It looks pretty boring,' said India. 'What do you think of while you're doing it?'

'Nothing,' he said.

'*Nothing?* That's impossible. Everybody has to think of something.'

He opened his eyes with a sigh. 'Sometimes it is very difficult, Miss Bentley,' he said. 'But it is not impossible.'

'Well, why do you do it?'

Tito thought for a moment. 'Because, when you think of nothing, then you start to see everything,' he said with a serene smile. India shrugged and settled into her bed. The way Tito talked reminded her of Calculus sometimes.

'Why did you become a monk, Tito?' she asked. 'I mean, I don't want to be rude, but your order seems a little . . . well, bonkers.'

'I see. And, if I might enquire, Miss Bentley, do you believe I am a little . . . bonkers too?'

India smiled. 'Well, no, I guess not. It just seems like a strange religion, what with the recycling and everything . . .'

Tito nodded. 'The Great Teacher came out of the wilderness, barefoot and carrying only the Bloodstone and a torch, with which he lit his way and fought off his enemies.' He spoke as though he had rehearsed the words many times. 'With these humble tools he brought wisdom to our forefathers. He showed us we all move in a cycle of birth, life and death. In the Brotherhood we recycle rubbish to remind ourselves that nothing stays the same and everything changes. When we understand that, then we are accepting of all the changes that life brings and we fear nothing. Not even death.'

'I see,' said India. 'Well, when you put it like that it doesn't sound so bonkers. In fact it sounds sort of cool.'

'Thank you, Miss Bentley,' said the boy, looking pleased.

'So is that what you do all day, just meditate?'

'Oh no, Miss Bentley,' he said. 'I have to study the writings of the Great Teacher, then there is rubbish to be recycled, holy relics to be cleaned, public ceremonies to—'

'But don't you have any time for friends?' she interrupted. The boy looked at her blankly. 'You do know what friends *are*, don't you?'

'Oh, I know all about friends, Miss Bentley,' he said brightly. 'The Great Teacher wrote about them. He said—'

'It's not something you can just read about, Tito. There's no substitute for having a real friend that you share everything with. You know, a *best* friend. Everybody should have someone like that.'

The boy looked slightly crestfallen. 'I see,' he said. 'May I ask: Miss Bentley, do you have a "best friend"?'

India caught her breath. 'I-I did have someone like that. His name was Calculus. He was kind and clever and he was very serious but somehow he always managed to make me laugh.' She smiled at the memory.

'And where is he now?' asked Tito.

India looked down at her feet. 'He died. He's gone now.'

Tito cocked his head on one side and looked at her strangely. 'No,' he said. 'I can see he is not gone, because you keep him alive.' He leaned forward and placed a hand on her heart. 'In here.'

India blinked at him, unsure of what to say. The boy settled back on to his makeshift bed with a smile. 'And now that I have told you about my life, Miss Bentley, perhaps you could tell me something in return.'

'Sure,' she said, snapping out of her daze. 'What do you want to know?'

'Tell me about your adventures as a tech-hunter, Miss Bentley,' he asked eagerly.

And so, while Tito huddled beneath his blankets, India told him about the bitter cold of Siberia and the perils of Angel Town. She described the sixteen-year-old outlaw, Sid the Kid, and his cruel father, and how they both died when their rig blew up. She told him about Captain Bulldog, who drove a vast moving oil rig called *The Beautiful Game*. Lastly, she told him about a wizened old woman called Nentu who sat on a mammoth-skull throne in the forest and was a Soul Voyager.

She found she enjoyed telling the story so much that it made her pine for the adventure all over again. And by the time she had got to the part where she returned safely to London with her father, she scarcely noticed that her audience had drifted off to sleep and that his round spectacles had slipped from his nose.

She woke the next morning to the sound of insistent knocking. She bundled the sleepy Tito and his meagre belongings into the space under her bunk before she opened the door, looking flustered and pink in the face.

'What are you doing in here?' said Verity, trying to peer into the room. 'What was all that scuffling?' India positioned herself to block the doorway and said the first thing that came into her head.

'Nothing, I was just, er, meditating.'

Verity squinted at her. 'Why are you out of breath?'

'It's, er, really hard work, meditating. All that thinking of nothing really takes it out of you.' She dragged a lock of hair out of her eyes and smiled winningly. Verity looked suspicious but decided it probably wasn't worth the effort to pursue the conversation. India politely declined her invitation to breakfast and shut the door as firmly as she could.

'That was close,' she said, pulling a slightly dusty Tito from under the bed. 'We need to find a better arrangement.'

As they moved into southern latitudes the air developed a keen edge and the seas began to heave like a grey shawl. The ship ploughed through the swell and the crew went about their duties with the same hard-working practicality she had seen in the rig crews in Siberia. When not keeping Tito company, India spent her time exploring every inch of the ship. She relished the smells of hot oil and coal smoke that drifted over the decks, poked around the wheelhouse, clambered in the hold and even scaled the narrow ladder to the crow's nest swaying dangerously high above the decks. She pestered the sailors to teach her to tie knots and to let her stoke the furnaces and, when she had exhausted all other entertainments, she would simply stand in the bows and let the icy spray run down her face.

She was relieved that Verity and Cael seemed to have reached a truce of some sort and one evening even spotted them sharing a drink together. Once a day, both adults attended Professor Moon's senior crew-briefing and India used the time to smuggle food from the mess for Tito. She was struck by how self-contained the boy seemed to be. Although he was always pleased to see her, he seemed equally content with his own company and spent a large part of his time meditating. She thought Tito must have lived a strange life in the monastery with only older, more serious-minded monks for company.

After nearly two weeks of ploughing south, the air turned bitterly cold and the ship began to buck and lurch, making everyone track zig-zag paths along the corridors and sending cups and plates sliding from the mess-room tables. Cold rain lashed the decks and the crew donned yellow oilskins and rubber boots. As Tito had left most of her cold weather gear on the quayside in Sing City, India waddled around the decks in borrowed sweaters and oversized oilskins until her face turned numb with the cold and she was forced to go below.

Tito was now spending most of his time ashen-faced on a makeshift bed of spare blankets, groaning and avoiding food. 'Come on,' she said one evening, when she could bear it no longer. 'You really need some fresh air.' Tito pleaded to be left to die in peace but, with the decisive manner of someone who is absolutely certain they are right, she pulled him to his feet and threw an oilskin over his head and shoulders.

After checking the corridor was clear, she ushered him out of the cabin and up the iron stairs. Darkness had descended and cold spray lashed the decks. There was no sign of life save for a faint yellow glow coming from the laboratory. She led Tito to the stern and sat him down, where, much to her surprise, he started to feel better.

'People are not meant to travel like this, Miss Bentley,' he said faintly. 'In future I think I will be the sort of tech-hunter that only travels by land.'

'It's all part of the job,' she laughed. 'I think it's a great way to travel.'

'What was that noise?' said Tito, cocking an ear. 'There's something down there, in the water.' They peered over the side but saw only the heaving, black waves.

'Well, there's nothing there now,' said India. The sound of approaching footsteps and muted voices made her glance over her shoulder. 'There's someone coming,' she hissed. 'Quick, in here.'

She pulled back one of the canvas lifeboat covers and manhandled Tito into the boat. They crouched uncomfortably on oars and coils of rope that smelled of diesel oil.

'I don't need excuses,' Professor Moon was saying as he rounded the corner. 'I need to know who is following us and where they are right now.'

India raised the edge of the canvas a fraction to peer out. Professor Moon was with Cael and a bald man with bad teeth whom she recognized as Mr Flatley, the ship's first mate. Flatley was frowning and the long wisps of hair that he normally combed over his bald patch streamed in the wind behind him.

'It's not as simple as that, Professor,' he said. 'Our radar has limited range. We've seen a couple of blips on the horizon but it could just be storm clouds.'

'It's Fang,' said the professor quietly.

'We don't know that, sir,' said Flatley. 'The weather conditions—'

'It's her!' said Moon emphatically. 'She's heard about our voyage and now she is coming after us.'

'I don't know if it's Lady Fang or not,' said Cael. 'But there are plenty of pirates in these waters. I suggest we head for Whalesong as quickly as possible. It's the nearest sheltered harbour and I have some influence there. You could arrange for your associates to meet us there.'

Flatley knitted his wiry brows. 'We don't need to run for shelter like some fishing vessel, Mr O'Hanlon. The *Ahaziah* is an iron-clad. We have heavy guns and if pirates or Lady Fang show their faces, we'll blow them out of the water.'

Professor Moon hunched his shoulders and gripped the rail tightly.

'Don't underestimate Fang,' he said. 'She's cunning and will have a plan. Tell the crew to be on alert and then send a Teslagraph to Captain Thor of the *Sea Wolf* asking him to meet us at Whalesong. If it *is* Fang, then she will know by now that I have acquired the monks' piece of the Bloodstone.'

A scuffling noise made India turn in time to see Tito lifting the canvas and clambering out of the boat. She realized with a start that, until now, Tito had no idea that Professor Moon had the monks' piece of the stone.

'Tito,' she hissed. 'Come back, you idiot!' But the boy had already dropped to the deck and was stalking towards the professor with a look of comic fury on his face.

'You are a thief!' he shouted at the professor.

'Oh, hell,' muttered India. She began to clamber after him.

Professor Moon turned to the boy with a start. 'What is this treachery?' he growled.

'You stole the sacred Bloodstone,' cried Tito, standing before the professor with clenched fists. 'I heard you admit it. Return it at once.'

‘Who the hell are you?’ roared Moon. He caught sight of India hovering behind. ‘And you again, Miss Bentley? What do you know of this?’

‘The stone is dangerous to those who do not understand its nature,’ said Tito, refusing to be deterred. ‘You don’t know what you’re dealing with. You must give it back.’

‘Silence! Identify yourself!’ demanded the professor. He pulled out his giant hand-cannon and levelled it at Tito.

‘Leave him alone,’ cried India, pushing Tito aside. ‘He’s just a boy.’

‘I’ve had enough of your insubordination, Miss Bentley. I can see it was a mistake to have ever trusted you. Stand aside. There is only one punishment for spies and stowaways.’

‘No, please!’ India blurted. ‘Don’t hurt him. It was my fault; I hid him in my cabin. I didn’t mean to—’

‘Silence!’ roared the professor. ‘I said, *stand aside*!’

‘Er, Professor,’ said Cael hesitantly. ‘I’m sure there’s a reasonable explanation. Maybe you should—’

Cael was cut off abruptly as a thick, glistening cable lashed out from the darkness, catching the professor across the face and sending his gun skittering across the deck. While the professor collapsed unconscious on the ground, the sinuous vine slashed at the air and wrapped itself tightly around Flatley’s neck.

The panicked first mate made weird gargling noises and clawed the slimy tentacle at his throat. Cael also tried to prise it away but found it impossible to get a grip on the writhing mass of sinew. The first mate began to turn a congested shade of purple.

India pulled her shock stick from her pocket and sparked it alight, but a second tentacle lashed from the darkness sending it flying from her hand. The coils snaked malevolently around the deck, seizing both India and Cael and pinning them both against the ship's rail. Flatley let out a noise like air escaping from a balloon and his eyes rolled up into his head.

'Stand clear, Miss Bentley!' yelled Tito, who was struggling to lift the professor's hand-cannon. A huge blast split the darkness, showering the deck with orange sparks and hurling Tito backwards.

The end of the tentacle pinning India and Cael exploded, showering them with green slime and shreds of flesh. A high-pitched scream filled the air as the water below the boat erupted in a mass of foam and the tentacles slithered back into the sea like scorched fingers.

India and Cael fell gasping to the deck as Tito popped up from behind a pile of rope, wearing a startled expression. The first mate was unconscious but his eyelids were flickering and Professor Moon was shaking his head groggily as he pulled himself upright. Shouting had broken out on the lower decks and someone was directing a powerful light on to the foaming water.

'What the hell was that?' spluttered India.

'I think we might just have been visited by one of the Leviathans,' said Cael, slapping the first mate gently around the face to rouse him. 'I've heard tales about them, but never this far north. It looks like we've entered the cursed waters.'

Professor Moon was peering over the side, his eyes staring and his hair in disarray. 'That was magnificent!' he declared. 'My guess is it was a subspecies of *Architeuthis princeps*, but I'd have to capture a specimen to make sure.'

'You want to catch one?' said India incredulously as she retrieved her shock stick from the deck.

'Of course,' he said. 'What else would a scientist do? Perhaps we could electrify the hull of the ship, which might stun one long enough to haul it up and take a good look. First thing in the morning I'm going to run some experiments to see if it would work. Of course, the long-term objective would be to try and capture a breeding pair.' He seemed highly excited, and all memory of his anger from a few moments earlier had evaporated.

'That was quick thinking, young man,' said Cael, gently taking the gun from a stunned-looking Tito. 'Mr Flatley here was very nearly squid bait.' He turned to the professor, who had pulled out a small pad and was making notes in pencil. 'So what would you like to do about your stowaway now, Professor?'

Professor Moon looked up vaguely from his jottings. 'What? Oh, yes, er, indeed. Well, in view of recent events, perhaps we should postpone making any decisions until the morning.' He cleared his throat and then nodded to

Tito. 'That was very well done, young man, very well done indeed.'

Cael helped the stricken first mate away as the professor directed the crew to shine more lights on the water, leaving India and Tito alone once more on the deck.

'That was an incredibly brave thing you did,' said India, replacing the oilskin around the boy's shoulders. Cael and I would have been killed for sure.'

Tito shivered and looked out to sea. 'I am not brave, Miss Bentley. I have never been so frightened in my life. I wanted to run away and hide.'

'But that's why you *are* brave,' India replied. 'Because you were frightened but you stayed anyway. That's what being brave is.'

He looked up and gave her a weak smile. 'You did not tell me, Miss Bentley, that the professor was the one who had stolen our stone.' He looked at her searchingly. 'And yet you must have known this.'

India felt a pang of guilt. 'I'm sorry, Tito,' she said. 'Really I am. I didn't think the professor would be too pleased if you just marched up to him and demanded it back. I just . . . thought it was for the best.' She lapsed into silence as Tito nodded.

'I fear you are right, Miss Bentley. I don't think the professor is ever going to give up the stone now.'

India eyed the black waters nervously. 'Come on,' she said. 'We'd better get below. Verity's never going to believe this.'

'You did what?' Verity spluttered her breakfast coffee across the table and looked aghast at India and the bashful figure of Tito by her side. India had thought it best to speak to Verity early before she heard about their adventures from someone else. So far, it was not going well.

'You brought a stowaway on board? What the hell were you thinking?'

'Please, Mrs Brown,' said Tito politely. 'This was not Miss Bentley's fault. It was I who decided to hide in her luggage. I did not mean to cause you any trouble.'

'You're already one heap of trouble,' said Verity angrily. 'If your mad monk friends knew you were here – then who knows what they might do?'

Tito wrung his hands and looked down.

'They *don't* know you're here, do they?' said Verity, raising an eyebrow.

'We-ell,' he said, examining his toes. 'Not *exactly*. But I did leave them a note saying I was running away to become a tech-hunter, like Miss Bentley.'

Verity groaned and sank her head into her hands. 'Oh, fabulous!'

'But it's a good job he is here,' said India, coming to Tito's defence. 'If he hadn't been on deck with us last night then the sea monster would have eaten Mr Flatley for sure.'

'Sea monster?' said Verity weakly.

So India took a deep breath and told Verity all about what had happened. By the time she had finished, Verity had turned quite pale.

'Holy rig pirates!' she exclaimed when India rolled up her sleeve to show her the bruises. 'That thing could have torn your arm off.' Her anger evaporated almost immediately. 'Take your jacket off. For all we know those things might be poisonous. We should get something on it straight away.' She fired a dozen questions at India as she pulled a foul-smelling ointment from her bag which she dabbed liberally on India's arm.

India began to wish Verity would go back to being angry. 'Stop fussing,' she said, pulling away.

'You should listen to Mrs Brown,' said Tito seriously. 'Last year Brother Lei was stung by a jellyfish when he was fishing. If we hadn't rushed him to the infirmary he would have died horribly, right there in the boat.'

'There you go,' said Verity. 'It was only your quick actions that saved his life.'

'Oh no, he still died horribly in the hospital,' said Tito.

'But at least he was in a nice bed when it happened.'

India rolled her eyes and Verity looked pained. 'I'm sorry,' said India. 'I didn't mean to hide anything from you but I didn't know what else to do. Do you think the professor will allow Tito to stay with us now?'

Verity put down the ointment and sighed. 'Look, India. In a job like ours it's a good idea to try and keep a low profile. So far on this voyage you've managed to upset the expedition leader, acquire a stowaway and nearly get yourself eaten by a giant squid. I'll talk to the professor but if you could manage to avoid causing mayhem until we get wherever we're going it would be much appreciated.'

'Oh, I know where we're going,' said India. 'We're headed for a place called Whalesong. Cael says he has influence there.'

Verity looked sceptical. 'Why does that statement fill me with dread?' she said. 'And didn't I tell you not to hang around with Cael O'Hanlon? Now why don't you leave me to finish my breakfast in peace?'

They left Verity muttering into her coffee and took a walk around the deck. A fresh wind was whipping the waves into foam and there was an icy bite in the air.

'Hi there,' called a cheery voice. Cael waved to them from the forward deck. He had pulled the tarpaulin from one of Professor Moon's machines – an iron vehicle the size of a small truck – and was attending to it with an oil can and a greasy rag.

'How are you both this morning?' he said. 'No nightmares I hope? That sea monster was enough to put the frighteners on anyone.'

Tito put his palms together and bowed deeply. 'On the contrary, Mr O'Hanlon,' he said. 'The Great Teacher says that we are most alive when we are closest to death. I found it quite . . . *exhilarating*.'

'How's the professor this morning?' asked India. 'He seemed pretty angry about everything last night.'

'He's fine,' said Cael. 'He's working on a plan to catch one of those sea monsters and he asked me to make sure his machines weren't getting corroded by the salt water. I'd say he's got over the shock of having a stowaway.'

India looked at the vehicle that Cael was oiling. It had wheels at the front and steel caterpillar tracks at the rear. There was a small cabin made of riveted iron plates and tiny windows of reinforced glass. But the most remarkable thing about the vehicle was the gigantic metal screw mounted on the front. It was the strangest-looking contraption India had ever seen.

'This is Orpheus,' said Cael. 'Apparently the professor invented it himself.'

'No doubt named after the mythical character who travelled to the underworld,' said Tito, enthralled. 'Truly this is a machine worthy of a tech-hunter.'

'A machine for drilling tunnels?' said India, sizing up the iron beast. 'Why does he need it out here in the middle of the ocean?'

'Don't ask me,' said Cael, 'I'm just the hired help around here. Why don't you give me a hand?' He reached into the tool box and brought out two grease guns, then showed them how to lubricate the steel tracks.

'So how did you meet Verity?' said India as they worked. Cael looked thrown by the question.

'Well, er . . . it was a long time ago,' he said. 'I was exploring a tech-mine in New Mexico when I ran into her.'

'She said she shot you for trying to steal from her,' said India gleefully.

'Oh, did she now!' said Cael, sounding miffed. 'Well, that's not the way I remember it. I barely had time to introduce myself before she pulled out a shotgun and opened fire. Fortunately the gun was only loaded with rock salt, but I caught both barrels in the backside.' India and Tito started to laugh uncontrollably. 'It might sound funny to you, but it damn well hurt,' he complained. 'Anyway when she found out I wasn't a pirate she was very apologetic and even helped to patch me up.'

'So what happened after that?' said India.

Cael shrugged. 'Well, it's hard to stay mad at someone when they've put sticking plaster on your bum,' he said. 'After that we started to travel around together, we made a good team.' He paused a moment to gaze into the distance. 'So now you tell me something,' he said, gathering his thoughts. 'She's changed her name since I knew her. Have you ever met *Mr* Brown?'

India snorted. 'No. I don't know anything about him. Maybe he was someone she met after you and she . . . you know.'

Cael nodded sadly. 'Yeah, I know.'

'So did you really steal all her money and leave her on her own in the middle of nowhere?' asked India.

Cael frowned. 'Look, I'm not proud of how things ended between us,' he said. 'But believe me, I had good reasons. Hey,' he said, slapping the side of Orpheus. 'Do you want to see inside?'

He fumbled with a set of keys and unlocked a small iron door. They crouched low and squeezed into the cramped vehicle. The cabin smelt of oil and diesel fumes and steel pipes ran around the iron walls, sprouting valves and gauges like odd flowers. There were hard benches for the passengers and a driver's seat surrounded by spindly levers and pedals. It reminded India of a smaller version of *The Beautiful Game*.

Tito clapped his hands with excitement. 'This,' he said an awestruck voice, 'is how a tech-hunter should travel.'

'Has anyone actually been underground in this?' asked India.

'Who knows?' said Cael. 'But I wouldn't want to be the first.'

'What are those?' asked India. On the back wall of the cabin was a steel gun rack holding the strangest-looking weapons India had ever seen. There were several hefty hand-cannons just like the professor's, some tall rifles and a blunderbuss with a huge trumpet-shaped barrel. But it was the object at the end of the rack that drew her attention.

A torpedo-shaped tank was attached to a harness of leather and brass, made to fit tightly around a man's body. It had two steel exhaust pipes, flared at the ends and discoloured as though they had been exposed to high temperatures.

'I think it's a rocket pack,' said Cael with a shrug. 'The professor reckons we'll all be using them to get around in a few years.'

'Does it fly?' said India, imagining what it might be like to soar into the clouds without the need for a plane.

'Sure it flies,' said Cael. 'Any idiot with a tank full of rocket fuel can fly. It's landing that's the tricky part.'

They spilt, laughing and joking, from the cabin, to find Professor Moon standing outside. He had resumed his stern expression from the night before.

'Mr O'Hanlon,' he said in a clipped voice, 'I do not pay you to act as a tour guide. Kindly get on with the job I asked you to do.' Cael nodded meekly and went back to the steel tracks.

The professor looked uncertainly at Tito. 'I . . . regret that I lost my temper with you last night,' he said.

Tito smiled but said nothing.

'Is it true that you are one of the monks of the Divine Brotherhood?'

Tito nodded.

The professor looked thoughtful. 'I was thinking,' he

said. 'It might be useful to have someone on our expedition who is familiar with the legends of the Great Teacher. If you would like to join us, there is a place here for you.'

'Thank you, Professor,' said Tito, his smile never fading. 'I will consider your offer.'

Professor Moon looked slightly put out. 'I can understand that you might be angry with me for taking the stone,' he said. 'But I would not have done it if I did not believe it was for the greater good.'

'The Great Teacher tells us that most evil deeds are done in the name of the greater good, Professor,' said Tito, without a trace of malice in his voice.

The professor's eyebrows met in a thick grey hedge. 'Nevertheless,' he said, tersely, 'the stone will remain safely in my laboratory. We arrive at Whalesong Station tomorrow, where I can arrange passage home for you if you wish it. In the meantime you will confine yourself to Miss Bentley's cabin and the mess room.' He turned abruptly and strode away.

'He was trying to be nice,' said India as they watched him leave. 'Did you have to antagonize him?'

'The Great Teacher tells us to always say what is in one's heart,' said Tito happily. 'This I have observed in you too, Miss Bentley. Is it not the way of the tech-hunter?'

'Yes . . . I mean, no.' She sighed. 'What I mean is, you shouldn't necessarily do what *I* do.'

'But if I wish to be a tech-hunter like you, what else would I do?' he said.

India groaned and rubbed her forehead. She was beginning to understand how Verity felt sometimes.

The following morning, a dark line appeared on the horizon which soon became a rocky island of green, snow-capped mountains and steep rock walls running down to the sea. The *Ahaziah* sailed around the island until it reached a gap in the sheer cliffs. Inside they found a broad bay with a dozen tough-looking boats anchored in the calm waters. As the crew gathered on deck, India watched thin wisps of steam rising from the black sand on the beach.

'Why is the beach on fire, Mr O'Hanlon?' asked Tito.

'Whalesong is built inside an active volcanic crater,' replied Cael. 'It's the only sheltered harbour in this region – but it's a strange feeling to know you could be blown sky high at any moment.' He turned to look at Verity, who had emerged from below deck. 'Hey, V. Do you remember that old tech-mine we found on the slopes of an active volcano in Bolivia? I rescued nearly a dozen fuel cells before the place got buried in hot ash.' He gave a satisfied grin.

'What I remember,' said Verity drily, 'is you losing those fuel cells and all our supplies to a group of local tribesmen in a game of cards.'

Cael frowned. 'They just had beginner's luck, you should have let me carry on playing.'

Verity rolled her eyes. 'What I should have done was let them eat you like they wanted to. If I'd been nice to them they might even have let me carve.'

The town of Whalesong stood on the far side of the bay, huddled in the lee of the mountains, a wind-battered collection of wood and corrugated-iron houses and tall, windowless sheds that billowed steam into the cold morning air. A row of iron boilers, shaped like pepper pots, stood along the water's edge, breathing coils of thick smoke. A short distance from the town, as though ashamed to be associated with it, a wooden church stood alone, stark white, with a cemetery that seemed too large for a town of this size.

On the shoreline, India could see men in leather aprons using long knives to slice strips of blubber from a grisly carcass winched up on the slipway. The water was red with blood and choked with slime and dirty ice.

'They still hunt whales here?' gasped India. 'How could anyone do such a thing?'

'There's not many that do it by choice,' said Cael grimly. 'It's a hard way to earn a living. A whaling man can count himself lucky if he lives more than two seasons out here.'

Long before they reached the shore, the smell hit them: a sweet rottenness that hung so thickly in the air it left a taste in the throat. India pulled her scarf closer but it failed to blot out the stench of death that hung over Whalesong like a cloak.

They berthed alongside working steamboats that looked rusted and unloved, each one carrying a fearsome-looking harpoon on the foredeck and a crow's nest set high up on the mast. A crowd of densely bearded men and raw-boned, hard-eyed women gathered to watch them as they tied up. Professor Moon emerged from his laboratory and surveyed the scene.

'Mr O'Hanlon,' he called from the upper deck. 'You say you know these people?'

'Oh yes, Professor,' said Cael, waving cheerily to the crowd. 'I spent an entire season here. I'm sure they'll remember me.'

'That's what I'm worried about,' muttered Verity.

'Very well,' said the professor. 'Mr O'Hanlon, you will accompany me ashore and make the introductions. Miss Bentley, perhaps you and Mrs Brown would join us. If the stone is nearby we might have use for your talents.' He frowned at Tito, who was looking up at him hopefully. '*You* will confine yourself to the ship until I'm certain you can be trusted,' he said gruffly. Tito's face fell.

The professor and Cael led the way as they descended the gangplank and approached the unfriendly crowd. India looked back and waved to Tito, who watched them glumly from the upper deck.

A barrel-shaped man with a face like a walrus approached them carrying a long bladed knife. 'Mr Larssen!' said Cael, turning on his brilliant smile. 'It's great to see you again, sir, and wonderful to be back in your beautiful town. Tell me, how is that lovely daughter of yours?'

Larssen's expression clouded like an approaching gale-force storm. 'I warned you, O'Hanlon, that if you ever came back here I'd have you cut up for fish bait,' he growled.

'Great news, Cael,' said Verity under her breath, 'it looks like they remember you!'

The smile on Cael's face faltered slightly. 'Look, if this is about that thing with the penguins and the whisky, I can explain everything.'

'We are God-fearing people, O'Hanlon, and we don't approve of violence,' said Larssen. 'But in your case we'll make an exception.'

Several of the larger men wielded sharp implements and wore expressions that suggested a strong interest in using them to explore the softer parts of Cael's body. He took a step backwards as Verity shifted a hand to the butt of her gun.

The tension was broken by a heavily accented voice booming from the back of the crowd. 'What's going on here? Move aside.' The group parted to make way for a giant of a man. He stood taller than anyone on the waterfront, broader than a warehouse door with a thick mane of blond hair that reached down his back. He looked as though he had been carved from solid rock. 'Professor Moon,' he boomed. 'I'm glad you made it.'

'Captain Thor!' said the professor, breaking into a relieved smile and pumping the blond man's massive hand. 'It's really *very* good to see you.' He eyed the crowd anxiously. 'Are the rest of your crew here?' The blond giant shook his head.

'Just the first mate and me,' he said. 'We got here

yesterday.' He turned and barked at Larssen in a language India had never heard before. The expression on Larssen's walrus-face relaxed slightly.

'My apologies, Professor Moon,' said Larssen in a slightly oily tone. 'I had not appreciated you were friends of Captain Thor's. You are, of course, welcome in Whalesong.' He looked at Cael and scowled again. 'But you had better keep a close watch on that sack of fish guts or I won't be responsible for what happens to him.'

Larssen began shooing the crowd back to their work and they drifted away with many backward glares at Cael. Thor looked Verity and India up and down, his face as unreadable as the cliffs.

'You said nothing about bringing strangers, Professor,' he said.

'Not strangers, Thor,' said the professor. 'This is India Bentley and Verity Brown who have agreed to help us in our search. This is Captain Thor of the *Sea Wolf*.'

Captain Thor ignored India entirely and took Verity's hand, pressing it briefly to his lips. 'It is a rare pleasure to meet a beautiful woman in a place like this,' he said, never taking his eyes from her.

'Why thank you, Captain,' said Verity, giving him her sweetest smile. India noticed she glanced briefly in Cael's direction and smirked.

'Where is your first mate, Captain?' asked the professor. 'We should talk immediately.'

Captain Thor jerked his head towards a ramshackle row

of buildings. 'We have rooms at the general store. He was on the night watch so we'll need to wake him.'

'The hell you will,' came a drawling voice from behind them. They turned to see the first mate of the *Sea Wolf* striding across the rough wooden planks. He was a tall, rangy youth, dressed in a seaman's sweater and an officer's cap, partially concealing a shock of thick black hair. A red scar ran down one side of his face and his eyes held a lean and hungry look.

It was a look that India had last seen while standing on a frozen lake in Siberia and it belonged to someone she thought was lost for good. He was taller and broader in the shoulders than when she had last seen him but there was no mistaking the pale figure that stood before her.

'Holy mother of all riggers,' she exclaimed. 'Sid!'

11 YOU'RE SUPPOSED TO BE DEAD

'What the hell are you doing here?' snapped Verity. 'You're supposed to be dead.'

'Well it's damned nice to see you too, Mrs Brown,' drawled Sid. 'I pretty much *was* dead, too, after you all abandoned me at Ironheart.' He cast a poisonous look towards India.

'Abandoned you?' spluttered India, 'I saw your father's rig blow up with you on board. We had no idea you were still alive—'

'Enough!' said the professor sharply. 'You needn't worry, Mrs Brown. Sidney is a reformed character from the young man you knew. I met him last year, shortly after his "accident" and I helped him find his feet again. He has joined Captain Thor's crew and risen through the ranks to become the first mate, a highly responsible position.'

Sid scowled and thrust his hands into his pockets, looking nothing like a reformed character.

'Come,' said Professor Moon brusquely. 'There will be plenty of time for you all to reminisce later. In the meantime I want to know what you have found out, Captain. Perhaps we could go to the general store to talk?'

They followed Thor and Sid towards the store as Cael looked back over his shoulder to make sure they were not being followed. The streets were laid with duckboards over the mud and cluttered with the debris of the town's trade. Whale bones the size of boat timbers lay in bleached piles among rope shards and bent harpoons, crusted with dirty snow. The stench of death followed them everywhere.

The general store was a two-storey wooden building with a hand-painted sign announcing that it sold dry goods and alcohol. Several men stopped drinking their soapy beer and watched in nail-hard silence as Captain Thor led them to a table at the back of the room.

Professor Moon fetched glasses of foaming beer for everyone, including India. She peered suspiciously at the brown liquid; after her disappointing encounter with wine she was not inclined to drink something that looked like the stuff her father used to weatherproof fences.

Verity squeezed on to the bench next to Captain Thor while Cael sat down morosely at the other end of the table. India watched Sid carefully from the corner of her eye. He still carried the same look of cold menace, but now there was something else there too. He had a coolness about him that was very different from the volatile young man she had first met.

'So, what news, Captain?' said the professor, settling into a seat at the head of the table. 'Where is the *Sea Wolf*?'

Captain Thor moved his untouched beer aside, and cast a sideways look at the whalers at the far end of the bar. 'We left the *Wolf* offshore, around the headland. A boat like that tends to get people asking too many questions.'

'Ah, yes, good thinking, Captain,' said the professor. 'And what of the Bloodstone? We have managed to trace the third piece to this area – but have *you* found anything more specific?'

'These whalers don't talk to outsiders much,' said Sid. 'But I heard a few things.' He dropped his voice and leaned closer. 'There's a man lives in these waters by the name of "Whaler John". They say that fifty years ago he fell overboard and got swallowed by a whale. When they cut him out he'd gone totally insane, said he could hear voices. From what I gather he became some sort of preacher.'

'Everywhere has its share of crazies,' said Verity, 'but where does the stone fit into all of this?'

'Whaler John reckoned he'd found some sort of artefact in the belly of the whale that let him speak to God,' said Sid. 'His followers call it the "Jonah Stone".'

'Sounds like that might be your Bloodstone,' said Thor.

'Yes, yes it might be,' said Professor Moon excitedly. 'Excellent work, Sidney. So where do we find this "Whaler John"? Is he in town?'

'That's just it,' said Sid. 'He never comes ashore. He spends his life at sea with his crew of followers so he can be closer to the voices. The last sightings of him were a couple of days south of here but that was all I could get before they clammed up on me.'

'It's not much to go on, Professor,' said Cael. 'Perhaps I could have another go at speaking to Larssen? I'm sure I could win him around.'

'I think we've had quite enough of your services as a guide, Mr O'Hanlon,' said the professor with a frown. 'Captain Thor, if this "Whaler John" is still in the area then the *Sea Wolf* is best equipped to find him. I suggest you take your crew and scout the area to the south while we wait here and see what else we can find out. You can send us a Teslagraph with your coordinates when you find him.'

'Are you sure it's safe to wait here?' said India, eyeing the grim crowd at the bar.

'Perfectly,' said the professor brusquely. 'These are just simple people and they're naturally suspicious of strangers.'

India thought of the 'simple people' of Hampstead who were quite likely to hang someone from a tree if they didn't recognize them. The men and women of Whalesong didn't seem that different to her.

The talk turned to weather patterns and fuel supplies and India's attention began to wander. But when she looked around she gave a start. Outside the window she saw Tito, waving his arms to attract her attention and pointing to something soft and shapeless in his hand. With horror she realized it was the leather pouch in which the professor kept the stones.

She looked around to see if anyone else had noticed. Sid, Thor and Cael were poring over a chart while Verity was telling Professor Moon she thought they needed to post more guards on the ship.

'I'm . . . er . . . just stepping outside,' announced India, slipping from behind the table. No one noticed her go.

Outside she dragged Tito away from the window. 'Tito, you idiot. How did you get hold of that?'

He grinned and stuffed the bag back into his pocket. 'After you had gone I told one of the crew that the professor had asked me to fetch something from his laboratory and that he had better not keep him waiting. He unlocked the door and I found this in the desk drawer.' He looked ridiculously pleased with himself. 'This is the sort of thing a tech-hunter would do, no?'

'No!' snapped India. 'The professor will kill you when he finds out and he won't be too pleased with me either.'

'The professor has no right to be angry,' said Tito firmly. 'He stole the stone from the brotherhood and I mean to return it.'

'He only stole one of the stones,' said India, 'the other one belongs to him, remember?'

'There is nothing I can do about that,' said Tito. 'As the stones can no longer be separated, I will have to take them both with me. The Great Teacher tells us that we must use our initiative. Thank you, Miss Bentley, your excellent tuition on how to be a tech-hunter has been a great help but now I must bid you farewell.'

He picked up his small black suitcase and started to walk down one of the narrow lanes that led back to the harbour.

'Where do you think you're going to go from here?' said India, running to catch him up. 'We're on an island in the middle of nowhere.'

Tito did not slow down. 'There are several merchant vessels in the harbour and I am sure one of them must be headed towards Sing City. All I have to do is explain that I am a monk of the brotherhood and Robert is your mother's brother.'

India frowned. 'I think you mean, "Bob's your uncle"?'

'That is what I said, Miss Bentley.'

She sighed and glanced back at the general store. Everyone was still inside; there might still be time to persuade Tito to change his mind. 'Look, if you start telling people who you are, they'll kill you for what you've got in your pockets. That's always assuming that the professor doesn't kill you first. I know you feel strongly about this, Tito, but you've got to put the stone back. Professor Moon will never stop chasing you if you don't.'

'I don't care!' Tito snapped. His normally serene face was suddenly contorted with anger. 'Professor Moon does not know what he is dealing with, Miss Bentley. These stones are not meant to be brought together until the end of the Great Cycle.'

He began scanning the ships in the bay and India wondered whether she should try and drag him back to the boat forcibly. 'There,' he said, pointing decisively to a blue and white merchantman on the far side of the harbour, bearing the name *Snow Petrel*. 'That one will take me to Sing City.'

'How can you know that?' asked India.

'Because I saw it in the port before we left, so I know it must go there.'

'Wait a minute,' said India. 'You saw that ship in Sing City? You must be mistaken.'

'There is no mistake, Miss Bentley,' he said firmly. 'I spotted it when I raised the lid of your trunk to get some fresh air. A tech-hunter must be observant at all times, no?'

'It's a bit of a coincidence that it should turn up here, don't you think?' said India. She looked closely at the ship. Now that she thought about it, it did seem to be well hidden away at the end of the harbour. As they watched, a door on the upper deck swung open and a tall man emerged, too far away to identify. He peered in their direction and then slowly raised a pair of binoculars.

India pulled Tito back into the shadows. 'This doesn't feel right, Tito,' she said. 'I don't know who's on that boat but I don't think you should go anywhere near it.' More people were emerging on deck now. Some were running towards the gangplank, carrying rifles. 'Uh-oh, this isn't good at all,' said India. 'We should get back and tell the others.'

Tito did not resist as India pulled him back up the narrow lane towards the general store. All of the boy's bravado seemed to have drained away. But as they were passing a darkened alley they were startled when a loose heap of rubbish stirred and something shadowy slithered out of sight.

'What was that, Miss Bentley?' said Tito in a half-whisper.

India peered into the alley. Although she could see nothing, a certain thickness in the shadows made her scalp prickle. 'It's just a rat,' she said with a swallow. 'Let's keep moving.'

They continued up the lane at a brisk trot, casting anxious glances over their shoulders.

'Miss Bentley,' said Tito, pulling on her jacket. 'Something just crossed the alley behind us. I don't think it was a rat, it was much . . . bigger.' There was an edge of panic in his voice.

A dustbin dislodged suddenly, sending the lid clattering across the cobbles and something heavy-bodied slithered past them into the shadows, settling behind a row of barrels.

'Well whatever it is, it's in front of us now,' said India quietly. Her legs felt shaky and she could hear Tito's breath coming in quick gasps. She couldn't explain why she felt so fearful but she felt certain now that they were being watched by malevolent eyes.

She grasped Tito's hand. 'Let's turn back – quickly.' They hurried back the way they had come, no longer caring that they were heading back to the harbour, when the pile of barrels crashed to the ground, spilling their contents across the cobbles. India thought she caught a glimpse of yellow eyes in the darkness.

'Run, Tito!' she yelled. Panic took hold of them both and they broke into a sprint, certain that some formless nightmare was pursuing them. Don't look back, thought India desperately. Whatever happens, *don't look back*.

As they reached daylight at end of the alleyway, a tall man stepped out and blocked their path. 'Get out of the way,' screamed India.

But as they drew closer it became obvious that it was not a man at all. India gasped and pulled Tito back and they both stumbled and fell to the ground. In nearly all respects the android before them looked just like Calculus – but somehow its stare was colder, its posture more menacing. The hideous hissing noise it made touched her heart with icy fingers.

'Stay very still,' she whispered to Tito.

'Have no fear, Miss Bentley,' said Tito unevenly. 'The Great Teacher said when we are faced with an opponent of irresistible force we should meet him with no force. I think that was good advice,' he added.

'Good work, Maximus,' came a cold female voice.

Lady Fang appeared beside the android, hands folded into the sleeves of her white fur coat. Skullet stood just behind, sporting a black eye-patch and clutching the collar of walrus-faced Mr Larssen. All of Larssen's earlier gruffness had evaporated to be replaced by a look of pure fear.

Fang slowly circled India and Tito, her heels clicking on

the cobbles. 'Search them both. They may have the stone with them.'

Maximus roughly turned out Tito's suitcase and their pockets, and Lady Fang's eyes widened when she saw the leather pouch.

'Both pieces of the stone,' she gloated. 'This is better than I could have hoped.' She turned the fused stone over slowly in her hand. When it caught the sunlight India winced as a sound like a high-pitched drill began in her head. She looked sharply at India and then back at the stone. '*Very* interesting,' she mused, before slipping the stone into the folds of her coat. She clicked her fingers and Skullet let go of Larssen and shoved him forward.

'Mr Larssen, we will leave immediately,' purred Lady Fang. 'Make sure that bumbling fool Moon and the others are killed when we are gone. I want no one following us.'

Larssen mopped his brow with a filthy handkerchief and licked his lips nervously.

'Killing was not part of our bargain,' he said. 'We agreed to stay quiet about your arrival and keep them occupied so you could search their ship. Nothing more.'

Lady Fang turned on him with her eyes ablaze. 'I am changing our arrangement, Mr Larssen,' she hissed. 'Take care I don't decide to let my Hellhound loose in your school before we leave.'

Larssen gulped and scuttled away before his deal with Lady Fang became any worse.

India felt sure the Hellhound must be the creature

that had stalked them in the alleyway. She shivered at the memory.

'Maximus,' barked Fang, 'round up your little pet and join us back at the ship.' Maximus nodded briefly and then disappeared into the shadows. 'Skullet, bring Miss Bentley with us. Kill the boy.'

'No!' cried India. 'He has nothing to do with this. Leave him alone!' She tried to stand but Skullet shoved her back to the ground. He hauled Tito to his feet and pulled out his knife, enjoying the boy's terror. Then his expression turned to a frown.

'Wait a minute,' he said. 'I know this one. He was on the High Priest's boat. He was the one holding the stone.'

Fang looked at Tito with renewed interest and stroked her chin. 'So what are you doing here, little monk? You're a long way from home.'

Before Tito could answer, a volley of gunshots broke out from the direction of the general store. Fang smiled. 'That will be Larssen's men taking care of your friends,' she said. 'Come on, it's high time we got out of this frozen stink-hole. Skullet, bring the boy, he might prove useful after all.'

Skullet marched India and Tito along the quay at knifepoint to a small boat, where a seaman waited to transfer them to the *Snow Petrel*. Lady Fang stepped expertly into the stern while Skullet shoved India and Tito into the front. He sat opposite India and lifted his eye-patch to reveal a ragged red socket. 'This is *your* doing, India Bentley,' he snarled, jabbing a finger at the wound. 'You cost me an eye and I mean to collect payment.'

India shrank back into her seat and tried not to look at the hideous wound. As the boat chugged towards the blue and white ship they heard more gunshots. India bit her lip and hoped that Verity and Cael were all right.

Tito looked thoroughly miserable. 'I fear I have made things worse, Miss Bentley,' he whispered. 'I do not think this lady will be a more responsible owner of the stones than the professor.' India was inclined to agree but could think of nothing to say that would make Tito feel better.

When they reached the *Snow Petrel*, Skullet shoved them up a ladder to the deck and began giving the crew orders to cast off. Maximus joined them a few minutes later, although India had not seen him return to the boat and there was no sign of the Hellhound.

The anchor clanked up from the seabed and the ship's powerful diesel engines burst into life, rattling the decks beneath their feet. As they began a slow turn in the bay, India saw several figures running along the decks of the *Ahaziah*.

'Maximus!' barked Fang. 'Make sure that ship can't follow us.' She gripped the ship's rail so tightly that her knuckles became white and bloodless. The android stepped forward and raised an arm. With the soft *schlick* of well-oiled metal, a compartment opened in his forearm and a tiny missile raised into position. It looked like a white bird, perched on his arm.

'No!' shouted India, rushing towards him. 'Please don't

hurt them, they're my friends.' The android pushed her aside as the little rocket left his arm with a whoosh that sucked the air from behind it as it went. The stern of the *Ahaziah* erupted with an explosion that rattled the wheelhouse windows in the *Snow Petrel*. A smoky ball of flame curled into the cold air over Whalesong and the figures on the deck of the *Ahaziah* scattered in all directions as they tried to extinguish the flames.

India watched with her hand to her mouth but there was nothing she could do, except to watch helplessly as the *Snow Petrel* passed unchallenged through the harbour entrance and into open sea.

12
WHALER JOHN

They sailed south for a day and a half. India and Tito were locked in a tiny cabin with a single porthole. It was even smaller than the cabin they had shared on the *Ahaziah* and contained only two small straw mattresses, a tiny table, a cracked sink and a steel bucket. When the weather turned rough and Tito's seasickness returned, the room was filled with the sour smell of vomit.

At the end of the first day, Lady Fang came to their cabin accompanied by the awful hissing vision of Maximus. She held up the two joined stones and India felt the familiar high-pitched whining start in her skull.

'The stones affect you in some way, don't they?' said Fang, passing them back and forth before India's eyes. India said nothing. 'Perhaps that is why Moon was so interested in you. *Perhaps* he is hoping you can help him find the third piece?'

She studied India carefully for a few moments and then

abruptly tossed the stone down on the table. 'Pick it up,' she snapped.

India looked at the stone apprehensively and the noise in her skull became a little louder. 'I-I can't,' she stammered.

Lady Fang frowned. 'Perhaps you just need the right motivation.' She looked into the cracked mirror above the sink, and lightly touched the lines on her face. 'It's a shame. We might have got a good ransom for the boy from the monks, but my need is becoming urgent. Sacrifices will have to be made.'

With the speed of a viper she grabbed Tito and wrapped an arm tightly around his neck. She pulled her other hand from her pocket and unfolded a set of silver claws with wickedly pointed blades, tearing the boy's glasses from his face and placing the thumb and index finger blades against his right eye. She smiled. 'Of course, I could just get Maximus to crush the boy's skull, but there is a certain artistry in removing an eye. Now, I will ask you one more time, pick up that stone and tell me where I can find Whaler John.'

'Tell her nothing, Miss Bentley,' gasped Tito. 'She must not have the stones. She must—'

He yelped as the blades pinched at the skin around his eye. India gasped and her head swam with the horror of what was about to unfold.

'I'll do it, I'll do it!' She hurriedly picked up the stone, feeling it thrill in her fingers. A pain like broken glass stabbed her through the eye and the noise in her head rose to a bone-sawing shriek. She closed her eyes and willed herself to focus.

She felt a wrench, as though she were being pulled away from the little cabin and the *Sea Petrel* itself. Then she was outside and she was flying: skimming the across the wave-tops at the speed of thought.

An image flashed before her like a night scene, lit by lightning.

A ship, pale and fragile on the high sea, a crew of hollow-eyed sailors and, at the helm, a man with hair and skin as white as bone and eyes of blue and brown that pierced her soul. She knew that this was the man they called Whaler John and that there was madness behind those eyes.

'Twenty leagues sou'-west is where we lie,' he cried. 'Find us if you wish but you will know the wrath of the beast if you do.'

She opened her eyes with a gasp and the stone fell back to the table with a clatter.

'Well?' said Fang eagerly.

'He's south-west of here,' she said, blinking rapidly. 'Twenty leagues. And he knows we're coming.' She was not sure how she knew any of this, but felt certain her vision was correct.

Lady Fang mouthed a silent 'Ah!' and released Tito, who staggered weakly to his mattress. 'Excellent,' she breathed. 'We shall undoubtedly want to make further use of your talents, Miss Bentley.' She glanced at the android and jerked her head towards the window. 'Maximus, make sure that porthole is properly secured. I want no ill-advised escape attempts. As for you two, I strongly advise you not to try and leave this room, or you might find something very unpleasant waiting for you outside.'

She laughed spitefully and whisked out of the room with the stone in her silver-clawed hand. India hugged Tito, who looked pale and frightened and was gingerly touching the cuts around his eye.

'Are you OK, Tito?'

'I believe so, Miss Bentley,' he said faintly, reaching for his fallen glasses.

They sat in silence while the android checked the window. A thought occurred to India as she watched him.

'Excuse me.' The android stopped and turned to look at her. 'I was wondering if I might have a word with you?' The android looked at her impassively and a faint hiss escaped from beneath its helmet. She suddenly felt that this might have been a bad idea.

'I was wondering if . . . That is, I wanted to ask . . .' She stopped. This was not at all like talking to Calculus. It occurred to her that she had never heard Maximus speak.

'I'm sorry,' she said quickly. 'Can you talk?' The silence that followed lasted several seconds. She heard Tito swallow loudly beside her.

'*Of coursssse.*'

The voice sent a trickle of ice water down her spine. It was as unlike Calc's as it was possible to imagine. Instead of a richly amplified tone, he spoke in a dark whisper, each word accompanied by a hydraulic hiss. It was a cold and pitiless voice, the very essence of a machine.

'I u-used t-to have a friend who was like you,' she stammered. 'I was w-wondering if you had heard of him. His name was—'

'*I am aware of the unit called Calculuss*,' he said. '*I know of all of the earlier Matssushito modelss. Their sspecificationss. Their weaknessess.*'

'Weaknesses?'

'*The unit, Calculuss, was a five-thousand series. An altogether inferior model, prone to ssentimentality and other human failingss.*'

India shivered. 'He wasn't weak,' she said firmly. 'He was my friend.'

'*As I ssaid*,' Maximus replied, '*prone to ssentimentality*.'

India took a deep breath. As much as she had loved Calculus, so this machine seemed thoroughly hateful to her. Still, she was determined to ask her question.

'If he was still alive, w-would you know about it?'

The android said nothing for a long while and India wondered if he had understood.

'*Yess*,' he said eventually. '*But he is not. That unit has ceassed to function*.'

'I see,' she said, trying to hide her disappointment. 'But is it possible that he might be alive somewhere? Even though his body was destroyed?'

There was another long pause.

'*All Matssushito droidss are built with an independent consciousness*,' he hissed. '*Our mindss can be transsferred to a new unit in the event of damage*.'

India nodded. Calculus had once told her something similar. 'So how long could an android's mind live outside its body?'

'*An android'ss mind can only be sstored within a computer core*,' said Maximus. '*Much dependss on how powerful the core is. Usually a few hours, no more*.'

'I see,' said India. 'But if the computer was really powerful, I mean like the most powerful computer in the world, how long could an android's mind survive then?'

The android scrutinized her for a long while. '*Potentially, indefinitely*,' he said at last.

India caught her breath.

'Thank you,' she said. 'Thank you very much.'

The next day, Maximus brought them to the wheelhouse, where Lady Fang was looking through a pair of binoculars. Skullet was applying a file to his teeth and testing the sharpness of their points with his tongue; he glared at them with his good eye. Two-Buck Tim looked up from a small box of wires he was prodding with a screwdriver and gave them a cheery wave. Then he promptly remembered where he was and his face fell sombre again.

A tall-masted ship with furled sails stood at anchor about a mile off their bows, pale and delicate . . . and looking exactly as it had appeared in India's vision.

'Lower the boats,' said Fang. 'Maximus will take charge of the boarding party.' Skullet bristled at this. 'Miss Bentley,' Fang continued. 'You and the boy will come with me, but don't get any ideas or I'll tie you both to the anchor and throw you overboard.'

The *Snow Petrel* approached the tall ship from the rear. The name on the stern identified it as the *Jonah*. At first sight its decks looked deserted. But then India spied the crew, around a dozen men, clustered on the foredeck. They appeared to be having a meeting.

The crew of the *Sea Petrel* lowered the two motor launches into the sea. A dozen heavily armed sailors went in the first boat, while India and Tito travelled in the second with Lady Fang, Skullet and Maximus. When they reached the *Jonah*, the crew slung heavy grapples over the ship's wooden rails. Two men scaled the ropes and lowered a rope ladder. Lady Fang managed to look elegant while being carried up by Maximus, while India and Tito followed and tried not to look down into the heaving, grey waters.

The *Jonah* was neat and well-kept with carefully coiled ropes and decks scrubbed to the colour of bleached driftwood. None of her crew had moved from their position on the foredeck and now that India saw them more closely it looked as though they were at prayer with their heads bowed.

Maximus barged his way through the group, scattering the crewmen who shrank back at the sight of the black android in their midst. One man, however, did not move. He stood at the prow facing the visitors and everyone stared at the sight of him.

His skin, hair, eyebrows and lashes were all bleached as

white as paper, as though all the colour had been sucked out of him. He looked like the ghost of an ancient mariner. His clothes were made of pale wool and he carried a long staff made from some kind of sea ivory marked with a spiral groove running around the shaft. India recognized him immediately as the man in her vision: it could only be Whaler John, the man who had been swallowed by a whale and had lived. He raised his staff into the air and called out over the howling of the wind.

'She comes, O brothers,' he cried, staring at Lady Fang. 'The one who would deliver us from this curse has come at last. And see –' his eyes shone in ecstasy – 'she brings Death with her.' He pointed to Maximus. 'Be not afraid of him, brothers, for Death is a friend who will take us from this place.'

'Mad as a coot,' muttered Skullet under his breath.

'Spare me your babbling, preacher,' said Fang. 'We've come for the stone. Give it to me now and we'll let your men go unharmed.' Whaler John clasped his hands together and a smile cracked his weathered features. The pinkness of his mouth looked like a raw wound in the ghostly face. 'None of us will leave unharmed from the lair of the Leviathan,' he cried. 'He leaves his mark on all who come here.'

'Enough,' barked Fang. 'Maximus!' She snapped her fingers. In a single movement the android grasped the collar of the nearest seaman and hurled him into the water. There was a single shriek and the man was gone – disappeared beneath the heaving swathe of grey.

Neither Whaler John nor his men showed any reaction. 'It makes no difference,' he said. 'We are all dead men here.'

'Where is the stone, you lunatic!' yelled Fang, her teeth bared in anger. 'Give it to me now or you will all perish.'

It was becoming difficult to be heard over the wind now. Deep grey cloud had begun to circle overhead like a whirlpool. Some way off the stern, India could see the *Sea Petrel* pitching and tossing in the swell.

'You have only to ask and it shall be given,' said Whaler John. 'Step forth and take it.' Lady Fang looked at him apprehensively. Clearly she did not like the idea of going anywhere near the mad preacher. 'The girl!' she said suddenly. 'Make her fetch the stone.'

Skullet grabbed the scruff of India's jacket and shoved her forward. The crew parted to allow her through and she approached the stark-white figure of Whaler John who stood, arms outstretched, as though welcoming her home. Up close she could clearly see his mismatched eyes of brown and blue that glittered with madness.

'You seek the stone, child?' he asked in his soft preacher's voice.

She nodded, vaguely aware that the howl of the wind was growing steadily louder.

'Then take it,' he said. 'But beware of what you take upon yourself. For fifty long years we have sailed these oceans, plagued by demons who whisper to us while we sleep, telling us dark tales about the curse of the Bloodstone. So take it now and bring me welcome death.'

The cloud above them whirled like a hurricane's eye and a crack of lightning split the sky. The *Jonah*'s timbers groaned and thick rods of rain began to lash the decks. 'The time is here,' Whaler John gasped. 'Quickly!' He grasped at his shirt front and tore open the buttons. Hanging by a leather thong was the third and final piece of the stone, broken-edged and covered with tiny hieroglyphs, just like the others. The skin of Whaler John's chest where the stone had lain was red and twisted like the aftermath of a terrible burn. India recoiled from him involuntarily.

'Take it!' gasped Whaler John. 'The beast is nearly come.'

'The beast?' said India. She glanced nervously at the boiling waters.

'Aye, the one with ice blood and cold jelly for a soul, but I will go to him gladly if you take this burden from me.' He thrust his chest forward. India reached out gingerly and lifted the thong from around his neck. She thought she heard him let out a sigh as the stone left his skin.

Lady Fang immediately snatched it from India's hand and pulled the other pieces from her pocket. 'Where is Atlantis?' she screamed at Whaler John. 'Make the stones tell me.'

Whaler John raised his hands up to heaven as a bolt of lightning seared the air, and struck the mast with a splintering crack, scattering men across the deck. 'Only a Soul Voyager can point the way,' he said. 'The girl has taken the stones upon herself and now they will speak only to her.'

Lady Fang turned on India like an angry tiger. 'Take them!' She thrust the stones into India's hands. 'Make them show me the way.' India was uncertain what she should do, but as she held them she felt the familiar energy coursing through them and they grew suddenly hot in her hands so that she dropped them with a cry. As they hit the deck, the final piece snapped together with the other two to make a perfect circle of green stone, flecked with red.

Lady Fang shoved India aside and crowded forward eagerly to look at the completed Bloodstone. A faint light began to emanate from within it and some of the hieroglyphs on the surface began to glow with their own light, standing apart from the others.

'It's a message,' gasped Fang. She reached out a hand but the boat gave a violent, splintering lurch and the stone slid away across the deck.

'The beast is here,' cried Whaler John. 'Praise be, brothers! Death has found us.'

All around the boat came a rushing and roaring like a great waterfall accompanied by a screeching almost beyond the range of human hearing. A vast tentacle burst from the waters, as thick as a tree and tapering to a hook-lined pad at its tip. India had a clear view of suckers the size of dinner plates along its length.

Lady Fang's crew shrank back and retreated towards the motor launches.

'The stone, you fools,' screamed Fang. 'Get the stone!'

A second tentacle lashed across the deck, wrapping itself

right around the *Jonah*, splintering deck rails and cracking the ship's ancient timbers. The whole boat shuddered and heaved as the stone skidded further along the deck, coming to rest against a coil of rope. Tito dashed forward to where the stone lay, and used a small square of cloth to wrap it up and place it in his jacket pocket.

'Not so fast, sonny!' Skullet flicked his wrist and a long silver knife snapped open with a machined click. 'Say your prayers, little monk,' he sneered. But as he lunged at the boy, the air was torn by more hideous screeching and Skullet turned just in time to see a slippery, sinuous tentacle lash out from the spray and whip around his neck.

He dropped the knife and clawed frantically at his throat, desperately trying to suck air into his lungs, but the slippery coils tightened mercilessly, jerking him from his feet and dragging him down into the boiling grey waters.

Whaler John's men had resumed their prayers amidst the chaos but Fang's crew were now in disarray, pushing each other out of the way in their panic to get into the launches. India saw Maximus with Lady Fang in his arms, leaping from the deck to the launch fifteen feet below.

Tito scrambled across the deck towards India. 'Miss Bentley,' he cried over the howling wind, 'I have it. The stone is safe—'

His words were cut short as another slimy limb snaked around his skinny body and dragged him from the deck. India screamed and ran to the rail, frantically searching the boiling waters for some sight of him. The *Jonah* was completely encircled by a seething mass of tentacles and Lady Fang's motor launches were now fleeing at full speed towards the *Sea Petrel.* She spotted Tito being tossed around in the water, his mouth open in a silent scream. At the centre of the writhing mass a huge red maw with wickedly hooked teeth pulsated obscenely as the boy was hauled towards it.

India had no sense of having made a decision, yet somehow she found herself clambering over the rail and hurling herself into the waves. The bitterly cold water shocked her rigid, and her heavy clothes instantly filled with water, dragging her down. She clawed her way, coughing and choking, to the surface and struck out towards Tito, narrowly avoiding a barbed tentacle. Against all odds she managed to grab the young monk by his collar.

'It's OK,' she gasped, 'I've got you!'

But then he was gone, torn from her grasp by the relentless force of the creature – leaving her clutching an empty jacket.

'Tito! No, no, NO!' she screamed. She twisted and turned frantically in the swell, searching for his small body. But he was gone.

A great splintering tore the air as the spine of the *Jonah* finally broke under the pressure of the beast and the ship was pulled beneath the waves, taking the last of her crew with her. India gasped as a thick tentacle wound itself around her body and pulled her down, squeezing her ribs to breaking point. Deeper and deeper she was dragged until the light faded to black.

In her heart, she knew this was the end.

Then, without warning, the giant squid released its hold and propelled itself away into the depths and India found herself floating alone, still clutching Tito's empty jacket. Her body screamed for air so that she scarcely registered the huge surge of bubbles that had erupted all around her or the monstrous black shape that rose from the depths beneath her.

She felt a hard, flat surface lift her up and up until she breached the surface and was brought, choking and gasping back into the light. Trembling with fear, she raised her head and realized that what she clung to was not another creature but a great, windowless submarine with water cascading over its black flanks. There was only one vessel that this could possibly be: the *Sea Wolf*.

13 THE *SEA WOLF*

A succession of images flashed past India's eyes as she clung to the deck of the submarine. A hatch crashing open. A glimpse of heavy boots as Sid strode past her. Rough hands pulling her up. She watched in a dream-like state as the *Snow Petrel* turned in the water and began to bear down on them. Sid stood at the front of the submarine, his black coat whipping in the wind and a pistol in each hand, letting loose volley after volley at the approaching ship, each shot finding its mark on the wheelhouse. Just when it seemed that the *Snow Petrel* must surely run them down, the ship pulled hard to port and swept past them.

'Get her below,' yelled Sid above the roar of the waves.

India was half carried, half pushed through a steel hatchway and into a dimly lit control room. Sid was the last man in, sliding down the ladder and slamming shut the hatch in a single movement. Captain Thor appeared beside him and together they tightened the hatch wheel.

The crew scurried to their stations like determined rats as an explosion rocked the submarine violently. Somewhere a klaxon began to sound.

'That damned robot's armed with enough explosives to break us in two,' barked Sid.

'Dive! Dive! Dive!' boomed Captain Thor. 'Take us down to fifty feet and bring us around on their stern.' He pulled on two rubber handles and a periscope slid smoothly into place. Everyone fell quiet as he squinted through the ground glass of the eyepiece.

'Open the outer doors on tubes one and two. I want to give them something to think about.'

Sid crouched momentarily in front of India and inspected her as though she were a piece of broken machinery. 'Is she gonna be OK?' he asked, as though she couldn't hear him.

'She'll be fine,' said a voice from behind her.

Someone prised Tito's jacket from her frozen fingers. She tried to speak but a suffocating weight on her chest made it hard to breathe and for a moment, it felt as though she was underwater again. Then, slowly, blackness crept in at the edge of her vision and she knew nothing more. Somewhere in her dreams came a noise like two banshees taking flight, followed by the deep boom of a distant explosion. And then there was peace.

India's eyelids flickered against the brightness as a huge figure loomed above her, blocking out the light. 'Captain Thor,' she croaked.

'You're awake,' he said, stating the obvious.

Every muscle in her body felt on fire and her throat was raw and dry. She pulled herself up on one elbow and winced. She lay beneath a rough blanket, her sodden clothes were gone and she was dressed in a dry boiler suit.

'The medic says you have multiple contusions and that you may have cracked a rib,' said Thor without any trace of sympathy.

'I'll be OK,' said India, trying not to let the pain show on her face.

'Good,' said Thor. 'You can keep the bunk for now. The rest of the crew have to take it in turns to sleep in shifts.'

'Oh,' said India, thinking that Thor's bedside manner was somewhat lacking.

The bunk room was long and narrow with a curved ceiling, like a tube. Steel beds with thin mattresses were suspended at every level in the cramped space, several of them occupied by sleeping crew members. India took stock of her injuries. Apart from the sore throat, her sides ached and she felt bruised and beaten as though as though she had been wrestling with a wild beast. Which, she had to remind herself, she had.

A memory stabbed at her. 'Tito?' she said.

'We saw the android pulling something from the water,' said Thor. 'It could have been a body but we don't know. Alive or dead, the monk belongs to Fang now.'

India bit her lip and turned to hide her tears, determined not to show her true feelings in front of this cold man. She couldn't believe that Tito was dead, not yet. No one was ever truly dead until you gave up on them, until you *let go* of any hope of getting them back.

'And . . . what about the *Ahaziah*?' she said, wiping her eyes on the sleeves of the boiler suit. 'Is Mrs Brown all right, and Cael?'

Thor nodded gruffly. 'We were attacked by Larssen's people just after you left, but they were no match for my first mate's pistols. Your Mrs Brown is a fair shot too,' he added approvingly. 'After the townsfolk surrendered, the professor repaired the damage to the *Ahaziah* and he and his crew headed south while we came looking for you and the boy.'

'I have to let her know I'm all right,' said India. She tried to get up but was hit by another wave of pain. Thor placed a hefty hand on her shoulder and laid her back down.

'I've sent a message to the professor and Mrs Brown to let them know you're alive,' he said. 'And that you managed to retrieve this.' He reached into the pocket of his pea-jacket and pulled out a perfect circle of polished green stone.

'The Bloodstone!' said India in wonder. 'But how?'

'It was inside the pocket of the boy's jacket,' the captain replied.

Forgetting her discomfort, India pulled herself upright to get a closer look at the stone. Now that it was complete, it no longer had the appearance of an ancient and broken artefact; it looked glossy and smooth with no trace of the jagged edges where it had been broken into separate pieces. Most strikingly, some of the hieroglyphs on its surface now stood out in gold as if the stone had finally chosen to reveal its hidden message. She reached out a hand but Thor quickly returned the stone to his pocket.

'The professor gave me specific instructions to keep it safe,' he said. He jerked his head towards one of the crew who sauntered over to India's bunk. 'This is Lily,' he said. 'She'll show you the boat. I advise you not to get in her way. Not much room for passengers on a submarine.'

Lily was a short, barrel-shaped woman with arms like a pirate rigger. She wore grease-stained overalls and had a pair of welding goggles pushed up into her cropped hair. She looked disdainfully at India.

'Crewman Lily Strong,' she said. 'I'm the Chief Engineer around here and don't you forget it. I catch you meddling with my engines and I'll blow you out of the tubes, d'you understand?'

India didn't understand but assured Lily that she wouldn't meddle with her engines. 'Come on then, I'll show you around – better wear these.' Lily gave her a pair of canvas shoes with rubber soles which India pulled on to her bare feet. Then she climbed painfully off the bunk and followed Lily.

The submarine was a windowless steel tube with all of its sections laid out in a straight line, each one separated by a watertight hatch. If a person wanted to walk from one end of the boat to the other they would have to squeeze past every other member of the crew on the way.

Lily first showed her the rear torpedo room, where the propeller-driven torpedoes that she called 'fish' were kept. After that came the battery and engine rooms which provided the sub with power. She patted the two huge diesel engines fondly.

'These beauties are over two hundred years old. Overhauled 'em myself,' she said, glowing with pride. 'They'll get us anywhere we need to go.'

'Where are we going?' asked India, suddenly realizing that she had absolutely no idea in which direction the submarine was headed.

Lily frowned. 'You mean you don't know either?' India shook her head and Lily stroked her chin thoughtfully. 'The captain don't tell us grunts much.' She moved closer to India, speaking in a low voice. 'I heard we was headed south, to the Quartermain Mountains.'

'We're going to Antarctica?' said India.

'That's right,' said Lily. 'I heard Moon was looking for lost treasure. What do you know about that?' India was suddenly aware that the other crewmen had stopped work and were listening to their conversation intently.

India looked around at the expectant faces, feeling suddenly like a mouse in a room full of cats. She shook her head. 'Nothing.'

Lily scowled and banged her fist on the engine cover. 'Damn it. Well, we'd better all get our share of what's coming or the captain's going to end up with a mutiny.

Get back to work, you bums,' she barked at the men. 'You, come with me.'

India followed Lily back towards the front of the submarine. Everywhere she looked, the boat seemed to be wearing its innards on display. The walls were studded with pressure gauges, steel valves and fuse boxes and the air was heavy with the smell of diesel and human sweat. India was reminded of the giant mobile oil-prospecting rigs she had seen in Siberia which had a nasty tendency to blow up if you mistreated them. She seriously doubted that a two-hundred-year-old submarine was any safer.

She saw Sid only briefly, giving orders in the control room, and he did not acknowledge her. After that he retreated to the cabins at the front of the boat where, Lily told her, only the officers were permitted to go.

Her tour over, India spent the rest of the evening sitting on her bunk watching the crew spend their leisure time. There were about eighty men and women on board, a number that included grizzled veterans and steely-eyed youngsters. Their principal hobbies seemed to be cleaning their guns, of which they owned a great number, griping about the captain, and arm wrestling, a sport at which Lily was the undisputed champion.

That night the dreams came again.

A solitary albatross followed the boat, floating on the slip-stream like a lost soul. India stood on the deck and looked up into its brown and blue eyes.

'Here is where I must turn back, Soul Voyager,' said the albatross. 'This conversation is between you and the Elders only.'

'What should I say?' said India.

'Say what is in your heart and nothing more,' said the albatross. 'Or the end of the Great Cycle will be the end of us all.'

The albatross rose higher on the wind, looking for the air currents that would carry it north.

'But what about Calculus?' India said. 'Will he be there?'

'He knows what he must do,' replied the albatross. 'He will play his part as must you.'

'But what do I have to do?'

The albatross was quiet for a long time. It slipped back and forth across the wind, as though anxious to be gone.

'You must cross the veil of cold,' it said eventually, 'and be reborn from death.'

And with a flick of its wings it was gone.

The water turned steadily colder and the submarine's walls became icy to the touch. With Lily's help, India managed to dry out most of her clothes in the engine room, although her leather jacket was beyond saving and she was forced to borrow an oversized seaman's sweater and an oiled canvas jacket. On the second morning she was allowed to sit up on the flat, slatted deck, where she breathed in the gin-clear air and took in the view, glad to be out of the claustrophobic submarine and its grim crew.

They had arrived at a rugged coastline where sheer black cliffs rose straight out of the sea for a thousand feet, their sharp peaks laden with snow and ice. Between the mountains, glaciers flowed into the sea like thick slabs of frosted icing. Icebergs of the deepest blue drifted past like ghost ships or lay grounded in the shallows where the wind carved them into abstract sculptures.

As she stood on the narrow deck, a loud snort sounded off the port bow and a cloud of sea vapour erupted into the air. A grey back, as broad as a road, with a spine like a steel cable, arched through the water and a pair of giant tail-flukes lifted high into the air as the whale sank into the depths. India smiled broadly; it felt like a personal welcome to the Antarctic.

'Humpback,' said a voice behind her. She turned to see Sid looking down on her from the watchtower.

'I didn't know whales lived all the way down here,' said India, watching the calm pond on the surface where the whale had dived.

'Whales live everywhere and nowhere,' said Sid. 'They spend their lives roaming the planet just taking what they need. That's why I like 'em,' he added.

She watched as he scanned the horizon and looked at the angry, ragged scar that tracked down one side of his face. 'How are you still alive, Sid?' she asked. 'I saw the explosion that blew up your father's ice rig. It was blasted to pieces and then fell through the ice. How did you survive?'

Sid shrugged. 'When I started fighting with my Pa I couldn't think of nothin' 'cept wanting to kill him for all the things he done to me,' he said. 'But then I got to thinking about what you said. About how you can always change if you really want to make it happen.'

'I remember,' she said.

'Well, I remember thinking, while we were fighting, that I didn't want to die. I tried to jump off the rig just as the engines blew up. I reckon I got hit by a piece of stray metal because I woke up alone and bleeding on the ice. I should have died, but instead it felt like being born again.'

'Well, how did you end up here? This is a pretty responsible job compared to being an outlaw, isn't it?'

Sid gave a snort of laughter. 'Outlaw or first mate, they ain't so different.' When his laughter had subsided he assumed a serious face. 'After the "accident", I met the professor in Siberia. He was the one that introduced me to Captain Thor.'

'And Captain Thor made you his first mate?' said India.

'Hell, no!' laughed Sid. 'I joined the crew as a grunt, same as everyone else. The first mate was a drunk and a bully and used to beat up on us. One night he beat one of the junior ratings unconscious. He would have killed him too if I hadn't shot him dead. After that the captain promoted me, he said I had "natural ability".'

'Oh, I see.'

An awkward silence fell between them.

'You want to see the officers' quarters?' he asked suddenly.

India nodded. He led her through the control room to

the front section of the boat. She listened to him describe the principles of negative buoyancy and how the bow planes worked. She watched intently as various crew members approached him with questions and she saw the looks of respect and trust that the others gave him, even though he didn't seem to notice it himself.

'What happened to you, Sid?' she said suddenly, interrupting his monologue about the forward torpedo room. 'When I first met you, you were this angry and dangerous kid that people were really afraid of.'

'I can still be pretty damned dangerous, you know,' he said. 'Don't let anyone tell you different.' His face fell sombre. 'You know what makes people angry?' he said. 'Fear, that's what. I used to be afraid of plenty. I was afraid I couldn't be what my pa wanted me to be; afraid I'd be a disappointment to him. You hate yourself so much for being afraid that you start hating everyone else just to feel better.'

'Wow!' said India with a smile. 'Did you figure that out all by yourself?'

A frown creased Sid's brow. 'Hey, I can figure out plenty for myself.' For a moment India thought she might have pushed him too far, but then the clouds lifted and he smiled. 'There's someone I want you to meet,' he said. 'She's real special to me. Come on.'

India followed him along the passage to the officers' quarters. She'd heard no suggestions that Sid had a girlfriend among the crew and had no idea who he might be about to introduce her to. She found her heart was beating slightly faster.

He opened the door on a minuscule and immaculately tidy cabin. The bed was perfectly made and Sid's pistols were laid neatly on an oilcloth on the bedside table. The only other thing in the room was a parrot with steel-grey plumage. As soon as it saw Sid, the bird squawked and shuffled along its perch to have its neck rubbed.

'Bad boy, Sidney!' it said. 'Sid's a baaaaaad boy.'

India laughed out loud. 'You keep a pet, Sid?' she said.

'Crackers ain't no pet,' he said defensively. 'She's a friend. She cares about me more than most people and she's smarter too.' He pulled a Brazil nut from his pocket and gave it to the bird, who held it in one claw while she cracked it effortlessly with her beak.

'She's beautiful, Sid,' said India. 'Can she say anything else?'

'Dive, dive, dive!' squawked Crackers in a passable imitation of Sid's voice. They both laughed, and even though it hurt India's ribs like hell, it felt good. When they had finished laughing, the silence fell between them again.

'So how's the tech-hunting thing working out for you?' he asked her. India was taken aback. She had never known Sid to ask a personal question before.

'It's OK, I guess,' she said. 'Verity's pretty cool and we've had some great adventures. I just wish she wouldn't treat me like a kid sometimes.'

Sid made no comment; his own youthful looks had led

many men to make the fatal mistake of dismissing him as a 'just a kid'. India turned her attention to the pistols laid out by his bed.

'What I really want is one of these,' she said enviously. 'Do you know where I could get hold of one?'

Sid snorted and shook his head.

'Forget it, India,' he said. 'You ain't a gun person.'

'What's that supposed to mean?'

'Just what it says. Getting a gun's a bad idea for you.'

India frowned, the colour rising in her neck. 'You think I'm just a kid too, don't you?'

Sid laughed. 'No, you ain't no kid, India. But you ain't no gun person either. I been around guns all my life and I know gun people and you just ain't one, that's all there is to it.'

'You think I couldn't shoot straight?'

'I think the only way you could hit something is if it was the size of a truck and standing still,' he said.

India scowled, but then saw the smile at the corner of Sid's mouth and relaxed.

'So what happened to you between the explosion and meeting the professor?' she said, changing the subject.

Sid drew a deep breath. 'Like I said, I was hurt pretty bad in that blast,' he said. 'I got found by some nomad hunters and they patched me up as best they could.' He touched the scar on the side of his face absently. 'But they couldn't fix what was going on inside my head. By the time the professor found me I was mad as hell with you.'

'With *me*?'

Sid looked down at his feet, embarrassed. 'I was angry,' he said. 'I figured you'd left me there to die cos I'd served my purpose.'

'But I would never—'

'I know it ain't true,' he said quickly. 'After I met the professor, he showed me that the only reason I ended up lying on that ice was because of the choices *I'd* made. He taught me to believe in myself and he found me a place I could belong, here on the *Sea Wolf*. He's a great man, the professor.'

A slow realization was dawning on India. 'So it was *you* that told the professor I was a Soul Voyager? That's why he came looking for me in Sing City, wasn't it?'

Sid shrugged dismissively. 'Yeah, what of it? The professor said he needed my help to find Atlantis and he wanted to know what had happened at Ironheart. Nobody ever said they needed me for anything before.'

India frowned. 'So you let him involve me and Verity in his crazy plan?'

Sid's eyes narrowed and he jumped to his feet. 'You think he's crazy? Don't talk to me about crazy, India Bentley. I've been all the way to crazy and back and I know what it is to burn for something. The professor's going to find Atlantis and he's going to make us all rich. Then you, me, *everybody's* going to be better off, you'll see.'

India was on her feet now too. 'Better off? Try telling that to Tito!'

Sid's face went black with fury and India was suddenly frightened. 'You listen to me, India Bentley,' he snarled. 'I'm sorry about your friend but that's just the price you pay for doing great things. The professor's going to find Atlantis and I'm going to help him. You and me might have some history but that won't count for nothing if you get in my way. Nothing!'

India gasped, in less than a minute she had witnessed the return of the old Sid, unpredictable, dangerous and terrifying. She turned and fled from the little cabin with the noise of Crackers's squawking following her down the corridor.

'Bad boy, Sidney, bad boy, Sidney, bad boy!'

On the third morning after coming aboard the *Sea Wolf*, India awoke with the feeling that something was different. She raised her head and looked around the bunk room but there was only the usual collection of huddled shapes and the sounds of snoring.

But when she looked beneath the covers, she saw that her bracelet had begun to flash again. Her immediate instinct was to hide it from anyone who might tell the professor. She dressed quickly, concealing the bracelet beneath long sleeves, and, ignoring the smells of breakfast coming from the mess room, climbed the ladder to the top deck.

Since arriving at Antarctica they had continued to cruise the coastline and India had taken to spending as much time as possible up here, breathing in the spirit-clear air and taking in the alien scenery. She found her usual spot, out of the wind behind the conning tower, and rolled up her sleeve.

The bracelet was flashing a complex repeating pattern of long and short pulses. It made no sense to her but it looked as though it carried some sort of meaning. It must be Calculus, she thought. But if it was, then what was he trying to tell her?

She sighed, and wished for the hundredth time that Verity was here. The previous day, Thor had sent another message to the *Ahaziah* by Teslagraph and had arranged to rendezvous at a remote sound that Thor had said would still be relatively ice-free. India couldn't wait to be reunited with her friends; after three days on board the *Sea Wolf*, she had no desire to spend any more time with its surly crew and volatile first mate.

She looked up into the clear blue sky and spotted a familiar shape hovering in the air over a nearby glacier. It took her a moment to recognize it.

'It's the airship!' she cried, jumping up and pointing. 'It's Professor Moon's airship.' Captain Thor was already on the conning tower, looking through his long binoculars, and soon others clambered up from below to watch. The *Sea Wolf* followed the slow-moving airship around a rocky headland and into a clear blue sound surrounded by glaciers and sheer black cliffs. The *Ahaziah* stood at anchor in the bay directly beneath the airship, which was now casting mooring lines down to eager hands on deck.

A shout went up from the decks of the *Ahaziah* and the crews from both vessels began to spill from the hatchways and on to the decks. In no time at all, the remote bay was filled with the sounds of celebration as the crews on both sides cheered and traded light-hearted obscenities across the water. India scanned the decks of the *Ahaziah* and spotted Verity standing at the rail with Cael and waving excitedly. Verity pointed to a stony beach where a steady stream of row boats was ferrying packing crates, oil drums and equipment to a growing pile of supplies.

'See you on shore,' she mouthed over the noise of the cheering.

India waited impatiently for the *Sea Wolf* to weigh anchor and for one of the *Ahaziah*'s impossibly ponderous lifeboats to make its way across to them. Then she pushed her way on board and stood in the prow of the boat as they rowed slowly for the shore, feeling that the frustration might kill her.

She arrived just as Verity and Cael disembarked from another boat and splashed excitedly through the shallows towards them. She threw her arms around Verity and buried her face in her shoulder, surprised to find she was sobbing.

'Tito's gone. I-I tried to save him, I really did, b-but I couldn't.'

'I know,' said Verity gently, 'I know. Thor sent us a message.' The older woman pulled away and looked at India with deep concern. 'I'm sorry about Tito, I really am,' she said, squeezing India's shoulders. 'But I'm so relieved you're OK. Too many people have been hurt by this adventure already.' She stroked India's hair and gave her another hug. 'Come on, let's get out of this cold water.' She led India up the beach to where Cael was waiting. He picked her up and spun her around several times until she was giddy and laughing.

'How you doing, kid?' he said with a wink. 'Great to see you still in one piece. I've just been talking to Captain Thor – he tells me they virtually pulled you from the jaws of a sea monster.'

India caught Verity's horrified expression. 'Perhaps we'd better sit down and I'll explain,' said India hastily.

Cael guided them towards some upturned crates while Verity went to fetch some food. An enormous bonfire had been built from discarded packing crates and the smells of burning pine and Grunion's cooking mingled pleasantly on the keen air. They ate oily, fried fish, squashed between slices of fresh bread, while India recounted the story of Lady Fang and Whaler John and their encounter with the Leviathan. When India told them about Maximus and the Hellhound, Verity's expression became serious.

'So where's the stone now?' said Cael.

'Captain Thor took it straight to the professor to see if he could decipher those hieroglyphs,' said India.

Verity looked worried. 'If Lady Fang has a fully armed android, then that's really bad news,' she said. 'But a Hellhound? I'd heard rumours about things like that but I had no idea that they really existed. This expedition just got a whole lot more dangerous than we thought.'

'There's no profit without danger, as my old ma used to say,' piped up Cael. 'If the professor's right about Atlantis, then this expedition could make millionaires out of all of us.'

Verity narrowed her eyes. 'That's all you think about, isn't it, Cael? You couldn't care less what happens to anyone else just as long as you make a fat profit.'

'Now wait a minute . . .' said Cael, his face turning red.

'Stop it, both of you,' cried India. 'I know it's dangerous, Verity, but we can't give up now. When I was on board the *Sea Wolf* I had another dream message from Nentu. She said if we found Atlantis then we'd find Calculus. Then, this morning, this happened . . .' She pulled back her sleeve and held out the bracelet, still pulsing the same patterns, over and over again.

Verity looked at the bracelet for several long seconds and turned pale. 'Does anyone else know about this?' she said quickly. India shook her head. 'Good, let's keep it that way.' She looked again at the flashing bracelet. 'This is Morse code. Calc and I used it to signal each other in emergencies.'

'What does it say?' asked India.

'It's just four letters,' said Verity. 'C – A – L – C.' The three of them fell silent and watched the blue light pulsing in the Antarctic sunshine. Verity looked visibly shaken.

'He's calling to us, Verity,' said India.

Verity was silent for a long time. 'All right then,' she said in a voice that cracked slightly. 'I believe *someone* is trying to send us a message. It still doesn't prove that it's Calc though.'

'But can't we at least try to find out?' said India exasperatedly. 'Don't we owe him that much?'

'She's right, V,' said Cael. 'Besides, even if it's not Calculus, someone's trying to get your attention pretty badly. Doesn't that make you even slightly curious?'

Verity blew out her cheeks. 'Well, now we're in the middle of nowhere with no ride home, I don't see that we have any choice but to go along with the professor's plans. But I'm warning you, India, I'm not putting anyone else's life at risk. At the first sign of Lady Fang and her mechanical hound I'm pulling us out, no arguments. Agreed?'

'Agreed,' said India with a smile.

Verity was quiet for the rest of the meal. She gazed across the bay, stealing occasional glances at the flashing bracelet on India's wrist. When they had finished eating she made an excuse and went for a walk by herself.

Elsewhere on the beach, preparations for an expedition were in full swing. The crew were breaking open packing crates and repacking tins of dried food, snow shoes and warm clothing into smaller packages. The imposing bulk of Orpheus had been brought from the ship and gleamed blackly in the late afternoon sun. Nearby, two delicate sledges made of canvas and wood were also being loaded with provisions. Instead of reindeer teams, each sledge carried a small petrol engine at the rear, attached to a large propeller.

'Another of the professor's inventions,' said Cael. 'He wants to test them out on the journey.'

They joined a small crowd watching two crewmen as they attached heavy sandbags to the harness of one of the professor's rocket packs. India saw Sid talking to Thor on the far side of the group; he didn't seem to notice her.

'The professor thinks he's perfected the design on these,' said Cael as they watched the final preparations. 'He claims it can carry a man for over a mile in complete safety.'

The crewmen finished tying the sandbags and propped the rocket pack upright. One of the men pulled on a large red tape attached to the fuel tank and then retreated quickly to a safe distance.

The rocket made a noise like air escaping from a balloon for several seconds. Just as India began to believe that nothing was going to happen, a jet of flame erupted from beneath the exhausts and a flash of heat washed over them, making them all cover their faces. The rocket surged into the air with a roar, exhaling dragon breath behind it and travelling faster than anything India had ever seen anything move in her life.

For a few heart-soaring seconds everything seemed to go well. The rocket flew straight and true across the clear blue sky, billowing thick, pillow-white smoke behind it. But then a wobble appeared in the flight path and in moments the rocket was corkscrewing wildly out of control. It spiralled into the side of the nearest mountain, where it exploded in a ball of orange flame, bringing an avalanche of snow crashing down from the mountain's icy battlements.

'Well,' said Cael, as they watched the wreckage of the rocket pack crash into the valley. 'I guess it still needs a little work.'

Cael fell into a heated discussion with one of the crew on the finer points of rocket packs while India spent a happy hour chasing the comical, waddling birds that Grunion had told her were called 'penguins'. By the time she rejoined the main group, the sun had dipped behind the mountains and the air had turned chill. The work of loading and packing had stopped for the day and the crews of the *Ahaziah* and the *Sea Wolf* gathered around the fire.

India spotted Cael and Verity sitting near the flames. Despite their earlier argument, India had a sense that something had shifted between them while she had been aboard the *Sea Wolf*. They seemed more relaxed in each other's company; Verity laughed at Cael's jokes and Cael watched her all the time from the corner of his eye, even though he pretended not to.

India accepted a blanket from one of the crew and spied Sid on the far side of the campfire, talking with the professor. He was leaning close to catch the professor's words, and nodding seriously, his eyes wide and trusting.

After a while a bottle of rum was passed around and one of the crew began to play a jig on a small fiddle. A group of sailors began to sing a song which made India blush, although Cael and Verity both seemed to know all the words and joined in enthusiastically. Professor Moon was in an excellent mood, accepting a glass of rum and leading several choruses of the bawdy song before raising his glass to the group.

'My friends, we are on the brink of the greatest discovery in the history of mankind. One that will rewrite the history books and spell an end to the misery of the Great Rains.' He gave them a broad wink. 'Not to mention making us all rich, eh?' There was much cheering at this, particularly from the crew of the *Sea Wolf*. The professor held his hand up for quiet.

'I won't pretend the next part of our journey will be easy. There are many natural perils to face. But I have not come this far just to give up! I will not rest until we have forced Atlantis to surrender its secrets.' His eyes gleamed in the light of the campfire. 'Are you with me?' The crew let out a resounding cheer that reverberated around the bay. 'Then raise your glasses to a toast. To Atlantis: may she yield her secrets to us, and us alone.'

'To Atlantis!' they roared. India caught a look of unease in Verity's eye. When he had finished his speech, the professor spent some time exchanging jokes with the crew and slapping backs. It seemed to India that Sid was not the only one who idolized him. As soon as he saw India he strode towards her.

'The hero of the day,' he boomed, clapping India on the back. 'Finder of the last piece of the Bloodstone.' He lowered his voice. 'I was sorry to hear about the boy. A sad business.'

India frowned. 'We don't know that Tito is dead,' she

said firmly. 'We might still be able to rescue him.'

'Yes, er ... quite so, quite so,' said the professor hurriedly. 'In any event, what I meant to say is that your success in recovering the stone is a job very well done, Miss Bentley.' He reached into the pocket of his heavy greatcoat and pulled out the stone, now a completed circle of burnished green. The hieroglyphs on its surface gleamed gold in the firelight.

'The Bloodstone, reunited for the first time in twelve thousand years,' he whispered, as though he were in church. 'For so long I have dreamed of this moment.' He put on a pair of delicate wire-framed glasses. 'These hieroglyphs pre-date Sumerian clay tablets by at least six thousand years,' he said. 'Even though I am fluent in fourteen ancient languages it still took me some hours to decipher them. As finder of the stone I believe you should be among the first to hear this, Miss Bentley,' he said. He cleared his throat, then began to read aloud.

'*When giants stand in line before a black sun, and ancient blood returns to Azatl. Then Heaven's terrible gates will be cast open and the sacred Ziggurat will burn with stonefire.*'

'Hmm, they weren't great poets, those ancients, were they?' said Cael. 'I prefer something with a bit of a rhyme, me.' The professor gave him a black look.

'What does any of that mean?' said India.

'I don't yet understand all of it,' said the professor. 'But "Azatl" is one of the ancient names for Atlantis and "stonefire" must be a reference to the energy produced by the Sun Machine. It tells me that we're on the right path.'

'What about this stuff about giants and a black sun?' said Verity.

'I'm not sure about the giants,' said the professor. 'Possibly this is a reference to something we will find at Atlantis . . . a statue maybe? But the "black sun" can only be a reference to the solar eclipse.' He pulled a yellowed chart from his pocket and spread it on the ground before them. It showed a section of the Antarctic coastline and a sweep of mountains extending inland from the sea. 'There is a full solar eclipse in three days' time. It will be visible in the southernmost part of the Quartermain Mountains – here.' He pointed to a large shaded area. 'I'm willing to bet that Atlantis is somewhere within this region.'

'That's still a mighty big area to search,' said Cael. 'There's over a thousand square miles of nothing there.'

'What's a ziggurat, Professor?' asked India.

'It's a sort of pyramid.'

'Well, what about this?' She pointed to a lone mountain on the chart, standing apart from the rest of the range.

'Pyramid Peak!' read the professor. 'How could I have been so blind? It's an extinct volcano, named for its unusual shape, and it's slap bang in the middle of the eclipse zone.' His eyes glittered. 'My friends, I believe that could be it! We should start our search there. It will take about two days to reach the mountains. We should make preparations to leave immediately.'

'What about the other stuff in the message?' said India.

'The stuff about "ancient blood" and "Heaven's terrible gates"?'

'I don't know,' said the professor. 'I assume it refers to the other treasures we'll find at Atlantis.'

'"Heaven's terrible gates will be cast open",' said Verity. 'It sounds more like a warning to me.'

'I prefer the treasure theory,' said Cael. 'Professor, when do we get going?'

The professor folded away his map. 'We leave tomorrow at first light. In view of Miss Bentley's recent encounter with Lady Fang, I believe speed is of the essence. We will travel quickly with a small team. Mr O'Hanlon, I will need your help to drive Orpheus.' Cael bowed slightly. 'Mrs Brown, Miss Bentley, I request your continued presence as my specialist advisers.'

'What about protection, Professor?' They turned to see Thor standing behind them with Sid at his shoulder. 'The crew of the *Sea Wolf* has an interest in this venture too, and you will need backup if you encounter Lady Fang. I recommend you take a team of my men.'

The professor shook his head. 'Our advantage lies in moving quickly. Fang doesn't have the stone and she doesn't know where to start looking for Atlantis.'

'But she has a Hellhound,' said Thor, leaning in so that the firelight cast craggy shadows across his face. 'From what I've heard, those creatures won't give up, even if they have to follow a man into the jaws of hell. Or a girl,' he added, looking pointedly at India.

The professor shook his head again. 'A large team will require extra supplies and will slow our progress too much. But I will take young Sidney. His, er, special skills will be invaluable.' The captain narrowed his eyes and muttered something into Sid's ear.

'Good, then it's settled,' said the professor. 'Everyone get a good night's sleep and be ready to leave at first light.'

Cael left with the professor to help him pack some of the instruments he would need for the journey. India watched them go with a frown.

'I'm worried, Verity,' she said. 'The professor thinks this "Sun Machine" is the answer to all of our prayers, but Tito seemed afraid of it and Whaler John said it was cursed. I'm not sure the Sun Machine is what the professor *thinks* it is.'

Verity snorted. 'That's the least of our worries,' she said. 'Not only are we being hunted by Lady Fang and her androids, but we're travelling with a mad professor, an unreliable drunk and a reformed psychopath. I knew this expedition was dangerous but I don't know if I'm more afraid of their side or ours.'

Tito opened his eyes and knew at once where he was. Fronds of blue-grey smoke curled up into the green dome of the temple. Around the walls, a thousand candles made from recycled cooking fat sent sooty plumes up the plaster, filling the air with the smell of fried food. A single spear of sunlight pierced the smoky haze and illuminated a small statue on the high altar.

The Great Teacher.

'What do you think when you look on him, Tito?' The voice was familiar: soft, but underpinned with steel. Tito hesitated, searching for the right answer from the countless scriptures he had committed to memory.

'That I should try to emulate the Great Teacher, Brother Amun,' he said eventually.

'Ah!' Brother Amun walked softly around the boy and into view. He was carrying a candle in a holder that sent dark lines of shadow up his face. 'And are you ready to do that, Tito?'

'I have studied the scriptures diligently,' said Tito evenly. 'And I have meditated on all the lessons handed down by the Great Teacher. There is no aspect of his life I have not memorized.'

'But are you *ready*, Tito?' The monk's black eyes bored into Tito as though they would suck the answer from him. At times like this, Tito understood why others were so afraid of Brother Amun.

'I . . . I don't know, Brother.'

Brother Amun's face relaxed. 'The Great Teacher came into the world alone at the start of the Great Cycle. Alone, Tito. Have you ever pondered what that means? However much you have listened to the teachings of your tutors, at some point you will be alone in the world. Will you know what to do when there is no one there to ask, and your inner demons make you doubt yourself?'

Brother Amun moved closer. 'Everything you see is just an illusion, Tito. In the end, the only thing that matters is the belief you have in yourself.'

'I see,' said Tito. He chose his next words carefully. 'Then, if I may be permitted a question, Brother Amun . . . How is it that I am speaking to you in the Temple of Reclamation when I know for certain that I am asleep in a cabin on board Lady Fang's ship?'

Brother Amun smiled. 'As I said, Tito, everything here is an illusion. Our order has many secret ways and dreamspeaking is one of our oldest tools. You are indeed on board Lady Fang's ship. But you are also here, talking to me – both places are real and both are an illusion.' He stroked his beard thoughtfully. 'So I return to my question, Tito, the only question that is important. Are you ready?'

Tito swallowed. 'I am not certain, Brother. Ready for what?'

Brother Amun leaned in close. 'The Brotherhood of Reclamation are the descendants of the Great Teacher, Tito,' he said quietly. 'And some of us are fortunate enough to have been given the gift of destiny. It is a gift we must be careful not to send back, lest we offend the gods. Your destiny involves the girl.'

'Miss Bentley?' Tito blinked at the older monk with wide eyes.

Amun nodded. 'She has successfully reassembled the stone and now she intends to take it to the resting place of the Elders.'

'She is looking for her friend, the android,' said Tito quickly. 'She believes she will find him there.'

'That is irrelevant,' said Amun abruptly. 'The girl has no understanding of what she will find there. I believe she will try to start the Sun Machine.'

'The Sun Machine?'

'It is not India Bentley's destiny to complete the Great Cycle, Tito. You must stop her.'

'Stop her how, Brother?'

'By any means possible, Tito,' said Amun. 'By – any – means – possible.' He breathed each word clearly and slowly.

Tito frowned. 'But . . . I don't understand. Why must I do this, Brother?' he said.

Amun smiled and leaned in towards the boy. He was so close now that Tito could feel the monk's hot breath on his cheek, even though he knew this was a dream.

'I'm going to tell you a secret, Tito,' he said. He began to whisper into the boy's ear and, as he did so, Tito's eyes grew rounder and his mouth dropped open.

'Do you understand me, Tito?'

'I think so, Brother.'

'Good,' said Amun brightly. 'Time to wake up then!'

In a single swift movement, the dark monk grasped Tito's wrist and held his hand over the candle.

Tito cried out and sat up in bed, clutching his hand. But there was no candle, no burn, just the sick sensation of a receding nightmare. He looked around the tiny cabin and listened to the creaking ship sounds – yes, he was still aboard Fang's ship. But the conversation with Brother Amun, that had been real too. He was sure of that.

He lay back down and stared up into the darkness for a long while.

'I believe I understand now, Brother Amun,' he whispered quietly in the dark. 'I understand and I am ready.'

The early dawn smeared pinks and purples across the sky as the crew reassembled on the beach to prepare for departure. The packing crates and fuel drums had gone and in their place stood a neat convoy of vehicles, heavily laden and lashed down against the wind.

At the front of the line was Orpheus, drill blades gleaming in the sunlight. The noise of its engines beat a tattoo on the sharp morning air and clouds of black diesel billowed from the stacks. Orpheus towed a high-sided trailer, packed with supplies, and behind that were two of the Professor's propeller sledges.

The sun had yet to chase away the night chill and India was glad of the thick padded coat and mittens that Cael had found for her in the stores. As she walked up the beach with Verity they were hailed by Professor Moon.

'We're almost ready to leave. You two will travel with me in Orpheus.'

India was startled by Crackers, alighting on her shoulder. The grey parrot nuzzled her neck. 'Pretty girl,' she cackled. India laughed.

'Go away, flatterer, I don't have anything for you.' A short distance away, Sid was barking at a crewman as he hauled several wooden boxes off the sledge.

'Take it all off!' he was yelling. 'This damned dynamite has degraded in the cold, and it's sweating nitro. One jolt and it'll blow the sledge into a million pieces, and me with it.'

As the crewman scurried away with the boxes, Sid narrowed his eyes at India and she felt her stomach flop. They had not spoken since their argument on board the *Sea Wolf*.

'You look after Crackers,' he growled. 'She can't spend too long outside.' India gulped and nodded, and Sid turned away. He spun the propeller on the sledge and the engine burst into life, sending penguins scuttling for the water.

'Good day to you, ladies, and may I say how lovely you're both looking this morning.' They turned to see Cael, in thick oilskins and wearing a brilliant smile that showed off his perfect teeth.

India grinned back and Verity raised an eyebrow. 'You can keep your flattery, O'Hanlon,' she said. 'We look like a pair of overstuffed sofas.' They climbed into the narrow cabin and India settled Crackers on to a wall pipe. The heat from the engine was intense and India immediately shed her outer layers and opened the hatch.

There were some last-minute delays as the final few packages were added and the professor settled into the driving seat, then they were off. Orpheus lurched across the ice with the rumble and clank of grinding metal, and the two propeller sledges followed close behind. As soon as they reached the brittle ice crust on the top of the glacier, the roar from the sledges increased and Sid and Cael streaked past to take the lead.

'The sledges will scout ahead to make sure we don't encounter any hidden crevasses,' shouted the Professor over his shoulder. India hung from the open door, screwing up her eyes against the snow glare. 'Take these,' said the professor, handing her a pair of dark goggles. 'They'll keep away the snow blindness.'

'I never knew Antarctica could be so hot,' said India as she fitted the goggles.

'That's because it's summer here,' said the professor. 'Eighteen hours of sunshine a day can make it surprisingly warm. But don't let that fool you – the weather can turn lethal without warning.'

They travelled for several hours along the unbroken ice sheet, and India was extremely glad when they pulled to a stop for a sparse meal of hard tack biscuit and leathery, dried meat that was like eating old shoes.

After lunch, India begged to be allowed to ride on the propeller sledge with Cael. Following a long lecture on safety from Verity, India was finally allowed to sit astride the packages. Cael gunned the engine and promptly overtook Sid, and India wore an irrepressible grin as her hood blew back and her hair streamed out behind her. 'This is brilliant,' she yelled to Cael over the roar of the wind. 'Make it go faster!'

Cael twisted the throttle control and the noise of the propeller increased as they shot forward. India tightened her grip on the packing ropes. The tremor in the sledge suddenly started making the light wooden framework judder violently. Cael throttled back the propeller, but too late: one of the front runners snapped under the strain and the corner of the sledge dug into the snow.

The next moments unfolded in slow motion as the sledge toppled sideways and India slipped from her perch, landing painfully on the hard ice. Cael struggled to regain control but was also thrown off as the sledge spewed food, tents and equipment in all directions before sliding to a halt twenty feet away. He sat up, rubbing the back of his head. 'Are you OK, India?' he called across the wreckage.

India tested her limbs. She was bruised but otherwise uninjured, and gave Cael a thumbs-up. 'I'm fine. I guess we ought to start picking up this mess.'

Before Cael could answer, a deep groaning issued from beneath them and a rapidly widening crack shivered along the ice. With a terrifying roar, the propeller sledge disappeared suddenly into the crevasse that had opened beneath it. India and Cael found themselves lying at the edge of a bottomless blue-black pit which had swallowed the sledge and all their supplies.

'Jumping rig fairies!' spluttered Cael. 'That's about as close as it gets!'

'Uh-oh,' said India as the Orpheus drew to a halt nearby. 'This isn't good.'

Professor Moon jumped from the cab and stalked across the ice like an approaching storm, closely followed by Verity.

'Mr O'Hanlon,' he roared. 'You have lost one of our transports and approximately a quarter of our food and fuel. Thanks to your schoolboy antics, we will endure reduced rations for the remainder of the journey.'

Cael winced and looked apologetic.

'The hell with the food,' yelled Verity. 'You nearly cost me my assistant.'

'It wasn't Cael's fault—' began India.

'Be quiet, India,' snapped Verity. 'Get back inside, there'll be no more joyriding from now on.'

After that they proceeded at a more sedate pace, with Sid leading on the remaining sledge, testing the ice as they went. Inside Orpheus, Cael did his best to make amends by volunteering to do the driving, while Verity kept her head buried in a book she had borrowed from the ship's library and India hung out of the hatchway, watching the endless white desert roll past.

After a few more hours in the stuffy cabin India was feeling overheated and more than a little bored and she was highly relieved when the professor pulled over once more.

'We've made good time,' he said, 'but we'll not make it to the peak before sunset. We need to find somewhere to stop for the night.'

'Storm's coming,' said Sid, pointing to a clutch of thick, black clouds that were clawing their way over the distant mountains.

'All the more reason to find shelter quickly,' said the professor. 'We certainly don't want to move anywhere in a blizzard.'

They set out again, heading for a nearby group of hills, and India stuck her head from the hatch to watch as the setting sun turned the glaciers flame-orange. She was about to close the hatch again when something caught her eye: a flash of colour that had no place in the natural landscape. She called out, and the professor stopped Orpheus to scan the horizon through a pair of black binoculars.

'It looks like an abandoned research station,' he said. 'Well done, Miss Bentley, it will afford us much better shelter than the hills.'

By the time they reached the cluster of buildings, the weather had begun to close in and they were forced to shield their faces from the driving sleet. The research station was huddled against an outcrop of black rocks and was made up of several long, low buildings built of wood and tar-paper, plus a hangar made from corrugated iron. A lone radio mast pointed skywards like a skeletal finger.

The smaller buildings were in different stages of being ripped apart by the wind, but the main hut was still in relatively good repair. Inside were several rooms, including a workshop, a dormitory with bunk beds and threadbare blankets, and a tiny kitchen with a stove and a dining table.

A fine layer of frost covered everything.

Sid and the Cael went outside to patch up the broken windows while Verity lit a fire in the grate and the professor and India investigated the kitchen. The cupboards contained some mouldy dry goods and several dozen tins which seemed intact, even though most had lost their labels.

'Looks like someone was here in recent years, judging by the provisions they left behind,' said the professor.

As Verity's fire warmed the kitchen, India and the professor played a game of 'Guess the Contents' with the tins. The first one contained sardines which had turned black and slimy, but the next few contained beans which were surprisingly edible. Best of all, they found an enormous tin containing a spongy brown pudding, slathered in sticky treacle. The professor warmed the pudding on the stove and gave India a large bowlful, which she consumed vigorously, savouring its sticky sweetness.

Sid came inside and began his usual activity of cleaning his gun and saying nothing while Verity sifted through a filing cabinet in the corner of the room, looking for something else to burn.

'It looks like this was a meteorological station until about five years ago,' she said, rifling through a sheaf of papers. 'Probably set up by one of the whaling stations. It all looks fairly normal – regular weather reports, that kind of thing. But this is strange . . .' She opened a black book she had found in a bottom drawer. 'It's the log of the station captain, a man called McNab. There were six people stationed here and they made occasional trips into the mountains to take readings. Listen to this. "*Denton and Scott returned from the mountains reporting more strange readings from the volcano called Pyramid Peak*",' she read. '"*Denton has a theory that it may be moving into an active phase.*"'

'Pyramid Peak?' said the professor, looking up from a tin of corned beef.

'How about this, from a week later?' said Verity. '"*Denton has recorded high levels of radioactivity from the peak. I have agreed that tomorrow he and Banks will take the sledges and investigate further.*"' She flipped a few pages and read on. '"*Denton and Banks are two days overdue. After four hours of searching in worsening weather, we found their bodies at the foot of the mountain. At first we suspected an accident, but closer examination revealed the dreadful truth. Both men had been drained of every last drop of blood. The dogs refused to pull the sledge with their bodies and we were forced to bury them where they lay.*"' Verity stopped reading and they looked at each other uneasily. She turned a few more pages.

'This is the last entry,' she said. '"*The deaths of Denton and Banks haunt us all. The crew have a terror of this place. I fear my authority will not be enough to make them stay at their posts and, in any event, I am inclined to agree with them. Tomorrow we will take the helicopter and fly out of here, and not one of us will be unhappy to see the back of this cursed place.*"'

She stopped reading and closed the book. In the silence that followed, India found she suddenly had no appetite for her second helping of pudding and pushed it away. The door burst open, and they all jumped as Cael barged his way into the kitchen, bringing a blast of cold air and stamping the snow from his boots. He was in a highly excited state. 'You'll never believe what I've found,' he said. 'You have *got* to come and see this.'

They donned their oilskins and followed Cael outside. The wind was howling through the station now, tearing at the loose corners of corrugated roofs and scouring any uncovered patches of skin. They pulled their hoods low and followed Cael's torch beam to the corrugated hangar. There were two small ice tractors parked outside, looking battered and unloved, but inside was a very peculiar-looking vehicle indeed. It had a long tail and a boat-shaped cabin that stood on three wheels, with three long blades on the roof that bent under their own weight. Cael grinned and rubbed his hands together.

'Isn't she beautiful?' he said. 'It's a Sikorsky S-62 fitted for cold weather operations.'

'What is it?' said India. The weird machine did not seem very practical for driving anywhere.

'A helicopter of course,' said Cael. 'I learned to fly in onc of these babies.'

'They let you fly helicopters?' said Verity. 'When there are monkeys available?'

But Cael wasn't listening; he had hauled up the engine cover and was running his hands over the greasy engine block, groaning with pleasure. 'Isn't she an absolute darling?' he said.

'It's a heap,' said Verity. 'It looks like it hasn't moved in five years. I'd sooner ride out of here on one of the professor's rocket packs.'

'Nonsense,' said Cael, checking the oil and frowning. 'They built these things to last. All she needs is a bit of tender loving care.'

'Kindly don't waste too much time on this machine, Mr O'Hanlon,' said the professor gruffly. 'This is doing nothing to help us achieve our goal.'

'It tells us one thing,' said Sid sullenly from a corner of the hangar. 'The crew of this station didn't leave on their helicopter like they planned. So what happened to them?'

They left Cael with his head under the engine cover and walked back to the hut. The wind had now reached near-hurricane proportions, driving steel-hard sleet into their faces. Back inside, Verity threw more weather reports on the fire and they did their best to stop up the remaining gaps in the dormitory windows and doors. By the time Cael returned, he looked frozen to the core.

'Holy rig fairies, that wind comes straight out of hell,' he gasped as he shook off his coat. 'Damn near blew me away.'

They settled down for the night in the dormitory, swaddling themselves in musty grey blankets. Despite the fire in the kitchen, the deep cold had penetrated right through the little cabin, and India felt compelled to sleep fully clothed. The gale raged outside like an angry beast but the hard labour and excitement of the day had taken their toll and, one by one, they drifted off to sleep.

Deep in the night, the storm ceased and the suddenness of its passing woke India. She lay for a few moments listening to the even breathing of the others before climbing out of bed and pulling on her boots. The door to the hut made a cracking, splitting noise as she opened it, and she stepped out into the disturbing stillness.

After the storm had come a cold, so deep that India felt it might fracture the rocks. It was like a living thing that had crept over the valleys, laying a death-white shroud over the landscape and sinking deep into the mountains. She blew on her hands, forming thick plumes of steam, and glanced down at her bracelet, still stuttering out its message. She shivered again but not from the cold this time. Her determination to find her friend seemed to flutter and fade in this hostile landscape and the words of Nentu's dream message came back to haunt her.

'You must cross the veil of terrible cold and be reborn from death.'

The following morning everyone was up early. Thick mist had descended over the station, smudging the outlines of the buildings, and the unnatural stillness subdued all conversation. The mood was not improved when they discovered that the shed in which Sid had stored the remaining sledge had been torn from its foundations by the storm, taking the sledge with it. Professor Moon picked up a piece of broken propeller and stared at it.

'That's most of our supplies gone and all of our back-up transport,' he said grimly. 'By rights we should turn back now.' He tossed the propeller aside. 'But there'll be no turning back from this mission. There is only success or there is death: there is nothing in between. If anyone wishes to argue, then speak now.'

'Well, I'm OK with the success option,' muttered Cael under his breath. 'But the death one . . . not so much.'

'Do you wish to say something, Mr O'Hanlon?' asked the professor.

'Absolutely not, Professor,' said Cael, flashing his brilliant smile. 'Success or death all the way, that's me!'

'Chickenchickenchickenchickenchicken . . .' cackled Crackers from her perch on Sid's shoulder. India stifled a grin.

'Good,' said the professor. 'Then let's gather as many of the supplies as we can find and get moving.'

Within the hour they were back inside Orpheus, which was now considerably more cramped. Nevertheless, India was glad to shut the hatch on the bitterly cold air and soak up the heat from the engine. Cael took the driver's seat and the station receded into the mists behind them. The professor consulted his charts as Orpheus began to climb a steep escarpment towards higher ground.

'Pyramid Peak is less than ten miles from here,' he said. 'We should have first sight of it once we reach the top of this plateau.'

Sure enough, as Orpheus crested the ridge, the mists

cleared and they saw a desert of white laid out below them. Only one feature stood out on the landscape, a cone-shaped mountain with steep sides rising to a snow-capped point.

The wind howled across the plain, and clouds of snow billowed like dust in a dry river valley. 'The weather's closing in again,' said the professor, looking anxiously at the horizon. 'We must hurry if we are to avoid the storm, Mr O'Hanlon.' The thought of being caught in another gale spurred them onward, but progress was painfully slow. What had looked, from a distance, like an unbroken plain turned out to be treacherous terrain punctured with knife-sharp rocks and tall ridges of ice. They took wide detours to avoid the crevasses that cut across their path and after nearly an hour, the peak seemed as far away as when they first saw it.

'This is taking too long,' complained the professor. 'Over there, Mr O'Hanlon. We have a clear run at the peak in that direction.'

Cael shook his head. 'I don't know, Professor. This whole area is riddled with crevasses.'

'For once, he's right, Professor,' said Verity. 'We should stick close to the rocks even if it takes longer.'

'The storm is coming and we can't risk further delay,' said the professor. 'Take us forwards now, Mr O'Hanlon. I'm giving you an order.'

'Professor, you have no right to endanger everyone's lives,' said Verity calmly. 'The longer route is safer.'

Nobody spoke. Sid's eyes flicked watchfully between Verity and the professor as Crackers made small noises and nestled nervously in his shoulder.

'Is this a mutiny, Mrs Brown?' enquired the professor. His eyes narrowed, dangerously.

'Just applying some common sense,' said Verity. 'I want to get there as much as you do, but preferably in one piece.'

'I'll not stand for a challenge to my authority, Mrs Brown,' the professor roared. He yanked his hand-cannon from its holster, but Verity was quicker and with a swift blur, her own gun was in her hand.

'Have you both gone nuts?' yelled Cael. 'Put those down!' He jumped from the driver's seat and tried to wrestle the gun from the professor. The hand-cannon discharged into the roof with a deafening roar, blasting out the light and showering them with sparks and broken glass.

There was a moment of shocked silence while everyone caught their breath and Orpheus rumbled, driverless, across the ice. The professor leaned against the bulkhead and panted for breath. He was about to speak when a great splitting and cracking sounded from under the hull, and Orpheus shuddered and tipped forward at an alarming angle.

'The ice,' cried Verity. 'It's giving way!'

They rushed to the little window to find themselves staring into a vast crack that had opened beneath them. 'Damn it, O'Hanlon,' roared the professor. 'It's a crevasse! You've killed us all!'

And before anyone could react, Orpheus plunged into the endless blue-black abyss.

Orpheus dropped into the chasm in a plunge that sucked the breath from India's lungs, filling her with undiluted terror. The vehicle bounced off the hard ice walls, flinging them around the inside of the cabin until they hit the bottom of the crevasse with an organ-jolting crunch.

India lay still in the darkness, trying to regain her breath and tasting blood in her mouth. 'Everyone all right in here?' A torch beam snapped on and Professor Moon swung the light on to each of them in turn. Cael and Verity had cracked their heads together and Cael had broken a tooth. Sid had fallen on the engine cover and burned his arm, which he was now binding with a strip of rag, and the professor had a cut over one eye which trickled crimson. He shone his torch out of the front windows.

'Looks like we fell about thirty feet,' he said. 'We're stuck in a crack in the ice sheet.' Through the tiny window India saw a blue-black ice tunnel sloping away from them.

'We have ropes in the back,' said Cael. 'Perhaps we could—'

Before he could finish the vehicle gave a loud groan and began to move forward slowly.

'Brace yourselves,' shouted the professor. Orpheus was now sliding along the crack in the ice, gradually picking up speed until it was rushing through the narrow space like a ball bearing in a chute.

'What's happening, Professor?' India juddered as she clung to one of the benches.

'We're sliding along a flaw in the ice sheet,' he shouted back. 'It's taking us deeper under the ice – but hold tight, it could stop at any moment.'

At that instant, Orpheus gave an enormous shudder and slewed sideways before grinding to a halt with a groan of tortured metal. Once again testing their limbs for serious injury, the battered crew picked themselves up slowly off the floor. Crackers flapped and squawked in a blind panic and Sid had to grab her to calm her down while Verity began to shut off a broken pressure hose that was filling the cabin with steam.

'D'you reckon it might have been a good idea to look where you was goin'?' drawled Sid. Cael looked about to argue when, very slowly, Orpheus began to slide backwards. 'Hell, what now?' muttered Sid.

India peered out of the tiny rear window. As her eyes grew accustomed to the dim light, she could see that Orpheus was perched precariously on the edge of a deep chasm. She also saw the reason they were being dragged backwards.

'The trailer!' she gasped. 'It's gone over the edge. It's pulling us in.'

Sure enough, the heavy trailer had tipped over the side of the gorge and was dangling beneath them like an oversized Christmas bauble, spilling fuel drums and crates into the chasm below.

'Mr O'Hanlon,' called the professor. 'Give us some forward traction. Now, if you please.'

Cael engaged the engine and the caterpillar tracks clattered and scraped uselessly against the rocky floor. 'We don't have enough power,' gasped Cael. 'It's going to drag us in.'

'We need to lose some weight, *fast*,' said Verity. She snatched up one of the professor's heavy pistols from the rack at the back of the vehicle and tucked it into her belt before hauling open the hatchway. 'Keep the drive wheels engaged, I'm going to blast that coupling.'

'No!' cried the professor. 'My instruments!'

But Verity was gone. India watched through the window as Verity found handholds on the outside of Orpheus, working her way around to the back of the vehicle like a rock climber. Holding on with one hand, she leaned out over the abyss and took aim at the steel coupling that bound them to the dangling trailer. The rear caterpillar tracks were already hanging over the edge and, in another moment, they would all be dragged into the pit.

The pistol fired and a column of flame leaped from the barrel, blasting the coupling and flaying the metal like torn paper. Like a reluctant child, the wagon clung obstinately to Orpheus by a shred of twisted steel until the coupling snapped. Relieved of its burden, the great machine leaped forward as the wagon plunged into the gorge, sending thunderous echoes around the cavern walls. Cael disengaged the drive wheels and applied the brakes. Now the only sound was the hot pinging from Orpheus's cooling engines.

They spilt from the cabin and rushed to the back of the vehicle. The remnants of the coupling hung down like tattered rag, but there was no sign of Verity.

Cael's face turned ashen. 'Oh no, no, no!' he cried, sinking to his knees at the edge of the gorge. 'V, where are you?' India's throat constricted as she peered over the precipice, but then she stepped back in surprise. A slim brown hand reached up from below, followed by Verity's head as she hauled herself up. She grinned at Cael's panic-stricken face. 'What's up Tech-Boy? Did you miss me?'

As soon as they had hauled Verity safely on to the ledge, India threw her arms around her. 'Don't ever do that to me again,' she said in a tight voice as Cael looked on, pale and shocked.

'Now you know how I feel most of the time,' said Verity with a smile.

As Verity dusted herself off, they took in their surroundings. They were standing on a narrow path at the top of a rocky valley, with sheer cliffs on either side.

Overhead, where the sky should have been, the valley was capped by a vaulted ice roof that groaned like the rafters of an old house. Every surface was covered with a layer of ice frost and their breath clouds hung in the air with no breeze to dispel them.

India looked up at a wide fracture in the roof above them, which she took to be the place where they had emerged through the ice. 'Ain't no going back that way,' said Sid, echoing her thoughts.

'No going back,' squawked Crackers unhelpfully.

'Incredible,' muttered the professor. 'It seems my minor error of judgement has led us to a momentous discovery. We are standing on the very bedrock of Antarctica, at least a mile beneath the ice cap. The last time this valley was in the sunshine would have been over twelve thousand years ago.'

'Somehow that doesn't make me feel any better,' said Cael. 'So what do we do now? If we take a wrong turn down here, we won't be seeing any sunshine for a few thousand years either.'

The professor checked his compass. 'This way,' he announced, confidently pointing down the valley. 'If my bearings are correct, I believe this rift will lead us towards Pyramid Peak.'

Verity rolled her eyes. 'Why does it always have to be underground?' she muttered. 'Doesn't anybody ever hide stuff in a place with natural daylight?'

The professor snapped shut the compass. 'We will

proceed with caution. Two of us will walk in front of the vehicle at all times to make sure the path is safe.'

It was agreed that Verity and India would complete the first shift. Verity collected her satchel from inside Orpheus and they began to walk, slowly, a few yards ahead of the vehicle.

'Do you think there's anything dangerous down here?' asked India.

Verity snorted. 'I suspect the most dangerous things down here are the people we came with. Let's hope everyone behaves themselves long enough to find a way out.'

After an hour of painfully slow progress they stopped for a break so that Cael and the professor could take over.

'This place is vast,' said Cael, looking around like a small boy lost in a cathedral. 'What do you think made it?'

'These are probably lava tubes,' said the professor. 'With luck they'll probably lead us right into the heart of the volcano.'

'With luck?' spluttered Cael.

'Have no fear, Mr O'Hanlon,' said the professor. 'Pyramid Peak is quite extinct.'

'Hey, Prof,' called Sid. 'There's something over here, take a look.' They crouched down to see what Sid was pointing at. A tiny creature was scuttling along the side of the rock wall, no larger than a cockroach, its many legs working furiously to propel itself out of the torch beams.

'It's just a spider,' said Cael derisively.

'Down here?' said Sid. 'I don't reckon it's catching many flies.'

'It doesn't look like any spider I've ever seen,' said Verity. 'It looks like it's made of metal.'

Sid reached out to pick it up. 'Careful, Sid,' said India. 'You don't know anything about it.' Sid threw her a contemptuous glance and placed it on his palm, where it scooped the air with its front legs. It was small, but definitely mechanical-looking, with a square-sided body and tiny, articulated limbs jutting from a steel-blue carapace.

'You're right, it does look as though it's made of metal,' said the professor. As he leaned in for a better look, Sid let out a yell and threw the bug on to the floor. A bulb of scarlet welled up on his finger.

'Hell! The dang thing bit me!' Before anyone could stop him, he drew his gun and fired three shots at the scuttling creature, which immediately turned to a spattering of metal on the rock face.

'Nice going, cowboy,' said Verity. 'Are you absolutely sure it's dead?'

'Astonishing,' said the professor. 'Sidney, I do believe you have discovered an example of a nanomite.'

'What in hell's name is a nanny mite?' snarled Sid, sucking his finger.

'A nanomite,' said the professor patiently, 'is a machine. A robot built on a tiny scale to carry out specific tasks. They used to make them before the Great Rains, but I've never seen anything like that one before. This could be the first evidence of an advanced civilization. We must capture a specimen.' He began to rummage in his bag for a suitable container.

'What use is a tiny robot?' said India. 'It's too small to do anything on its own.'

'Ah!' said the professor. 'But they're like insects. Put enough of them in one place and make them cooperate, and together they could have an enormous impact. That little chap and his friends might well roam these tunnels extracting valuable minerals from the rocks. He was probably after the iron in your blood, Sidney.'

A chill ran down India's spine. 'The log from the research station said the two men who were killed here had been drained of all their blood.'

Cael's jaw dropped open. 'You mean these tunnels are filled with blood-sucking mechanical spiders?'

'Fascinating thought, isn't it?' said the professor, picking up his bag. 'Come along, we have less than eighteen hours to find Atlantis before the solar eclipse!'

'Fascinating be damned,' muttered Cael. 'If there are vampire spiders, then I want a bigger gun.' He returned to the vehicle and selected the largest weapon he could find in the gun rack – a tall blunderbuss with a trumpet-shaped barrel – before rejoining the professor.

India and Verity climbed back inside Orpheus while Sid swore at Crackers, who had settled on the top of the vehicle and could not be persuaded to get back in the cabin. 'Stupid bird,' he muttered. 'Stay out here and freeze, see if I care.'

While Cael and the professor walked ahead, Sid took the driver's seat and pushed Orpheus forward, not seeming to care how close the iron tracks came to the edge of the gorge. After another half an hour of slow creeping along the path, Sid brought Orpheus to a halt.

'Why are we stopping?' said Verity.

'The professor's found something up ahead,' said Sid.

Once outside, they saw immediately why they had stopped. Stretching across the chasm to a path on the far side of the gorge was a bridge, a slender and graceful span made from copper-coloured metal and delicate cables.

'You have got to be kidding me,' murmured Verity under her breath.

'I'm seeing it but I don't believe it,' said Cael.

The professor was ecstatic. 'My friends,' he gasped. 'I have waited for this moment for half of my life. Here is the proof that there was an advanced race before us, able to build nanomites and bridges!' He rested a hand gently on one of the slender metal beams. 'Imagine,' he said. 'This bridge is more than twice the age of the Egyptian pyramids and yet it looks unblemished.'

'You're not planning to walk on it, are you?' said Cael. 'The whole thing could be rotten to the core. It could take all of us to the bottom of that pit.'

'I agree,' said Verity. 'Something that old is likely to turn to dust the moment you step on it.'

'I think not,' said the professor. 'I have faith in the abilities of the ancients.'

Before anyone could stop him, he had stepped on to the bridge and strode out to the middle. 'You see?' he announced loudly as he bounced up and down on his toes. 'Solid as a rock. Come on, we're running out of time. Sidney, please bring Orpheus across.'

Cael looked dubious as he stepped on to the bridge. He breathed a visible sigh of relief when it held his weight. 'You know, I think the old man's right,' he said with a grin. 'I reckon we'll be OK.'

'But Orpheus weighs several tons,' said India. 'How do we know the bridge will take it?'

'You worry too much, India Bentley,' drawled Sid. 'If the professor says it's OK, then that's good enough for me.'

'You take quite a lot on trust, don't you?' said Verity. 'Have you ever tried thinking for yourself?'

'She's right, Sid,' said India quickly. 'It's one thing trusting the professor but it's another thing having blind faith.'

'You can walk across if you want to,' snapped Sid. 'I'll see you all in hell!' He climbed into Orpheus and slammed the door with a clang.

Verity rolled her eyes. 'The professor and Sid make a right pair,' she said. 'One of them does anything he wants, and the other one does everything he's told.' She picked up her satchel with a sigh. 'And neither of them care whether they live or die.'

They walked across the bridge as though it was made of glass, the view over the edge reminding India of their earlier escapade with the jeep. They reached the far side without incident, then watched as Sid engaged Orpheus's drive wheels.

The bridge flexed and creaked under the weight of the machine – the way India had once heard an old oak tree do, just before it had come crashing down one winter's evening in her village. Sid's face could be seen through the window, frowning with concentration as he managed the controls.

India's heart beat like a piston. She placed a steadying hand on the bridge and then pulled it back quickly as a black bug scritched across the back of her hand and scuttled away along the handrail.

'Er, Professor,' she said.

'Not now, India,' he said, watching Orpheus intently. 'To your left a bit, Sidney,' he yelled, giving Sid a hand signal.

India spotted a second nanomite, then a third. Cautiously she leaned over the rail and peered into the gorge. What she saw made her catch her breath. The walls of the gorge were alive with a black carpet of nanomites swarming up from the black depths. When they reached the top of the gorge they surged along the spars of the bridge.

'Professor! Sid needs to get off that bridge now,' yelled India.

'Great Scott,' cried the professor, turning to see the bugs. 'They're attacking the metal structure!' He waved his arms frantically at Orpheus. 'Sidney, get out of there at once!'

The bugs moved with purpose, like a colony of ants, clinging to the bridge supports and swarming along the handrails. They appeared to be heading for the centre of the bridge, and for Orpheus.

Sid slammed Orpheus into reverse and tried to go back the way he had come, but more bugs were now advancing from the other side of the bridge, trapping the vehicle. The copper-coloured metal had turned into a seething mass that looked like it had been dipped in dripping tar.

'Sid,' cried India. 'Get out – before the bridge gives way!'

A cable snapped with a hiss of sliced air making the bridge lurch. A second cable snapped, then a third, and then Orpheus was sliding sideways towards the edge.

Crackers took to the air, squawking incoherently, as, with a final shriek of tortured metal, the bridge gave way and the machine plunged into the abyss. A distant crash in the darkness below them boomed around the cavern and confirmed the awful truth.

Sid was gone.

Silence fell over the tunnel, save for the frantic screeching of Crackers. The distraught bird flew in circles over the spot where Orpheus had fallen as the others looked on in voiceless shock. India was breathing hard and her legs felt watery, like she wasn't sure they would hold her upright.

'You OK, kid?' said Verity, placing a hand on her shoulder. India nodded dumbly and peered over the edge of the ravine.

'Maybe . . . maybe he's still alive,' India whispered. 'W-w-we could lower a rope down and look for him. I'm the lightest, I should be the one to go.' She was talking rapidly and wringing her hands as she spoke.

'India,' said Verity softly. 'All of our ropes were on board Orpheus. We have no way of getting down there. Besides –' she looked over the edge of the precipice – 'I don't think Sid could possibly have survived a fall like that.'

'You don't know that!' cried India. Hot tears began to

roll down her face. 'You don't know Sid, he's tough and he's a survivor and . . .' Her words tailed off and she wiped her nose noisily on her sleeve. 'It's all my fault!' she sobbed.

'You can't blame yourself, India,' said Verity soothingly, 'How could it be your—'

'It *is* my fault. If it wasn't for me being a stupid Soul Voyager, none of this would have happened. And if I hadn't wanted to find Calculus so badly, then maybe Sid and Tito would still be alive!'

'Sid and Tito made their own decisions to come, India,' said Verity gently. 'You couldn't have stopped them. However much you try, you can't control someone else's destiny.'

'I hate to break this up . . .' said Cael, pulling his gaze away from the ravine. 'It looks like most of those bugs fell into the ravine with the bridge, but we don't want to be hanging around if they decide to come back. I'm sorry about your friend,' he said to India, laying a hand on her shoulder. 'He was a very brave guy.'

Cael turned to the professor, who was still gazing absently at the spot where Sid had fallen. 'That was our only exit route, Professor. So what do you suggest now?'

The professor turned to look vacantly at Cael. Then he seemed to gather his wits; he shook his head and smoothed down his hair. 'We must go forward,' he said decisively. 'Atlantis lies ahead of us, and Sid's brave sacrifice must not be in vain.'

'Sid's brave sacrifice?' blurted India. 'He didn't choose

to die! You made him drive across that bridge. He trusted you, and you sent him to his death.' The professor's face darkened and Verity stepped in quickly.

'That's enough,' she said. 'It's bad enough that we've lost someone, without fighting amongst ourselves. The way I see it, we've got no transport and precious few supplies. Everyone, turn out your bags and let's take stock.'

Their supplies were a gloomy sight. India had some dried meat and biscuit in her satchel, and Cael had brought some tinned beans and pears from the research station. Verity was mostly carrying bits of old-tech, plus a knife, a torch, and ammunition for her pistol. The professor had brought some bottles of fresh water.

'We need to be thinking about survival,' said Verity, repacking her bag. 'From now on, we ration the food and the water and we waste nothing.' She took a last look at the broken bridge and picked up her belongings. 'Come on, let's move out.'

Crackers had been circling the place where Sid had fallen, but now she flew down to India's shoulder and nuzzled miserably at her neck. India offered her a small piece of biscuit, but the bird didn't want it.

'Sidney, Sidney, Sidney?' she cackled.

'I'm sorry, Crackers,' said India, wiping her eyes. 'This time I think he's really gone.'

'We've got a problem,' said Cael, interrupting her thoughts. 'Our friends are back – look!'

A short distance away, the seething mass of bugs was

again pouring over the edge of the ravine and working its way towards them. The hard metal carapaces gleamed blue-black in the half-light.

'We'd better move!' said Verity. 'And let's hope this path leads somewhere, or we're all going to be joining Sid pretty soon.'

India cast a last look back at the spot where Sid had fallen, as they started off along the tunnel at a pace. The bugs moved slowly and it was relatively easy to stay ahead of them, but they were relentless. Every time they slowed or stopped to rest, the bugs made up ground behind them, scritching at the rock with a tiny claws and making a noise like a million tiny typists rattling through the tunnel behind them.

'How much further?' gasped India after half an hour of trying to stay ahead of the creeping black horror.

'I don't know,' said Verity, 'but we can't afford to stop.'

'Hey, there's something here,' cried Cael from further up the tunnel. The path ended abruptly in a flight of stone stairs, worn smooth from use. At the top was a pair of copper-coloured doors, twice the height of a man, recessed into the rock face. 'First a bridge, and now a door,' said Cael. 'Where do you suppose it leads?'

'I don't know,' said Verity, looking over her shoulder at the advancing bugs, 'but pretty much anywhere is preferable to here. Professor?'

The professor mounted the steps to examine the doors. Their surfaces were engraved with an elaborate design: a pyramid structure arranged in five steps beneath a golden sun motif.

'The mark of the Sun Machine,' said the professor. He bent down to examine the golden sun, positioned in the middle of the door. 'It seems to be a locking mechanism of some kind,' he announced. 'Possibly one of the earliest known examples of—'

Verity yelped and stomped on a bug that had strayed too close to her boot. 'Ordinarily I'd find that fascinating, Professor,' she muttered, 'but perhaps you could focus on getting it open?'

'But of course,' said the professor, as though he'd been asked to open a window on a warm day. 'Now then,' he said placing his half-moon glasses on the end of his nose. 'Protecting the context of an archaeological find is critical. The door appears to be sealed with a simple warded mechanism so if I were to probe this area, it should—'

'Sorry, Professor, time's up,' said Cael, pushing him to one side. He unhitched the long blunderbuss from his shoulder and took aim at the lock. The blast assaulted their ears and the end of the gun spouted flame and sparks, knocking Cael to the floor with the recoil.

The smoke cleared to reveal a ragged hole where the lock had been. Verity and Cael kicked and shoved at the door, until it scraped open enough to allow them to squeeze through, one at a time. They heaved it shut again just as the first bugs began to surge over the top steps.

'Very subtle, Cael,' said Verity, stamping on a solitary

bug that had followed them through the gap. 'But quite effective.' She took off her jacket and stuffed it tightly in the hole. 'There, that should hold them for a little while.'

Cael was looking extremely pleased with himself, though his face fell when he discovered that the end of his blunderbuss had peeled open like an exploded trombone.

'Hey, Professor,' he said. 'I'm sorry, I broke one of your guns.'

But the professor wasn't listening. He was gazing in the other direction, and his jaw was hanging open. 'By the gods of Atlantis,' he murmured. 'Has there ever been a sight in Heaven or Earth to match this?'

They turned to find they were standing on a wide stone gallery, overlooking a cathedral of natural rock. The far side of the cavern was almost a mile distant, dark and indistinct, while the roof was lost in the blackness many hundreds of feet over their heads. The darkness was relieved by a pale blue phosphorescence that seemed to come from the rocks themselves. By the cold ghost-light they could see a frozen lake meandering across the cavern floor, fed by high waterfalls that had long since been hard-frozen in the act of gushing from the walls.

But it was not the natural scenery that made them stop and stare in wonder. The floor of the cavern was filled with dark buildings, crowding down the slopes to the shores of the lake on all sides. Great shadowy terraces, carved into the rocky cliffs, overlooked high walls, spires and broken towers – all made from the same tightly fitted green stone blocks. Narrow lanes twisted between the ruins, connecting broad avenues that were cracked and heaved with age.

'Holy mother of all riggers,' said Verity. 'This place is off the scale. It's a whole city under the ice cap!'

'Not just *any* city,' said the professor. 'This is where the kings of the Elder Race sent forth their wisdom to our fledgling civilizations. This, my friends, is the city of Azatl, also known as *Atlantis*!' He gazed starry-eyed at the cavern, like a small child in a very large sweet shop. 'Astonishing. It seems that the entire city is built inside the magma chamber of the volcano.'

'Magma chamber?' said Cael. 'You mean as in *molten lava*?'

'There's no need to worry, Mr O'Hanlon,' said the professor. 'This volcano has been extinct for at least twelve thousand years. I imagine the Elders chose their hiding place very carefully.'

'It's beautiful,' said India. 'It looks like the Emerald City in *The Wizard of Oz*, but darker.' She looked down from the high gallery at the tightly packed stone houses below. A soft wind sighed through the narrow lanes between the buildings, like the jealous whispering of ancient ghosts. She shivered involuntarily.

'Come along,' said the professor abruptly. 'We can't hang around here gawping. There's a whole city to be explored.'

He marched off along the gallery, and the others followed, with Cael muttering under his breath: 'I don't know about exploring, I could do with a sit-down. Doesn't anything ever slow this guy down?'

A flight of stone steps took them down to street level, where a thin layer of frost-smoke swirled around their ankles. The grey flagstones were shot through with feathery strands of crystal that split the light from their torches, giving a hint of life to the otherwise dead city. India looked up at the cavern roof and tried to imagine people living in the houses. It would be a strange place to live, she thought, where you never saw the sun and where the cold air whispered around you like a dead man's breath.

She was roused from her thoughts by a noise behind her, a faint rattling of stones, or maybe the sound of a broken tile sliding down a roof. She looked around, feeling the gooseflesh rise on her arms, but only the empty streets stared back at her. Crackers suddenly launched herself from India's shoulder with a squawk and flew off in a great wheeling arc around the city.

'Crackers!' she cried. 'Come back, you stupid bird. If I lose you, Sid will be—'

She stopped, remembering the empty space left behind by Sid. Crackers paid her no notice and India was forced to watch helplessly as the tiny grey speck disappeared across the lake and was lost in the blackness of the upper cavern.

'What is that building?' said Verity as India rejoined the others. Standing on an island in the centre of the lake, dimly visible in the poor light, was a squat stone pyramid built of flat slabs that rose up in stages.

'A tomb, or a place of worship perhaps?' ventured the

professor. 'I believe we may find the answers to some of our questions there.' They continued downhill through the ruined streets until they stood at the edge of the frozen lake. Now they were closer, they could see the pyramid was also built from carefully dovetailed blocks of stone, rising in five tall terraces with a narrow flight of stone steps running up the centre.

As they crossed one of the stone bridges that spanned the frozen lake, India remembered a story her father had told her about the river that formed the boundary between the Earth and the Underworld. She shivered as she looked up at the pyramid again. *We're going to the land of the dead,* she thought, and remembered her vision of Calculus, staring up at her from beneath the ice.

Once on the island, the professor started straight up the steps of the pyramid without pause. The climb was steep, and even in the icy air India quickly began to feel warm and sticky beneath her heavy clothes. She paused halfway up to gaze over the city, but there was no sign of Crackers, and she felt suddenly bereft, as though the last piece of Sid had taken flight and left her behind.

By the time they reached the fifth terrace, the sweat was running freely down India's face. She turned her face gratefully towards the freezing breeze and looked around. The top of the pyramid was a flat square, a hundred paces to a side. At the centre was a raised circular platform of carved stone, with a smaller platform to one side that looked like a ceremonial altar. Four slim stone columns, each about twenty feet high, were arranged at the corners of the altar. Most curious of all, on the far side of the terrace, was a solitary stone arch made from three heavy blocks of stone, one laid horizontally over the others. The arch seemed to lead nowhere.

'Magnificent!' cried the professor, pulling on his glasses and running his finger along a line of characters on one of the columns. 'This place clearly had some sort of ceremonial significance. These hieroglyphs say that the pyramid is forbidden to all but the high priests. Most of what's written here are descriptions of the terrible things that will happen to anyone who tries to enter.'

'What sort of terrible things?' asked Cael nervously.

'Let's see,' said the professor. He scanned the rest of the stone. 'It says trespassers will be consumed by sickness, suffer flaying of the skin, and will pass to the afterlife within two sunsets.'

'Sounds like a place I knew in Shanghai,' muttered Cael.

The professor scratched his head. 'I expect the warnings were put here to frighten away the general population.'

'Perhaps there's more to it than that,' said Verity. 'What if the pyramid really does contain something hazardous? Wouldn't they want to make sure no one went near it?'

'It's possible, I suppose,' said the professor. 'We should proceed with extreme caution.'

'I have no problem with "extreme caution",' said Cael. 'It's the "proceed" part I'm worried about. If there's something deadly in there, shouldn't we be heading in the other direction?'

'We have not come this far, simply to slink away, Mr O'Hanlon,' said the professor, sternly. 'If Atlantis is keeping any secrets, then they will most likely be found inside this pyramid. We must find a way in. Everybody look for an entrance . . . *carefully*.'

'How about this?' called Verity. She was examining an ornate grille, set into the stone flags of the terrace, made from the same coppery metal as the bridge they had seen earlier.

'It looks like a ventilation shaft,' said Cael, holding out a hand towards it. 'There's a breeze coming from down here, and it's warm. I never heard of a pyramid needing ventilation before . . .' He jammed the sharp end of his hunting knife into the gap and sprang the grille free with a clatter.

Verity shone her torch into the straight-sided opening.

'Black as a hole into hell,' she said, sucking her teeth. 'If only I had some climbing gear . . .'

India breathed a mental sigh of relief that Verity was not able to complete the thought.

Meanwhile, the professor was examining the low stone altar, taking out a handkerchief to brush away the accumulated dust. 'Good heavens, take a look at this.' As he cleaned away the dirt, he revealed a spidery lattice of crystal filaments spreading across the altar. The crystal threads snaked across the terrace and down the sides of the structure. When they looked out at the city, they could clearly see that all of the crystal veins they had seen running through the streets converged on the pyramid. 'It looks as though every part of the city is connected to this spot,' said the professor in a hushed voice.

'Look at this, Professor,' said India. In the centre of the altar was a carved circular niche. 'It looks about the same size as the Bloodstone,' she said. 'You don't suppose . . . ?'

'Upon my word, I believe you're right.' The professor fumbled in his bag and pulled out the stone. 'I believe it will fit in here precisely.' He slapped a palm to his forehead. 'Good grief, how could I have been so blind? The answer has been in right front of us. I think this entire pyramid is the fabled Sun Machine. If I am correct, then the Bloodstone is the key, and inside we will find the unlimited energy source of Atlantis.'

'You mean the crystal you told us about that turns the sun's rays into unlimited energy? The Heliotrope?'

The professor nodded. 'Precisely so,' he said. 'Here, help me place the stone on the altar.' He brushed away the last of the dust as Verity, India and Cael exchanged an anxious glance.

'Just a minute,' said Cael holding up his hands. 'Am I the only one who thinks that starting up a twelve-thousand-year-old machine is a really bad idea?'

'I agree,' said Verity. 'We shouldn't meddle with it. It probably does nothing, but then again, it might just vaporize us all on the spot.'

'The Sun Machine could be the greatest discovery in the

history of mankind,' said the professor. 'So I am not leaving here empty-handed just because you think that turning it on looks a bit risky. I came here to harness the technology of the ancients and that's what I intend to do.'

The professor's words were greeted by a peal of laughter that rose above the noise of the wind. The sound was as cold as a sliver of glass, and India knew instantly who it belonged to.

They turned to see the slender figure of Lady Fang, cresting the steps of the pyramid on the far side of the terrace. She was accompanied by a dozen guards carrying heavy guns, faceless beneath scarves and balaclavas.

'Unfortunately, Professor Moon,' said Fang with a thin smile, 'neither you nor your friends will be returning to civilization at any time soon.'

The broken remains of Orpheus lay on a rocky ledge like the carcass of a dead animal. Only the faintest ray of light penetrated the dusty windows, to fall across the pale cheek of the young man trapped inside. In the half-light he had the look of a sleeping angel, and only the hint of a frown line, and the red scar down his left cheek, suggested a more troubled nature.

Sid's eyes flickered as he struggled to free himself from a nightmare filled with memories of pain, and fire, and his father's fists. He felt again the horror of being trapped in the wreckage of a burning rig that seared his flesh, and he heard the sound of his own desperate screaming as he struggled to get out.

The nightmare woke him with a jolt and he lay gasping for breath, disorientated in the darkness. Slowly he remembered where he was and how he had got there. That damned bridge . . . The one the professor had said would be safe. That was the reason he was down here. He tried to move, and suffered a wave of pain in his ribs. He winced. It felt like one of his fingers was broken too.

Orpheus lay at a strange angle. He looked up at the faint glimmer of icy light through the partially occluded window. Would they be coming to rescue him? No, he decided quickly. None of them would risk their lives for him. Except maybe the girl; she sometimes made him feel like she cared about him. But they wouldn't let her try, he knew that. They'd written him off; once again, he was dead in their eyes.

He craned his head to see more from the window. It looked like Orpheus was stuck on a narrow shelf that had broken his fall. Not that this was much help. There was no way out; he'd be dead for sure, pretty soon.

He heard a faint scritching on the outside of the vehicle and for a moment he thought they had come to rescue him after all. Then he realized it was the bugs, digging away at the hull with their tiny claws. It wouldn't take long before they broke through, and then what? He imagined them crawling over his body, sucking him dry for the iron in his blood, and fought back the urge to panic.

As if on cue, one of the bugs crawled along the window above him, its metal legs clattering against the glass. 'Git outta here, bloodsucker!' he roared, making his ribs hurt. 'Let me die in peace!'

He forced himself to lie back and take a deep breath. Dying didn't matter, he told himself. But the way you looked when you died, *that* mattered plenty. Sid had seen enough dead guys to know that there were some ways he'd never want to look when he was dead. And once those bugs had finished with him, there wouldn't be anything left you'd want to look at. That thought, more than death, scared him cold.

A fresh wave of anger boiled up inside him as he looked at the bugs, now all but covering the window. 'It ain't fair,' he yelled. 'It ain't fair and it ain't right that it happens like this, damn you!' Tears of frustration ran down his face as he pounded on the controls in front of him, the pain from his broken finger fuelling the fire of his rage.

'Dang!'

He pulled his hand back sharply and looked at the fresh burn he had received from the oil gauge. 'Damn thing's still got pressure,' he muttered to himself. The animal part of Sid's brain began to turn. He tapped cautiously on the gauge again. Might just be enough juice left to drive this old hulk over the edge and into the pit, he thought darkly. There'd be no bugs down there. Sure, he'd still be dead . . . but at least he'd be a good-looking corpse.

With a shaking hand he reached out for the drive lever and the engine responded with a low rumble.

20

THE SUN MACHINE

Lady Fang's guards fanned out across the top of the pyramid, quickly relieving Verity, Cael and the professor of their guns. Maximus appeared behind his mistress, clutching a terrified Tito by the scruff of his jacket. He shoved the boy roughly to the ground.

'Tito!' India dashed to the fallen boy and hugged him until he squeaked. 'Thank goodness – you're alive – I thought you'd gone for good!' She held him at arm's length. 'You've lost your glasses. Can you see OK?'

He blinked at her with startled eyes. 'Without my glasses I am as blind as a hat,' he said. 'However, the Great Teacher himself was short-sighted, and if he could manage, then so can I. I am sorry I could not warn you about Lady Fang . . . I think I am not such a good tech-hunter, after all.'

India smiled. 'You managed to stay alive, Tito,' she said. 'I think you're doing just fine.'

Last to arrive was Two-Buck Tim, pink-faced and

hauling a large wooden box. He waved to them cheerfully, seemingly oblivious to the seriousness of the situation, then immediately shrank under the glare of Lady Fang. He set down his box and pulled out a short metal probe. The box made little clicking noises like a grasshopper and India caught a glimpse of ivory dials and flickering meters inside.

'How did you find us here, Fang?' demanded the professor. 'I thought the *Sea Wolf* had disabled your ship for good.'

Lady Fang laughed lightly. 'Dear Evelyn, you are so trusting. We only *pretended* to have been damaged by the *Sea Wolf*'s torpedoes. I knew as soon as you had all the pieces of the stone you would head straight for Atlantis. Using the Hellhound to track Miss Bentley was simplicity itself.'

India blanched. 'You used that *thing* to track me down?' She looked around quickly, remembering the half-seen creature from the alleyway in Whalesong. 'Where is it now?' she whispered.

'Roaming the streets of Atlantis,' purred Fang, 'in case any of you decide to make an ill-advised escape attempt.'

'You have no business here, Fang,' said the professor. 'Atlantis should benefit the whole of mankind.'

'Come now, Evelyn,' laughed Fang. 'Don't be such an idealist. No one ever does anything for the benefit of mankind. Besides, the only reason I know about this place is because of you.'

'What's she talking about, Professor?' said Verity.

The professor scowled. 'Fang and I have some history,' he said in a strangled voice. 'Some years ago she came to see me, posing as a wealthy investor interested in my work. By the time I discovered the truth about her she had already stolen most of my research.' He sighed heavily. 'Ever since then I have lived with the fear that she would steal the secrets of Atlantis for her own despicable ends.'

'So let me guess,' said Verity, scowling at Lady Fang. 'You're hoping the Sun Machine will turn out to be some sort of super-weapon that you can sell to the highest bidder.'

Lady Fang burst into fresh peals of laughter, colder than the frost-laden air. 'I have no interest in super-weapons, Mrs Brown. My interest in the Sun Machine is far more . . . *personal*.'

She stalked around the group like a cat that had chanced upon a flock of plump, flightless birds. 'Do you know the real secret of the Bloodstone?' she said. 'Do you know why men have sought it for thousands of years, killed for it, traded their kingdoms to possess a piece of it?'

'No, Fang!' cried the professor. 'You cannot speak of this; you will bring chaos down on all of us.'

'I'll tell you,' said Fang, ignoring the professor. 'Throughout history, pieces of the stone have been owned by kings, queens, emperors, explorers and priests. All of them wanted it for different reasons, but one thing united them all. There was not one among them who was less than a hundred years old when they died. It seems that ownership of the stone brings a long life.'

'That's surely just a coincidence,' said Verity. 'Just because some of its owners grew old doesn't mean the stone can extend someone's life.'

Lady Fang pointed to Tito. 'Tell them, boy.'

'It is true, Mrs Brown,' said Tito, timidly. 'All of the past High Priests in our order have carried the Bloodstone and every one of them was over a hundred and twenty when they died. Archimotos the Forgetful was said to be one hundred and sixty.'

'You're not seriously trying to tell me the stone makes people live longer?' said Verity.

'The Bloodstone has unique properties,' said Lady Fang, 'but it is only a part of the Sun Machine. Did Evelyn not tell you about the Heliotrope?'

India glanced at the professor, who was shaking his head forlornly. 'He said it was a crystal the Atlanteans used to generate energy,' she said quietly.

'But not just energy,' said Fang. 'The Heliotrope also bestowed health and long life on all those who lived within its light – did it not, Professor?'

'That may be true,' said the professor hesitantly. 'I found evidence to suggest that the Heliotrope produced some sort of regenerative field. It is possible that anyone exposed to it on a regular basis would have an unnaturally extended lifespan. But it was only a theory,' he added.

'Evelyn is too modest,' said Fang. 'His research papers were most illuminating. The Atlanteans lived in this city under the glow of the Heliotrope. It gave them power, wellbeing and an almost unlimited lifespan. The Heliotrope is nothing less than the fountain of youth, and I mean to have it for myself.'

'Do you mean to say,' said India incredulously, 'that you're doing this just because you don't want to grow *old*?'

Lady Fang's gaze swivelled to India. 'You are still young and pretty,' she growled. 'You could do great things in the world, India Bentley, as I have done. But do you know what stops greatness in its tracks?' She drew so close that India could see the network of fine cracks and creases in her make-up.

'*Death*.' Fang breathed the word as though it excited her. 'No matter how much care a woman takes of herself, age will rob her of her beauty and death will steal away her empire. Well, I am not prepared to settle for that. I want nothing less than immortality.'

'OK, she's officially a fruit loop,' muttered Cael.

Fang turned sharply to the Irishman. 'Is there something you wanted to say, Mr O'Hanlon? You're a long way from Sing City for a man who owes so much money to my gambling dens. Not running away, I hope?'

Cael gave an easy laugh that sounded a little too forced. 'Me? Of course not. As soon as we'd finished here I was coming straight back to Sing City to see you.'

Fang smiled. 'Well, I can save you the bother, Mr O'Hanlon. We're going that way – we'll give you a lift.'

The smile faded from Cael's face.

‘Enough of this,’ snapped Fang. ‘Two-Buck! Is everything ready?’

Two-Buck pointed the metal probe at the circular stone platform and the clicking noise became louder and faster. ‘I am registering a big build-up of radiation under the pyramid,’ he said, consulting the dials. ‘Whatever you’re going to do, best to do it now.’

‘Radiation?’ said Cael under his breath. ‘Underneath a twelve-thousand-year-old pyramid?’

Verity slapped her forehead with her palm. ‘Of course!’ she muttered. ‘The message on the Bloodstone said the pyramid would burn with stonefire. What if “stonefire” referred to something we know by a different name? Something like electromagnetic radiation?’

‘What could possibly be radioactive under a twelve-thousand-year-old pyramid?’ said India.

‘Well, whatever it is, it sounds like it’s waking up,’ muttered Cael. ‘So let’s add that to the list of reasons why we *shouldn’t* be here.’

‘Professor Moon, the stone if you please,’ barked Fang.

The professor clutched the stone to his chest. ‘Fang – don’t do this,’ he pleaded. ‘The Heliotrope could bring untold benefits to the human race.’

‘Evelyn, you are an idiot,’ said Lady Fang scathingly. ‘Human beings are like a nest of roaches, never living long enough to achieve anything worthwhile. But I will change all of that. When I am immortal, then all men will come to fear and worship me as a goddess.’ She smiled. ‘Then we'll see some *real* change around here.' She turned to the android. 'Maximus, bring me the stone.'

Maximus wrenched the stone from the professor's hands and moved to the altar, carefully placing it in the carved niche. Several long seconds passed; India realized she was holding her breath.

It was Lady Fang who broke the silence. 'Two-Buck, why isn't it working?' she demanded. She brandished her silver claws and Two-Buck shrank back.

'P-p-perhaps the girl should be the one to place the stone,' he stammered, pointing to India.

Fang's gaze flicked to India and a slow smile formed on her cruel mouth. 'Yes, yes of course,' she purred. 'The stone responds to you, doesn't it?' She snatched up the Bloodstone and thrust it at India. 'Here,' she said. 'Make it work.'

'I . . . I won't do it,' said India. 'The professor's right, if the Heliotrope exists, it should be used to benefit everyone.'

Fang frowned. 'I see. Well, let's see what we can do to make you reconsider, shall we?' She turned again to the professor. 'Evelyn, do you think this machine could save the life of someone who is close to death?'

The professor looked puzzled. 'Possibly, but—'

'Excellent.' In a single, fluid movement, Fang pulled a small silver pistol from her sleeve and whirled around to face Verity. 'Let's find out how Miss Bentley feels when someone she cares about is in danger. A single shot to the stomach should kill Mrs Brown in about fifteen minutes, plenty of time for you to start the machine and save her.'

Verity stiffened and turned pale but otherwise showed no emotion.

'No, wait!' shouted India. 'I'll do it. I'll turn the machine on for you. Just don't hurt her.'

'Too late,' said Fang with a smile.

The gun fired, sharp and loud like a firecracker. In the same instant, Cael flung his body sideways, knocking Verity out of the way. As the sound of the shot died away, Cael groaned and folded in half. Verity caught him under the arms and laid him on the floor.

'Cael!' she cried. 'Where are you hurt? Speak to me.'

Cael blinked up at her. 'You definitely owe me one now, Verity Brown,' he gasped. Then he groaned and clutched his stomach. 'Oh boy, that really smarts.'

Fang shrugged. 'Oh well. Wrong person, same result. Assuming you care about Mr O'Hanlon, you have around fifteen minutes to see if you can save him, Miss Bentley. Don't wait too long, will you?'

Verity was trying to staunch a blossoming red flower on the front of Cael's shirt.

'Do it, India!' she snapped. 'Do it now!' India did not need telling twice. She grabbed the Bloodstone from Lady Fang and ran to the altar, feeling its familiar energy coursing through her body. The stone scraped gently as it slid into place. Then she stepped back and they waited.

For a moment India thought the machine was still not going to work at all. Then, very faintly, a low hum began deep beneath their feet. As the sound grew louder, the pyramid began to shudder, and the accumulated dust of centuries danced on the surface of the stones. Then a new noise began: the hollow scraping of stone on stone.

'Look,' cried Tito, pointing to the circular stone platform. 'The pyramid is opening.' A hole was opening in the centre of the stone platform like a dilating eye, releasing a rush of fetid air. When the hole was about three feet across, a long column of copper-coloured metal began to rise from the darkness. At the top was a delicate cage containing a long, blue-white crystal, the size of a man's head. It continued to rise from the pyramid until it was taller than all of them, before slowly coming to a halt.

'By the stars,' gasped the professor. 'The Heliotrope!'

The crystal gave off a faint blue light of its own, making everything around it seem dimmer. Two-Buck pointed his metal probe towards the hole and consulted the dials on his machine with a worried expression. 'Radiation levels just jumped two hundred per cent,' he said shaking his head. 'There's something big down there and no mistake.'

Cael stirred and groaned. 'What happens now, Professor?' said Verity, desperately pressing both hands against Cael's stomach to staunch the bleeding. 'Cael won't last much longer.'

The professor did not answer. He was looking up at a brilliant white spot that had appeared in the roof of the cavern and which was steadily growing into a blue circle of sky. A shower of dust and small stones began to rain down on them, sending Fang's men running for cover. 'The top of the volcano is opening,' he said, breathlessly.

The volcanic pipe continued to widen, allowing brilliant Antarctic sunshine to flood into the buried chamber for the first time in millennia. When the first beams of sunlight struck the Heliotrope, the effect was immediate. The crystal crackled and hissed and began to glow brightly, turning first to a brilliant blue, then growing gradually brighter until it was an intense ball of searing white light. The air was filled with a noise like a high-voltage charge passing along an overhead cable.

'Look at the city,' cried India. From where they stood they could see a line of brilliant blue light carving its way through the glittering crystal paths of the stone city, lighting the streets and making the buildings glow with suffused energy.

The view above them had changed too. Instead of the rocky cavern roof, they saw a billion stars and galaxies, projected in perfect crystal clarity, as though distilled from the clearest of night skies. In their midst, rotating in vast sweeping arcs around the cavern, were the planets of the solar system: great coloured orbs in stormy reds and cool blues, swinging silently over the city as though they were solid and real.

'Ah, damn it,' groaned Cael. 'I've bloody died and gone to heaven!'

'The stone is creating energy from the sun's rays,' cried the professor excitedly. 'It's just as I predicted.'

'You can write a paper on it later,' snapped Verity. 'Right now we have to help Cael. Tell us what we have to do!'

The professor appeared uncertain. He looked at Cael and then at the brilliant light shining from the crystal. 'Let's get him on to the platform,' he said. 'Perhaps the energy being given off by the crystal will repair the damage in some way.'

'I'm not so sure,' said Cael weakly. 'I have very fair skin you know. I burn real easy.'

'Help me to get him up,' snapped Verity. She and the professor lifted Cael by the shoulders while the India and Tito grabbed his feet. He moaned as they dragged him to the platform while Lady Fang looked on.

They heaved Cael on to the platform and stepped back. The ball of light surrounding the crystal seemed to stretch and expand until it enveloped Cael like a cocoon. He cried out and arched his back and India clutched Verity as they watched him writhe in the beam.

'Enough,' cried Verity. 'Pull him out.' They dragged him from the light and lay him gently on the floor. Cael lay motionless and pale as Verity cradled his head.

'Cael, speak to me,' she said with tears welling in her eyes. No one spoke and only the awful sound of the crackling energy from the crystal broke the silence. Cael lay motionless.

'Is he dead?' asked Lady Fang, peering distastefully at the Irishman's limp body.

Verity gently lay Cael's head on the ground, then turned

on Lady Fang. 'You cold-blooded murderer,' she shouted. 'Cael never did you any harm.'

Maximus immediately stepped between them and pushed Verity away.

'He was expendable,' said Fang, disinterestedly.

'You'd only say a thing like that if you had never cared about anyone,' sobbed Verity. 'He may not have been perfect but he had more decency in his little finger than you have in—'

A loud groan made her break off in mid-sentence. Cael had propped himself up on his elbows and was blinking at them with a dazed expression.

'You really care about me, V?' he said in a small voice.

'You're alive!' gasped Verity. She immediately crouched down beside him. 'Are you OK? What about the bullet wound?'

Cael pulled open his bloodied shirt and felt the smooth skin of his stomach. 'Gone,' he said incredulously. 'I think I'm going to be all right. And you really care about me, too. So this is turning out to be a pretty good day.' His grin stretched from ear to ear. Verity scowled.

'Just be "all right" a bit quicker next time, will you?' she snapped. 'I could cheerfully kill you again right now.' She glared at him but Cael wouldn't stop beaming.

'Enough of this,' snapped Lady Fang. 'The machine works, that's all I need to know, now get out of my way.' Lady Fang consulted with Two-Buck while Maximus herded them away from the altar.

Cael looked pale but seemed to have recovered completely, although Verity continued to throw concerned glances in his direction. The professor was now looking up at the whirling stars and planets projected silently above their heads.

'You know, I think this actually an accurate depiction of the night sky immediately above us,' he said.

'That's very interesting, Professor,' said Verity in a whisper, 'but I think we should turn our attention to how we're going to escape. If Lady F is planning to expose herself to that light then we might have a chance to get away while everyone's distracted.'

'But you're missing my point,' said the professor. 'Look at the planets.'

'Those big ones are nearly in a line,' said Tito.

'Precisely,' said the professor. 'It's an alignment of the four gas giants, Jupiter, Saturn, Uranus and Neptune. An event like that would be incredibly rare and it looks as though it's about to happen now, at exactly the same time as the solar eclipse.'

'"*When giants stand in line in the light of a black sun,*"' said India, '"*then Heaven's terrible gates will be cast open.*" That was the message on the Bloodstone. It was telling us that there's something underneath the pyramid.'

'Well, I can't speak for anyone else,' said Cael, 'but I'm not in a hurry to meet anything that lives underneath a twelve-thousand-year-old pyramid.'

'Can you lot focus for one damned second!' snapped

Verity. 'As soon as Lady Fang steps into that light, every one of her guards is going to be looking at her. That's our cue to make a break for it.'

'Make a break to where to exactly?' said Cael. 'In case you hadn't noticed, we're standing on top of a pyramid in a lost city underneath an ice cap. Oh, and there's a robotic Hellhound roaming the streets. Did I leave anything out?'

'Well, how about down there?' said Verity, pointing to the ventilation shaft they had opened earlier. 'I doubt Fang's men will want to follow us and if it *is* an air vent of some kind then there may be drainage tunnels underneath the city. They might even lead us outside.'

'Oh, great idea, genius,' hissed Cael. 'Let's climb into a hole where the twelve-thousand-year-old radioactive thing lives.'

'Fine, stay here with Her Ladyship if you want to,' snapped Verity. 'But the rest of us are getting out of here.'

Lady Fang had finished her discussion with Two-Buck and had turned her attention to the crystal. 'Maximus, I need your assistance,' she purred. She took off her coat and handed it to the android. Underneath she wore a silk dress the colour of blood. 'I will spend five minutes in the light of the Heliotrope,' she said. 'If anything goes wrong then pull me out immediately. As for them –' she swept her gaze over India and her friends – 'if anyone tries to escape . . . kill them all.'

They watched Lady Fang step on to the stone platform. If she was nervous she didn't show it.

'You've got to hand it to her,' whispered Cael. 'Nerves of steel, that woman.' Verity shot him a glare.

Fang took a deep breath and stepped into the brilliant halo surrounding the stone. She immediately went rigid, as though electricity was coursing through her body. Her eyes went wide and her head jerked back, exposing her long white neck as her mouth opened in a soundless scream. Just as Verity had predicted, the eyes of every one of the guards were fixed intently on her.

'OK,' said Verity softly. 'Now's our chance.' She edged closer to the vent and peered in. 'I'll go down first, then you, Cael. Professor, you come last. Make sure nobody gets left behind.' She threw India a tight smile, then, without hesitating, she crossed her arms over her chest and dropped into the blackness. India looked around; no one seemed to have noticed Verity disappear.

Cael blew out his cheeks. 'Well I suppose someone has to watch her back,' he said. 'Here goes.' He swung his legs over the hole and dropped out of sight.

India edged closer to the hole. 'I'll go next,' she said.

'*You! Stop where you are!*' It was the death-cold voice of the android. Maximus moved away from the stone platform and crossed to where they stood in three strides. A sleek grey tube slid from his forearm. '*The penalty for escape is death*,' he hissed, taking aim at India. She gasped and backed away.

'Leave her be!' shouted the professor. He leaped for the android's gun but Maximus knocked him aside. The gun blasted once and the professor collapsed to the floor, pale and gasping for breath.

'Leave the professor alone, you bully!' Tito leaped on to the android's back and wrapped his arms firmly around Maximus's head, and the android began to thrash like a blinded animal.

Startled by the gunshot, the guards had abandoned the spectacle of Lady Fang. But as they ran to help Maximus, the android's gun began to fire indiscriminately. A spray of bullets scattered the guards, cracking flagstones and blasting a chunk from one of the narrow stone columns by the altar.

Maximus ceased firing and hurled Tito to the floor, where he landed with a groan. India raced to his side as the android once again raised his gun. But before he could fire again, there was a loud crack from behind him as the damaged stone column began to topple. Maximus turned and barely had time to raise an arm before he was bludgeoned into the ground by the weight of the falling pillar.

Lady Fang stepped out of the light and immediately collapsed to her knees, gasping like someone who has come up for air. The Heliotrope had done its work on her: her eyes burned like coals in her chalk-white face, her hair stood out in a demented halo, and she looked as though a high-voltage charge was running through her body.

'What have you done to my android?' she shrieked. 'Grab them, you fools! Don't let them get away.'

India pulled Tito closer as they backed away from the guards. She glanced at Professor Moon who lay pale and panting for breath, with a look on his face that made India fear the worst. As she took another step backwards, something knocked against her boot. It was the professor's gun that had been dropped in the confusion. She picked it up with both hands and waved it wildly.

'Stay back! I'll shoot if I have to.' Her voice was shaky and unconvincing but the guards stopped advancing and watched her with predatory eyes.

For a moment everyone stood in a frozen tableau. India's gaze flicked from the guards to Lady Fang and the ashen figure of Professor Moon. She was now cut off from the ventilation shaft and she realized there was only one place left they could go.

'Tito, up here!' Dragging the boy with one hand and holding the gun shakily with the other, she pulled him on to the stone platform. The Heliotrope was still blazing brilliant white like an angel, and India paused for a moment before it. The hole from which the crystal had emerged appeared black and bottomless and she had no way of knowing what lay in there.

She gritted her teeth. 'Time to jump, Tito,' she said.

'But Miss Bentley,' he gasped. 'I am not sure it is such a good idea to leap before you look. Perhaps—'

He was cut short as India shoved him headlong into the hole.

'India Bentley!'

Fang stood behind her with the crystal fire still blazing in her eyes. Maximus had extracted himself from beneath the pillar and was getting to his feet.

'Run if you wish but you will only prolong your agony,' yelled Fang. 'Submit to me now and I promise you will not suffer.'

India stared back defiantly. 'Go to hell, you old bag!' she growled, then plunged into the black hole after Tito.

Lady Fang stared thoughtfully at the hole after India had disappeared.

'*Do you wish me to follow them, my lady?*' hissed Maximus.

'No,' she replied firmly. 'It's time we gave Miss Bentley a taste of true terror. Go and fetch the Hellhound.'

The drop through the hole was dark and bruising. India tumbled after Tito, not knowing if she might be smashed against a stone floor like an egg at any moment. Somewhere in the back of her head she remembered a story about a little girl falling into an endless rabbit hole.

Without warning the tube flattened out and disgorged her on to flat ground. She rolled awkwardly and then tumbled straight over the edge of another drop. She threw out an instinctive hand and caught hold of a hard ledge, wrenching her arm painfully as she dangled, one-handed, in the darkness. Her fingers began to slip. India could see nothing beneath her but yawning blackness and her sixth sense told her that to let go would be fatal.

'Tito!' she cried out. 'I need help. Where are you?'

'Right here, Miss Bentley.' She heard him fumbling through the darkness and a small pair of hands clasped her wrist and began to pull. She scrabbled to get a purchase with her boots and with Tito's help she clawed her way back to the top of the ledge where they both collapsed panting.

'Hold tight a moment.' She reached into her pocket and sparked the shock stick alight. Tito's grubby face lit up before her.

'Are you all right, Miss Bentley?' He blinked at her owlishly.

'I'm OK, I think,' she gasped. 'Where do you think we are?'

She directed the light from the shock stick towards the tube they had tumbled from. It was made of polished stone and nearly vertical. 'Well, there's no going back that way,' she muttered. When she shone the light over the ledge she gasped. 'Holy rig fairies!' The ledge dropped into a straight-sided pit about twelve feet deep, lined with evil shards of black volcanic glass spiking upward at odd angles. To have fallen in would have meant certain death. She and Tito looked at each other and shivered.

'By the Great Teacher's beard!' exclaimed Tito. 'When I fell down my coat caught on the end of the pipe. If that had not happened we would have both ended up down there.'

India swallowed hard. 'You're right,' she said. 'This was obviously meant to stop anyone breaking into the pyramid. There may be more traps, further in, so we need to go carefully.' 'Where are the others?' asked Tito. 'I was unable to see much without my glasses.'

'Verity and Cael dropped down the ventilation shaft,'

she said. 'It might lead here or it might go much further down.'

'And what of the professor, Miss Bentley?' he asked in a quiet voice.

India saw that he was trembling. 'I-I think that Maximus shot him,' she said hesitantly. 'He looked in a bad way, Tito.'

Tito looked down and nodded sadly.

By the sputtering light they could see a low chamber built of the same tightly fitted blocks they had seen in the city. All the stone surfaces were covered in a fine layer of crystalline frost and the still air smelled like a mausoleum, full of dampness and death.

Tito shifted uncomfortably. 'I am worried, Miss Bentley. Mr Two-Buck said there was radiation in this place. Many times in the brotherhood we have come across radioactive waste. Some of the brothers became sick and died. We should not stay here.'

India held up the shock stick to penetrate the gloom on the far side of the chamber. 'I agree,' she said. 'Besides, Lady Fang might decide to send some of her men after us. It looks like there's a doorway over there. Come on.'

India picked up the professor's hand-cannon which had tumbled down the chute with her and they shuffled carefully around the edge of the pit. On the other side of the chamber they found a flight of stone stairs leading down into the darkness.

'It goes down even further,' said India. 'I thought this

pyramid was big on the outside but I think most of it is underground.'

'Look at this, Miss Bentley,' said Tito. 'Someone has been here before us.'

She crouched down to examine the floor where Tito was pointing. The dirt and dust had been disturbed as though something heavy had been dragged across the room from the edge of the pit. The marks continued down the steps. 'Keep your eyes open, Tito. There might be someone else in here.'

They followed the marks in the dust, punctuated here and there by dark stains on the stone, and tried not to breathe in the overpowering smell of ancient mustiness. 'Look, Miss Bentley,' said Tito. 'There's something down there.' At the base of the steps they saw what appeared to be a bundle of rags. When they drew closer they could make out the outline of a thin figure in ragged oilskins. A vicious black-glass spike protruded from its back.

'Oh my,' said Tito, faintly. 'That's not Mr O'Hanlon or Mrs Brown, is it?'

India's heart clenched as she moved closer and held out the light towards the bundle. The fine layer of ice crystals covering the body spoke of its age.

'It's OK,' she said, breathing a sigh of relief. 'This one's been dead for a long time. It's little more than a skeleton.' She looked down on the grinning skull of the corpse, sprawled on the bottom step. 'Whoever it was must have been caught on the spikes. Then they managed to drag themselves down here before they died. What a horrible way to go.'

She examined the skeleton more closely. It wore the clothes of an explorer but they were crude and old-fashioned.

'There's a piece of paper in his hand,' said Tito.

Trying not to touch the skeleton itself, India pulled a yellowed and cracked piece of paper from the bony fingers. She smoothed it on the ground and held the light over it. It was a note, written in spidery pencil. She read out loud.

> *It seems I am cursed to die alone in this place, having left all the things that were good in my life to come here. I alone have witnessed the wonders of the Elders and now their secrets will go with me to my grave. With my dying breath I can only hope that the things I have discovered here remain hidden forever. But to any who find and read my words, you should know that this place is not what it appears. Within its deepest recesses lie demons that might yet consume us all. Turn back, traveller, before their curse is visited upon us all. May God look after my family.*
>
> *Sir Vivian Moon.*

'Sir Vivian Moon!' exclaimed India. 'It's the professor's grandfather. He really did discover Atlantis after all!'

'What demons is he talking about?' said Tito, 'I don't

like the sound of it, Miss Bentley.'

'Look,' said India. 'There's something drawn on the back.' She turned the paper over and they squinted at a series of lines criss-crossing the sheet in faded brown ink. 'It's a map of the city,' she said. 'Look, here's the pyramid, and this looks like a network of tunnels running beneath it. If we can find Verity we might be able to use this to find a way out.' She held up the shock stick and peered along a narrow brick corridor. '*If* we can find Verity,' she added with a sigh. She reached into her satchel and pulled out some broken hard-tack biscuits and a few shreds of dried meat. 'Here, take this,' she said. 'It'll make us both feel better.'

They chewed on the unyielding, salty food and caught up on what had happened since they had last seen each other. India told Tito about their journey across the ice, how they had arrived at the city, and how Sid had been lost when Orpheus had fallen from the bridge.

Then Tito told her what had happened to him since India was rescued by the *Sea Wolf*. He explained how angry Lady Fang had been that India had escaped with the stone and how he thought she might kill him in her fury.

'In the end it was Mr Two-Buck who persuaded her that I might be useful,' he said.

'Two-Buck Tim?' said India, surprised. 'I wouldn't have thought Fang would listen to him. Perhaps he's not such a sleazeball after all.'

'She relies on Mr Two-Buck to maintain her equipment,'

said Tito, 'especially the Hellhound.'

India looked over her shoulder and shivered. 'Don't remind me. Just the thought of it gives me the creeps.' She forced her feelings back down and was packing the remains of the meagre meal into her shoulder bag when Tito touched her arm.

'Miss Bentley,' he hissed. 'What is that?' He was pointing a trembling finger towards the far end of the passageway, where a robed and hooded figure stood, bathed in a faint blue glow. It was looking directly at them and India had a sensation like cold ice-water dropping into her stomach.

'I-I've seen it before,' she said in a whisper. 'It was in a vision I had in the professor's laboratory.'

Tito reached out and clutched her hand. 'It's the ghost of Sir Vivian!' he said tremulously.

'There's no such thing as ghosts, Tito,' India said, with as much confidence as she could muster. 'Sir Vivian is nothing more than a bag of bones so it can't be him.'

'Well what is it then?' said Tito. 'There is no one down here except you and me.'

She opened her mouth and then closed it again. Her supply of rational answers had dried up. The spectre beckoned them with a shrouded arm, then turned and walked away.

'I think it wants us to follow,' she said, wiping her sweaty palms on her trousers. 'And seeing as this is the only direction we can go in, we don't have much choice.'

They crunched across the frozen dust to the end of the

corridor and emerged on to a wide gallery. There was no sign of the spectre anywhere. The walls were threaded with veins of blue crystal, running through them like the roots of an exotic weed. When India touched one, it made the skin on her finger tingle.

'The energy from the Heliotrope is being fed down here too,' she said. Her voice skittered away in a thousand whispers through the dark chamber.

'Why would anyone feed energy *into* a pyramid?' said Tito.

The acoustics told them they were standing in a huge space, an echoing stone chamber. India peered over the edge of the gallery and as her eyes grew accustomed to the dim light, she saw that the chamber was not entirely empty.

'Holy mother of all riggers!' she cried, looking down into the heart of the pyramid. 'What *is* that thing?'

Stretched across the pyramid floor was an elongated grey shape, partially buried in the sandy floor. It was difficult to gauge its size in the half-light, but India estimated it was several hundred yards long. It appeared smooth and sculpted, as though the air might slip easily across its surfaces, and graceful spiral markings traced its curves. Its dusty, grey skin gleamed like graphite in the soft, blue light.

'Miss Bentley,' said Tito in a hushed voice. 'That does not look like something you would expect to find inside a twelve-thousand-year-old pyramid.'

She nodded. The object looked completely out of place, like a giant seashell, washed up on an ancient tide.

But, there was something else about it that troubled her. As she looked at it, she had the strangest sensation that it was giving off waves of energy that sang beyond the range of normal human senses. It awoke feelings inside her that were chilling and primeval, as though she was looking at something from a childhood nightmare. It spoke to her of unimaginable distances and age beyond reckoning.

'It's old, Tito,' she whispered. 'Older than anything else in here. I don't know how I know that, but I do. And, what's more, I think it knows we're here.'

She searched her head for the right word to describe what she was seeing and feeling, but the only word that presented itself seemed too scary to use. It felt *alien*.

Tito was obviously thinking along the same lines. 'Miss Bentley,' he said in a small voice. 'Do you think that object might be a spaceship?'

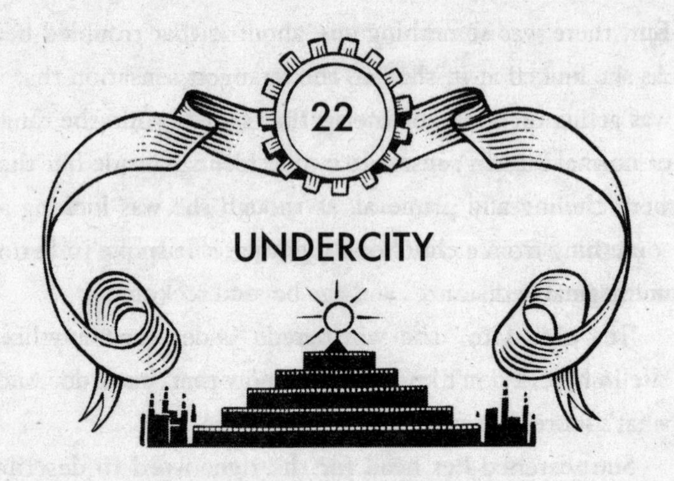

After a skin-scraping slide that seemed to last an eternity, Verity Brown slithered from the end of a stone pipe and dropped into twelve inches of freezing water. She swore and climbed to her feet, groping blindly in the darkness. There was a loud splash behind her followed by a groan.

'Cael! Is that you? Are you OK?'

'No! I am very much not OK,' came an angry voice. 'So far today I've faced death by falling, shooting and being eaten alive by mechanical bugs . . . and now my only pair of decent trousers are soaked through! Where the hell are we, anyway?'

Verity flicked on her torch. They were in a wide stone tunnel that disappeared in both directions as far as the torch beam would carry. A vigorous river of filthy water ran through the tunnel and Cael sat in the middle of it, glowering at her.

'We fell for a long way,' said Verity. 'I'm guessing we

went right through the pyramid and now we're under the city. It looks like we're in some kind of sewer.'

Cael jumped up quickly and began to brush down his sodden trousers. 'A sewer? Ah, hell, you don't mean to say this water is really—'

'Relax!' said Verity. 'I doubt anyone's had a pee in it for twelve thousand years.'

Cael was trying, unsuccessfully, to wring out his jacket. 'Well why the hell is there water down here anyway? Everything else is frozen solid.'

Verity wasn't listening. She was anxiously shining the torch back up the pipe. 'Where are they?' she muttered. 'They should all be down here by now.'

Cael shrugged. 'Maybe they ended up in a different pipe? I saw at least one side tunnel and there were probably others.'

'Maybe they got caught by Fang,' said Verity. 'Damn it! I shouldn't have gone first.' She hammered a fist angrily against the wall.

'Hey, hey, relax,' said Cael. 'India's a smart girl, she'll be OK.' He put his hand to his mouth and hollered India's name. But only an echo came back, receding into the distant recesses of the tunnel.

'If this really is a sewer system then it must join up somewhere,' said Verity. 'Come on, if they're not down here we need to find a way to get back up to the city.'

Cael looked up and down the corridor. 'So, which way?' he said.

Verity shrugged and looked down at her feet. 'Follow

the water, I guess,' she said. They splashed through the tunnel, with Verity leading, bowing their heads against the low roof. Along the way they passed side tunnels, disgorging more water into the main channel.

'Doesn't it worry you that it's so damned hot in here?' said Cael after a while. 'You know, what with this being an *extinct* volcano and all? And come to think of it, what is that stink? You didn't—'

'Don't be disgusting, Cael,' snapped Verity. 'It's sulphur dioxide; volcanic gas. I think the professor was definitely wrong about the volcano being extinct; it could be in the early stages of a new eruption. Hold on a moment . . . What's that?' As they rounded a bend in the tunnel Verity stopped and Cael walked into the back of her.

'Jumping rig rats,' he said, peering over her shoulder. 'Will you look at that?'

The tunnel ended abruptly in the side of a sheer rock wall and the water gushed past their feet and over the lip of the pipe in a long, splashy horse's tail. Verity leaned out and looked down. The cavern was far larger than the light from her torch could penetrate up or down; there was no telling how deep it might be.

Twenty yards away, a huge shape loomed out of the darkness. It was over a hundred feet wide and looked like a giant copper cauldron resting on a slender stem that rose from the pit below. At evenly spaced points around the rim, pillars of the same metal rose, curving gracefully like flowering petals. When Verity looked beyond the cauldron, she could see a second one in the darkness behind it, and a third one behind that.

'What are they?' said Cael in a hushed voice.

'I've seen these before,' said Verity. 'They generate energy, vast amounts of it. The one under Ironheart was powerful enough to shoot down an asteroid. Something down here must be using an awful lot of power, that's for sure.'

Cael shrugged. 'Well, there's no getting out that way. Come on, let's go back.'

They tore themselves from the sight and walked back in the direction they had come.

'Let's check out one of these side tunnels,' said Cael. 'There might be another way out.' The side pipe was smaller than the main channel and they had to crawl on hands and knees through the freezing water. After a short distance they emerged into a small room hewn from the rock and partly filled with water.

Cael caught Verity's arm. 'Look at this.' Arranged around the walls of the room were a dozen or more partially submerged stone chests. The lids were at least six inches thick, and too heavy for Cael to move, but the lid of the last chest was split down the centre. When Cael shone his torch into the gap, a thousand tiny points of light shone back at him.

'Quick, V, help me get this off.' Together they heaved the broken slab on to the floor and Cael let out a whistle. 'Holy mother of all riggers, will you look at these babies!'

The chest was filled with burnished gold coins and

brilliant blue-white gemstones, each one cut with a thousand facets that split the light a million ways. Cael picked up a gem the size of a pigeon's egg and turned it slowly in his fingers.

'Those Elders sure were fond of their crystals,' he said. 'This is a flawless diamond. At least a hundred carats. It's the best I've ever seen.'

Verity turned one of the coins in her fingers. 'It's embossed with the same sign we saw on the door and on the altar,' she said. 'I reckon this was where the Atlanteans stored their wealth.

Cael's eyes gleamed. 'There's a king's ransom in this room alone,' he said, 'and probably more in the others.' He looked around greedily. 'We have to check out the other tunnels.'

'What we have to do,' said Verity with a frown, 'is find India.'

'Yes, yes, of course. But don't you realize what this means? We're rich!'

'That may be so, but unless you can eat diamonds, we're going to be rich and dead pretty soon, so let's get moving.' With some difficulty she dragged Cael from the room, but not until after he had crammed his pockets and satchel with as many of the baubles as he could carry.

They returned to the main tunnel and continued walking, but they had not gone far when Verity yelped. She stopped to examine the small black creature she had trodden on. It lay on its back waving its broken legs in the air.

'It's another one of those bugs,' said Cael.

'And it's not alone,' said Verity. 'Look!'

The walls and roof of the tunnel ahead of them appeared to be liquefying as a metallic swarm of bugs seethed along the tunnel towards them, clicking and snipping their legs as they came.

Cael glanced anxiously up and down the tunnel. 'Looks like we have a choice,' he said. 'Get eaten alive or jump into the pit.'

'Not today, Tech-Boy,' said Verity. 'Quick, back into the storeroom.'

They scrambled back through the low tunnel with the bugs clattering and scritching behind them. They manhandled the broken stone lid across the low entrance, then began to shovel handfuls of diamonds and gold coins into a large heap behind it to keep the bugs out.

No sooner had they finished than a loud chattering began on the other side of the stone, like the noise of a million tiny jaws all working furiously. 'They're eating their way through solid rock,' said Verity. 'They must be pretty desperate to get our blood.'

They searched the room for some sign of another pipe or doorway and examined the stone chests to see if they might be moved, but to no avail. When they had exhausted all possibilities, they stood in the centre of the room and watched the barricade, which was now under a sustained attack from the other side.

'It's no use,' said Verity quietly. 'They're coming through, and I don't think there's anything we can do to stop them.'

India stared disbelievingly at the vast object below them. If it really was a spaceship, then it violated everything she knew about what was possible in the universe.

Once, when India and her father were gazing at the night sky over Lake London, he had explained to her just how far away the stars really were. He had started by telling her how fast a beam of light travelled. It was not something she'd ever really thought about before. If you turned on a light it was just there, instantly. But he'd explained that it just seemed that way because light travelled so quickly.

A tiny beam of light, he said, could travel thousands and thousands of miles in a single second. From here to the moon and back in a heartbeat. And as fast as light travelled was as fast as it was possible to go – nothing could go any faster than that.

But even at those unimaginable speeds it would still take years to travel to the nearest star, and it would take more than a lifetime to get to most of them. Some of them were so far away that it would take longer than the entire age of the Earth to reach them.

'There may be other life out there, India,' he told her. 'But we're never going to meet it. The Earth is like a tiny village in the middle of a vast desert that's just too big for anyone to get across.'

Yet here was the evidence that her father was wrong. Inside a pyramid, in the heart of a lost city, in a remote corner of the biggest wilderness on Earth, was a thing that should not have been there.

India tried to tell herself that this couldn't be a spaceship, that it must be something built by men before the Great Rains. Yet she knew in her heart that it could never have been built by men. The part of the craft that was visible above ground was over two hundred yards long and its graceful, organic curves reminded India of something that had grown rather than been built. Everything about it said it was not of this world . . . not *human*.

As their vision became more accustomed to the light, they saw that the crystal threads running through the pyramid stones all converged on the craft, creeping across its surface like strange, glassy vines. Faint blue light pulsed through the crystal at regular intervals.

'It looks like it's feeding on the energy,' said Tito in wonder.

Curiosity began to outweigh their fear and by unspoken agreement they started timidly down a flight of steps to the pyramid floor. Seen up close, the impression of the object as a giant seashell grew stronger. The section they could see seemed to be part of a vast, tapering spiral and the surface was smooth and encircled with graceful curving lines.

All around the spaceship, the floor was crowded with shapeless heaps that gleamed dull yellow in the faint light. Many of the objects were unrecognizable, decayed into mouldering wood fragments or flaky ashes of parchment. But the items made of gold gleamed in the soft light, unchanged by time. And there was so much gold.

There were golden statues, daggers with jewelled handles, coins that looked freshly minted and jewellery boxes teeming with rings, hair combs and necklaces. When they turned to look at each other their faces shone with reflected yellow light.

'I've never seen so much treasure!' whispered Tito. 'But why is it all here?'

'Look at this,' said India, holding up an engraved golden plate. She wiped away the dust to reveal the etching beneath. It showed a group of men and women wearing ceremonial robes gathered around an object that was clearly the spaceship. All of them were on their knees, bowing deeply towards the craft.

'They worshipped it!' said India. 'They must have thought it had come from the gods. I'm guessing they put the treasure in here as an offering.'

As India replaced the golden plate carefully, something else caught her eye. Among the finery was a small statue, three inches high and finely carved in green jade. But it was not the workmanship that made her cry out in surprise: the statue was a perfectly wrought representation of a tiny android.

'Tito! Look at this.' She snatched up the statue and thrust it towards him. Tito's eyes grew wide.

'It looks like Lady Fang's android,' he said.

'I know it looks like Maximus, but it isn't,' said India. 'I've seen a picture of it before. The professor said it was the demon that guarded the Sun Machine. But see here, there's a small crack across the visor and here, there's a tiny plate in its chest. This isn't Maximus, it's *Calculus*!'

'Your friend?' said Tito. 'But how can that be? This statue was made thousands of years ago.'

'It's a mystery, Tito,' she said. 'But it has something to do with this spaceship, if that's what it *really* is. I think we'll find the answers in there.'

Tito's eyes opened wider still. 'You're not planning to go inside, are you, Miss Bentley?'

'Yes, I am. I came to look for Calc and I'm not going to give up now,' she said defiantly.

'But have you considered there might be . . . *aliens* in there?'

India blinked. Up until that point, she had not remotely considered the possibility that anything might be alive on board such an ancient machine.

She took a deep breath. 'I'm still going to look,' she said. 'Calculus was my friend. If there's any way of finding out what happened to him, I have to do it.'

'Very well, Miss Bentley,' said Tito. 'Then I will help you. Although I am not sure I have enough training as a tech-hunter to deal with aliens.'

'I don't think they teach that sort of thing in tech-hunting school,' replied India. 'Come on, let's walk around it. But go carefully, I don't want to wake anything up!' She meant the comment as a joke but the words fell heavily.

They made a slow circuit of the craft. There was no obvious doorway and the outer skin was smooth and seamless. Only the faint latticework of glittering crystal growing over the surface gave any suggestion of life, like a trickle of moisture being poured on to a dead plant. When they reached the far side of the ship they found a perfect circle, inscribed lightly on the outer shell. India reached out her hand to touch it but pulled it back at the last moment; the surface was covered with a fine frost.

'Do you think this might be a door?' she said.

Tito didn't answer. He was peering at a small symbol inscribed on the surface of the craft. India followed his gaze.

'It's the mark of the Sun Machine,' she said. 'We saw it on the gates when we arrived. It's the same as the tattoo on your chest.'

Tito looked at her, aghast. 'But how is that *possible*, Miss Bentley? My tattoo is the secret mark of the Great Teacher. It is known only to the monks of our order; it should not be here, on the side of a spaceship!'

The boy's lip trembled and he backed away.

'There's probably a simple explanation, Tito,' said India.

'No there isn't,' said Tito hotly. 'Nothing about this journey is simple – the dreams, the sea monsters, the eclipse, none of it. I told you, the Great Teacher warned us that the three parts of the stone should not be brought together. Well, now they have been, Miss Bentley, and look what is happening. First the stone has led us to this place, and now the planets are coming into alignment for the first time in thousands of years. And if that wasn't enough, we've found a spaceship that carries the same mark as I do!' In a fit of anger he pulled open his shirt to reveal his tattoo.

'Tito, for goodness sake—'

There was a loud clunk from the hull. A thin ray of blue light needled out from the craft to dance briefly over the tattoo on Tito's chest, delicately tracing the line of the design.

A deep boom sounded in the depths of the spaceship, the sound of a millennia-old silence being broken. Then the circular line deepened and a round door slid upward as quickly and smoothly as a window shutter. A gust of humid air surged out like a great exhalation of breath, forming thick vapour clouds as it met the cold air of the cavern.

India and Tito stared at the open doorway as though they expected monsters to come rushing from the darkness towards them. But nothing came, there was only a faint wind as the last fingers of warm air rushed up from the bowels of the ship.

'How did you do that?' said India in a hushed voice.

'I don't know,' Tito whispered back, hastily buttoning his shirt. They eyed each other nervously.

'Tito, where did you say the Great Teacher came from?' asked India.

'I didn't, Miss Bentley,' said Tito. 'No one ever knew where he came from.'

'Do you think it's possible,' said India, 'that he had something to do with this spaceship?'

Tito shook his head in disbelief. 'I have always been taught,' he said, 'that the wisdom of the Great Teacher came from the gods themselves. Now I no longer know what to believe.'

'Perhaps the answers are in there,' said India, pointing to the doorway. 'Shall we find out?'

'Excuse me, Miss Bentley,' said Tito, aghast. 'Have you mislaid your marbles?'

'You mean *lost* my marbles,' corrected India. 'And no, I haven't. Listen, both of us came here to look for something. I came to look for my friend and you came to look for an adventure. Well, just look at this: a real-life alien spaceship. How much bigger would you like your adventure to be?'

'Well . . .' pondered Tito. 'Maybe just a little smaller?'

India grinned. 'I'll take that as a "yes". We'll make a tech-hunter out of you yet.'

'I am beginning to think,' said Tito as they stepped up to the door, 'that life inside the monastery wasn't so bad after all.'

*

Beyond the doorway, India could see a round corridor curving away into the ship. The ceiling, walls and floor were perfectly round and smooth like mother-of-pearl. It did not look like the corridor was made to be walked in at all. Watched by Tito, she clambered up to stand just inside the doorway. The air was warm and neutral-smelling and not foul or poisonous as she had feared it might be. A shiver of excitement ran down her spine: she was standing inside a spaceship!

'Come on then.' She held out a hand to Tito, loitering outside. 'Whatever happens,' she said as she pulled him up, 'remember what we came for.'

He nodded resolutely.

They walked forwards slowly through the dim passage, lit by a faint blue phosphorescence that permeated the walls. The corridor linked a succession of small chambers, each one empty and smooth with no corners anywhere. More corridors twisted away at strange angles into the walls and ceiling. At one point, a circular passage dropped straight down into the floor like a deep well and they skirted around it carefully, trying not to think about how far down it might go.

'How could anyone get around in here?' said Tito after a few minutes. 'It looks like you'd have to be able to fly.'

'My dad told me there's nothing to hold you down in space,' said India. 'You just float around.'

Tito gave her a scornful look. 'Really, Miss Bentley,' he

said. 'Now I think you're pushing my leg.'

'I'm not *pulling* anything, Tito,' she replied. 'There's no gravity in space, you ask my dad.'

'If we ever get out of here, Miss Bentley,' he said, 'I would be delighted to avail myself of that opportunity.' He looked anxiously over his shoulder. 'Maybe we should go back before that door shuts again. Otherwise it might be another twelve thousand years before somebody finds our skeletons.'

India laughed. 'Don't worry, Tito. Whatever used to live in here is long gone, there's no sign of life any—'

She broke off suddenly. The corridor ended in an opening that led to a perfectly spherical chamber. The room was in near darkness, not black but deep red, the colour of blood, and it was stiflingly hot.

'This feels familiar,' she muttered to herself. Her scalp prickled and her senses went on high alert. The room was dark and apparently empty but she could feel something watching her as surely as a prey animal feels the eyes of a wolf.

'What is it, Miss Bentley?' whispered Tito. 'What's wrong?'

She motioned Tito to be quiet and peered into the darkness looking for . . . for what?

And then she saw them.

Three shapes at the far end of the chamber: dark spheres, floating against the blood-red background. They made no sound, and yet India knew for certain that they were alive.

They were just as she remembered them from Ironheart – the three parts of the Machine Mind that called themselves the voices of Wisdom, Compassion and Logic.

They spoke in perfect unison.

'Welcome, Soul Voyager,' they said. A flurry of tiny lights danced across their surfaces. 'You have come, just as we knew you would.'

24 A WALK IN THE PARK

Verity dropped an armful of diamonds on the makeshift barricade and rammed them into place with her boot.

'It won't do any good, you know,' said Cael, looking disparagingly at the heap of precious gems that was keeping the small army of bugs at bay. 'Those things will be in here in five minutes.' Verity snorted and returned to the chest for more diamonds.

'Well, that's another five minutes I'm going to live then,' she growled. 'Which is more than you'll manage if you don't shut up.' She began to drag a heavy piece of the stone lid towards the door.

'All right, all right,' said Cael getting up wearily. 'I'd forgotten – you're not scared of anything, are you? Come on, I'll give you a hand.'

'Stay the hell away from me,' she snapped. 'I've had enough help from you for one day.'

'Meaning what exactly?'

'Meaning if you hadn't been so keen to fill your pockets we might have got out of here earlier instead of waiting to be sucked dry by a horde of mechanical roaches.' She hurled a heavy diamond at the wall in frustration.

'Look,' said Cael with a hint of annoyance. 'I'm sorry, but I needed those diamonds. Those bugs aren't the only things after my blood. I owe money to some bad people in Sing City and if I don't pay them off when I get back, then they'll do some very unpleasant things to me.'

Verity gave a dry laugh. 'It's the same old story, isn't it, Cael? There's always something you have to do that's more important than anything or anyone else. I guess that's why you dumped me in the jungle to fend for myself?'

'Look, V,' said Cael holding up his hands defensively, 'I know how it looked but I was trying to protect you. Not that you'd believe that.'

Verity turned on him with fire in her eyes. 'You're damned right I don't believe it. We'd been together for a whole year, I thought we were happy. Then one day I woke up and you'd just gone, disappeared without a trace, with all our money. I was twenty-one, Cael, and you left me on my own in bandit country, so don't give me the "I was only trying to protect you" story. You've never committed a selfless act in your life.'

'Oh yeah?' snapped Cael. 'Well perhaps you've forgotten who Lady Fang was aiming at when I got shot back there?'

Verity lapsed into sudden silence. Her mouth opened and shut a few times then she down heavily on a stone chest. 'You're right,' she said eventually. 'I never thanked you for saving my life.'

'Well,' said Cael, taken aback by the sudden change. 'You're welcome.'

'But then I saved yours right back,' she said quickly. 'So we're even. Aren't we?'

Cael gave a wry smile. 'Sure,' he said. 'Don't worry, we don't owe each other anything.' He sat down beside her and they listened in silence to the incessant scratching and scraping outside. It sounded much closer now.

'I never got a proper chance to tell you why I left you in the jungle,' he said after a while. Verity raised an eyebrow. 'About six months before I met you, I got into a dispute with some slave traders, really bad people. They came to a village where I'd been staying and tried to take the children. I tried talking them out of it, but there was an argument and I shot the ringleader. After that they put a price on my head. I kept out of their way for a long time and by the time I met you I thought it was all forgotten.' He smiled. 'Those twelve months were the happiest time I can remember, V,' he said. 'Then I got word that they were coming after me again. I was terrified they'd kill you too, so I decided to go and see them to sort things out once and for all.'

'You took on a bunch of slavers on your own?' said Verity. 'What were you thinking?'

'I was thinking that an Irishman can talk his way out of anything,' said Cael with a grin. 'I thought we'd have a quick chat, I'd apologize, pay them a little blood money and that would be that.' He looked down. 'But that's not quite the way it worked out.'

'What happened?' said Verity.

'They took all of our money and then put me to work on one of their slave ships for good measure. It was nearly a year before I managed to escape.'

'A year?' said Verity. 'I looked for you a lot longer than that. Why didn't you come and find me?'

'I did,' he said. 'I asked everywhere about you. I finally found out you were living in Shanghai. But . . .'

'But what?'

Cael looked away and sighed. 'Well, that was when I found out you'd become Mrs Brown. I figured you'd met someone else and you didn't need me any more. I couldn't blame you,' he said. 'After all, I had gone off and left you.' He gave her a sad smile. 'So, who was the lucky guy?'

Verity shook her head and then punched Cael hard on the arm. 'Cael, you stupid, thick-skulled, chicken-brained moron. Was that the only reason you stayed away from me?'

'W-what? Yes, but I . . . Ow!' He rubbed his arm. 'What was that for?'

'There never *was* a Mr Brown, you halfwit!' she cried. 'I made him up.'

'You made him up? But—'

'It wasn't easy being a twenty-one-year-old tech-hunter and a woman on my own in hostile territory,' she said. 'After you'd gone I got a whole lot more attention than I wanted – for all the wrong reasons, so I invented a husband.

It kept most of the sleazebags away, and for anyone who didn't get the message, I had my pistol.'

Cael's mouth had dropped open and he stared, unable to speak for several seconds. 'But this is terrific!' he spluttered eventually.

'What? How exactly is it terrific?'

'Well it means that you and I . . . I mean, we could still . . .'

A sudden avalanche of diamonds from the barricade made them both jump to their feet. A large piece of stone fell away and thousands of tiny black bugs immediately began to surge through the hole. Verity and Cael shrank back to the furthest corner of the room and watched the horror unfold.

'Do you think this will be quick?' said Verity in a shaky voice as she eyed the creeping death.

'I reckon so,' said Cael. 'It'll be a walk in the park.' He smiled but his eyes were sad.

Verity returned the smile. 'OK, Cael, I'm officially scared now,' she said taking his hand.

Cael reached into his pocket. 'There was always something I meant to ask you, V,' he said. 'And I reckon this is the last chance I'll get.' He pulled out one of the larger pear-cut diamonds and handed it to her. The room seemed to light up in its presence.

Verity looked at the stone and smiled. 'You always were one for grand gestures, Cael,' she said. 'So, what are you saying?'

He looked suddenly boyish and shy. 'Well, I know it's a bit late and everything . . .' He was turning pink as he spoke. 'But I was wondering, if you would consider, that is, I mean would you be—'

'Shut up!' Verity pushed him away suddenly. She frowned and cocked her head to one side, suddenly becoming the cold-eyed tech-hunter once more.

'What the . . . ! V, what's going on?' he protested.

'Be quiet and listen,' she snapped.

'Listen to what?' huffed Cael. 'All I can hear is about a million bugs that want to drink our blood. For heaven's sake, V, don't you have a sense of occasion? We're about to die here.'

'Maybe not today,' said Verity, pressing her ear to the wall. The bugs were now most of the way across the floor. 'Here,' she said. 'Behind this wall, can you hear it now?'

Cael put his ear to the stone and heard a low growling and rattling that shook the ground and vibrated the walls. 'It's an engine!' he said. 'But how—'

'Get back!' cried Verity. She leaped away from the wall and threw her weight on top of Cael, pinning him to the floor as the rear wall of the chamber exploded in a fountain of loose rock and earth. The pointed end of a giant rotating screw burst into the room in a cloud of debris closely followed by the black iron hulk of Orpheus.

'What the . . . ?' spluttered Cael. 'Where did . . . ? How did . . . ?'

The first of the bugs took advantage of his distraction to

sink its metal fangs into his leg, making him yelp. Orpheus lurched to a halt in the middle of the chamber and the side hatch clanged open.

Sid leaned against the door for support. He was as white as a sheet and a streak of blood ran down his forehead. Two of his fingers were tied together with an old rag and he looked ready to collapse.

'Sid!' cried Verity. 'I never thought I'd be pleased to see you. You look like hell!'

The boy looked down at the pair of them on the floor and curled his lip. 'Well, I'm having a bad day,' he growled. 'So if you two'd rather stay here then just say so. Otherwise get your backsides up here and let's get going.'

India watched the floating spheres and felt the knot in her stomach tighten. They hovered silently, just as they had done when she first saw them at Ironheart. She was vaguely aware of Tito breathing heavily behind her.

'Once again you have come before us, Soul Voyager,' said the middle sphere. Red and gold lights danced over its surface and its voice combined male and female qualities. India remembered it as the voice of Wisdom.

'And . . . you have brought others to this place,' said the sphere to its right. 'You can no longer be trusted.' It sounded cold and irritable, and rippled green lights. India swallowed. She remembered the voice of Logic from their first meeting, when she had formed the distinct impression that it didn't like her at all.

'If you mean Lady Fang,' said India, 'we didn't bring her here, she followed me. We were trying to get away from her when we escaped down here.'

'You have come to destroy us, Soul Voyager,' said Logic coldly. 'The short-lives always destroy what they do not understand.'

Tito let out a small whimper and India reached out in the dark to take his hand.

'That isn't true,' she said, boldly. 'And that isn't why we're here. You trusted me before, when we met at Ironheart. At least, I think it was you,' she added, uncertain how to tell one sphere apart from another.

'It was us,' said the third sphere. It spoke in a cool, female voice: the voice of Compassion. 'We trusted you once, India Bentley, but you are not the same person you were a year ago. Nor are you the same person you will be a year from now. Our trust cannot always be taken for granted.'

'We haven't come here to destroy you,' said India, squeezing Tito's hand tightly. A bead of sweat began to trickle down her neck; the heat was becoming intolerable. 'We came here because we thought this was an abandoned place, a dead city.'

'We are not dead,' said Logic. It sounded even more irritated than usual.

'No,' said India quickly. 'I didn't mean that.' She took a deep breath. If anything, the spheres seemed to have become even more touchy. 'I came here to find my friend, Calculus. I dreamed he was alive, and then my bracelet kept flashing, and the professor found drawings in a temple that looked like him and . . .' She paused and took a breath, aware of how lame this all sounded. 'What I'm trying to say is that you were the last ones to see him, so you must know what happened to him. Please, tell me, is he still alive?'

'If we tell you,' said Wisdom, 'will you do what we require?'

India was taken aback. 'Well . . . what do you want me to do?'

'Whatever we ask, Soul Voyager,' said Logic. 'That is what we want you to do.'

Tito tugged insistently on her hand. 'Miss Bentley, I am not sure that is what Mr O'Hanlon would call "a good deal".'

'I'm pretty sure it's not, Tito,' she whispered, 'but I think it's the only way I'm going to find out what happened to Calc.' She took another deep breath. 'OK, then,' she said. 'Whatever you want me to do, I'll try and help. But you have to tell me what you know.'

The spheres moved closer together, and India had the impression they were conferring about something. 'We will hold you to your word, Soul Voyager,' said Logic. 'The Messenger will explain what you need to know. Now we must rest.'

When Logic had finished speaking, the lights faded from all three spheres and they became still and lifeless, like grey stones against a blood-red background.

'What happened?' said Tito. 'Have they gone?'

'Maybe they're sleeping,' said India.

'They're dying,' said a voice behind them.

They jumped violently and turned around. Silhouetted

in the pale light of the doorway was the spectral figure they had seen earlier. They instinctively backed away.

'Who are you?' demanded India.

'I will not harm you,' said the spectre, its voice little more than a whisper. 'I have been sent to speak with you. I am . . . I *am* . . .' It paused as though it had not previously considered the question of who it was.

'I saw you in my vision,' said India, taking a step towards the spectre. 'You showed me Calculus, trapped beneath the ice. Is he here?'

'Calculus?' said the spectre vaguely. 'It is hard to remember. So many thoughts . . . so many lives.'

'Calculus was my friend,' said India impatiently. She stepped closer to the spectre, trying to see under its dark hood. 'If you know what happened to him, please tell me.'

The spectre hesitated, sifting memories. 'I remember now,' it said slowly. 'He was a creature without a heart, a tin man.'

India nodded. 'Like in *The Wizard of Oz*,' she said enthusiastically. 'I gave Calculus a copy of the book and I told him he reminded me of the Tin Man.'

'Your friendship was what made the Mind decide to preserve him,' said the spectre. 'Thanks to you, he is immortal.'

It raised its head to look at her.

'I remember,' it said after a long pause. 'I *remember* now. There is no need to be afraid of me, India Bentley.'

It reached up and pulled back its hood.

India gasped and the blood drained from her face. She felt giddy and clutched at Tito's hand for support. Underneath the hood, the spectre wore a long helmet. There was a large dent in its skull and a thick crack ran across the visor. Through the folds of his robe, India could see the piece of rusty sheet-steel that had been riveted into place across his chest.

Her hands flew to her mouth as Tito stepped backwards in fear. 'Calc!' His name escaped her like a sob. She took a step forward and then stopped, unsure. 'Is it really you? Are you really here?'

The android removed a hand from the folds of its sleeve and looked at it in wonder.

'I am here,' he said absently, as though speaking to himself. 'After so long living in dreams, I *am* here.'

'Oh, Calc,' cried India. 'They said you were dead but I wouldn't believe it. It was you who sent me those messages on the bracelet, wasn't it?'

Calculus looked down at her bracelet, as though trying to remind himself of a dream, and nodded.

India beckoned Tito over. 'It's all right,' she said. 'This is my friend, Calculus. Nothing bad will happen to us while he's here.'

Tito hung back. 'He looks like Maximus,' he whispered.

'Well, he's not Maximus,' said India, a little annoyed. 'He's nothing like Maximus and now that he's back—'

She stopped. 'But . . . *how* are you back, Calc? You were

uploaded into the Mind weren't you? I guessed that much when I spoke to Maximus.'

Calculus spoke like a person waking from heavy sleep. 'You are correct, India,' he said eventually. 'When Ironheart was destroyed, the Mind thought I was interesting enough to be preserved. It was fascinated to learn that a machine could have had a friendship with a human like you.'

'Mr Calculus,' interrupted Tito, 'I have a question. If you were destroyed in an explosion, then how is it that you are here?'

Calculus folded his arms back into his sleeves. 'What you see here is just an image created by the Mind from my memory files,' he said.

'But I saw you in my dreams,' said India. 'You gave me a message and said I had to come here and find you!'

'The Mind can only send my image a certain distance,' said Calculus. 'Beyond that, I had to use other means. I have to confess that communicating in dreams is not as easy as Nentu makes it look.'

'Then,' said India in a small voice, 'you're not really here at all?'

'I am a projection, nothing more,' he said. 'I am here only because the Mind remembers me.'

India felt as if she had been given something precious, only to have it whisked away again. 'But you're here and you're talking to me,' she said, with a note of desperation in her voice. 'And the professor showed us pictures of you on the walls of an ancient temple. How can you not be real?'

Calculus let out a sigh. 'I have learned,' he said, 'that the distinction between past, present and future is a stubbornly persistent illusion.'

India backed away from him. 'You're not making any sense, Calc,' she said accusingly. 'You sound strange . . . not like you at all.'

'I am sorry, India,' he replied. 'If I sound strange, it is because I have seen strange things. Now you must listen to me. The Mind sent me here as a messenger. There is something important I have to show you. Come on.'

Without waiting for a reply he turned and walked away along the corridor. India and Tito followed at a safe distance, still holding hands.

'How do you know where you're going?' asked Tito, as Calculus led them through a succession of identical chambers.

'I am a projection of the Machine Mind. Whatever they know, I know too.'

'But . . . if you were created by the Mind,' said India, 'how do you know your thoughts are really your own?'

'How do any of us know that, India?' asked Calculus. He turned suddenly and led them through a circular doorway.

'We are here,' he said.

They were standing in a tall, cylinder-shaped room. Floating in the air a dozen feet off the ground was an object that looked like a figure of eight, lying on its side. It seemed to be made from a band of pure energy that turned lazily in the air, throwing dappled light on to the walls like sunlight through water. India had a strong sense that it was something out of place: an object that somehow violated the rules of nature.

'This,' said Calculus, 'is the infinity engine. It is the heart of the ship.'

'Do you mean like a control room?' said Tito.

'In a way,' said Calculus. 'It creates a gateway through which the ship can pass.'

'Pass to where?' said India.

'To anywhere,' he replied. 'Or indeed to any when.'

'Any when?'

'As I said, past, present and future are all just illusions. This ship can move between them, just as one might walk back and forth across an open field.'

India was struggling to cope with what Calculus was saying. 'Do you mean it can travel through time? But that's not possible – the past isn't a place you can go to, it doesn't exist any more.'

'The corridor we just walked along didn't stop existing after we passed through it,' said Calculus. 'You can return there as long as you know the way. So it is with the past.'

'So the people who made this ship were time travellers?' said Tito. He seemed to be much more at ease with the concept than India, and he looked at the hovering shape with interest.

'They were just *travellers*,' said Calculus. 'They were a race we know only as "the Long Lives". Their ship crashed here fifteen thousand years ago when the climate was warm and temperate. The primitive tribes of humans who lived here at the time worshipped them as gods. They helped to hide the ship and protect the visitors, and in return the Long Lives shared as much of their science as the tribes could understand. Together they built the city you saw outside. They also built machines like the one we found at Ironheart to protect the Earth. It was the first example of cooperation between people from different galaxies.'

'So that was how the legend of Atlantis began,' said Tito in an awestruck voice.

'Indeed,' said Calculus. 'When early explorers found this place they went home telling tales of a golden race who lived in a miraculous city.'

'So are the Long Lives still here?' said India. She glanced around, half expecting to see creatures emerging from the shadows, but the ship seemed just as dead and empty as before.

'Earth was not a hospitable environment for them,' said Calculus. 'Within a few hundred years, the last of them had died out, leaving only their machines behind to watch over the ship.'

'But why did they stay?' asked Tito. 'Why didn't they just repair their spaceship and leave before they all died?'

'The spaceship is repaired,' said Calculus, 'but it cannot leave. Not yet.' He spread his arms before the rotating shape overhead. 'Every one of the Long Lives' ships carries a device like this. It allows the ship to travel to other dimensions. But once it has stopped working, it requires a strong gravitational wave to start it again.'

Tito's forehead had become increasingly furrowed as Calculus was speaking. 'But what would cause such a thing to occur, Mr Calculus?'

'A number of things might suffice,' said Calculus. 'Usually a major celestial event such as the collapse of a star, the presence of a black hole or—'

'Or the alignment of all the biggest planets in the solar system,' said India. '"*When giants stand in line behind a black sun.*" That's what the message means, doesn't it? The stone is counting down to the eclipse.'

'Yes,' said Calculus. 'The professor was right about that. But even he did not guess the true purpose of the Sun Machine. In about three hours, the four giant gas planets in our solar system will come into alignment with our moon and the Earth. Their combined mass will create a gravitational wave of massive proportions. When it reaches the Earth, the Heliotrope crystal will amplify the wave's energy and use it to restart the infinity engine. This is what the Sun Machine was built for and it has waited over twelve thousand years to fulfil its destiny.'

No one spoke. In the silence that followed, India became aware that the infinity engine was making a faint singing noise, like a wet finger running around the rim of a wine glass.

'So why am I here, Calc?' she said after a while. 'Why did you go to so much trouble to get me to come?'

Calculus looked up at the infinity engine. 'The Long

Lives' technology responds only to their telepathic commands,' he said. 'The Machine Mind cannot control the ship by itself. Only a living being with a telepathic link to the ship can give the order for it to take off.'

'You mean me, don't you?' said India. 'You think that because I'm a Soul Voyager I can talk to this spaceship? You're crazy.'

'It's what a Soul Voyager is, India,' said Calculus. 'When the Long Lives realized they were dying, they knew there might be no one here to give the order. So they seeded their DNA in the human population. They created a few humans who could communicate telepathically with their machines, so that when the time came, their descendants would be able to give the instruction. Every mystic, shaman and holy man who ever lived has had some part of that DNA inside them. It enabled them to hear the voices of the Machine Mind. You have that DNA, India. That is why you were brought here.'

'So you're saying the ship needs me?' She bit her lip and looked up at the infinity engine, listening to its faint song. 'What does it want me to do?'

'Not much,' said Calculus quickly. 'When the eclipse starts, you must be ready to give the order to the Machine Mind. After that the ship will take care of itself. You and the others will have plenty of time to get away from here before it takes off.'

'I don't understand, Mr Calculus,' said Tito. 'Why does the spaceship need to take off at all? All of the Long

Lives are dead – you said so yourself.'

'Not all of them,' said Calculus. 'The crew are dead but there are still over a million souls on board this spaceship. They are refugees from the Long Lives' home world, stored as crystallized memory engrams deep within the cells of the ship. If this ship is destroyed, then the last survivors of their race will be gone forever.'

'A million souls?' said Tito. 'We have to help them!'

'Yes,' said Calculus. 'We really do.'

India gave a dry laugh. 'It's not that simple, Calc,' she said. 'Lady Fang and her goon squad were waiting for us when we got here. She thinks the Heliotrope will make her immortal and she's going to take it back to Sing City.'

Calculus looked startled. 'Lady Fang has the crystal?' He placed his fingers against his temples. 'But this cannot be allowed to happen,' he gasped. 'Without the crystal, the ship cannot take off. It will be a disaster!'

'I know,' said India. 'But I don't know what we can do to stop her.'

'It wouldn't just be a disaster for the Long Lives,' said Calculus. 'The ship is nearly drained of energy. The nanomites are scavenging for raw materials to repair it but they are fighting a losing battle. If the ship runs out of power, the systems that have protected it from the volcano for the last twelve thousand years will fail.'

'I'm guessing that's a bad thing, right?' said India.

'Yes, India,' said Calculus. 'That is a very bad thing. The infinity engine is an immensely powerful device. As long as the ship is intact it is safe. But if the ship is consumed by the volcano then it will cause an explosion that will scatter radioactive material over half the planet. Millions will be killed.'

'The Great Teacher was right,' gasped Tito. 'This really is the end of the Great Cycle!'

'India, you have to find a way to stop Lady Fang,' said Calculus.

'How are we supposed to do that?' said India. 'She has a dozen men with guns, an android, and some kind of killer Hellhound on her side!'

A low rumble echoed through the space ship. The blue light permeating the walls flickered once and then went out. Calculus switched on his visor, filling the room with harsh white light.

'What was that?' whispered India. 'What just happened?'

Calculus looked up at the ceiling. 'I am guessing that Lady Fang has removed the Heliotrope from the temple,' he said. 'It has stopped sending power to the ship. We only have a limited amount of time before —'

His image flickered before their eyes.

'Calc, what's happening?'

'The power is failing,' he said through a hiss of static. 'You must find Fang and persuade her to return the stone before the eclipse.'

'But what will happen to you when the spaceship takes off?'

Calc's voice was becoming crackly and indistinct. 'The

Machine Mind will release me,' he said.

'We'll do it, Calc,' said India determinedly. 'Tell the Machine Mind that we'll get the crystal back and save the Long Lives.' She looked at the flickering image, wondering if Calc could still hear her. 'And we'll save you too, Calc,' she said, reaching out to touch him. 'I promise.'

The image blinked out and they stood alone, lit only by the faint glow from the infinity engine.

'What happened to your friend, Miss Bentley?' said Tito in a small voice.

'I'm not sure, Tito,' she said, her hand hovering in empty air. Her brain was struggling to process everything she had seen and heard. 'But we have to try and help him. We have to get the Heliotrope back.'

'Lady Fang wishes to be young again,' said Tito. 'I don't think she will give up the crystal easily.'

'I don't know how we're going to do it,' said India, 'but the first thing we need to do is get out of here.'

They left the infinity engine singing quietly to itself and fumbled their way back to the corridor. At the end of the long passage they could make out a patch of pale grey against the blackness. 'Come on, we're nearly there,' said India.

But as they ran towards the door, Tito stopped abruptly and jerked on India's arm, his eyes stricken with terror.

'Tito, what is it? What's wrong?' she whispered. Then she felt it too. A sudden overwhelming fear that made her skin prickle and turned her legs to rubber. Behind them in the corridor she heard a faint hiss, followed by the dry scraping of reptilian scales rubbing against one another. Fighting the instinct to run, she turned and saw a black shape, coiled near the roof of the corridor. It was darker than the darkness, save for two points of bile-yellow light shining at them. The shape growled, a deep and resonant sound that vibrated the air.

'Miss Bentley,' said Tito, his voice quaking. 'I b-believe that may be Lady F-Fang's Hellhound.'

And as though it had been waiting to be announced, the Hellhound began to unwind its sinuous body from the roof and slid silently to the floor. Then watching them through septic eyes, it began to creep liquidly towards them.

26
THE HOUND FROM HELL

They had not had a clear view of the Hellhound before. Now, as they peered into the darkness, they could see its powerful, armoured body making sinuous S-shapes as it slithered towards them on short, muscular legs. Its head was wide and held low behind bunched shoulders, and inside the partially open mouth they could see rows of gleaming steel teeth with cutting edges that closed together like scissor blades.

The creature moved slowly, confident of its prey, with no mercy in its yellow eyes. It seemed to India that her fear increased with every step the beast took towards her, though she knew that to run would be a fatal mistake. She grasped Tito's hand and found he was trembling.

'*The gun, India. Use the gun.*' It was Calc's voice. She could not tell where it had come from, but it prodded her into action. She groped in her bag and pulled out the iron hand-cannon. Using both hands, she levelled it at the approaching beast.

'Tito, run. I'll hold it off with this.'

'Miss Bentley, I—'

'GO!' she yelled. The Hellhound's jaws yawned wide as it leaped: a hate-filled blur in the darkness. The hand-cannon bucked in India's hand, hitting her in the face as the blast knocked her down.

She sat up, bleary-eyed, ears ringing. The corridor was full of dense smoke and the Hellhound was rolling on the floor, shaking its head to clear its vision. India scrambled through the doorway and collapsed on the ground outside. When she wiped her mouth, her hand came back bloody.

Tito was pulling on her arm now, his voice indistinct, as though she were underwater. 'Hurry, Miss Bentley, I think the creature is stunned only.'

Another growl made them turn around – to see the Hellhound standing in the ship doorway: its demonic features were mutilated by buckshot and one of its bile-coloured eyes was gone. India tried to lift the gun again but her strength failed her and it clattered to the ground.

'Stay back, beast!' yelled Tito. He began to walk towards the Hellhound, holding up his hands.

'Tito, what are you doing?'

'I am not afraid, Miss Bentley,' he said. 'I am following The Great Teacher's advice. He said when we are faced with an opponent of irresistible force we should meet him with no force.' The Hellhound lowered its head and glowered at him. Its jaws snapped at the air.

'Tito,' screamed India. 'That thing will tear you apart.'

But Tito was not listening. A look of steely certainty had settled on his face. 'Leave us alone, beast!' he yelled. 'Leave us or perish.'

The Hellhound bared its teeth and braced to leap at the boy and, at the same instant, Tito tore open the front of his shirt. The blue needle-light danced briefly across his tattoo and the great door slammed downward like a guillotine, breaking the back of the beast and crushing its steel bones like matchwood.

For a few tense seconds, the Hellhound gnashed wildly as it lay trapped, furiously snapping its jaws and thrashing its powerful body like a whip. Then the struggling became weaker until the beast gave a final shudder and its remaining eye blinked out.

Silence descended over the pyramid as the boy and girl stared at the creature, now reduced to a broken pile of steel with sticky blue fluids leaking from its mouth.

'Are you all right, Tito?' asked India quietly. The boy did not answer. 'Tito?'

'Why do men build such things, Miss Bentley?' he said. India was not sure if it was a question she was supposed to answer.

'I don't know, Tito,' she said. 'But we should really—'

'Life is a precious thing, don't you think?' he went on, staring at the dead Hellhound. 'So why do we behave like it doesn't matter?'

'I don't know,' she replied with a small smile. 'But if you keep asking questions like that, then I don't think you can be such a bad monk after all.' She climbed painfully to her feet and put her arms around the trembling boy.

'Are you sure it's dead, Miss Bentley?' he whispered.

'I think you killed it pretty good, Tito,' she said as she bent down to retrieve the professor's pistol. She looked around the vast chamber. 'Well, we can't go back the way we came in, so let's see if we can find another way out of here.'

They walked around the outside of the spacecraft, examining the walls of the pyramid carefully, but there was no sign of another way out. When they had completed two circuits, India sank down on a pile of gold coins for a rest.

'If we cannot find a way out of here,' said Tito in a matter-of-fact tone, 'then we will end up as skeletons, like Sir Vivian.'

'Well, *you're* a great comfort in an emergency,' said India, failing to keep the note of irritation from her voice.

'I'm just saying, Miss Bentley,' he continued. 'We could be entombed here forever. Always assuming that the bugs don't eat us alive first, or that the ship doesn't blow up, or the radiation doesn't—'

'Enough!' snapped India. She was about to give Tito a lecture on the importance of remaining positive when the ground began to shake beneath them. She jumped to her feet, causing a small avalanche of gold coins. 'What now?'

The vibration grew more intense until it shook the soles of their boots. As they clutched each other for support there was a sudden eruption of dust and rock on the far side of the chamber, and a black mechanical hulk burst into the pyramid, exhaling thick diesel clouds and scattering gold coins and priceless treasures into the air.

'It can't be,' said India under her breath. 'It's Orpheus! But that must mean . . .'

'You friend Mr Sid is alive!' said Tito excitedly.

Orpheus idled its engines amidst a pile of earth and gold trinkets as India and Tito sprinted towards it. When they drew close, Tito pulled urgently on India's arm. 'Miss Bentley,' he gasped. 'The bugs . . . Look!' A river of bugs was swarming from the hole made by Orpheus and spreading rapidly across the floor.

'Don't stop,' panted India, 'or they'll have us for lunch.' She grabbed Tito by the hand, and they jumped on to the footplate, yelling and hammering on the steel hatch for attention.

'They can't hear us, Miss Bentley.'

India pressed an ear to the metal. 'Can you hear something?'

'It sounds like an argument,' said Tito.

Over the grumbling engines they could hear three sets of raised voices inside the vehicle. India pulled out the professor's gun and used it to hammer on the door. This time the voices stopped and the door swung open. The startled faces of Verity, Cael and Sid peered out.

'India!' Verity threw her arms around India and dragged her into the narrow cabin. 'Damn it, I swear you're going to give me a heart attack one of these days. I know you're indestructible but I'm not. And as for you . . .' She turned to Tito, who was being helped through the hatch by Cael. 'The last I heard, you'd been eaten by a sea monster.'

Tito grinned broadly but refused to be hugged, and insisted on formally shaking hands with everyone. India threw her arms around Sid's neck.

'Sid! I'm so glad you're alive.'

He winced and scowled as she hugged him. 'Yeah, well, get over it. I could be back to being dead in no time.'

An awful thought occurred to India. 'Sid, I'm so sorry, but . . . Crackers . . . I mean, she flew away. I tried to call her back but she wouldn't come.' She saw a momentary stab of pain the boy's eyes. Then it was gone and the hard look returned.

'Yeah, well, who cares about a dumb bird anyway?' He turned back to the controls and wouldn't look at her again.

'Where's the professor, India?' asked Cael. 'Isn't he with you?'

'He didn't get away,' said India, suddenly filled with remorse that they had left him behind on the pyramid. 'He was shot and I think Lady Fang may have taken him prisoner . . .'

Sid's expression had turned black at the news. 'You *think*?,' he snapped. 'Well, he ain't staying her prisoner. We're going back to rescue him, and no arguments.'

'Look, Sid—' began Verity.

'I said no arguments!'

Cael was looking out of the cabin door. 'Holy mother of

all rig fairies,' he gasped when he saw the spaceship. 'What *is* that?'

Verity peered disbelievingly into the gloom, 'Is that a . . .' She ran out of words to describe what she was seeing.

'It's a long story,' said India. 'But right now those bugs are everywhere. We need to move before we get eaten alive.'

'Hang on a minute,' Cael spluttered, catching sight of the piles of treasure gleaming softly in the darkness. 'Is that *gold*?'

'Damn it!' said Sid, kicking away a bug with the toe of his boot. 'They're going to eat the dang machine. Let's git!'

'But . . . the gold,' spluttered Cael. 'Just give me five minutes out there!'

'If I give you five minutes out there you'll be coming back with no legs,' snapped Sid as he reached for the door. 'We need to get our priorities straight and first up is getting out of this damned pyramid!' Cael groaned as the hatch slammed shut.

'Strap yourselves in,' yelled Sid as he gunned the engines. 'This might be a bit uncomfortable.' He yanked on the levers and Orpheus began to rattle as though it might shake itself apart.

'W-w-what's h-h-happening?' asked India in a juddery voice.

'Engaging the drill blades,' said Sid. Through the windscreen India saw the pointed nose of Orpheus begin to turn like a giant screw. Sid aimed the vehicle at the inside wall of the pyramid while Verity and Cael pressed themselves against the rear window.

Orpheus hit the stone wall with a crash that sent India sprawling. As the steel blades bit into the heavy blocks, the juddering and vibrating increased. Broken rock and gravel clattered against the toughened glass windscreen and two rows of steel claws began to scoop away the debris and hurl it out behind them like a burrowing mole.

'H-h-how m-m-much l-l-longer?' shouted India after they had been going for a few minutes.

'W-w-we're going as f-f-fast as we c-c-can,' Sid yelled back, 'b-b-but I reck-kon we g-g-got some of them b-b-bugs in the air v-v-vents.'

It was clear that Orpheus was labouring heavily now. The engine coughed and spluttered, and a metallic, grating noise reverberated through the cabin like a hundred sets of fingernails being dragged along a blackboard. Just when India felt sure the machine would stutter and die, they burst through the outer wall of the pyramid and Orpheus crashed back to a horizontal position, wheezing like a sick patient. Pale light began to filter through the dust and grime on the windscreen.

'We're back in the city,' said Verity. 'Nice going, Sid!'

'Please remember to tip your driver,' drawled Sid as he shut down the engines. Silence filled the cabin and only the faint tinking of the engine could be heard as the hot metal began to cool. Sid kicked open the hatch and jumped out to inspect the damage. One by one, the others followed, stretching cramped muscles and taking stock of where they were.

Orpheus had created a ragged hole in the base of the pyramid, scattering perfectly cut stones in a wide circle of debris. The crystal veins running through the rock had returned to a dead, grey colour and the spectacular astronomical display had disappeared. There was no sign of Lady Fang. The roof of the volcano remained open, however, and they looked up hungrily at the tiny, visible patch of night sky five hundred feet overhead.

'Fang's gone,' growled Sid, swatting the last of the bugs from the vehicle and crushing them beneath his boot. 'She must have taken the professor with her.'

'And the crystal,' said India.

'Then our priority is to get out of here,' said Verity. 'The volcano is becoming unstable and we need to make some distance before we become part of the geological record.'

'But we can't leave now,' cried India. 'Calculus said we had to return the Heliotrope to the pyramid or terrible things would happen.'

'Calculus?' said Verity with a sigh. 'What are you talking about, India?'

India took a deep breath and blurted out their story, interrupted at frequent intervals by Tito. She told them about the spiked pit, showed them Sir Vivian's map and recounted the incredible discoveries they had made inside the pyramid. When India described how Tito had destroyed the Hellhound, the boy flushed with pride.

When she had finished talking, she looked expectantly at the faces of Verity, Cael and Sid, but was met only with expressions of bafflement.

'A spaceship, India?' said Verity eventually. 'I don't know *what* that thing was in there – but I don't believe it's a spaceship.'

India was startled. It was not the reaction she had been expecting. 'But it's true!' she cried. 'Tito and I went inside it. And Calculus said we have to return the crystal before the ship can take off.'

'It is true, Mrs Brown,' piped up Tito. 'I too saw Mr Calculus and spoke with him.'

'A spaceship and a dead robot?' muttered Sid. 'You have got to be kidding me.'

'OK, OK,' said Verity, holding up her hands in submission. 'Let's just say for a moment that there really is a twelve-thousand-year-old spaceship in there. How do you know you were really talking to Calculus?'

'What do you mean?'

'You said it yourself, India,' said Verity. 'The ship, if that's what it is, is under the control of the Machine Mind. The same devious and dangerous Mind we met at Ironheart. Don't you think they might have created an image of Calculus just to manipulate you into doing what they want?'

India was lost for words. She had been bursting to tell Verity the good news about Calculus but now she felt like an overexcited child at a birthday party who has just been told to calm down. 'I-it wasn't like that,' she stammered. 'I *know* it was Calc, I talked to him!' She wiped away an angry tear. 'At least let's see if we can find Lady Fang. We might be able to persuade her to give up the stone.'

'Don't be so naive, India,' said Verity. 'Fang's a ruthless killer. I'm not about to put all of our lives at risk on the word of—'

'Of a child?' said India. 'Was that what you were going to say?'

There was an awkward silence. Cael looked at his feet while Sid sat on the caterpillar tracks, engrossed in rebinding his broken fingers together with a piece of his shirt.

'All right then,' said Verity eventually. 'You want the truth? For the last year I've watched you grieving for Calculus. I've seen how you think about him all the time and I've heard the way you talk about him. When you got it into your head that he was still alive I tried to persuade you it wasn't real but you wouldn't listen. So I thought it might be good for you to follow it through and to see, once and for all, that he's really gone. But I can see now that it was a bad idea and I'm sorry.'

India felt like the world was falling away beneath her. 'You were *humouring* me?' she said weakly. 'You didn't think I was old enough to be told what you really thought, just like you didn't think I was old enough to have a gun. Well, I've got news for you. I was talking to Calculus not half an hour ago and if I hadn't had this –' she pulled out the professor's gun and waved it in the air – 'then Tito and I would both be dead by now.'

'None of this matters more'n a rigger's curse,' growled Sid, sliding off the tracks. 'Fang's gone. She's taken the professor and the stone and she's most likely halfway back to the coast by now, and, in case anyone hadn't noticed, them bugs are right behind us. So I'm gonna find a way out of this volcano and then I'm gonna go after Fang and rescue the professor – and you lot can either come with me or you can stay here and get eaten.'

The bugs were indeed right behind them. They were now pouring from the hole in the pyramid like a black river.

'We don't have time to argue,' said Verity. 'Everybody get back in, we're going to find the nearest tunnel out of this troll-cave.'

Nobody spoke as they clambered back on board Orpheus. India sat in the corner and glowered at the back of Verity's head while she and Cael pored over Sir Vivian's map and Sid fired up the engines.

'Here,' said Verity, jabbing a finger down on the map. 'It looks like there's a side vent in the volcano on the western side of the city. With luck it will take us to the surface. Straight ahead, Sid.'

Sid pushed forward on the drive levers. Orpheus gave a lurch and began making laboured, grinding noises. They were barely moving.

'We're losing oil pressure,' said Sid, tapping a gauge that was flickering dangerously in the red. 'Reckon we got some of them bugs in the manifolds. We need to lose some weight or we're never going to make it.'

'Start shedding the excess baggage,' said Verity. 'We can start with these.' She went to the gun rack at the back of the vehicle and began pulling down the heavy blunderbusses that looked like instruments from a bizarre orchestra.

Cael opened the hatch and threw out the first armful of weapons, which crashed to the ground outside. As soon as the door was opened they could see what had been causing the problems. The outside of Orpheus was now overrun with bugs. They crawled over the metal surfaces, attacking the engine covers, creeping into the air vents and being crushed beneath the metal tracks.

'Keep them out of the cabin,' yelled Sid. 'Or we'll all be roach food.'

Tito picked up a large spanner from the rack and began to hammer at the bugs that strayed inside the doorway while India helped Cael to pull the professor's rocket pack off the wall. 'Well, I won't be sorry to see the last of this walking bomb,' he said as they flung it from the open doorway.

Lightening their load seemed to have done the trick. Orpheus picked up speed as they rattled across one of the bridges to the main part of the city. While Verity shouted instructions, Sid wove the iron vehicle through the warren of narrow streets, until they arrived at the edge of the city where the buildings met the sheer cavern walls.

'There should be a volcanic vent right here,' said Verity, scanning the map.

'What about over there?' said Cael. Nearby was a frozen waterfall which was now melting rapidly. 'It could be behind there.'

'Only one way to find out,' said Sid. He re-engaged the drill once more, which made screechy, metal-on-metal noises. The icy sculpture shattered easily and they smashed their way through to uncover a narrow tunnel.

Sid manoeuvred the vehicle carefully into the cavity. The ground was rough and uneven and the vehicle's forward beams picked out walls lined with rocky teeth, like the mouth of some primeval creature.

'We're in the vent,' said Verity. 'Let's hope there haven't been any cave-ins since Sir Vivian drew his map.'

Progress through the pipe was slow. Orpheus was on its last legs now: the engine was making a noise like a bucket of nails in a cement mixer, and thick black smoke billowed from beneath the engine cover. When they reached a particularly steep part of the tunnel, a deep metallic fracturing came from somewhere inside the machine and they ground to a halt.

They climbed out to inspect the damage but it was clear that Orpheus was beyond any attempt at repair. The outer skin of the vehicle was pockmarked and ravaged by bugs and one of its steel tracks had unravelled in the tunnel behind them. Oily flames licked around the engine bay and sticky black fluids poured from underneath. Orpheus looked like a giant beast that had been fatally speared and was now bleeding to death before their eyes.

'Now what?' said Cael. 'We're not going to get very far without transport.'

A colossal boom came from the cavern behind them, followed by a thunderous shaking, as if a giant were attacking the very roots of the mountain.

'We're running out of time,' said Verity. 'Let's see what's up ahead and then decide what to do. Perhaps the weather outside will be good enough for us to walk to the research station. We could try and get one of their vehicles working.'

They continued along the tunnel, with India bringing up the rear, each step feeling like a betrayal of what Calculus had entrusted her to do. The tunnel emerged in a broad-mouthed cave that opened on to the slopes of the mountain and their first proper view of the outside for nearly twenty-four hours.

If they had been hoping for a break in the weather they were disappointed. A howling blizzard of terrifying ferocity raged outside the cave. Ice, sleet and snow raced horizontally past the entrance, threatening to tear the skin from anyone who ventured out in it. It was impossible to see more than a few feet and, even in the relative shelter of the cave, the wind penetrated their clothes like steel knives.

'So much for the escape plan,' said Cael. 'It would be suicide to try and walk anywhere in this.'

'And from the sound of the volcano it will be certain death if we stay,' said Verity grimly.

27 CAT'S CRADLE

They ransacked the bones of Orpheus and turned out their bags, looking for anything that might improve their chances of survival. But the assortment of items they collected on the floor of the cave was a sorry affair.

The most useful pieces of equipment were the two sets of cold-weather gear that Cael found in a locker in the back of the vehicle. Apart from that they had one of the professor's handguns, some climbing rope, three torches, a compass and some dried meat. It was not much.

'No one can go outside in this weather without the right clothing,' said Cael. 'They'd be dead before they got off the mountain.'

'But I don't think this mountain is going to be here for much longer, Mr O'Hanlon,' said Tito, glancing into the tunnel behind him. Despite the deep cold outside, the air inside the cave had become distinctly hot.

'The research station is less than ten miles from here,'

said Verity. 'Cael and I will take the cold-weather gear and head there. We'll get one of the ice tractors working and come back for you. We should be able to do the round trip in less than four hours.'

'If you don't freeze to death on the way,' said Sid. 'And if you can get a five-year-old tractor to work. And if the volcano doesn't blow its stack in the meantime. That's a lot of "ifs" for one sentence.'

'Well, I don't hear any better ideas,' snapped Verity, shrugging on a padded jacket.

'Why do *you* have to be the one to go?' said India. She knew there were at least a dozen good reasons, but somehow it felt good to be challenging Verity.

'You know why,' said Verity. 'You're not—'

'Old enough?' spat India.

'Experienced enough,' said Verity firmly. 'This weather is a killer if you don't know what you're doing.' India folded her arms sulkily while Verity stepped up to the mouth of the cave and peered anxiously into the maelstrom.

'Four hours,' she shouted over the noise of the storm. 'Just sit tight until then.' She gave India a look that was both determined and slightly sad at the same time. Then she and Cael stepped from the cave and were immediately swallowed up by the storm.

No sooner had they left than India was filled with a horror that she might not see either of them again. She ran to the cave entrance and called after Verity but the wind whipped away her voice and the suffocating snow was so thick that she could not see six feet in front of her. Verity had gone and the time for apologies had passed.

She sat down heavily next to Tito who, as usual, appeared quite calm. Sid too seemed unperturbed by events and was pressing his ear to the wall at the back of the cave.

'Come and listen,' he said after a while. 'What do you think this is?'

India and Tito both pressed their ears to the rock. There was the faintest vibration through the rock. 'It's an engine,' said Tito excitedly.

'Yeah,' said Sid. 'Diesel engines, three of them, somewhere inside the cavern. It must mean that Fang is still here – and so is the professor.' He returned to their supplies and slung the climbing rope across his shoulders.

'What are you doing?' said India, fearing she already knew the answer.

'The professor treated me better'n anyone did before or since,' he said. 'And I ain't leavin' him in the clutches of that witch.' He pointed towards the roof of the cave. 'There's another tunnel up there and I think it leads back into the main cavern. I'm going to climb up and take a look.' He checked the chambers in his pistol.

'Mrs Brown said we should wait here,' said Tito.

'Since when do I need Verity Brown's permission to do anything?' said Sid, holstering the gun. He swivelled his pale eyes on India. 'Are you coming or are you going to do what you're told, like a good girl?'

India hesitated. 'But Verity will be expecting—'

'Pah!' Sid turned away and began to climb. 'Stay here then. I'm sure Mrs Brown'll give you a great report card at the end of term.'

India felt her face flush. 'Wait!' she said. 'I'm coming.'

'Then I must come too,' said Tito.

'Tito, I don't think this is a good idea . . .' began India.

'The Great Teacher said friends do not abandon other friends, Miss Bentley,' said Tito, firmly. 'Mr Sid must go after the professor, and you must go after Mr Sid, therefore I must go after you.'

'Great,' said Sid. 'Now I got a whole school outing to contend with. OK, everyone follow me and keep your mouths shut.'

At the back of the cave they found a fissure in the rock that led upward, like a narrow chimney. Sid jammed his back against one side and his feet against the other as he climbed. Almost immediately he dropped to the ground and grimaced, clutching his ribs.

'Sid, are you OK?' said India. 'Maybe you shouldn't do this right now. You were beaten up pretty badly—'

'Shut the hell up!' Sid whirled on her, making India recoil. 'I told you not to try and stop me, India Bentley. Professor Moon's the only person who ever gave a damn about me and I'm going to rescue him. So either help me or go to hell.' Hot tears streamed down Sid's face and he wiped them away angrily with the back of his sleeve.

'We'll help you, Sid,' said India gently. She placed a hand on his arm. 'We'll rescue the professor together.'

'Whatever it takes, Mr Sid,' added Tito seriously. 'We will be fearless in the face of Lady Fang.'

Sid stared incredulously at Tito for a moment and then laughed in a jerky sort of way as he wiped away the last of his tears. 'Holy mother of all riggers,' he gasped. 'Ain't we the sorriest rescue party you ever saw?'

He straightened himself up and then gave them both a nod. 'All right then, let's go. But keep up, I don't go back for stragglers.' He started up the rock face with renewed energy, climbing like a cat and feeling for tiny handholds in spite of his broken finger. India and Tito did their best to keep up, not daring to complain.

After a half an hour of climbing, India ventured a look down and wished she hadn't. When she looked up again, Sid had disappeared from view. She cupped a hand to her mouth and shouted, and Sid's angry face immediately appeared over the ledge above her. 'Shut yer hollerin' and get up here,' he hissed, before disappearing again.

'I have noticed,' said Tito in a whisper, 'that Mr Sid seems to carry a lot of anger. Perhaps he would benefit from some meditation.'

'I'm not sure Sid is the meditating type,' said India. 'Come on, let's catch up.'

They found Sid crouching in the mouth of another small cave. When they looked out, India gasped at the sight. The cave was high up inside the main pipe of the volcano with a panoramic view of the city and the lake several hundred feet below. 'It's beautiful,' she said.

'Look at the lake,' said Tito in a hushed voice. The lake around the pyramid had been replaced by boiling yellow mud that burped great, sulphurous bubbles. Even at this height, the heat rising from the city was intense and the fumes made their eyes burn.

'Over there,' said Sid, pointing urgently. 'It's Fang – look!' Just below the cave was a rough track, wide enough for a single vehicle. It ran around the inside of the volcanic pipe like a helter-skelter, rising up to the lip of the crater. A convoy of three half-track vehicles were parked in a row, heavily laden with supplies, and several guards lounged against them, smoking quietly.

'So that's how she got in,' said India. 'She came down the inside of the volcano. But why are they waiting around? I thought they'd be gone by now.'

'That's why,' said Sid. A little higher up, a gap in the track was spanned by another copper-coloured bridge, supported by a fine network of cables. A small team was making repairs with a welding torch that was sending brilliant blue sparks cascading into the cavern below.

'The tremors must have damaged the bridge,' said Tito in a whisper. 'Lady Fang is trapped in here.'

'That won't hold her up for long,' said Sid. 'As soon as they've repaired the bridge they'll drive straight out of here with the professor.' As he spoke, Lady Fang appeared around the side of the truck with one of the guards, and they promptly ducked down to avoid being seen. Fang still looked wild-eyed and manic.

'The bridge is fixed, my lady,' the guard was saying. 'But I don't trust the welds on this strange metal. We should only cross one truck at a time.' Fang waved him aside impatiently.

'We're not going anywhere until I get some answers,' she said. 'Get that old buffoon out here now!' Two guards hurried to the last vehicle in the convoy. One of them removed a small wooden crate from the driver's cabin while the other hauled a bloodied and dishevelled figure from the back.

'It's the professor,' hissed Sid. 'She's got him trussed up like a chicken.'

The professor was dragged over to Fang and pushed to his knees. He was in a bad way. His hands were bound and the front of his shirt was soaked in blood. At a nod from Fang, the first guard opened the lid of the crate and a thousand tiny points of crystal light lit up their faces.

'It's the crystal,' hissed Tito.

Lady Fang leaned over until her face was level with Professor Moon's. 'Why won't it work for me?' she yelled.

The professor looked at her with tired eyes. 'Do you mean the Heliotrope?' he said calmly.

'Yes, idiot,' yelled Fang. 'It's meant to convert sunlight into energy, isn't it?' She picked up the crystal from the crate and held it up towards the daylight. The storm had abated and the first rays of a weak morning sun were filtering into the volcano but there was no perceptible change in the crystal. She tossed it back into the crate angrily. 'Nothing,' she hissed. 'Why doesn't it work?'

The professor began to laugh and then lapsed into a fit of coughing. 'Haven't you been paying attention, Fang?' he said. 'The Heliotrope is a sophisticated piece of Elder technology. It will only work in the presence of a Soul Voyager.'

'The girl?' growled Fang.

'Yes, and you let her escape. Without her, the Heliotrope is little more than a Christmas decoration and you will grow old and die like the rest of us.' He began laughing again until one of the guards clubbed him with the butt of his gun and he fell to the floor. Sid started from his hiding place and had to be restrained by Tito and India.

As the guards bundled the professor back into the truck, Fang screamed at the top of her voice: 'Maximus! Where are you?'

The android stepped from the truck.

'What's happened to that damned Hellhound? It should have found the girl by now.' Maximus bowed stiffly.

'*It hass been out of contact for the lassst two hourss*,' he hissed.

'Then go after it,' barked Fang. 'Find the girl and bring her back. I don't care if you have to kill all of her companions – just make sure you fetch her alive.'

Maximus bowed again and withdrew.

'My lady,' said the first guard. 'It's too dangerous to wait here. The men are becoming restless.'

'We wait until Maximus returns with the girl, Commander,' said Fang. 'If anyone disagrees, send them to me.'

The commander gulped visibly. 'Yes, my lady,' he said.

'But perhaps I could at least move the supply trucks to the other side of the bridge. The dynamite is beginning to degrade in the heat.'

Fang waved him away. 'Fine,' she snapped. 'We'll take them up to the crater rim and wait there.'

The commander looked relieved and began to bark instructions to his men. 'Move them across in single file; I don't trust those new welds.' The lead truck revved its engine and trundled slowly across the bridge while the commander climbed into the second truck with Lady Fang.

'Two-Buck!' he called to the driver of the last vehicle. 'Wait here until we're across and then follow on.' Behind the windscreen Two-Buck Tim gave a thumbs-up and grinned a mouth full of tombstone teeth.

'Now's our chance,' said Sid urgently as the second truck started out across the bridge. 'There's no one in that last truck except the professor and the driver. Everyone else is on the far side of the bridge.' He pulled out his pistol, holding it awkwardly in his bandaged fingers. 'You still got that hand-cannon?' he said. India nodded. 'You ever shoot anyone before?'

She licked her lips. Her mouth suddenly seemed too dry to speak. 'I shot the Hellhound,' she said.

'I don't mean a machine,' said Sid. His eyes bored into hers, searching for something. 'I mean, did you ever shoot a real person, made of blood and muscle?' India shook her head.

'Well listen up,' said Sid. 'We're gonna rescue the

professor and you may have to shoot someone pretty soon.' He outlined his plan to tackle the driver but India found it hard to listen. A rushing noise had filled her ears and her heart thumped louder and louder as though it wanted no part of this.

'. . . and we'll get the professor into the tunnels before anyone realizes he's gone.' Sid turned his attention back to the truck.

'Sid, I can't do this,' she blurted suddenly. She felt hot and sweaty, and sure she would be sick. Sid's eyes narrowed.

'Now listen up,' he said. 'I said you wasn't a gun person; well, now's the time to prove me wrong. If someone comes at you, you aim for the centre line and you shoot straight. You got that?' India nodded dumbly.

'This will be splendid!' said Tito brightly. 'We will be like the three mountaineers!'

India stared at Tito's happy expression and suppressed a hysterical giggle. 'It's *musketeers*, Tito,' she said automatically. 'Three *musketeers*. And I'm sorry, but you can't come with us. It's too dangerous and you're too—'

'Too young, Miss Bentley?' said Tito, raising an eyebrow. 'Is that not the same argument you were just having with Mrs Brown?'

India's mouth opened and shut.

'I . . . er, well maybe she had a point after all,' India muttered. 'I just want you to be safe, that's all.'

'Then at least allow me to keep watch?' said Tito

earnestly. 'I will warn you if any of Lady Fang's men approach. Please?'

India blew out her cheeks and nodded.

'Great,' said Sid, rolling his eyes. 'Now that Mighty Monk's on guard I feel safer already. Come on, enough talk, let's move.'

They scrambled from their hiding place and moved as silently as possible over the loose rock. Sid approached the parked truck from the rear, so that they could not be seen from the bridge. He yanked open the driver's door, catching a startled Two-Buck in the act of picking his nose. Sid dragged him from the cab, and shoved the end of the pistol up his left nostril.

'Don't kill him!' said India suddenly.

'What?' spluttered Sid. 'Well, why the hell not?'

Two-Buck's eyes flicked nervously between Sid and India.

'I don't know,' said India, flustered. 'But I know him. He's just a bit . . . pathetic.'

Two-Buck nodded as eagerly as he could manage with the end of a gun up his nose.

'Oh yes. I'm damned pathetic, me,' he babbled. 'You won't ever find anyone this pathetic – no, sir.'

'Shut up!' snapped Sid. He gave India an exasperated look and sighed. 'Damn it, I must be going soft. All right!' he said, turning back to Two-Buck. 'Prove to me you're worth keeping alive. Tell me how to take that bridge out.'

Two-Buck looked at him with startled eyes. 'W-what?'

Sid shoved the gun barrel further up Two-Buck's nostril. 'The *bridge*. We're on one side; your friends are on the other. If we take out the bridge they can't follow us.'

Two-Buck blinked quickly. 'Lady Fang is going to blow up the bridge as soon as we're across,' he said. 'The lead truck is full of dynamite, but there's still one case in the back of this one. Very degraded,' he said seriously, 'very dangerous.'

'My favourite kind,' said Sid. 'OK, Mr Pathetic, keep out of sight of the other trucks and start running. If you try to warn any of your friends we're here I'll come after you personally, and I eat pathetic things for breakfast.' He pulled the gun away. 'Now git!'

Two-Buck did not need telling twice. Staying out of sight behind the larger rocks, he began a panicked scramble up the loose scree towards the lip of the crater.

Sid and India went to the back of the truck and opened the canvas flaps. The professor lay in a crumpled heap, surrounded by crates of supplies.

'It's OK, Professor,' said Sid, jumping inside. 'Me and India have come to get you out.'

'Sidney, my boy,' said the professor, turning his head weakly. His breath came in harsh, ragged gasps, as though the threads of his life were strained to breaking point.

'And Miss Bentley, too. You should not be here, Lady Fang is looking for you, she will stop at nothing—'

'We know,' said Sid. 'Quiet now.'

Despite the adrenalin coursing through her veins, India watched in amazement as Sid cradled the professor's head and gently released his bonds. She handed Sid her water bottle and watched as he held it up for the professor to drink. She had never imagined Sid to be capable of such tenderness.

'What now?' she asked. 'They'll be back to see why this truck isn't moving in a few minutes.'

Sid didn't answer. He scanned the crates piled high in the truck until he found the one he was looking for.

'Dynamite!' He helped the professor to sit up, and then reached down a small wooden crate with rope handles and the words 'High Explosive' stencilled on the side. He levered off the top and pulled away a sheet of greaseproof paper to reveal neat rows of tightly wrapped cylinders. A layer of fine crystalline powder clung to the outside of each one.

'He was right,' muttered Sid. 'This stuff is sweating nitroglycerine. The slightest knock could set it off.' He replaced the lid and tucked the box under his arm. 'I'll plant this down by the bridge supports. Then we'll back off to a safe distance and set it off with a gunshot. By the time Fang realizes what happened, the bridge will be at the bottom of the crater.'

'Then what?' said India.

'We take the truck and use the map to find another way out. We'll head for the research station, see if we can catch up with Mrs Brown, and then make for the coast.'

'Calculus said we have to return the Heliotrope to the pyramid,' said India determinedly. 'I'm not leaving until we do.'

Sid shook his head. 'We ain't got time, we need to—'

'Professor,' said India, cutting across Sid. 'When we were underneath the pyramid I spoke to the Machine Mind. It told me we have to return the crystal before it's too late or there'll be an explosion that could put the whole world in danger. Where is the Heliotrope?'

The professor raised his head and focused on India. 'You spoke to the Elders?' he croaked. His voice was paper thin and he gasped for breath between words.

'I talked to the machine they left behind.'

'Then it is true! This really is the last resting place of the Elder Race.' He sank back to the floor. 'My life's work has not been in vain!' He closed his eyes.

'Professor, we need to return that crystal! It's not ours to keep, the Long Lives . . . the Elders still *need* it.'

'Leave him be,' snapped Sid. 'Can't you see he's hurt?'

'Hush now, Sidney.' The professor placed a hand gently on Sid's. 'India is right. The crystal is not ours to keep. I was a fool to think I could control its power. Look over there.'

India found the box in the corner and pulled off the lid. The inside of the truck lit up with a faint blue glow.

'I don't care about no crystal,' said Sid as he smoothed the professor's blood-stained hair. 'But I care what happens to you. I gotta go and blow that bridge before they find us here, but I'll be right back.'

Sid tucked the box of dynamite beneath his arm and jumped from the back of the truck, pulling the flap closed behind him. He turned away from the truck just in time to see a matt-black shadow lunge at him with lightning speed.

*

Inside the truck, India waited with the professor. She fed him some more water from the bottle and wondered what was keeping Sid. Just as she was thinking of going outside to look for him, she heard a familiar voice that made a cold shiver run down her spine.

'India Bentley,' called Fang's voice. 'I have your friends out here with me. Come out if you value their lives!'

India looked aghast at the professor.

'Don't go out there, India,' he whispered. 'Don't fall into Fang's clutches. She'll make a puppet of you like she did with me.'

India bit her lip. 'I'm no one's puppet,' she said. 'But if my friends are in trouble I have to help them.' She picked up the professor's gun and checked the chambers; there was only one bullet left.

'No!' he said quickly. 'Don't take a gun out there. They'll shoot you down where you stand.' He raised a hand to stop her but it fell back ineffectually.

'Don't worry, Professor. I'll just take a quick look, I promise,' she lied.

The scene outside the truck chilled her to the core. Fang was standing in the centre of the bridge with her hands folded into her sleeves. Sid was on the ground and appeared to have taken a beating. Maximus stood over Sid, while simultaneously dangling Tito over the edge of the bridge with one hand. The monk's eyes were wild with terror and his legs bicycled feebly in the empty air.

'Nice of you to join us, Miss Bentley,' said Fang with a twisted smile.

'Tito hasn't done you any harm,' said India, holding the gun out in front of her. 'Let him go.'

'A bad choice of words, India,' said Fang. 'I might decide to take you literally.' Maximus began to shake Tito so vigorously that he squealed in terror and one of his shoes fell off, tumbling end over end as it dropped into the cavern.

India pointed the gun at Fang. 'Put him down – *safely*,' she shouted. 'I'm warning you. Do it or I'll—'

'No you won't,' interrupted Fang. 'For one thing, Maximus will drop your monk friend into the volcano, and for another I have bathed in the light of the Heliotrope. I cannot be harmed by you or your comical weapon.' She smiled thinly. 'Besides, India, true cruelty is an art form and you just don't have what it takes. You can wave that gun around all you like, but we both know you're not going to use it.'

'India, don't give her nothing,' yelled Sid, earning a kick in the ribs from Maximus.

'Stop!' cried India. 'Please stop hurting my friends! I'll do whatever you want.'

Fang smiled and gave another nod to Maximus. The android lifted Tito back over the barrier and set him down next to Sid. India was vaguely aware of Lady Fang's men watching and waiting on the far side of the bridge.

'It appears that the crystal does not work without the services of a Soul Voyager,' said Fang. 'Soon I will need to bathe in its light again and when I do I will need you to make it work for me. So here is my proposal. I will let your friends live, including Verity Brown and Cael O'Hanlon. In return you will work for me as my personal Soul Voyager.'

'You mean . . . forever?' said India.

'It's a bargain, India,' purred Fang. 'The lives of five people in exchange for your own. Surely you don't think you're worth more than that?'

India blinked at Fang and pondered the awful prospect of living as her slave.

'Too slow deciding,' said Fang, shaking her head. 'Maximus, kill the boy.'

'Wait!' cried India. She dropped the gun to the ground with a clatter. 'I'll do it. I'll come to Sing City and work for you.'

'Miss Bentley,' cried Tito. 'You can't become Lady Fang's slave. You—'

'Silence,' shouted Lady Fang, striking Tito across the face. 'We have a deal, Miss Bentley.' She turned to Sid and Tito. 'You can both leave now, but not this way. The dynamite will take care of the bridge and you can take your chances inside the volcano.'

'That's not fair,' cried India. 'They'll be killed if they can't find another way out.'

'You should have thought of that before you struck a deal,' hissed Fang. 'Now come with me.'

Sid spat blood on the ground and then spoke in a scathing voice. 'This is exactly why I said you weren't a gun person, India,' he said. 'You finally got that gun you wanted, but you're too damn scared to use it!'

'Sid, I'm sorry—' she began, but Sid hadn't finished.

'It's like I said before, India,' he said, holding her gaze. 'There's only one way you could ever hit something. You know what I'm saying?'

India frowned and looked curiously at Sid. The way he was looking at her made her think there was something else beneath his words. 'Come along, Miss Bentley,' said Fang. 'I haven't got all day.'

India's frown deepened. 'The only way I could ever hit something . . .' she murmured. She looked at the gun and then back at Sid.

Moving very slowly, Sid linked one of his arms around a bridge support and with his free hand he reached out and grasped the scruff of Tito's jacket. Then he nodded imperceptibly and, in that moment, India knew exactly what she must do.

Time slowed down and became drawn out like toffee.

She stooped and picked up the gun. The smile vanished from Fang's face as India raised the pistol and aimed it at the covered truck parked on the far side of the bridge. The red-stencilled boxes were clearly visible, stacked behind its canvas flaps.

'The only way I could ever hit something,' she said out loud, 'is if it was the size of a truck and standing still.'

She pulled the trigger.

Time speeded up like a freight train running full tilt into the buffers.

The truck exploded in a ball of flame, hurling flaming wreckage across the bridge and sending out a shockwave that punched everything out of its path. A blast of heat and noise washed over them, throwing India backwards into the dirt.

When she opened her eyes, the view was fogged by smoky blue clouds and her ears were ringing. She was sitting on the edge of a cliff, looking down into the city below. The bridge was gone, torn from its supports and scattered into the cavern.

The two lead trucks had been completely destroyed, leaving behind only their wheels and some burning pieces of metal. She could not see the truck with the professor, nor was there any sign of Sid and Tito. When she peered over the edge of the path, her stomach lurched.

The cables that had supported the bridge so delicately had collapsed in a tangled mess and were now slung, like a poorly made cat's cradle, across the gap. Hanging, nose down in the midst of the tangled mess was the professor's truck, suspended by a knot of cables that strained and creaked under its weight.

'India, we're over here.' On the far side of the gap she saw Sid and Tito, clinging to another tangle of cables and torn metal.

'Thank goodness you're alive!' she cried. 'Where's Lady Fang, and Maximus?'

'The android went over the edge in the blast,' called Sid. 'I reckon Fang bought it the same way. Can you see the professor from there?' India looked at the truck hanging below her, but there was no sign of life. She shook her head.

'Can you climb down to the truck?' yelled Sid.

India swallowed hard. The truck swayed slowly back and forth, like a child's swing, hundreds of feet above the city. 'I don't think I can, Sid,' she said nervously. 'It's too high, I—'

'Just do it, India,' he snapped. 'Those cables could give way at any second.' He began to inch his way along the thickest cable that hung across the divide. India could see that it would take Sid several minutes to reach the truck from where he was and that it might easily fall before then, taking the professor with it. She had no choice but to climb down and help him.

The thought of what she was about to do made her legs go weak. She took a long slow breath, trying to quell the rising panic. Then, without looking down, she reached out over the ledge and grasped the cable nearest to her. It was thick and heavy and attached to several twisted pieces of metal that had once been part of the bridge.

'Please be careful, Miss Bentley,' called out Tito.

She jumped out and wrapped her legs around the steel cable, which swung like a jungle vine. For a moment she thought she might lose her grip out of pure fear. Then, moving slowly and gripping with the rubber soles of her boots, she began to climb down to the truck. She tried to ignore the creaking of the cable and focused on placing one hand carefully after another. After several painful minutes she lowered herself gently on to the tailgate of the truck and peered through the canvas flaps.

The crates and boxes had all slid to the front of the truck where they lay in a broken pile. She could see the professor lying among the wreckage, eyes closed and breathing heavily. 'I can see him,' she called to Sid. 'He's unconscious.'

Sid was still some distance away, inching his way slowly along the cables. 'You've got to get in there and help him before the cables give out,' he yelled back.

India took a deep breath and lowered herself gently into the truck, feeling it lurch sickeningly downward with the extra weight. As she pulled away the broken boxes that had fallen on the professor, his eyelids flickered and opened.

'It's all right, Professor,' she said, as gently as she could manage. 'We're going to get you out.'

'No!' He grasped feebly at her arm. 'You can't save me, India, I'm done for. You must return the Heliotrope to the pyramid before it's too late.' He pointed to the blue-white crystal lying among broken crates.

'We can save you *and* the crystal,' she said, trying to lift his head. 'There's still time.'

'There isn't,' he gasped. 'The crystal, India! At all costs save the crystal.' He slumped back and closed his eyes. India looked around and found a canvas tool bag in the corner which she emptied out, placing the crystal carefully inside.

'What's happening in there? Is the professor all right?' Sid was peering down at them from the tailgate and looking anxiously at Professor Moon.

'Sidney, my boy,' said the professor in a hoarse whisper, squinting at the light. 'Take the crystal to safety and then come back and help India.' Sid looked dubiously at the heavy bag in India's hand.

'We ain't got time for that, Professor,' he said. 'This truck's headed for the bottom of the crater at any second.'

'Do it now, Sidney!' barked the professor, some of his old authority returning. Sid flinched and then reluctantly reached down to take the bag from India.

'I'll be right back for you both as soon as I've got this up top,' he said. He turned away and began to shin back up the tangled mess of cable and metal towards the cliff path.

India tried to help the professor to a sitting position. 'Listen carefully,' he gasped. 'I want you to take care of Sid for me when I am gone. He is a good young man, but he has had a savage start to life. I fear my death may hit him hard and send him back to his old ways.'

'Professor don't talk like that—'

'Promise me!' The professor coughed violently and a thin trickle of blood ran from his mouth. 'Don't let him be consumed by his anger.'

India nodded gently. 'I promise,' she said. 'Now let's get you—'

She stopped in mid-sentence as five claw-like blades suddenly punched through the canvas wall of the truck. They ripped their way down the awning and the rabid face of Lady Fang appeared. Her lips were pulled back in a hideous grin and the veins on her face and neck stood out as though they might burst.

'You piece of vermin,' she spat. 'You could have been my faithful servant, but now you will die for your treachery.' The blades slashed at India with lightning speed, slicing through her jacket and cutting into her flesh. India screamed and scrabbled to get away over the boxes. But as Fang raised her claws for a second strike, the professor burst into life. He launched himself across the truck and clamped his meaty hands around Fang's throat.

'Die, you witch!' he gasped. Fang slashed wildly at his face but his grip remained firm as the truck lurched and shuddered.

'India, up here.'

India looked up to see Sid leaning into the truck and extending a hand towards her. Without pause she reached up and grasped his forearm. In that same instant, the last remaining cables holding up the truck snapped and the vehicle plummeted towards the boiling lake, taking Fang and the professor with it. Sid gritted his teeth and held on to India as he gripped the cable with his legs and his free arm.

With a huge effort, he hauled her up beside him and they climbed to the relative safety of a twisted piece of the handrail, where they lay for a long while, gasping for breath and not speaking.

When they finally managed the climb back to the path they found Tito waiting for them, clutching the bag. 'Oh, Miss Bentley, Mr Sid,' he cried, embracing each one of them in turn. 'I was sure you had both licked the bucket.'

India stared at him with exhausted eyes. 'It's *kicked*, Tito,' she whispered hoarsely. 'And no, we didn't.' She turned to Sid but the he looked away, his shoulders heaving with great racking sobs. 'Sid,' she said, tentatively placing a hand on his shoulder. 'Sid, I'm so sorry about the professor.'

Sid shook away her hand. 'What about him?' he shouted. 'He was just someone I worked for, that's all.'

'Sid, I know how much he meant to you. It's OK to be upset.'

'I ain't upset,' he spat. Sid seemed so furious that India took an involuntary step backwards. 'I was on my own before he came along and now I'm on my own again. I don't need him, I don't need you, I don't need *anyone*!' He turned and stalked away down the path, leaving India and Tito to stare after him.

'Miss Bentley,' said Tito tentatively as she watched Sid go. 'There is something you should know.'

'I know what you're going to say, Tito,' she said. 'But Sid's just upset because he's lost someone he loves.'

'It's not that, Miss Bentley,' said Tito. He pointed to the patch of clear sky above the crater where the sun was peeping through the clouds. At first there seemed to be nothing unusual, but then she saw it. A dark shadow-bite had appeared in the side of the sun's yellow disc. The eclipse had begun.

28 THE DOOR OF STARS

The professor's death hung over them like a shroud as they returned to the city, and the changes they found there only served to underline their black mood. The constant earth tremors had toppled walls and archways, and noxious fumes rose from the deep cracks in the streets. Atlantis was dying.

The path from the top of the volcano brought them to a point close to the pyramid. They looked dubiously at the great structure which now stood in a lake of a boiling, mustard-yellow mud, belching bubbles the size of dinner plates and spattering fountains of hot goo.

'I don't think the volcano is dormant any more,' whispered Tito.

India checked the progress of the moon across the face of the sun. 'We have to get to the top of the pyramid,' she said. 'We don't have much time.'

Sid's anger had subsided on the long walk down and he now seemed resigned to going wherever India led him.

Braving the hot, rotten-egg smell, they picked a careful path across one of the bridges and began the ascent to the top of the pyramid.

'You sure you want to do this?' asked Sid as they mounted the steps.

India nodded. 'I know you don't believe me, but I *saw* Calculus inside that spaceship. If we don't put the crystal back, then half the world will be destroyed.'

Sid frowned. 'If it was just down to me, I'd say the hell with it,' he muttered. 'But the professor thought it was important so I'll go along. For *now*,' he added.

The scene at the top of the pyramid was much as they had left it. The Bloodstone was still in place on the altar and the long column still projected from the top of the pyramid; only the Heliotrope was missing. High above them the encroaching black disc of the moon had nearly consumed the sun. It was now or never.

India reached into the tool bag and pulled out the crystal, feeling it thrum in her hands, eager to do its work. But as she walked towards the platform there was a blur of movement to her left. The air shimmered as a lithe black shape rushed from the shadows, sending Tito sprawling. The android immediately turned on Sid, striking him a vicious blow, so that he tumbled down a dozen steps and lay still.

India stared at Maximus in shock. The android had suffered badly in the fall from the high bridge. He was spattered with gobs of volcanic mud, his visor was cracked, and his pristine black paintwork was badly dented and burned.

'*Give me the cryssstal.*' The words came off him like cold breath. '*It belongss to the misstress.*'

India clutched the Heliotrope to her chest and backed away.

'Your mistress is dead,' she said.

'*The cryssstal hass the power to resstore life where there wasss none before*,' he hissed. '*I will find the misstress's body and use it to revive her.*'

India gulped, imagining the horror of seeing Lady Fang's mangled body brought back to life. She glanced quickly right and left, but there was no way she could outrun a fully armed war droid and nowhere to go if she did. She reached for the familiar hardness of the shock stick in her pocket. Its small charge was of no possible use against a creature like Maximus, but in that thought the germ of an idea formed.

'*The cryssstal*,' said the android. '*I will not ask again.*'

India forced herself to focus. 'All right, here it is.' She held out the Heliotrope towards Maximus. 'But tell me something: can that crystal really magnify any energy that goes into it?'

'*At leassst a thousssand-fold*,' said Maximus, grasping hold of it.

'Good,' said India. 'Then this is going to hurt a bit.'

In one swift movement she whipped out the shock stick and pressed its crackling tip to the blue crystal. The effect was immediate. There was a brilliant flash as the charge from the shock stick was instantly intensified by the crystal and surged through the android's body.

Maximus began to shudder uncontrollably. His spine arched as though it might snap, and a crackling fountain of sparks erupted from behind his visor, filling the air with the smell of burning plastic. As the charge died away, India removed the shock stick and held her breath. The android remained rigid for several seconds and then, very slowly, began to topple backwards, crashing to the stone flags like a steel mannequin, still clutching the crystal.

India peered nervously at the body. There was no sign of movement from the android and only some faint wisps of blue smoke curled into the air from behind his visor.

'I think you have killed it, Miss Bentley,' said Tito, appearing at her shoulder. His eyes were as round as marbles.

'I certainly hope so,' she said. Her legs were suddenly wobbly, and she felt filled with a nervous, shaky sort of laughter. They found Sid in a crumpled heap on the steps. He moaned softly when they turned him over.

'I think he is just knocked out, Miss Bentley,' said Tito. 'Perhaps you should replace the crystal before you do anything else?'

She looked up at the sky. A supernatural twilight had crept over the city as the last gleams of sunlight slid behind the moon. 'You're right,' she said. 'It has to be now.'

She removed the crystal from the android's lifeless

hands and placed it on top of the column just as the moon's shadow swept overhead, plunging the mountain into darkness. Very gradually, the crystal began to glow, but not with the blue light they had seen earlier. Instead it radiated a strange blackness, like a substance drawn from the eclipse. Long, dark fingers extended through the crystal like veins of diseased blood. They trickled through the stone column and traced the crystal threads across the terrace and down the sides of the pyramid.

'Miss Bentley, look,' said Tito excitedly. He pointed to the space under the stone archway, which had begun to shimmer. As the archway grew darker, it revealed spiral galaxies and vast nebulae that glowed in reds and purples and a billion stars that glittered like gems scattered on velvet.

'Miss Bentley,' said Tito in a whisper. 'It is a doorway to the stars.'

'It's a portal of some kind,' said India breathlessly. Without understanding how it was possible, she felt with absolute certainty that they were looking out on real space.

'It is the heart of the infinity engine,' said a voice behind them. They turned to see the three spheres, hovering in a tight group at the top of the steps. 'This is the place where all points in space and time meet,' said the voice of Wisdom, shimmering in red and gold.

'Where's Calculus?' said India at once. 'You said you would release him when I brought the crystal back.'

'So we will,' said the voice of Logic.

'Well, where is he?'

'Your friend exists only within the boundaries of the Machine Mind,' said Compassion. 'When our ship leaves, we will release him. He will become part of the never-ending stream of the universe.'

'Do you mean he won't be coming back?' said Tito.

'Not as you understand it,' said Wisdom. 'But energy can never truly be destroyed. The memories of Calculus will always be a part of the universe. Like all things, he is truly immortal.'

'But I did what you asked,' yelled India. 'You cheated!'

'Calculus knew what to expect,' said Wisdom.

India sank slowly to the stone floor and held her head in her hands. 'Then I've failed him,' she sobbed. 'Even though we saved the world, I couldn't save my friend.'

'Your task is not yet complete, Soul Voyager,' said Logic. 'The infinity engine can only be controlled by a Soul Voyager, one who must pass through the portal and guide the ship to its destination.'

'What?' said India, thinking she hadn't heard correctly. 'You expect me to go in there?'

'It is the only way to complete the task,' said Logic. 'Or all will have been for nothing.'

India sized up the portal and the glittering starscape beyond. 'But . . . how do I get back?'

'There is no *back*,' said Wisdom. 'There is only forward. The portal joins all parts of the timeline. From here you may travel to any point in space or time but you may not come back.'

India's brow creased as the words sank in. 'You mean that wherever the portal takes me is where I have to stay?'

'Your sacrifice will save the lives of millions,' said Wisdom. 'It is a fair exchange.'

'It isn't fair at all,' shouted India. 'I thought you were an advanced race of beings, but you're not, are you? You lie and cheat to get what you want, just the same as we do.'

'We do not expect you to understand,' said Logic. 'Humans have such a limited capacity for self-sacrifice.'

India was cornered. If she didn't help the Machine Mind, a million souls on board the ship would be lost and millions more would die from the radioactive fallout when the infinity engine exploded. But if she agreed to go . . . then what? She walked up to the portal and peered into it.

'Miss Bentley?' said Tito nervously. 'You're not thinking of going in there, are you?'

'I'm just looking, Tito,' she said absently.

'There is not much time left, Soul Voyager,' said Wisdom. 'The eclipse has nearly passed.'

India did not answer. As she stared into the door of endless stars she saw images swim briefly to the surface and then fade again. She saw a family, laughing as they picnicked by the shores of a lake on a summer afternoon. The man was a younger version of her father, and the woman was beautiful and young, with a face India remembered only from a photograph.

'It's my mother!' she said in a small voice. 'I remember this day. It was my birthday, the year before Bella was born.' She smiled. 'Mum had saved enough eggs to make me a cake and she didn't tell me until we got there. Then afterwards we went swimming and I rode home on Dad's shoulders.'

'Is this the place you have chosen?' asked Wisdom.

India tore herself away from the vision to look at the spheres. 'I could go there?' she said.

'We can return you to that point in the timeline,' said Compassion.

India looked into the portal again and watched the happy faces of the family by the lake. 'I think I know what I have to do, Tito,' she said.

'But, Miss Bentley,' he said, with tears in his eyes. 'You can't go, you are my teacher.'

'You already have a teacher, Tito,' she said with a smile. 'Besides, this is what Soul Voyagers were made to do.'

The tears ran freely down Tito's face, making her sob along with him. They hugged and she kissed the top of his bald head. 'I have to go now,' she said. 'Make sure you and Sid get out safely and say goodbye to Cael for me.' She paused. 'And tell Verity . . . Tell her I only ever wanted to be like her.'

'I don't want you to go, Miss Bentley.'

'I'll be all right, Tito. I'm going back to the past. Things are always better in the past.'

'Miss Bentley,' he said tearfully. 'Might I have something to remember you by?'

'If you like, Tito.' She smiled. 'What do you want?'

'I was wondering if perhaps I might have your shock stick?'

India was taken aback. 'Really? Well, OK, I guess if that's what you want.' She pulled the shock stick from her pocket and held it briefly, remembering the many times it had saved her skin. 'I hope it's as lucky for you as it has been for me.'

'Thank you, Miss Bentley,' he said, sparking it alight and watching it crackle. 'I shall always treasure it. And I hope in time you will find a way to forgive me.'

India frowned. 'Forgive you? Forgive you for wh—'

Her words were cut short as Tito jabbed her hard with the shock stick.

A blinding, blue-white rush of electricity surged through her brain. Every muscle in her body snapped taut, forcing her legs rigid and jerking her head back. She slammed to the ground, banging her head on the stones, her limbs twitching uncontrollably. Then . . . there was nothing.

She had no idea how long she lay like that. She had been having a wonderful dream about her mother but then someone started calling her name from the next room. The voice was insistent and the dream was slipping away faster than she could grab it back.

'Miss Bentley, you must wake up, NOW!'

She opened her eyes and was deeply disappointed to find she was still inside the volcano. The heat was stifling and the cavern was being rocked by bone-shaking explosions.

She sat up shakily, still feeling the after-effects of the shock stick. Sid was still motionless and there was no sign of the spheres or of Tito.

'Tito, where are you?' she called, struggling to her feet.

'I am right here, Miss Bentley,' he replied. His voice came from the archway and she saw that the portal had changed. The stars had disappeared, replaced with angry swirling colours and she knew at once where Tito had gone.

'No, Tito!' she cried. 'You have to get out of there, it's not safe!' She reached out an instinctive hand but the portal crackled with energy, sending a painful shock up her arm.

'You cannot follow me, Miss Bentley,' came Tito's voice. 'I have taken the Bloodstone. The portal is now sealed.'

'You can't do this, Tito!' she shouted. 'Only a Soul Voyager can control the infinity drive.' She began to feel her way around the stonework, looking for another way in.

'You are not the only Soul Voyager here, Miss Bentley,' said Tito. 'Brother Amun told me that I also carried the blood of the Elders.'

She stopped. 'Brother Amun told you?' she said faintly.

'He came to me in a dream,' said Tito's voice. 'He said it was my destiny to enter the portal – not yours. I am sorry I deceived you, Miss Bentley, but I had to take your place.'

India walked all the way around the arch but there was no way into the portal. 'Where are you now, Tito?' she asked quietly.

'I am among the stars,' he said. He sounded distant – as

though he were being distracted by something momentous. 'It feels like I can see forever, Miss Bentley.'

'But I can't see you, Tito,' she said.

'And I can't see you either, Miss Bentley. So I suppose my journey has already begun.'

A loud humming began to vibrate the archway and the portal crackled with energy once more. 'What's happening, Tito?' said India urgently.

'The infinity engine is starting,' he said. His voice sounded fainter. 'I think this will be an adventure worthy of a tech-hunter, no?'

'Tito, I don't want you to go,' she cried.

'I remember now what the Great Teacher said about friends,' said Tito. 'He said there was more treasure in a friendship than in a thousand scriptures; I think he must have known someone like you. Goodbye, Miss Bentley, I will not forget you. Thank you for being my friend.

India pressed her face to the stone as she felt the gulf open between them. 'I'll always be your friend, Tito,' she whispered softly. 'We'll be friends forever.'

'For even longer than that, Miss Bentley,' came Tito's distant voice. 'For even longer than that.'

She did not know how long she sat watching as the colours of the portal faded to black. She was roused by a voice behind her.

'India, what the hell happened here?'

She turned to see Sid, clutching his head and staring

dazedly at the lifeless form of Maximus. 'Where's the monk?' he said eventually.

India looked at him wearily. 'He did the thing he was meant to do,' she said quietly. 'He fulfilled his destiny.'

Sid looked at India, and then nodded knowingly. 'I'm sorry about the kid,' he said, 'but this place is about to blow. We need to get out of here, and I mean *now*.'

India shook her head. She looked up and screamed into the air. 'You cheated me! You took Calculus and now you've taken Tito. I hate you all. I hope you leave and *never* come back!'

And as though she were being answered, a new sound began beneath the pyramid. A deep pulsing that throbbed through the cavern and seemed to distort the air.

'Damn it, India,' yelled Sid with a note of panic in his voice. 'If you don't come now I'm gonna leave you here to burn.'

She allowed Sid to drag her towards the stairs. 'Wait!' She stopped beside the charred hulk of Maximus. 'Is he really dead?'

'I don't know what you done to him but he's as dead as they come.'

'Then help me to move him.'

'India, there ain't no time,' Sid said through gritted teeth.

'Then go, I don't care!' screamed India. Sid stared at her for a long moment then, shaking his head, he began to help her move the android. 'Quickly,' gasped India. 'Get him on to the altar.'

It took all of their combined strength to move the machine, Sid with his hands beneath its arms and India carrying the feet. The black light still pulsed weakly through the crystal as the last vestiges of the mysterious energy drained away. 'Now, get him into the light – quickly.'

'Are you crazy? You've seen what this light does. Do you want to bring this thing back to life?'

'Not Maximus,' she said. 'Someone else.'

They laid the giant android on the stone platform and watched the last of the black light surround his body. 'Give him back to me!' she screamed into the air. '*Please* do this one thing for me!'

They waited as the city crumbled and the molten rock made its way relentlessly towards the island, and all the while the deep thrumming under the city grew louder and faster.

But then the black light from the crystal flickered and died. When India looked up, the first brilliant bead of sunlight was emerging from behind the moon.

'It's over,' said Sid. 'He's gone, and we gotta go too.'

India felt drained. She followed Sid in a daze down the pyramid steps to the edge of the island, but all the bridges had collapsed and the ground was now swarming with metal bugs, scuttling to stay ahead of the advancing lava flow.

'Hell and damnation,' said Sid, their last hope of escape gone. He sat down heavily on the steps and looked out over the blazing ruins of the city. Beneath their feet, the pulsing reached a crescendo.

India looked up at the pyramid and wondered if they could climb it to gain a few precious minutes. If only there was a way to reach the circle of clear blue sky at the top of the volcano, she thought. Then something caught her eye: partially buried in the debris, a harness fashioned from leather and brass. It was the professor's rocket pack!

All at once the desperate desire to survive ignited inside her. She might not have saved Calculus, but there were others out there who cared just as much about her: her father, her sister and Verity. All she had to do was to find a way to live!

'Sid, look at this,' she gasped. 'Help me – quickly.'

'Forget it, India,' said Sid wearily. 'It's too late and I'm too tired.'

She dropped the leather straps of the rocket pack and walked over to where he sat. 'You're tired? Tired of what? Tired of life?'

Sid shrugged and India felt a sudden surge of anger. 'So you're just going to give up? Is this because the professor died?'

Sid turned on her suddenly. 'You don't understand,' he yelled. 'I lost the one person who believed I could be *better*!'

'I lost people too, Sid,' she shouted back. 'My mum, Calculus . . . Tito. But I'm not ready to just lie down and die just yet.'

'Well, maybe *I* am!'

'Is that how you're going to repay the professor? By throwing away everything he did for you?'

'What? I—' he spluttered.

'Professor Moon loved you like a son,' she said. 'And if you ever cared for him, then you have to go on. That's how you remember someone, Sid. You live in a way that would make them proud and you keep them alive –' she leaned forward and placed her hand on his heart – 'in here.'

Sid said nothing for a long while. Then he sighed, and all the hardness drained from his face. He looked at the harness and a slow smile crept across his face. 'You're as crazy as a snake, you know that?'

'I learned it from you,' said India, smiling back at him. 'Are you up for it?'

He broke into a broad grin. 'Why the hell not?'

As Sid was the taller, India helped him into the harness, tightening the straps and opening the fuel valves on his back. Then she faced him while he wrapped the waist belt around both of them and pulled it tight, so that their bodies pressed together. He grasped the red ignition tape and looked her straight in the eyes.

'You know we're gonna die now, right?'

India grinned. 'Better to die trying than die without trying,' she said. 'You told me that once.'

'Yeah, well,' he said. 'We're still gonna die.'

On a sudden impulse, she stood on tiptoe and kissed him. 'Then we'll die together,' she said. When she drew away, he was smiling.

'OK,' he said. 'Let's do it.'

And he pulled hard on the tape.

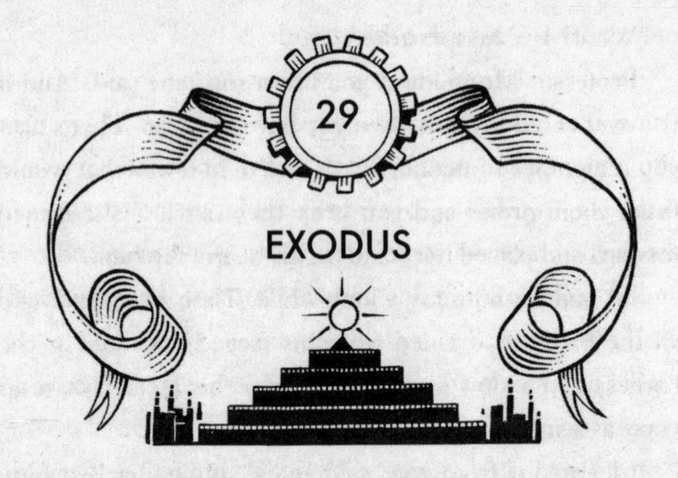

Nothing happened.

Almost nothing. There was the faintest hiss like gas escaping from a balloon. Sid and India looked at each other nervously, each searching the other's face for some sign that it was going to be all right. India spoke first.

'Do you think it's—'

The rocket exploded into life with a deafening bellow and a great tongue of flame spewed out behind Sid. In the same instant they were brutally jerked upward as though on a taut wire. The belt cut into India's back and she instinctively clutched at Sid.

And then they were flying, being dragged relentlessly upward, faster and faster and faster, the rocket twisting in a demented, bone-shaking spiral up into the volcanic pipe. India clenched her teeth and tried to ignore the shrieking blur of scenery, the bubbling lava below and the jagged walls all around. They locked eyes, the only constants in each other's world.

They burst from the top of the volcano in a streak of flame, like a hot cinder being spat from a fire. The rocket choked once and died beneath them. And then they were tumbling, free-falling, to crash-land on the snowy slopes in an explosion of white powder. They rolled over and over amidst steam and hissing and the smell of scorched metal until they came to a tangled halt on the upper slopes.

Sid jumped up and tore at the leather straps, hauling off the glowing rocket pack and swearing as he slapped out the flames that licked around the edge of his jacket. Between them they hurled the smouldering tank as far away as they could manage, sending it bouncing and rolling down the slopes before it came to a hissing rest in a bank of snow. Then they stood panting and staring at each other with scared, disbelieving eyes.

'We did it!' gasped Sid after a few moments. 'We did it! We damn well rode that death trap out of there.'

India grinned back. But when she looked around her smile faded. It was as though they had escaped the fires of hell only to land in a war zone. The crater glowed deep red and a column of hot ash billowed into the sky like a thick line of charcoal. Gobs of hot cinder thumped into the ground around them, hissing loudly as they burned deep sockets in the ice and thick worms of fire crawled down the black sides of the mountain, stinking of sulphur and cutting off their descent.

'There's no way down, Sid,' said India. 'We're trapped.'

Sid was not listening. He was staring up at the crater. When India followed his gaze she saw a small black dot high overhead, being buffeted by the thermals. Then Sid's face lit up. 'Crackers!' he cried excitedly. 'It's Crackers! Over here, girl!'

The beleaguered bird fluttered towards them but refused to land. She flew round and round them, flapping and screeching until she finally landed on Sid's outstretched arm with a joyful squawk. Her feathers were soot-stained and bedraggled but she immediately hopped up his arm and nestled into his neck as he smoothed her gently and spoke softly into her ear. 'I knew you wouldn't leave me.'

'Sid, there's something else up there too,' said India, tugging at his arm. 'She pointed to a black shape that was now swinging around the mountain and skirting the ash cloud. It looked like a long-tailed insect, with sparkling, whirling wings. The volcano was roaring like a fire god but there was a new sound now too, an incessant *thwop-thwop-thwop* that chopped the air above them.

'It's the helicopter,' cried Sid. 'Over here! Hey! OVER HERE!'

They screamed and waved like wild creatures, suddenly aware of how insignificant they were on the slopes of the volcano. The helicopter was clearly visible now, fat-bellied with a bright orange underside and a large sliding door. It wavered in the air and, for an agonizing moment it looked as though it would turn away. But then the nose of the craft dipped towards them, the side door slid open and there was

Verity Brown, waving and grinning.

The helicopter touched down lightly on a level slab of snow, keeping the rotors turning, and Verity leaped from the door and sprinted towards them. She ran full tilt into India, hugging her tightly.

'I thought you'd gone for good this time,' she gasped. She turned and pointed at the helicopter. 'Cael was absolutely brilliant. He got this machine working in less than an hour, but when we got back the volcano was spewing out lava and ash. I was convinced you were all dead. It was Cael that spotted Crackers.'

A window slid back at the front of the craft and Cael's head popped out.

'We need to get moving. That ash could choke the air intakes at any moment.'

Verity glanced around. 'Where's Tito?' India didn't reply and Verity read the answer in her eyes. Before she could speak the ground quaked beneath their feet and a ripple of energy pulsed outward from the volcano, making the earth shiver like water.

'That was no ordinary earth tremor,' said Verity. 'Come on, let's get in the air.' She pulled them towards the waiting machine but India was looking at the bracelet on her wrist.

'India, come on,' pleaded Verity. But then she saw what India was looking at. The bracelet was pulsing its brilliant blue signal over and over.

India looked up to the lip of the crater, feeling as though an invisible cord was tugging at her, as though her name was being breathed on the wind.

'There's something up there,' she said. 'I can feel it.'

A lone figure climbed over the lip of the crater and emerged from the smoke. It was tall and lean and stumbled slightly as it walked towards them. No longer pristine and matt black, it was battered and burned, almost beyond recognition, and smoke rose from its hot metal skin.

'Holy mother of all riggers,' said Sid under his breath as Crackers pushed deeper into his neck.

'I don't believe it,' said Verity weakly as the android approached them. They all held their breath as it drew near.

'Hello, Mrs Brown,' said Calculus. 'It's very good to see you again.'

The sounds of delighted shrieking broke out across the slopes of the volcano as India and Verity rushed to embrace Calculus. He stopped them with an outstretched hand.

'I would not advise touching me, Mrs Brown,' he said, calmly. 'The temperature of my outer skin is well over a hundred degrees.'

They had to content themselves with hovering a few feet from Calculus and grinning at him maniacally. 'But . . . how did this happen?' Verity kept saying over and over again.

They were interrupted by Cael who came running across the snow towards them with one of the professor's pistols in his hand.

'Stay where you are,' he barked at Calculus. 'Verity, India, move away from him right now!'

'It's OK,' said Verity, placing a soothing hand on Cael's arm. 'It's not Maximus. *This* is a very old friend of mine.' Cael looked around suspiciously as though everyone had taken leave of their senses. 'Where's Tito?' he asked eventually.

'We all deserve some explanations,' said Verity, looking at Calculus again. 'But first we need to get off this mountain. Now! We can talk once we're in the air.'

Seen up close, the helicopter was battered and decrepit. The stuffing hung from the seats and one of the windows was missing. As soon as Calculus confirmed that his skin had cooled sufficiently, they clambered into the cramped space. Verity continued to stare, wide-eyed, at Calculus while Cael gave the android suspicious sidelong glances in between checking the dials and running quick fingers across the overhead switches.

'Strap yourselves in,' he shouted over his shoulder. 'That volcano could swat us like an insect at any moment.' The noise of the rotors increased in pitch and the helicopter lurched up and forwards, briefly filling the windscreen with a view of the ground and making everyone reach out to steady themselves.

Despite having landed successfully on the volcano, it was obvious that Cael was an extremely poor pilot. The helicopter wobbled and dipped alarmingly and at one point spun around in the air several times before heading back towards the volcano.

'Perhaps I should give Mr O'Hanlon a hand,' said

Calculus. 'I maintain several piloting sub-routines and I am fully versed in Sikorsky S-62 helicopters.' Verity nodded, still looking slightly dazed. When Calculus sat down in the co-pilot's seat, Cael let out a string of expletives.

'It's all right, Cael,' said Verity. 'You need to trust him, otherwise you're going to fly us all into that damned mountain.'

'We ain't out of the woods yet,' said Sid. 'There's something big happening down there.' He pointed out of the window where deep cracks were opening in the ice, around the volcano. Large sections of the ground had dropped away to reveal an abyss where something pulsed in the darkness. The insistent thrumming had grown louder now, shaking the air like a great turbine under the earth.

'There's someone down there,' said Calculus, pointing to a lone figure that was running and falling and scrambling to stay ahead of the collapsing ice.

'It's Two-Buck Tim,' cried India. 'He must have made it out of the volcano. Let's pick him up, *please*?'

Calculus dipped the nose of the helicopter towards the fleeing figure and left the controls briefly to Cael as he leaned out of the cabin door. Poor Two-Buck turned to see an ancient helicopter swooping from the sky and a large android reaching out to grab hold of him. He barely had time to let out a shriek before he was snatched into the air and the helicopter soared away again.

By now, the sheet ice had fallen away completely, revealing a black pit more than a mile across in front of the volcano. An ice-blue light pulsed deep inside it like a living thing taking its waking breaths.

Two-Buck forgot his terror as they all pressed against the windows to watch. Very slowly, a shape began to rise from the pit, emerging into the Antarctic sunlight for the first time in twelve thousand years. India recognized the graceful organic lines as belonging to the craft she and Tito had seen, half buried in the floor of the pyramid, but it was clear that it was far larger than they had ever imagined.

'We only saw the tip of it,' she murmured. 'It's huge!'

The craft rose gracefully from the pit, like a shimmering sea creature, in living pinks and greens that danced lightly across its shell. Hundreds of feet high, it occupied their entire field of vision, blocking out the sun and dwarfing even the volcano. The rhythmic thrumming from the ship drowned out the noise of the helicopter and the light from its skin grew in intensity until all the colours in the cabin were bleached to pure white, forcing them to shield their eyes.

For a moment, India fancied she could hear a high-pitched tone, like a finger running around the rim of a wineglass, then, with a roar like a departing hurricane, the light vanished.

The helicopter was immediately caught in a violent wash of turbulence that spun them around and around. A klaxon sounded in the cabin and several yellow oxygen masks dropped in a tangle from the cabin roof. Crackers took flight, shedding sooty feathers and out-shrieking the klaxon until Sid grabbed her and tucked her inside his coat.

When Cael and Calculus finally brought the helicopter back to level flight they crowded to the windows once more. The spaceship had gone, leaving an empty crater the size of a small town into which rivers of lava poured like scarlet ribbons. After a few minutes, Calculus turned the helicopter away and flew fast and low across the ice, avoiding the thick clouds of ash and smoke that rose into the air behind them.

In the far corner of the helicopter, Two-Buck Tim sat with his knees drawn up, staring wide-eyed at the collection of misfits that had rescued him from certain death. He reserved his most suspicious looks for Sid who, as soon as the danger had passed, had pulled his hat down over his eyes and gone to sleep.

Verity crouched in the cockpit between Cael and Calculus, looking at the android with a disbelieving smile. 'But how did it happen?' she said for the fifth time.

'All Matsushito droids maintain an independent consciousness, Mrs Brown,' he said. 'When Maximus was killed, India realized the Machine Mind could download me into his dead body.'

Verity looked down at his battered frame. 'You mean, this is really . . . ?'

'It was Maximus, but he is gone now.'

Verity looked as though she was trying to work out a particularly difficult sum in her head. 'So, it really is you then?'

Calculus made some minor adjustments to the controls. 'I am as sure of that as I can be, Mrs Brown,' he said. 'However, there remains a possibility that I am someone else pretending to be me and that part of me that is me has not detected the subterfuge. If that is the case, then the only safe course of action would be to—'

Verity laughed out loud. 'Don't worry, it's you all right,' she said. 'I'd recognize that twisted logic anywhere.' She smiled fondly at him. 'It's good to have you back, Calc. It's going to be like the old days again with the three of us back together.'

Calculus shook his head and looked past Verity to where India sat, looking out of the window. 'I don't know, Mrs Brown,' he said. 'I'm not sure we all made it out of Atlantis undamaged.'

Verity made her way to the back of the aircraft to where India sat alone. The girl did not turn around. 'India,' she said softly. 'I'm really sorry about Tito. I know how fond you were of him.' India continued looking out of the window as though she were seeing a different view altogether.

'It's OK,' she said absently. 'I know where he went and I'm glad for him.'

'What happened to you back there, India?' said Verity. 'What did you see?' There was a long silence and Verity wondered if India had heard her properly.

'I looked into the heart of the infinity engine,' said India eventually. 'I can't really explain what I saw, not properly.

Tito once told me that when he meditated he could see everything and that's what it was like, Verity. It felt like I could see everything and nothing was ever going to scare me again, not even death. It was . . . beautiful.'

Something in the girl's voice made Verity feel chilled inside. 'India, are you OK? You sound . . . *different*?'

'I'm not sure,' said India in a distant voice. 'I feel fine, but I also feel like some part of me will never be the same again.' She turned then to look at Verity and the older woman let out a gasp. For when she looked into India's eyes she saw that one had become the colour of rich brown earth while the other had turned to the clearest blue, like an Antarctic sky.

By late afternoon they had reached the coast and Calc had located the secluded bay where the *Ahaziah* and the *Sea Wolf* lay at anchor. The helicopter clattered to a stop on the stony beach and was immediately surrounded by a group of suspicious crewmen. Verity was required to do some fast-talking when they saw Calculus.

Sid went to report to Captain Thor while Verity evaded questions about the professor until she and Cael were able to speak to the first mate on board the *Ahaziah*. Before they left, Verity grabbed Two-Buck Tim by the arm and handed him over to Grunion.

'Here's your new kitchen boy,' she said. 'Just make sure he washes his hands before he touches anything.'

Grunion looked at the cringing Two-Buck as though someone had just placed him in charge of a particularly unhygienic ape, and then led him away, muttering as he went. 'Come on, son, let's see how well you can make chips.'

*

Some hours later, when their tales of Atlantis and Professor Moon's heroic battle with Lady Fang had been told a dozen times over, the two crews met on the deck of the *Ahaziah* around a blazing brazier to toast the memory of their late captain. India knocked back the small shot of resinous brown liquid that Verity had given her and promptly wished she hadn't. It felt like a small, malevolent creature was doing something unpleasant in her stomach.

After they had drunk the toast, Grunion served everyone a surprisingly good fish stew prepared by his new assistant and they listened to the mournful voices of the sailors singing a slow ballad.

Verity explained how she and Cael had made their trek through the storm and how Cael had used all of his mechanical skills to get the helicopter working. 'He was amazing,' she said as Cael looked bashfully at his boots. 'He stripped down the carburettors and primed the fuel pumps and charged the batteries with an old hand-crank.' India listened to the admiration in Verity's voice and saw the light in her eyes and thought about how much had changed since Verity had punched Cael unconscious on their first meeting.

Then there were more calls for India and Sid to retell the story of their battle high above the ancient city and how the professor and Lady Fang had fallen into the volcano. 'What a horrible way to die,' said Verity with a shiver.

'What makes you so sure Fang's dead?' asked Cael.

'She spent quite a bit of time in the light of that crystal. How do you know she's not still alive somewhere in the heart of that volcano?' A chill silence fell over the group as they contemplated the prospect of Lady Fang's living death.

'I guess there really are worse things than dying,' said India to no one in particular.

'One thing I don't get,' drawled Sid, looking at Cael. 'If they put you in that crystal light, does that mean you're gonna live forever too?' Cael looked taken aback as though he had not considered the question before.

'Hell, there's an easy way to find out,' said Verity, pulling out her pistol with a grin. 'Hold still, Tech-Boy, this won't hurt a bit.'

'Whoa, whoa!' said Cael, putting up his hands. 'If you don't mind I'll just live without knowing.' They all laughed. 'Anyway,' said Cael, reaching into his bag, 'now that Fang's dead I guess I won't be needing all of these babies.' He pulled out a knotted scarf and unwrapped it to reveal a dozen diamonds as large as beach pebbles that burned blue and gold in the firelight. He tossed one each to India, Verity and Sid. 'I reckon you all earned a fair share.'

Verity raised an eyebrow. 'A fair share, Cael? What are you planning to do with the others?'

Cael grinned. 'I was thinking I might go into the old-tech business. From what I hear, Lady Fang's got a whole boatload of it sitting in Sing City that she doesn't need any more. Once I've helped myself I'll be the biggest dealer in the city. These little baubles will give me the capital I need to get started.'

'Not so fast, Mr O'Hanlon.' They looked up to see Captain Thor standing over them with the first mate of the *Ahaziah*, Mr Flatley, by his side. A group of grim-faced seamen were gathered close behind. 'You are forgetting there are two crews that need paying for this little adventure and those diamonds will do nicely. So if you don't mind?' He held out his hand.

Cael stared at him open-mouthed. 'Now wait a minute,' he stammered. 'You can't be serious. I mean, not *all* of them. At least leave me a few . . .' He tailed off as Thor plucked the scarf from his grasp and placed it in the pocket of his pea-jacket.

'I suppose you'll want ours too?' said Verity, raising an eyebrow at Thor. He smiled and bowed low in her direction.

'I wouldn't dream of it, Mrs Brown,' he said, smiling and bowing politely. 'It's been a rare pleasure to make the acquaintance of such a beautiful woman. The *Sea Wolf* sets sail in the morning and I wish you all luck on your travels. Come along, Sid.' He bowed again and walked away with the rest of his men close behind. Sid got up and began to follow. He had been quiet for most of the evening and India knew he was brooding about the professor again.

'Come and say goodbye before you leave in the morning,' she said hurriedly.

Sid nodded curtly. 'Sure,' he said. And then he was gone.

Cael trailed after the captain and Sid as the rest of the

crew headed below decks. 'Gentlemen!' he cried enthusiastically. 'Of course, everyone should have a fair share. And just to prove there's no hard feelings, how about a glass of whisky and a friendly game of cards? Everyone's welcome, we could even have a small wager to make it interesting?'

India smiled as she watched him go. 'Do you think he'll manage to win back his diamonds?'

Verity gave a snort. 'I doubt it. He's terrible at cards. I always took his money when we played.'

'Are you going to go with him to Sing City?' said India gently.

Verity shook her head sadly. 'He'll never change, India,' she said. 'Sometimes you've just got to let a person go, however much you might not want to.'

Verity made an excuse about wanting some sleep and went to her cabin, leaving India alone. The young Soul Voyager breathed in the chill night air, feeling relieved to be by herself at last. Since they had arrived back she had felt uncomfortable in the company of other people. She had noticed some of the crewmen staring at her and whispering when they thought she wasn't looking. Right now there was only one person in whose company she felt truly comfortable.

She found Calculus standing alone at the back of the ship. He was removing heavy pieces of steel hardware from the hidden slots in his arms and body. A sizeable collection of machine pistols, knives, rocket launchers and a miniature flamethrower lay in a tangled heap at his feet. As India approached he succeeded in extracting a small missile from his forearm and tossed it into the black waters.

'That would be worth a lot of money in Sing City,' she said.

Calculus sighed. 'I learned many things in the last year,' he said. 'The Machine Mind showed me everything we do has a consequence, like ripples on water.'

He looked down on the guns at his feet. 'Maximus used these weapons to cause terror and destruction and that is not how I wish to be remembered.'

India watched while he tipped the rest of his hardware into the water, then she reached into her own bag and pulled out the professor's gun.

'I reckon Sid was right,' she said. 'I'm not a gun person either.' She tossed the hand-cannon into the water. They stood in silence, watching the expanding ripples.

'Why was your picture on the walls of an ancient temple?' she asked him suddenly.

Calculus looked unflinchingly into her blue-brown eyes and she felt with an absolute certainty that if he had eyes of his own they would be the same colour.

'The infinity machine is not something we should have been exposed to,' he said. 'It joins all points in space and time and it allows things to happen that should not be possible.'

'You mean like time travel?'

Calculus nodded. 'You and I, India, have seen more than most people could ever conceive. More than is good for us.'

'I feel that too,' she said. 'When I looked into the infinity machine what I saw was terrifying and beautiful all at the same time. Then, when Tito went in my place, it felt like I'd lost something precious.' She looked up. 'I want to go back there again, Calc, it's all I can think about.'

Her words hung on the air. Calculus didn't try to say something comforting and India didn't want him to. She was grateful for his silence because she knew it meant he felt the same thing.

They stood by the ship's rails for some time, looking up at the crystal-clear night and feeling the first sharp tendrils of winter. Then Calculus turned towards the gondola, still tethered to the deck beneath the silken gas balloon. The door stood open, spilling soft yellow light across the deck. 'There is someone in the professor's laboratory,' he said.

As they approached, Sid emerged from the door with Crackers on his shoulder, he looked surprised to see them.

'Sid, what are you doing in there?' asked India. 'Aren't you meant to be getting ready to leave on the *Sea Wolf*?'

He frowned and dug his hands into his pockets while Crackers fluffed her feathers in the chill evening air. On the floor of the gondola behind him she could see his duffel bag packed and ready to go.

'The professor always said we shouldn't be afraid to die but we *should* be afraid of not living,' he said. 'I never knew what he meant until now.'

He ran a hand along the gondola's wood panelling. 'I've had enough of thieving and killing and the stink of a submarine. So me and Crackers are going to see something of the world. I reckon the professor would be pleased about that.'

India smiled. 'Yes, I think he would.' They stood awkwardly for a moment. 'You've changed, Sid,' she said eventually. 'I think Professor Moon would be proud of who you've become.' She stroked the grey parrot so she wouldn't have to look at Sid. 'You look after him, girl,' she said, her voice cracking.

'Pretty girl,' said Crackers softly.

'And you look after yourself too, India Bentley,' said Sid. 'I won't never forget you.' He bent down and kissed her on the cheek.

They watched him cast off the mooring ropes and then stand in the laboratory doorway as the airship lifted gently into the night sky, briefly silhouetted by the full moon as it sailed towards the horizon. 'I hope he'll be OK,' said India softly.

'I think Sid is more than capable of taking care of himself,' said Calculus as they watched the airship disappear into the clouds.

They stood silently for several minutes until, somewhere in the depths of the *Ahaziah*, a klaxon began to sound. India looked around, startled, as crewmen began to rush up from below decks. Her first thought was that they were going to pursue Sid, but nobody seemed concerned about the missing laboratory. Instead the crew rushed to their stations or pressed against the rails, pointing into the darkness. 'What's going on, Calc?' she said. 'What's happening?'

Calculus looked out across the bay and she heard the optics behind his visor whirring into place. 'There's someone else out there,' he said. 'Three ships heading this way.'

India peered across the bay and saw what he was pointing to: three distant sailing ships with square sails, each one bearing the sign of a hand holding a torch.

'It's the monks from Tito's order,' said India under her breath. 'They must have followed us all the way here!'

Verity arrived, pulling on her leather jacket, with Cael close behind. Verity had her pistol in her hand. 'Stay alert, Calc,' she said, not taking her eyes from the boats. 'These guys weren't too friendly the last time we met them.'

'We would appear to have them heavily outnumbered,' said Calculus. 'They would be unwise to attempt an attack now.'

They watched in silence as the ships weighed anchor in the bay and a single rowing boat was lowered to the water. India recognized the dark-robed figure standing in the bow as Brother Amun and she shivered. Even from a hundred yards away she could feel his stare. The boat pulled alongside the *Ahaziah* and Brother Amun exchanged a few muttered words with Mr Flatley before being allowed up the ladder with two other monks. Once on deck, all three of them dropped to one knee before India and bowed their heads. As India and Verity exchanged puzzled glances, Brother Amun stood and folded his hands into his sleeves.

'Thanks to you, Miss Bentley, our task is at an end. The Great Cycle is complete and the ark of the Elders has returned to the heavens.'

India frowned. 'The "ark of the Elders"?' said India. 'Do you mean—'

'The spacecraft, Miss Bentley,' said Brother Amun. 'The one hidden beneath the city of Atlantis.'

'You knew about that?' said Verity incredulously.

'We have always known,' said Brother Amun. 'Our order was founded by the Great Teacher himself, specifically to make sure that the spaceship would have the help it needed to return to the heavens after twelve thousand years. He left a prophecy telling us to expect the appearance of a warrior-girl who would reunite the Bloodstone and bring about the end of the Great Cycle.'

A slow dawn of realization crept over India's face. 'Do you mean *me*?'

'Yes,' said Brother Amun. 'I knew it the moment I saw you on the High Priest's boat.'

'Well, your High Priest didn't seem to know it,' snapped Verity. 'He threw India in jail, or have you forgotten?'

'My apologies, dear lady,' said Brother Amun. 'The High Priest is merely a figurehead, a comical figure we keep in case anyone should decide to investigate us too closely. Our true authority lies in the secret order of which I am the head. For thousands of years we have passed down the secrets of the ancients to a select group of monks, a circle within a circle, waiting for the time when the prophecy would be fulfilled.'

'But I didn't fulfil any prophecy,' said India. 'I wasn't the one who entered the portal – Tito went in my place.' A single tear tracked down her face.

'It was never meant to be you,' said Brother Amun softly. 'That task was for Tito alone. It was *his* destiny to pass through the portal and return to the start of the timeline, not yours.'

India shook her head. 'I don't believe any of this. How could you have known I was this "warrior-girl" just from seeing me on the boat?'

'I have something for you,' said Brother Amun. He gestured to the monk behind him and Brother Scrofulous shambled forward, bearing a small wooden casket and scratching his backside vigorously with his free hand.

Amun took the casket carefully. 'When the Great Teacher emerged from the wilderness to bring wisdom to our forefathers,' he said, 'he was carrying two things. The first was the Bloodstone which was the key to the Sun Machine. The second was a sacred object with which he lit his path and defended himself from his enemies.'

'The torch of the teacher,' said India. 'Tito told me about it.'

'Tito was a very diligent student,' said Brother Amun. 'But did he tell you the torch had been passed down through six hundred generations for safe keeping and that it was kept in the catacombs beneath our monastery? It is our most sacred possession.' Amun caressed the box like a cherished pet. 'Before he died, the Great Teacher left specific instructions that the torch should be given to the warrior who brought the Great Cycle to a close.'

India was puzzled. 'Me? But why?'

'Open it,' said Amun, passing her the box. It was made of dark wood, turned almost black from being stored in a hundred sooty caves. The lid opened with a squeak, revealing a slender piece of iron about six inches in length. The metal was heavily corroded and pockmarked and was scarcely recognizable as a man-made object. But when she picked it up, something about its size and weight was familiar to her.

'It feels like a shock stick,' she said looking at Amun in amazement.

'Turn it over.'

On the underside she could make out some faint marks scratched into the metal. 'It says "IB",' she said in a tight voice. 'My initials. But this is—'

'*Your* shock stick, Miss Bentley,' said Amun. 'It was carried back through the portal to the start of the time loop created by the spaceship.'

India's thoughts began shouting at her like argumentative people all demanding to be heard at once. 'But that means that Tito . . .'

'. . . was the Great Teacher,' said Amun. 'He was a

humble student who had committed all the Great Teacher's writings to memory. He was perfectly equipped to bring civilization to the ancient tribes. He was always the one who was destined to enter the portal, not you.'

'I don't believe it,' said Verity. 'You mean that kid . . .'

'. . . is the reason that all of human civilization is here,' said Amun. 'I am honoured to have known him. And you too, Miss Bentley,' he added.

He bowed again to India and the other monks followed suit, then they promptly turned and walked back towards their boat.

'Where are you going?' India called after them. 'Won't you stay?'

'I cannot, Miss Bentley,' called Amun as he climbed down the ladder. 'The Great Cycle may be over but there is much wisdom in the words of the Great Teacher. I have devoted my life to bringing his lessons to those who have not heard them. There is still much to do.'

They watched the sailing ships draw up their anchors and slip back into the night. 'Are you all right, India?' asked Verity, laying a protective hand on her shoulder as the girl gazed out to sea.

'Yes,' said India distantly. 'I really am, Verity. And now I know what it is I have to do next.'

Dawn broke in a violet line over the jagged Siberian mountains, sending golden rays slantwise through the beech trees and casting a blood-red sheen over the fresh snow. High in the forest, a lone Samoyed raised its snout from its forepaws and sniffed at the scent of approaching spring after a hard winter.

The dog yawned and turned its attention to the crest of a nearby hill, narrowing its blue-brown eyes against the sun. For a long time there was no sound that a human could discern. Then a faint tremor in the ground became the rumble of distant engines carrying the smell of diesel fumes and men. It was time.

The dog padded towards a lone tent in the trees, painted with elaborate reindeer designs and hung with sage and brushwood, and slipped quietly between the heavy hide flaps covering the entrance.

With the percussive rattling of diesel engines, a battered

hulk crested the hill, spewing blue smoke into the crisp morning air. The vehicle was iron-clad, once white but now streaked with red oxide along its flanks. On its roof a rat's nest of cables and drilling equipment spilt over the sides and its great steel tracks bit into the snow, bending and splitting the young beech trunks in its path. The giant rig ploughed down the hill, making the forest path considerably wider as it went, and pulled to a halt beside a frozen lake. The engines clattered to a stop and the sounds of the forest rushed back to reclaim the silence.

A steel door clanged open and a stout, barrel-chested man in a heavy jacket, clambered out over the steel tracks and jumped to the ground. He stretched his arms wide and inflated his substantial chest.

'That's what fresh air should smell like,' he declared in a voice that frightened a flock of small birds from the trees. 'Air that ain't been breathed by a dozen other people before you get to it. Know what I mean?'

Verity Brown climbed stiffly from the cabin and cat-stretched. 'I don't know about fresh air, Bulldog,' she groaned. 'I'd happily suck on an exhaust pipe if it meant getting out of that tin box.' She turned to look at the great mobile oil rig, *The Beautiful Game*, that she and India had travelled in the previous year. It looked exactly as she remembered it, making soft pinging noises as it cooled and dripping hot oil on to the virgin snow.

'I thought you were going to fix this thing up? It looks more decrepit than ever.'

'Now, now,' said Bulldog looking hurt. 'I've just tried to preserve her "unique" character, that's all.'

A woman with long blonde hair and high cheekbones appeared in the hatchway behind them. She looked at Verity as though she was something that the cat had regurgitated before turning her venomous glare on Bulldog.

'Damn it, Bulldog,' she spat. 'How long are we going to have to spend in the middle of nowhere? This is not good for me in my condition.' She placed her hands in the small of her back to emphasize her pregnant bulge.

'No longer than we have to, Tashar my sweet,' said Bulldog, turning on a sugary smile. Tashar scowled and shot a final glare at Verity that carried enough venom to make a cobra run and hide.

'I can't believe you actually married her, Bulldog,' said Verity in a hushed voice, after Tashar was safely back inside. You two always fought like cat and dog.'

'She's really a sweet girl once you get to know her,' said Bulldog cheerfully. 'Besides –' he lowered his voice – 'it's hard to get good rig pilots these days. I had to find some way of getting her to stay.'

'Bulldog!'

He grinned at Verity's shocked expression. Then his face became serious. 'How's India doing?'

Verity cast a quick glance over her shoulder. 'I really don't know, Bulldog,' she said. 'Most times she's the same India that she always was but at others . . .' her voice tailed off. 'Since Antarctica, it's like something's changed under the surface. I keep catching her staring into space and I know her nightmares have got worse. But, she was adamant that this was where she wanted to come.' Verity pulled her jacket tighter and looked up the hill towards the lone tent. They had followed India's directions to the place where she said the old shaman, Nentu, lived, but there was no sign of activity. Verity wondered idly if the old woman was still alive.

'Do you think she knows we're here?' she said.

Bulldog looked up at the tent and nodded. 'Oh yeah, she knows all right. I don't pretend to understand this stuff but I've lived here long enough to know there's a lot we can't explain. If India thinks this is where she needs to be, then she's probably right.'

There was more scrambling from the hatch and India emerged into the sunshine, closely followed by her father, John Bentley and the slender figure of Calculus.

Verity looked at India and her father together and thought, not for the first time, that they seemed to have switched places. A year ago John Bentley had been ragged and scrawny from living under the Siberian mountains, but now he was fit and well-groomed. Instead it was India who was now scarecrow-thin, with a haunted look in her eyes that made Verity's heart ache whenever she looked at her.

John Bentley was drawing in lungfuls of the mountain air. 'I didn't think I'd miss this place after I'd spent a year inside Ironheart,' he said. 'But I'd forgotten how beautiful it is. Everyone should get a chance to see Siberia!'

'That's exactly what Bella said,' said India with a smirk. 'I don't think my sister is going to forgive you in a hurry for not letting her come with us.'

John Bentley gave a sad smile. 'Well, perhaps another time. When we can all be together, eh?'

India gave Bulldog a huge hug. 'Thanks for bringing me, Bulldog,' she said warmly. 'Give the baby a kiss from me when it arrives.'

'No worries,' said the big man. He looked like he was about to burst into tears. 'Me and Tash will look in on you now and again when we're in these parts. By the time you're done here I'll most likely have a new sign for the rig. "Bulldog and Son – Freelance Prospectors".' He imagined the sign with a sweep of his hand.

India grinned mischievously. 'It might be "Bulldog and Daughter", you know.'

'Eh?' Bulldog looked confounded, as though this had never occurred to him. India laughed and then moved on to Verity. They looked at each other for a long time, unable to speak. Then they hugged fiercely; when they separated they were both crying.

'You sure you'll be OK out here?' said Verity, wiping away a tear.

'Sure,' she replied. 'If any cannibals turn up I can just hold them at bay with some witty conversation, remember?' They giggled and India smiled. 'I'll be fine, honest. Tito showed me that we all have a destiny to fulfil. I need to start being a Soul Voyager and Nentu is going to show me how.'

She bit her lip. 'I'm not sure how long it will take, but when I'm done can I come and find you?'

Verity smiled. 'Whenever you're ready, Soul Voyager,' she said. 'I'll be here.'

India backed away, releasing Verity's hands slowly. Before she left she rummaged in her bag and handed Verity a small box. 'This is for you,' she said shyly. 'I'm sorry you won't have the real thing.' Verity gave her a puzzled look and went to open the box but India stopped her. 'No. After I'm gone,' she said with a smile.

India picked up her bag and walked up the path with her father, who placed a protective arm around her shoulder. As they approached the tent, one of the flaps was pushed aside and a tiny figure emerged into the sunlight, to peer at them with clouded eyes. Looking like a wizened bird stripped of its feathers, Nentu raised a single, clawed finger and mumbled something they couldn't hear. Then India and her father embraced before she followed the old woman into the tent and was gone.

Verity realized she had been holding her breath and let out a long sigh. She looked at her companions and an awful thought struck her. 'Calc? India didn't say goodbye to you.'

The android nodded. 'We spoke about it and agreed some time ago,' he said.

'Agreed what?' Verity had a sense that something was amiss.

'India risked everything to save me, Mrs Brown,' he said. 'She showed me that no life is unimportant, not even an android's. I intend to stay here and ensure no harm comes to her while she is with the shaman. I am sorry, but I cannot come back to work for you.'

Verity bit her lip as a fresh set of tears began to prick at her eyes. 'It's OK, Calc,' she said. 'You can go wherever you want. That's what it means to be a free person.'

She hugged him then because there was nothing else she could do or say that would change things. The android started up the path after India, stopping to exchange a few words with John Bentley on the way.

Verity leaned against the steel tracks, feeling the cold bite of the frosty metal, and opened the box that India had given her. Nestling inside on a bed of tissue paper, was a small jade statue. It was a slender figure about three inches high wearing a long helmet with the faintest hint of a crack across the visor: a perfectly rendered image of an android from a time before history. Beneath it was a small card that read simply, '*Never give up on someone you love*'.

'Well, Mrs Brown,' said John Bentley, breaking in on her thoughts. 'There's nothing more for us to do here. What do you say to a joining me for a drink in Angel Town?'

Verity looked up from the statue and a slow smile crept across her face. 'Thanks for the offer, John,' she said. 'But there's someone I need to find in Sing City.'

When everyone else had gone inside, Verity stayed on her own, taking a last look at the Siberian wilderness. A single line of brown, peaty smoke had begun to rise from the tent, drifting lazily through the fresh green pines as they shed the last of the winter snow. And at the crest of the hill, silhouetted against the morning sun stood Calculus, a lone sentinel in the wilderness, keeping vigil over the child he loved.

Verity smiled then. She turned without looking back and hauled herself on to the footplate of *The Beautiful Game*. She felt the tremble of the deck plates beneath her feet as the rig fired up its engines and the breeze in her face as the great machine turned to the west. She relished the tang of diesel on the fresh mountain air and found, when she breathed it in deeply, that it made her heart beat faster.

It smelled like adventure!

ACKNOWLEDGEMENTS

I would like to thank everyone who has helped me to turn *Bloodstone* from the loose collection of 'cool scenes' inside my head into this beautiful finished book. In particular my gratitude goes to Rachel Kellehar for her extraordinary editorial talent; to the team at Macmillan for consistently managing to make me look good; to my agent, Julia Churchill, for her unfailingly frank and sound advice; to the team at Antarctica XXI, who got me to the white continent and back in one piece; to my beta readers Christian, Alice, Harry and Aisling for 'giving it to me straight', and of course to Ryan, Kate and Carol for tolerating my eccentricity in all its varied forms.

My thanks doesn't seem enough for what you have all done, but it's what I have.

Thank you.

REFERENCES

Fingerprints of the Gods: The quest continues, by Graham Hancock, first published by William Heinemann Ltd, 1995

Arctic Dreams, by Barry Lopez, first published by Charles Scribner's Sons, New York, 1986

South: the Endurance *Expedition*, by Ernest Shackleton, first published by William Heinemann Ltd, 1919

The Mammoth Book of Antarctic Journeys, edited by Jon E. Lewis, first published in the UK by Robinson, an imprint of Constable & Robinson Ltd, 2012

The Lost Continent of Mu, the Motherland of Men, by James Churchward, first published in 1926, reissued 2010 by Kessinger Publishing

DESCRIP
Other uses
Could be used
Bloodstone must
How?
Atlantis
From the desk of
Sir Vivian Moon
To: The President of the Royal Society
Sir,
Discrepancies regarding the his
I wish to beg your indulgence regarding a mat
light in the course of my studies. The enclosed
from an ancient text of unknown origin, said to
Although the map predates the discovery of the
of geological sonar of my own design, I have
the map is an accurate portrayal of the coast
covers Antarctica.
I will return with evidence that will
Sir Vivian Moon
TIWANAKU, BOLIVIA - LEGEND TELLS OF A CITY BUILT 'IN A SINGLE
NIGHT' USING METHODS THAT WERE ABLE TO 'LIFT GREAT STONES
MIRACULOUSLY'. EVIDENCE OF AN ANCIEN
OLOGY AT WORK?
SOME INDICATION
OBJECT BURIED DEEP
EXAMINATION SUGGESTS -
BE IN AN OBJECT 12,000 YEARS OLD?
VISIBLE ON THE ANTERIOR OF THE STONE ARE
INCOMPLETE AND PARTIALLY OCCLUDED. HOWEVER, I BELIEVE THEY
POINT TO A REGION OF THE CONTINENT AT 72 DEGREES 16 MINUTES
SOUTH, 165 DEGREES 35 MINUTES EAST.
ANTARCTIC COASTLINE MUST HAVE BEEN MAPPE
A PERIOD
BETWEEN 4,000 BC AND 13,000 BC - WHICH
FABLED
CIVILIZATIONS COULD BE RESPONSIBLE?
LEMURIA
MU
ATLANTIS - YES!
I WILL GO - EVEN IF I MUST GO ALONE!

Atlantis
FINGERPRINTS OF
I must journey south from Bolivia
using the artefact that I
is a part of the ancient
guide me. As
expeditions, the
towards the white
more I can feel
be leading me
of the
of Azath? For
meticulously
links between
by time and
legends that
race of elders
sure they are
whose secrets
the ice caps. I feel
of greatness.

FIND OUT WHERE THE ADVENTURE BEGAN IN

ALLAN BOROUGHS

Since her father went missing, life has been tougher than ever for India Bentley. Little does she know that he was actually searching for Ironheart, a legendary fortress containing the secrets of the old world. A place that could save humanity . . . or destroy it forever.

Accompanied by tech-hunter Verity Brown and her android bodyguard Calculus, India must make the journey to remote Siberia to find her father and finish his work. But there are others looking for Ironheart too, outlaws led by the merciless oil baron Lucifer Stone – and what lies beneath the ice is a far darker secret than any of them could imagine.

IF INDIA FAILS, IT WON'T JUST BE HER FATHER WHO PAYS THE PRICE. IT WILL COST HER THE EARTH.